NANDI TAYLOR

wattpad books

wattpad books **W**

Copyright © 2021 Amanda Taylor. All rights reserved.

Published in Canada by Wattpad Books, a division of Wattpad Corp.
36 Wellington Street E., Toronto, ON M5E 1C7

www.wattpad.com

First Wattpad Books edition: January 2020

ISBN 978-1-98936-563-2 (Trade Paper edition)
ISBN 978-1-98936-505-2 (eBook edition)

Library and Archives Canada Cataloguing in Publication
information is available upon request.

Printed and bound in Canada
1 3 5 7 9 10 8 6 4 2

Cover design by Jeff Brown
Illustrator © Jeff Brown
Map illustration by Jason Flores-Holz
Typesetting by Sarah Salomon

To anyone who feels like they don't quite belong—
may you find your tribe.

1

Yenni made her decision as her cousins slithered through the grass like log snakes, hemming the creature in from all sides.

They would hate her for this.

She pulled energy through her focus rune—a band of white painted across her eyes—and felt its warm tingle on her skin as it sharpened her vision. Ahead the *n'ne* shimmered in the sunlight, the black hair of its haunches flashing blue, then green, then gold. It grazed, its graceful neck bent forward and its tall horns curved and gleaming like blackwood. Four long legs, suited to loping sprints, disappeared into the tall grass. Such a gorgeous animal. Small wonder her cousins wanted to skin it, put its head on display, and make a cape of its pelt.

But n'ne were highly intelligent. It was rare to see more than one or two at a time, and the scholars theorized that they sacrificed themselves to draw predators away from the main herd. In fact, Yenni was certain it knew they were there. At any moment it would draw on *ach'e*, the divine energy that ran through all things, and put on a magical burst of speed to dart away. She planned to help it escape.

Yenni heard a bird trill, high and sweet, and recognized it as the signal that one of her cousins, or perhaps her younger brother, was in place. Another bird call, and another. They would not attack with fire—that would singe the creature's hide. No, they would chase the poor thing this way and that until they could catch it, and then someone would snap its neck with their bare hands. If she let them.

Yenni moved through the grass clumsily, causing it to shake and shiver around her. The formation was still incomplete.

Run, she thought desperately.

As if it had heard her, the creature took off, its legs glowing with ach'e as it galloped through the tall grass. Yenni flared the speed runes on her thighs and calves, relishing the familiar warmth of energy coursing through her, and shot after it. Two of her cousins jumped up out of the grass. "Weh! Weh!" they shouted, waving their arms. The n'ne zipped right, where her younger brother, Jumi, kept pace, his runes blazing blue-white on his dark legs. He dove, arms wide to tackle the n'ne, but it slipped free and left him tumbling. Yenni grinned, until she realized the creature now ran right at her. If she scared it, it would turn tail and head straight for her cousin Ade-Ige. He would no doubt catch it and then . . .

Yenni sprang out of the path of the runaway n'ne, flattening herself to the grass. The ground vibrated as it thundered past and she heard her cousin let out a frustrated curse.

"Mothers and Fathers! It's escaped into the forest, we'll *never* find it now!"

Standing, Yenni brushed herself off while mentally tensing

against the tirade to come. She did feel a small stab of guilt for ruining the hunt, but it was her last trip for a long while to come, and she refused to taint the memory—the pale grass of the plain against the soft blue of the sky—with the tang of the beautiful animal's red blood.

When Yenni looked up, the others—all eight of them—stood across from her with their eyes glittering in accusation under their white focus runes.

"Why didn't you chase it toward us?" Ade-Ige demanded. Yenni stood straighter, raising her chin to meet his gaze, saying nothing. But her cousin was too far gone in his irritation to afford her proper respect.

"You let it escape on purpose, didn't you? Probably due to some foolish notion of it being too pretty to kill." He threw up his hands. "This is why I dislike hunting with women!" He kicked at the grass like a petulant child.

"Ah! It wasn't *me* who let it escape!" cried Ade-Ige's younger sister. She looked like a feminine version of him, right down to the fire in her eyes. "Don't lump us together!" A second later she sent Yenni a frightened glance before fixing her gaze on the ground.

Yenni huffed. It was one thing to bring down a boar for a feast or defend a village from a pack of emboldened hyenas, but rare and intelligent creatures—especially those that could channel ach'e—had always been Yenni's weakness. Though she loved to encounter such animals in the wild, to stalk and study them, she was loathe to kill them. "Yes, I found it beautiful, as did you, which is why you wanted to capture it."

"And now it's gone!" Ade-Ige shouted. "I don't know who you think you are!"

Her temper flared hot in her face. "I am Yenni Aja-Nifemi *ka Yirba*, and you would do well to remember that!"

Ade-Ige and the others bowed their heads, all except her brother, and Yenni winced. She'd promised herself she would use her prowess as a tracker, not her title, to win their respect. But pigheaded Ade-Ige always got under her skin.

"Let's return," she said, and before anyone could answer, she turned and pulled ach'e through her speed runes, dashing toward the white houses of the city and the gleaming gold palace perched on the top of the hill.

$$\Delta$$

Later in the day, Yenni sat in her bedroom on a wide reed mat beside her hammock, mixing runepaint. Once it was the right consistency, and the perfect shade of blue-tinged white, she took up her runebrush, dipped the coarse boar's-hair tip in, and started the rune for strength on her bicep. As she drew she sang the hymn of strength, and her song infused the paint, making it glow, until she tied the hymn off with a final low note and the rune set, seeping into her skin. It would stay there until she used it up.

She nodded in satisfaction and went back to mixing. The circle of prongs that made up her new blackwood whisk clacked against the shiny, matching bowl—a going away present from her older sisters. Blackwood was incredibly hard to come by, but it was best for blending the purest runepaint. Typically only the Masters, in their temples along the coast, had access to the sacred wood. How her sisters had come by the set she had no idea, but the two of them were bright eyed, sweet voiced, and charming, and tended to get their way more often than not. Yenni had not inherited their same powers of persuasion, but she *had* been able to sway her parents on the thing that mattered most: tomorrow she would leave for the Empire of Cresh.

Three sharp raps sounded on her door. It had to be a servant, or her brother Dayo. He was the only member of her family who waited to be invited in.

"Enter!" she called, and frowned at the chalky paint on her fingertips.

Sure enough, her oldest brother strode into the room, dressed as always in a long, regal kaftan tied around the middle with a thick golden sash, his gold prince's cape over one shoulder. She couldn't understand why he insisted on such formal attire at all times, and in this heat. Yenni preferred her hunting clothes: a simple shift tied over one shoulder—or perhaps a half-shirt and skirt—and her hide sandals.

"How go your preparations, *Kebi*?" he said, using the informal address for a younger sister.

She smiled and embraced him. "Well, thank you, *N'kun*," said Yenni, returning his greeting with the term for an older brother.

He frowned at her. "Why aren't you dressed?" Dayo ran a hand along his beard, as he always did when he was irritated. "Kebi, could you at least *try* to look like a daughter of the chiefclan? This feast is to celebrate your birth, after all."

Yenni sighed. Dayo would make a fine chieftain once their parents stepped down, if for no other reason than his rigorous observance of propriety.

"I'm sorry, N'kun," she said, "but I just returned from hunting, and I became so caught up in mixing runepaint—"

"Yes, the hunt," her brother said, cutting her off. "I received a complaint from our cousins that you impeded their kill. Again."

She had the grace to look sheepish, but said nothing.

"You are too old to still be hunting, Kebi," he scolded. "Whoever heard of a woman of seven . . . no, *eighteen* rains still roaming the hills and plains?"

Yenni folded her arms. "I am not married."

"No, and I suspect you intend to remain so. Forever, if you could, but you cannot."

Yenni caught the flicker of concern in her brother's eyes and knew he was referring to their shaky political position. At present, their tribe was the most powerful on the Sha Islands, but their father's health was failing, and with each meeting he missed, the wolves within the other tribes sniffed closer. A political marriage would do much to help them regain their footing.

"You have a duty to strengthen the tribe, Yenni. The same for all of us who bear the name ka Yirba."

"Then why aren't *you* married?" she grumped.

He looked at her out of the side of his eye but didn't answer, and she knew she was approaching disrespect. Yenni didn't exactly envy her older brother's position. He was in training to become a general, and besides that, he spent more and more time in political meetings with their mother, acting as a stand-in for their father and resolving their people's disputes. But he was only five years older than her, and she knew the other leaders did not yet respect Dayo as they did her father. He would likely be forced into a strategic alliance himself soon.

"Apologies, N'kun," she said, and bowed her head. "But I know I will find a way to cure *N'baba* abroad, the Sha will guide me. Once he is well and active again, perhaps I won't need to—"

But Dayo was shaking his head. "You are all but engaged to

Prince Natahi ka Gunzu. How would we explain to the Gunzu that you don't want to marry their second son? They already believe we look down on them, Yenni. You know that would cause them grave insult."

That was Dayo, ever the strategist, just like their mother. "I see," Yenni said softly, resigned that she would come home to the shackles of responsibility.

"Sending you away for a year is bad enough, but it can't be helped now. Come, I'm going to find our sisters to help you dress. You must look your best tonight."

Yenni grimaced. She must look her best *not* because it was her birthday but because the *Gunzu* would be there.

"All right, N'kun," she said wearily. "Send them along."

Dayo hugged her, chuckling against the top of her head, but his laughter soon died away. He pulled back and squeezed her arm affectionately. "I'll miss you, Kebi. Not a day will go by that I won't pray for your safe return, and not just for the sake of the tribe."

She rested her hand on his. "Thank you, but I'll be fine. The Sha will protect me while I'm away, and if nothing else, I know which end of the spear is for stabbing."

Dayo chuckled again. "That you do. See you tonight."

He left and Yenni went back to grinding and mixing ingredients, so focused that the faint creak of the doors to her sitting room barely registered. It wasn't until her bedroom doors burst open, spilling forth a flock of pretty, chatty women and girls, that Yenni whipped her head up from her work. The group was led by her sisters, twin paragons of Yirba style and grace. They surrounded her in a flurry of color, clacking beads, and the musky-sweet scent of shi-shi root oil, and Yenni smiled despite herself.

"Time to dress, Kebi dear," chirped high-cheeked Ifeh.

"N'kun is looking more harassed than usual," said doe-eyed Jayeh. "What did you—ah!" She gestured at Yenni, her gold bracelets jangling. "You're really going to make us work today!" She eyed Yenni's paint stains as she kissed her back teeth.

"You call it work? All you do is supervise and dictate," said Yenni.

Ifeh fanned her nose. "Draw a bath," she called to no one in particular. "Oh, don't you pretend not to like it. You always come out stunning." She flashed Yenni her charming, gap-toothed smile.

"Yes," said Jayeh, and winked. "Almost as pretty as us."

Her cousins giggled. Yenni wanted to seem angry, but she couldn't help but laugh at her sisters' teasing. Tonight they coordinated in slim, flowing gowns that showed off the flawless, dark skin of their arms. Both dresses had a pattern of bird feathers: one orange and blue, the other pink and yellow. And each sister wore a tall, regal head wrap: Jayeh's gold, Ifeh's a shimmering rose. A wave of sadness chased Yenni's mirth. She would miss them greatly.

They had her stand on the tile of her sitting room, trying on this and that, as they held up earrings and necklaces, and occasionally having girls run to their wing to get something from their own stock. As the sun made its path across the sky Yenni's mood soured. No matter how she loved her sisters, nothing would convince her that getting dressed was meant to be such a production. How did they all stand it every day?

At last the twins settled on a vibrant green gown, the material sheer and layered, the sides accented with yellow beading that emphasized Yenni's figure, and it did not escape her that green and yellow were Gunzu colors. They sat her down among a pile of printed cushions and had her young cousin Bisini, the maid with the nimblest fingers, oil and rebraid her hair.

"Why must my hair be perfect if it will just be under a wrap?" Yenni said, wincing as her maid pulled her hair against her scalp.

"Because that is what's proper," said Ifeh.

Finally Yenni's hair was done, twisted up in thick braids to a small cone on top of her head that would help hold her head wrap in place.

"You have such nice, healthy hair, but I wish you would stop cutting it," said Jayeh. When not wrapped up Jayeh's hair fell in neat locks down to the middle of her back.

"It's better for training," said Yenni. Her sister frowned, but the other twin gently took Yenni's chin. "Hmm, I think it suits her." Ifeh preferred to shave her hair close to her head. It was how most told the two apart. But Yenni found both styles too much upkeep—most of the time, Yenni preferred a row of neat braids that fell just below her jawline.

They put on the final touches: a sparkling gold chain that draped from a hoop in her ear to her nose, thick gold bands on her arms, and an ostentatious royal head wrap in gold and green, to match her gown. Her sisters beamed at her.

"You look like, well, like a princess!" cried Ifeh.

"Is it over?" asked Yenni. "I'm starving."

"I suppose this will have to do," Jayeh teased, then clapped her hands. "All right, everyone! Let's give them an entrance to talk about!"

Δ

Yenni's sisters knew how to throw a party. They had overseen all the preparations, and the celebration started off with a sumptuous feast featuring Yenni's favorite foods: fragrant chunks of goat in gravy with rice; hot pepper soup; cassava, boiled and sweetened; spot-beans with thick pepper sauce; sweet stewed chicken; breadfruit; coconut; and the juiciest mangoes she'd ever eaten.

The courtyard was alive with drums and singing and chatter. Stilt walkers lumbered about in colorful costumes while musicians plucked out beautiful, happy melodies. There had been dancers, singers, and an exciting battle between two clacking and towering rune puppets, and now Yenni sat with her parents at the high table while her siblings mingled with the crowd. Once again she glanced at her n'baba. He sat straight backed in his kaftan of Yirba colors: midnight blue with gold accents. He smiled benevolently at the guests who came to greet them, but every once in a while Yenni saw him clench his jaw, and sweat beaded on his forehead. He was in pain, but too proud to leave. He might even need assistance to make it down the steps from the high table and back inside, and she knew the last thing he wanted was for their guests to see him leaving stooped and weak on the arm of his wife or his guard.

This, *this* was why she had pestered and pleaded with her parents to make the pact of *Orire N'jem* and travel abroad. None of their healers knew what to make of her father's condition. The most celebrated healers among the Yirba, the Shahanta, the Fuboli, and even the Gunzu could not figure out the cause of her father's waning strength, so at last her mother had sent scholars to Cresh, the empire to the north. They had returned only a few weeks back, with reports of Creshens suffering a condition similar to her father's. The Creshens had yet to find a cure themselves, but were reportedly working toward one.

I will find a way to help you, N'baba, Yenni thought as she watched her father smile through his pain. *I swear it by all the divine Mothers and Fathers.*

For now, perhaps she could make some kind of diversion so that he could at least slip away and stop tormenting himself.

"Blessed Birthday, Yenni Aja-Nifemi."

Prince Natahi bowed before her seat. He'd used her whole name, as was proper, but somehow the way he said it seemed familiar, like a caress. The prince wore the vibrant-green pelt of a rare emerald leopard draped over his shoulders and down his back, not quite hiding his warrior's physique. His skirt was made of the same material—*Hopefully from the same poor animal,* Yenni thought—and a headdress made of blue-green peafowl feathers sat perched on his head. No runes, at least none that were visible, appeared on his body. It would be insulting to show up to another palace covered in paint as if expecting a fight.

"Sha-blessed chieftain and chieftainess," he said, addressing her parents. "Thank you for inviting my family and me to your festivities. I am greatly enjoying myself."

Yenni's father bowed his head sagely while their mother answered. "We're happy to hear it, Prince Natahi."

"Princess, would you do me the honor of accompanying me on a stroll around your grounds?"

Yenni slid her eyes to her mother, even as her heart jumped to her throat. Was the prince planning to ask for her hand already? Surely her parents would not have finalized their union without telling her?

But her mother remained as calm and regal as always. "What a wonderful idea," she said neutrally. Her face gave no hint of her emotions.

"It would be my pleasure," Yenni said, and took the hand he offered, stepping down from the dais of the high table.

Well, this will certainly create gossip, Yenni thought. But it would have been unwise to refuse. Besides, Prince Natahi was not so bad. The few times she'd met him he had been polite and charming. He was also passionate about runelore, like her. And he was handsome. If she *had* to get married, she could do worse. They walked arm in arm through the palace's back garden, between women in tall hats or bright head wraps that crowned their heads like sunrise, and among men in fine kaftans who flashed them white smiles.

There, by a lone iroko tree, she made out Jayeh and her husband chatting with the Fuboli chieftain, the three of them balancing wooden bowls of palm wine on their fingertips. Yenni narrowed her eyes. A few days earlier, the Fuboli had announced that due to bad harvests they would be increasing the price of rice, which Yenni's tribe imported from them regularly. However, her mother had it on good authority that they had increased the price more for the Yirba.

"How go your runes?" asked the prince, bringing her back to the present.

"Oh! Well," said Yenni. "I've gotten much better at pain ward."

"Hmm, yes, a tricky one."

The pain ward rune was more complicated than most, and needed to be painted down one's spine to be effective, which required much practice.

"I am happy to see His Blessedness the chieftain is looking well," said Prince Natahi, then lowered his voice. "Princess, are you aware of the current political climate on the Sha Islands?"

"I am," Yenni said cautiously.

"So you know that your father's illness has made brave some of the other tribes—the Fuboli, for example. They came to us to try to foster an alliance, and insinuated that together we would hold more power than the Yirba. To what end, they didn't exactly specify, but . . ."

"Do my parents know of this?" Yenni asked sharply.

"Of course. My father told them. The Gunzu and the Yirba were once one tribe, after all. And the last thing we want is strife among the Islands." His face went dark. "Not with the Creshens waiting to swoop in as if we were carrion."

Yenni paused at that. It was Gunzu ancestors who had refused to enter into trade with the Yirba centuries ago, and the current Gunzu chiefclan upheld that proclamation, so why was Natahi now going on about them once being of the same tribe? They must truly be serious about a marriage alliance.

"But Cresh is not a threat to us," said Yenni at last. "We have a treaty."

Natahi gave her a pitying look that sent the blood rushing to her face in anger. "They are savages, Princess. They attacked us once, they will do so again. It is their nature to take what does not belong to them. Remember: they stole a third of the Sha Islands, ravaged them, imposed their false gods, and have the nerve to call it civilization, as if they were doing the Islands a favor."

"That was over three hundred rains ago—"

"They exterminated *all* of our dragons," Prince Natahi continued, as if she hadn't spoken. His eyes blazed with righteous anger. "Not a single dragon left on all the Islands. Even in their so-called colonies they slaughtered them all, even those that surrendered."

"I know my history," said Yenni coldly.

He seemed to catch himself. "No doubt you do, Princess. My apologies, I can get carried away. I have little love for Cresh."

He would not be happy to learn of her upcoming journey then. Perhaps she would not have to worry about a betrothal on her return after all.

Prince Natahi took one of Yenni's hands in his. "I meant no offense. You are a beautiful, intelligent Island woman and I don't care what people say, any man would be lucky to have you."

"Thank you—what? What do you mean 'what people say'?"

"Ah," he looked uncomfortable. "You do have a reputation for being somewhat . . ."

"Yes?"

"Unladylike."

She pulled her hand free and blinked at him, stunned.

"But surely you know this? Your study of runelore, your love of the hunt and combat, these are not womanly things."

"Many girls hunt with their brothers!"

"Girls, yes—not women."

"And there are female Masters of runelore!"

"Masters are different. They hold no lands and have no children. They are devoted to communion with the Sha."

"As for my combat training, I train in the spear and jabdanu wrestling. Since you are so well versed in history, I trust you know that both those disciplines have been traditionally practiced by *women* as far back as the Island Wars five hundred rains ago, when women defended our homelands from raiders while the men were away."

"Yes—"

"And I can only assume, with your extensive knowledge of history, that you are well aware of how integral women were in defeating Cresh during the War of the Continent. We sent our women to fight while they did not," Yenni finished, her face flushed and warm with her irritation.

"Oh, indeed," said Prince Natahi. "Though our runes and domestication of flying mounts tipped things in our favor as well. But that was then, and this is now. We are at peace. Women no longer need to fight and hunt," he said soothingly.

"So you would have me give up these things?" asked Yenni.

He gave her a flirtatious smile. "While I may find your quirks charming, there are certain societal expectations that must be observed, and more so for royalty."

Yenni folded her arms. "Forgive me, but did you not say you were concerned about a future attack from Cresh? What would you have Island women do then?"

"The women of the Sha Islands are by far our greatest treasure," he began, but he was interrupted by a sudden shout. A pack of guards rushed past them, and as the music and drums died down Yenni heard her mother's voice ring out strong and commanding above the confused chatter.

"Summon a healer!"

N'baba!

2

The low and soothing *coo, coo, coo* of the night birds was a welcome contrast to the chaos of earlier. Yenni's father had at last given out and slumped forward in his chair. Yenni's mother and youngest brother had rushed off with her father, while Yenni forced herself to push back her anxiety and remain with Dayo and her sisters to attend to their guests and assure them that everything was fine. Her siblings were far better at hiding their fear than she was, but she did her best.

At long last they'd bid everyone farewell, and now she knelt beside her parents' softgrass mattress, holding her father's hand and wondering how by all those divine she would leave tomorrow.

"For the last time go to sleep, all of you," the chieftain said, glancing around at his family. Yenni hated how weak and breathy his voice sounded. "We have a big day tomorrow."

She would receive her final blessing and runes tomorrow. She would leave for Cresh. *Tomorrow.* Yenni closed her eyes and breathed deeply to still her fluttering heart, smelling the familiar sweetness of the tree violets, and relishing the hot breeze blowing in from the gap between the roof and the wall. Home.

Her brothers and sisters each came up to hug their father and say good night, but Yenni didn't want to leave his side, even as Dayo, the last of her siblings to go, called to her from the doorway.

"I can stay," she insisted, ignoring her brother.

"You know you cannot," said her mother sharply. She was seated on the other side of the large mattress, still wearing the beautiful blue and gold gown she'd put on for the feast, though it was now crumpled. Yenni knew her mother well enough to know the bite in her voice was not due to anger, but worry.

"Your *iyaya* is right—you cannot," her father agreed. "You made a pact with the Sha."

Tears pricked Yenni's eyes. Her father squeezed her hand and sighed. He pushed himself upright. "Dayo, fetch me my rune-paint, there," he said, pointing to a dark shelf in the left corner of the room. Her brother hurried to obey.

"Now, leave us. I would talk to your sister in private."

Dayo bowed, touching his fingertips to the ground. "As you wish, N'baba. Good night."

With Dayo gone, Yenni's father turned his attention back to her. "I had hoped to do this tomorrow after your final blessing from the Masters. But come, give me your hand. I will teach you a new rune."

Yenni's eyes went wide. Each tribe had certain runes they kept carefully hidden from the others. Some were passed down only among the royal family, and only as the Masters deemed royal children ready and worthy. Some were known strictly among the Masters alone. Slowly, reverently, Yenni gave her left hand to her father.

"Now, listen carefully." He sang her a rune hymn she had never heard before, the wordless tones of his voice bittersweet. As he sang his voice no longer shook, but came out strong. The hymn was not long, and he had Yenni repeat it twice after him.

"Very good. Watch and do as I do."

He dipped his brush in his paint and drew an unfamiliar rune, this one fluid and interconnecting, on her palm. His hand remained steady and sure. Yenni felt a brief warmth as the rune set, and her father kissed her hand before dropping it and handing her the brush.

"Pull on your rune as you draw the same one for me."

As Yenni pulled ache to the rune she found it easy to re-create it on his palm.

"Well done. Now, with your iyaya as well."

Once Yenni had completed the same set of runes with her mother on their right hands, her father sighed and leaned back against the blankets.

"These runes will keep you connected to us. If they fade, so does our health. If they disappear, so too have we departed this world."

Yenni could not stop a tear from falling. "I understand, N'baba."

"By the Sha, that will not be for a while yet. A good night's rest and I'll be fine tomorrow."

"Come," said Yenni's mother, drawing her down to sit beside her. "Tell us a story, the way you used to when you were a child. It will be a good distraction to all of us. Tell the story of Orire N'jem."

Yenni sniffed, wiped a tear away, and began.

"Many, many rains ago, when the Sha still walked the world of man, three of them had a disagreement . . ."

The story went that Father Sho, patron of hunters, insisted that only a hunter's skill determined their success, but Mother Ib and Father Ji, twin Sha of fortune, argued that luck was most important. They argued for five nights and days, until wise Father Ri came upon them. He suggested they each choose a hunter and give them from one rain to the next to catch a vicious king baboon that liked to steal children to eat. The Sha could protect their chosen from harm, but must not bestow their divine aid— not fortune and not proficiency. Should their hunter succeed by skill or by luck, therein would the Sha find their answer.

And so Yenni weaved the tale of two young champions, the pioneers of Orire N'jem. The first, a preening prince, was lazy and failed to catch his prey. Due to his failure his whole tribe was cursed with a terrible harvest. However, the second young hunter, a princess from a seasoned mountain tribe, was able to lure out the baboon king and stab him through the heart. So impressed were the Sha by her determination that on her return home they showered her tribe with blessings, including the rune of focus.

It was tradition ever since that in times of dire need, princes and princesses would make journeys to faraway lands in search of some creature or plant or sacred place, and dedicate their journey to the Sha in the hope of winning their favor, even asking specific boons of them. The journey was always completed alone, with all faith placed in the Sha's divine protection, and always one year long.

Thus Yenni had begged to go to Cresh on Orire N'jem. At last her parents had relented, and took Yenni's case to the tribal Masters. They had conferred and, to Yenni's joy, agreed that she should go, but under one strange condition: she must ask the Sha not to heal her father, but to protect the tribe from harm. She could not leave on Orire N'jem without the Masters' blessing, so Yenni agreed. Her father was part of the tribe, after all, so should not the Sha's protection extend to him as well, thus saving him?

"You have always been a skillful storyteller," said her father sleepily when she was done.

"Iyaya, N'baba, thank you again for trusting me to go on Orire N'jem. I will not fail the tribe, and I will not fail you."

Her mother took her hands and rose, urging her to stand as well. She kissed Yenni's cheek. "It is late. We will both be there on the shore to see you off tomorrow, my sweet daughter, so go to sleep."

"Yes. Good night," said Yenni softly. She touched her finger-tips under her chin and bowed to her parents before leaving the room.

Δ

The seabirds called and the ocean shushed against the sand. Yenni lay on the warm stone of the temple dais as Masters Keema, Ollu, and Joko prepared to paint her. All three wore the same style of dress, even though Master Keema was a woman and Masters Ollu and Joko were men. Large headdresses of golden sunbird feathers surrounded their heads, and each was draped in lavish robes reflecting the colors of the Sha they especially worshiped. Master Ollu wore the green and black of Father Gu the warrior, Master Joko's robes were the blue and yellow of Father Sho the hunter, and Master Keema wore blue and white for Mother Ye, protector of women. They all had pale, watery eyes—the result of the constant pulling of runes and communion with the Sha. It was impossible to tell how old they might be.

The chiefclan—Yenni's mother, her father, Jayeh and Ifeh and their husbands, and her brothers, Dayo and Jumi—sat in a semi-circle on glittering embroidered cushions, all silent. A ship waited in the harbor and once Yenni received this final rune, she would depart.

She'd considered flying her field sphinx, Ofa, across the sea, but she didn't know where she would stable him in Cresh. She decided it was better to leave him home, safe and sound. She'd gone to the royal stables to say one final good-bye that morning. As she scratched the sandy fur of his head, his feline face was long with sorrow.

Now, beams of dusty sunlight streamed in through the high windows of the temple, and the air smelled of the sea. The atmosphere was hushed and reverent.

The three Masters arranged themselves around her.

"Daughter," began Master Keema.

"Receive this rune, the holy blessing of the Mothers and Fathers bestowed upon the Yirba," continued Master Joko.

"The Sha's divine protection," Master Ollu finished.

As one they dipped their fingers directly into their bowls and began to sing, their voices blending in beautiful union. Yenni struggled not to squirm as they traced the complex rune on her abdomen. She felt them moving in a circle, drawing branches and lines out from the center.

Their voices coalesced into a final note, two voices high, one low, and abruptly they stopped, tying off the rune. Without looking, Yenni knew the chalky paint was now one with her skin.

"This rune will alert you to threats on your life," said Master Keema.

"If you feel its heat against your skin . . ." began Master Joko.

". . . beware," Master Ollu finished.

Yenni stood and bowed to the Masters.

"Praises be to the Mothers and Fathers," she responded, a little breathless as her heart thudded in her chest.

Her family departed the temple in silence, and too soon they were at the docks, where Yenni's ship waited. She hugged and kissed each one of them, exchanging tears and shaky good-byes, until she came to her father.

"I'll see you when the rains come around once more," she whispered, staring fiercely into his eyes. He pulled her close and kissed the top of her head.

Each step up the ship's wooden gangplank felt heavy with cause to Yenni, and at last she was staring down at her family, blurred by her tears, as the sailors called and prepared to depart. Yenni's aunt, Morayo, head of ships, met her at the top. She squeezed Yenni's shoulder as she made eye contact with Yenni's mother and nodded. Then all too soon the sails unfurled, and the ship shuddered as it pulled away from the shore.

$$\Delta$$

Yenni kept track of her days at sea by lining gold figurines along her cabin wall. She often received tiny sculptures, carved in intricate detail, of her favorite creatures as gifts—quick-footed n'ne and glorious sunbirds, fleet cats and giant river fish with tails longer than she was tall. They were some of her most prized possessions, and she planned to sell them all once she reached Cresh. From the moment she left home she must make her own way without the aid of others, lest she break the Sha's rules and upset them, so she could not accept gold from her family. However, selling her own possessions was an acceptable sacrifice.

Two figurines and they reached the Shahanta's island, where they replenished their stock of provisions. Six more figures joined the line as they passed the chain of small islands that made up Fuboli territory. Another eight as they cut through Gunzu waters, again stopping to restock, but Yenni stayed onboard to avoid awkward questions. And at last they were on the home stretch to Cresh. Though they would pass the small, single island of the Watatzi tribe, they did not plan to stop there. The Watatzi were a strange and reclusive people.

Their ship made good progress, sailing pleasantly when the wind was favorable, the crew urging the ship along with wind runes when it was not. Yenni very much appreciated that her aunt had left hanging her responsibilities as head of ships to see Yenni across the sea. The head of ships was almost always a woman, as it was known that water—oceans, rivers, and lakes—behaved far better for women than men, offering up its bounty of fish or allowing them smooth passage.

Yenni spent her days studying Creshen language, history, and politics, grilling her aunt about her travels to the Empire, or simply standing above deck and watching the white wake of the ship frothing on turquoise seas as she contemplated the task that awaited her in Cresh.

Over and over she recalled the day when she'd flown her field sphinx down into Father Ri's sacred cave, to the ancient shrine at the bottom. How it was bathed in streams of sunlight and strips of shadow. She'd taken her divination stones, etched with pictures in the language of the Sha, and offered them up to the faceless statue of wise Father Ri.

"I, Yenni Aja-Nifemi ka Yirba, princess of the Yirba tribe, have come to pledge myself to the royal rite of the sacred journey, to embark on Orire N'jem," she'd said. "I ask that you protect my tribe from any looming threat, and in return I will journey to the Empire of Cresh. Tell me, Oh wise Father, what would you have me do there?"

She'd cast her eight-sided divination stones, and they'd clattered on the rocky floor, echoing through the silence. When at last they'd settled, one showed an open eye: search or find. The other depicted a flame—the symbol for the energy that ran through all things: ach'e.

Thus instructed, Yenni had devised her plan. She must travel to Cresh and study the Creshens' use of ach'e—"magic," as they put it. She would gain entrance to their best academy and learn all she could. To what end, she was not yet sure, but the Sha had spoken and her faith was strong. The key to understanding her father's illness must somehow be tied to Creshen magic, she was sure.

She had twenty-three figurines all in a line when they docked at the Island of Sainte Ventas, the biggest of the islands colonized by Cresh and a hub for commerce. Yenni marveled at the stilted houses dotting the hills in flashes of bright pastel colors: pink and blue and yellow. Captain Morayo took her into the island proper, among the noise of rumbling donkey carts and calling vendors. The scents of fried fish and coconut. White painted storefronts with tall and welcoming arches. The people here looked so different! Some were dark skinned, like her, but some had skin the color of a sandy shore. Were these native Creshens? She had never seen a Creshen in person before, but she'd heard they were pink skinned, and the people she saw were more of a golden brown. Perhaps they simply had Creshen heritage.

Either way, most everyone she met was incredibly friendly, even the trader who'd bought her figurines. As her aunt had warned, he'd offered a sum so low that she'd had to counter ten times as much. Though he spluttered and cajoled, and she hadn't understood half of what he'd said due to his strange Island dialect, they eventually met in the middle. With a sad sigh Yenni gave up her beloved treasures for a thick stack of Creshen duvvies.

Though she wanted to stay and explore, Yenni headed right back to the ship. She had to register for the entrance test and she would rather not tempt Father Esh, trickster and troublemaker that he was. Though she had no figurine to mark it, it took all night to navigate from Saint Ventas to the coast of Imperium Centre. The honeyed globe of the sun was just rising over the ocean, like a goddess stepping from her bath, when at last the towers of Cresh appeared on the horizon. It was also around this time that Yenni spotted her first dragon.

They were like a streak of fire, with scales that glittered orange in the light of sunrise. Yenni stood captivated on deck along with most of the sailors as the dragon swooped into the city. Beautiful but dangerous. Her conversation with Prince Natahi suddenly came to mind. Frowning, she fished a pot of runepaint and a brush from the pack on her hip. The Songs of the Sha said the first dragons were birthed from the fires of Father Gu's forge, and their only weakness was water, thus she softly sang the hymn for water as she painted a rune on the back of each hand.

Soon their ship pulled into harbor, and it was time for Yenni to depart. Her eyes were wide as she took in the streams of people bustling along the docks. *These* were Creshens. Their skin was quite pale and their hair flowed like seaweed. But people of many different hues, including more northern Islanders, like those of Sainte Ventas, threaded through the crowd as well.

She felt a tap on her shoulder. "This is where I leave you, Yenni," said her aunt. Yenni reached back and felt for her spring-spear, then felt for the small knife strapped to her arm. She looked at her left palm, where her father's rune marked her skin.

"I am ready. Thank you for seeing me here safely." She embraced Morayo and felt the taut strength of her aunt's arms, muscle corded from a lifetime of ship's labor. "May the Mothers and Fathers smile upon you," she said.

Watching Morayo return to her ship, Yenni fought down a bubble of anxiety. She had never been this far from home, and never on her own. But she had her wits, her runes, and the divine guidance of the Sha. Bowing her head, she prayed.

From this moment on, I undertake this sacred journey in your name. Oh Most Divine, watch me and guide me, your servant.

Yenni hitched up her back-satchel and set off to follow the crowd leaving the docks.

3

Four guards stood in front of a large archway made of pale stone and decorated with flowery Creshen carvings. It was part of a high wall that stretched off to either side of the docks, cutting off the wooden boardwalk. The guards seemed to let most people through, but when Yenni's turn came, one of them put out a gloved hand and stopped her.

"Hold. Your business?" he demanded, a wiry beard parting to reveal his mouth.

"Hello! I am here to apply for admission to Prevan Academy for Battle and Magical Arts!" said Yenni.

Another guard, younger, with big ears that stuck out from either side of his head, like those of a rodent, glanced between Yenni and a sheet of paper, scribbling furiously with what looked like a bird's feather even as the two others continued to wave people through. Her interrogator turned and spit whatever he was chewing on the grass. "Where are you from, en? Dressed like that. One of the Islands?"

"The Sha Isl—I mean the Moonrise Isles," said Yenni, pleased she'd remembered the Creshen name for her home in time. All four sets of eyebrows went up.

"Huh," said the bearded guard. "Well then, welcome to Imperium Centre. We accept any and all. You'll hardly find a more sophisticated city in all the world."

"Name?" asked the man as he scribbled her portrait.

"I am Yenni Aja-Nifemi ka Yirba."

"Right. You want to repeat that?"

Eventually the scribe took down her name. "Your writ of passage," he said, handing her one roll of paper. "And a map of the academy," he said, holding out another. "It's just there, you can't miss it." He gestured with the paper at a collection of towers and outbuildings that looked like the Creshens' version of a palace— tall, gray, and stately. "Can you read?"

"Yes, why would you think otherwise?"

He shrugged. "It's true your Creshen is good for an Islander. And from the Moonrise Isles at that, en?"

"I see. Thank you." Yenni knew he was trying to compliment her, but something about his statement made her uncomfortable.

He opened the map. "Right then. I'm an alumnus of Prevan myself, you know. Registration is at Bertrand's East, it's right next to the bell tower here." He drew a circle on the map and handed it to her.

The bearded guard pointed at her weapons. "Arms are allowed in the city, but don't go making trouble, or the peacekeepers will be on you in half a second."

"I . . . do I seem like the type to cause trouble?" Yenni asked, confused.

"Just a warning," he said. "That's it, then—you're free to go."

Yenni nodded and stepped through the arch. She soon found herself caught up in the crowd moving north from the docks, and the sights of the city around her drove all thoughts of the uncomfortable encounter with the guards from her mind. Cresh was so different from home. So much of everything was columns and rows. Rows of pastel houses—tall, skinny, and pointed. Rows of intersecting streets paved in slick, smooth stone. Rows of people, rows of carts. Rows of trees planted just so. Yenni longed to wander down the lanes and alleys, to peek into every glass window, to discover the source of that syrupy scent teasing her nose, but she had a mission. She fixed her gaze firmly on the tall, sprawling compound in the distance and soldiered on.

$$\Delta$$

Excitement and nerves fluttered like bottleflies in Yenni's chest. Creshen architecture soared around her, all height and pillars and hard, sharp angles. The Creshens had a curious habit of letting leaves grow on the surface of the stone, like animal fur, but it was pretty and exotic.

Yenni found she could hardly look up from her map without catching someone's curious gaze. It must be her runes. White paint made swirling patterns all over her dark skin: strength runes on her arms, speed runes on her legs, water runes on the backs of her hands, and wards against pain down her spine. Once more Yenni glanced between her map and the academy grounds, searching for the bell tower. Straight ahead a long, white structure blocked her path—the entrance surrounded by thick columns.

She swiveled her head left and right, trying to get her bearings, and made eye contact with a man standing far off, across the grass. He squinted at her, but unlike the others, he didn't immediately dart his eyes away. He continued to stare, unabashed, and Yenni squinted right back. She wasn't about to let some brute intimidate her. From what she could make out, he was tall and well muscled. He wore his dark hair in a thick braid that fell over his left shoulder and his shirt was open, showing his chest. His skin was a few shades darker than the other Creshens around.

Whoever he was, she had no time for him. Yenni shook her head and focused on the building ahead. It was pretty in its way. True, it lacked the gold and tile embellishments so common back home, but it had many beautiful windows made of panes of colored glass. Sleek columns supported a stone awning above the entrance, which was engraved with words she couldn't make out due to the loopy, stylized writing.

Pretty as it was, the building stretched like a barricade, blocking her view. She craned her head upward, standing on her toes to see, and a sound like sails snapping in the wind echoed through the air before a shadow fell across her. A screeching roar pierced the quiet. Before she could even think to run a black beast swooped in like some overgrown demon hawk and touched down on the grass beside the whitestone path, right across from her. He blinked huge, violet eyes and lazy trails of steam drifted from his large nostrils as he rumbled at her, deep and guttural.

Oh Mothers and Fathers protect me.

Instincts honed from years of hunting told her not to make any sudden movements, but she slowly brought her hands up, backs out, showing him her water runes.

"I want no fight, Dragon," she said as she retreated. The dragon stalked after her, claws clicking on the path. Her back hit rough stone, an outbuilding of some kind, and the dragon stopped as well. She kept her shaking hands before her but hesitated to attack. The beast didn't plan to kill her—the Masters' rune gave her no such warning, but that could change in an instant. He seemed more curious than anything, and she didn't want to antagonize him.

He turned his long, scaled head to the side and regarded her out of an eye as big as her palm, the slitted pupil a dark, elliptical discus floating in amethyst. Though adrenaline flooded her veins and her muscles tensed to run, she couldn't help thinking that the dragon before her was even more stunning than the one she'd seen flying into the city; maybe even more beautiful than the n'ne on the plains at home. She marveled at how his scales flashed from black to violet in the sun.

"What do you want with me?" she demanded.

A gleaming claw shot out at her. Yenni dove and rolled to the right, straight into the hard scales of the creature's tail. She jumped up even as the dragon curled leisurely around her, sinuous and deadly. Yenni whipped up her hands and unleashed twin jets of water at the beast.

He snorted and flicked out a pink lizard's tongue, lapping at the water.

Mothers and Fathers, water does no harm! The dragon lay flat, still eyeing her, his body a wall of scales. Tall, regal horns curved up and back from his head.

Yenni's stomach was a twisted knot of nerves, yet she heard no screams, no shouts, no indication that anyone else noticed the grumbling beast surrounding her. She'd seen students everywhere coming and going, and though a few spared curious glances for the unfolding drama, none stepped in to help her; not even the man who'd stared her down so boldly moments ago.

The dragon turned. Yenni flared her speed runes and dove, but too slowly, and a forked tongue slid rough and wet against her thigh. The dragon jerked his head up, twin plumes of smoke hissing from his nose, and nimbly jumped to his feet like a fleet cat, rising up to more than twice her height. Then he turned away from her, opened his bat-like wings, and flapped them, fanning her with heat. He took off with a screech, flashing purple and black as he soared into the azure sky. For two heartbeats Yenni stood stunned, watching the beast disappear, then she grabbed the straps of her back-satchel and ran like an emerald leopard was on her heels.

She didn't stop until she was in an open square of bright, green grass, where at last she flicked her eyes back to the sky, relieved to see it dragonless. Panting, she glanced around. The other students gave her strange looks, but none seemed particularly disturbed. What by all the Sha was going on? She didn't imagine the whole thing, did she?

She looked up again, tense, alert for the sound of wings beating the air, but the atmosphere around her was calm, almost pastoral. Perhaps it had been some kind of hallucination brought on by stress. But that heat and those gemlike eyes . . . the dragon felt real enough. Yenni looked to the sky yet again. Still no dragons. She bit her lip. If she retraced her steps she could find the main gate again and go from there. Hallucination or not, she wanted to get out of the open as quickly as possible. She turned to head back and froze.

A very strange person was making her way through the sprinkling of students in the square. Yenni blinked. Was this another trick of her mind? She shook her head, but the woman didn't disappear. Yenni knew it was rude, but she stared openly. She couldn't help it: the woman was blue!

All the Creshens she'd encountered so far were pale, but this woman was so light skinned her complexion had a blue tinge. Her face was angular, with high cheekbones and eyelids that folded over in a way Yenni had never seen before. Truly, all manner of people resided in Cresh.

The woman smiled as she approached, her steps gliding and graceful under her long ivory skirt. She didn't seem to be a threat. Still, Yenni stood ready to call on her runes. This was a strange place where no one batted an eye at dragon attacks, and she wasn't taking any more chances.

"Let me guess, you're looking for admissions?" said the woman.

Yenni let her shoulders drop. "Yes, I am."

"Allow me to show you where to go. I'm volunteering with the student service committee and it's my job to stalk the grounds looking for lost lambs to lead. I'm Kiyozui Duval. Call me Zui."

She held a hand up, palm forward, and it took Yenni a moment to remember that in Cresh women greeted each other by touching palm to palm. She placed her hand against Zui's, holding back a grimace at the awkwardness of it.

"Nice to meet you. I am Yenni Aja-Nifemi ka Yirba, and I'm from the Moonrise Isles."

"I should have guessed. I've never seen anyone like you before. Your hair is really something. May I touch it?"

"Touch it?" Yenni felt a trace of unease that she couldn't quite understand. "Oh. I—I suppose . . ."

Zui ran one of Yenni's black braids through her hand. "Pretty," she said.

"Thank you. Your hair is quite interesting as well. May I?" Yenni gestured to the swath of pale-blue hair draped like sea grass down the woman's back.

"Oh! Well, I suppose it would be rude of me to refuse after you were so accommodating." Zui was about a head taller than Yenni, and she bent awkwardly so that Yenni could run her fingers through her hair.

"Incredible," she said, fascinated by how the blue hair slid lazily through her fingers.

After a while Zui cleared her throat awkwardly. "I'm beginning to feel a bit like a pony on a petting farm," she said and laughed nervously.

"Ah!" cried Yenni, the source of her earlier discomfort clicking into place. "Yes! That was how I felt as well."

"Oh my, I do apologize then." Zui blew out a breath and changed the subject. "These white markings on your skin are quite striking, Do they have a purpose or meaning?"

"They do, but"—Yenni glanced at the sky again—"I am in a hurry. I will tell you about my runes on the way to admissions. Please lead the way."

"Oh! Of course."

As they walked Yenni took in the hard lines of the strength rune painted on her right bicep. She'd never thought of runes as being striking, but she supposed the white paint did contrast highly with her dark skin.

"These are runes, for pulling ach'e—no. What is the word? Magic," she explained. "These ones are for strength, speed, and wards against pain," she said, touching the designs painted on her upper arms, calves, and spine respectively.

"Incredible! Things are quite different on the Moonrise Isles. I was born in Minato myself, but I moved here when I was just a baby."

So that was it! Zui wasn't actually Creshen, but from the Minato Empire to the east. Yenni smiled, glad she no longer had to come up with a way to ask the woman why she was blue. She did, however, want to know more about dragons.

"Welcome to Prevan Academy for Battle and Magical Arts," Zui continued. "You're right to be in a hurry, I'm sure there'll be quite a line."

"Oh?" Sharp anxiety pierced Yenni's chest. "That many are vying for entrance to the academy?"

"Why yes!" said Zui. "It's like this every season."

"And will everyone be let in?"

Zui put a delicate hand to her chest and laughed. "Not even close! A quarter, if that. Come, it's this way."

Yenni followed Zui, all thoughts of the dragon wiped away. She had not expected such competition, and anxiety slowly unfurled in the depths of her belly.

Stop it, she chided herself. *I will gain entrance to these Creshens' academy. I'm top of my class, I speak five languages, and I am a princess of the Yirba. I will not fail.* She squeezed her left hand shut, encompassing the rune there. *I cannot fail.*

Δ

The bell tower rang out twice in the time Yenni spent standing, then sitting, then standing in the line that snaked out of Bertrand's East. The other applicants chattered and whispered around her, though none engaged her directly. Yenni ignored them, letting her thoughts drift back to home. At last it came her turn to show her writ of passage and to answer a few questions. She exchanged her paper for two tokens, one carved with a flame, the other with a sword. They would grant her entrance to the battle aptitude and magical aptitude tests in the following days.

At last Yenni jogged down the wide flight of steps and moved off the path to the grass. Free of the crush and noise, she closed her eyes and breathed deeply. Her next move was to secure lodging at the guest residences for prospective students.

Yenni's stomach rumbled, bringing her back to the present. As she rummaged around in her bag for the dried plantain she'd bought in Sainte Ventas, someone called her name. Zui Duval weaved through the sea of students, followed by someone just as colorful. Yenni smiled and returned the blue woman's frantic waving with a casual flash of her hand.

"Hi, Yenni!" Zui called. Yenni flinched at Zui's casual address, but met her palm.

"To be honest, my name is Yenni Aja-Nifemi," she said. "Though Yenni Ajani will do. I know that in Cresh you are used to shorter names, but on the Moonrise Isles those are somewhat informal, reserved for family and close friends."

"Oh! I apologize, Yenni Ajani. This is my husband, Harth." Zui gestured to the man beside her.

"Only?" It wouldn't do to call him by a name with just one sound. One-sound names were reserved for the Sha. "Do you have any other names?"

"Well, my full name is Harth Raynee Duval," he said, and stuck out a hand. Yenni remembered just in time that men in Cresh greeted each other, and women they weren't familiar with, by clasping the forearm. She grabbed his arm loosely.

He was tall, and she had to look way up to meet his eye. "I am happy to meet you, Harth Raynee Duval," she said, emphasizing each name.

Her mouth stayed parted for a moment more, a question heavy on her tongue, but she shut her lips and swallowed the words. This was a new place with many new customs to learn and people to meet. Yenni didn't want to seem rude or ignorant, so she was having a hard time coming up with a way to ask Harth Raynee Duval why his skin was green.

He wasn't a vivid green, only greenish, darker at spots like his elbows and knuckles. His hair, now that was vivid green, and pulled back in a short horsetail. His eyes were friendly and shone like polished jade.

"Back at you, en?" he said. "So, Yenni Ajani, you are easily the most interesting person I've seen in a while. Where are you from?"

"The Moonrise Isles!" cried Zui. "Isn't that something?"

"Oho! So it is. What brings you all this way?"

"I—I wanted to be the first woman of the Moonrise Isles to study in Cresh," she said. It was best not to tell people about Orire N'jem, should they inadvertently intervene in a way the Sha deemed unfit.

Harth looked impressed. "A pioneer! I must ask, what are these white markings? They're very striking."

Yenni laughed. "Your wife said that exactly." She briefly explained her runes. "And I could say the same for you. Are you also from Minato?"

He looked astonished. "Of course not! I'm Creshen through and through. What would give you that idea?"

Yenni faltered. "You look similar, so I thought . . ."

They looked at each other and spoke as one. "We do?"

"Yes. Your coloring . . ."

"But I'm blue and Harth is green," said Zui, as if one just happened upon blue and green people as a matter of course.

"We're both dragons, if that's what you mean," said Harth.

Yenni stared at him. Blinked. "I'm so sorry, but my Creshen is not very good. I thought I heard you say you were dragons."

"Your Creshen seems fine to me, and yes, I did."

Yenni's mouth worked as she tried to form a sentence. "I—I didn't realize . . ."

Harth burst out laughing. "But how could you? We blend in so naturally with everyone else, en?"

Yenni narrowed her eyes at him, anger rising up her throat like bile. She did not like being ridiculed, made to feel ignorant. After all, it wasn't her fault there were no dragons left on the Sha Islands.

Zui glanced at her face and smacked her husband on the arm. "Ow!"

"Don't mind him," she said. "There aren't any dragons on the Islands are there?"

"Not for three hundred years," said Yenni. She cut her eyes at Harth. "Our dragons were exterminated by Cresh during the Colonial War, after all, so I have never met a dragon in person."

Harth cleared his throat. "Ah. Yes. Then you couldn't have known. Understandable."

Yenni frowned in thought. "To be honest, I did meet a dragon earlier, but perhaps meet is not the most accurate word. He accosted me."

"En? Truly?" said Harth. At last, someone was having a reasonable reaction.

"Yes, a big violet-black one."

"Ooooh," they said together. "Weysh."

"He's . . . mostly harmless," said Harth.

"Well, he licked me."

"What?" said Zui. "He licked you? With his *tongue*? That *is* uncivilized, even for Weysh."

"Oh, speak and the spoken appear," said Harth. He waved at someone behind her. "Ho! Weysh!"

The same man who'd stared her down earlier strode toward them, his pace eating up swaths of the green grass. Up close he was tall, perhaps even taller than Harth Raynee Duval. He still wore his shirt open, and Yenni saw he had the build of a warrior, the muscles of his abdomen plainly sculpted. His hair still hung in that braid over his shoulder, and his dark eyebrows were drawn down over violet eyes that bore into hers shamelessly.

"Weysh!" called Harth. "I hear you're going around licking unsuspecting women now."

The man ignored him and came to stand right before Yenni.

"What's your name?" His voice was deep, resonant. Was this really the dragon who had cornered her earlier? Yes, Yenni could believe it. There was something powerful about him, almost as if he radiated heat. And sections of his hair shone violet in the sunlight. Yenni stood straighter.

"I am Yenni Aja-Nifemi ka Yirba," she answered. "I'm from the Sha . . . no. Moonrise—"

She gasped as the man lifted her up like she was a clay doll, buried his warm face against her neck, and sniffed. She was too shocked to stop him. He put her down and stared, like he'd taken a blow to the head and lost his wits. Yenni could only stare back, utterly lost for words.

"It's really you," he murmured at last, and reached for her again.

Yenni struck out like a hood snake, kicking his arm away.

"For the blessing of Byen!" he roared. Zui gasped beside her.

She yanked her spring-spear from the holder on her back, twisting the mechanism to make it extend, and pointed it at him. "Understand that if you touch me again I will run you through."

Harth glanced back and forth between the two of them, his mouth agape.

The dragon cradled his arm to his chest and had the audacity to look at her like she was at fault. "En?"

"Stay away from me, Dragon."

He looked absolutely perplexed. "But . . . you're my Given!"

4

The Island girl—his Given—pointed the sharp tip of her metal spear right at his throat. Weysh blinked at it, bewildered.

"What does this mean, *Given*?" she demanded.

"En? It means we're bonded through the will of Byen."

How could she not know that? He took her in, not only the heady scent of her, but her stance and her attire. White paint made strange marks all over her body, and her shirt was nothing more than a swath of yellow material that wrapped around her middle and looped over each shoulder, leaving her arms bare and showing a tantalizing hint of her midriff. A brown leather skirt hugged her hips. It was far more skin than he was used to seeing a woman show in polite society, not that he was complaining. She didn't look like any Islander he knew, certainly not like his cousins. Where had she said she was from? Weysh's eyebrows shot up. Did she say the Moonrise Isles? Well, *that* would be why she had no concept of Given. In fact, she continued to glare at him in obvious confusion.

"It means we'll be married soon," he clarified.

Her eyes went wide, then angry. "*Lunacy*," she said. "I refuse to wed you, Dragon."

"What? You can't say that." Weysh turned to Harth. "Can she say that?"

Harth shrugged. "Apparently so."

Weysh turned back to Yenni. "Look, lovely, I'm sorry if I've done anything to offend you, but we're Given—it's natural that we should be familiar with each other, en?"

"What do you not understand? Stay away from me!"

"Oho!" shouted Harth, that ass boil. He was probably enjoying every second of this mess. Weysh tuned him out.

"Don't you have a mouth on you," he said, and then he was distracted by her mouth. A small mouth with full lips he very much wanted to kiss.

"I am leaving. Follow me and you will regret it."

He raised his hands in surrender. "All right, lovely. As you say."

She jerked her spear away and marched off, her hips swaying hypnotically as she disappeared down the whitestone path, bound for the sharp spires of Lelond Hall.

"Watcher above, Weysh!" cried Zui, and took off after his Given. Weysh wanted to run after her, too, but it was best to give females space when they got like that. For now he'd make do with the scent of her. It still clung to his nostrils like perfume on his sheets the morning after he'd taken a woman home. He wasn't even in dragon form and he'd been able to catch her scent from yards away. She smelled like flowers. No, soil! No. Sun? Meat? Grass? Hmm . . . no. She smelled like . . . *forever*.

A goofy grin spread across his face. He'd resigned himself to his fate, sure that due to the circumstances of his birth, he was a severed dragon, Givenless. But then here she was, like a summer squall. He wanted to shout it across the square. He'd met his Given!

Slow clapping brought his mind back from among the clouds.

"I must say, well done, Weysh."

As was often the case with Harth, Weysh couldn't tell if he was being serious.

"Erm, thank you?"

"Yes, that's the fastest I've ever seen you incite a woman to murderous rage."

"She'll come around," Weysh grumped. "She must. Others do, and she's my Given."

Harth opened his mouth as if to say something, closed it, opened it again. "You're sure?"

Weysh gave one firm nod of his head. "Absolutely. It's her scent, Harth. It's like . . . it's . . ."

"Sharp, new, and tantalizing, but with notes of something cozy and very familiar."

"Yes, that's exactly it!"

"Well, then, I suppose congratulations are in order! But it seems like you have a bit of a gap to bridge, en? I will forever treasure the look on your face when she threatened to spear you like a fish." Harth sputtered and laughed.

"It's not funny, Harth!"

"Well, you deserve it! You should know not to manhandle a woman like that."

"She's not *a* woman, she's my Given!"

Harth shrugged again. "All the more reason to treat her with kindness."

Weysh frowned. Had he been unkind? "Listen, if my Given

asks me to, I will pluck the scales off my back and give them to her."

Harth held up his hands. "Yes, I know—"

"And my dragonling will have the best father to walk the realm of folk. He will want for nothing."

"I understand that, but—"

"I would never do to her what my *sire* did to *his* Given, and to my maman and others. *Never!*"

"No one said you would, but—"

"She's too sensitive," Weysh concluded. "Most women are. I just have to show her I'd never hurt her. Once she realizes that, she'll come running with open arms."

"I see. Well, please let me know how that works out for you. In the meantime, what on Byen's hallowed soil do you plan to do about Carmenna?"

Weysh's insides went so instantly frigid it was as if he'd swallowed a bucket of ice shavings. Kindly Watcher, he really was a dung worm—he'd completely forgotten about Carmenna, the woman who right until a few moments before he'd been convinced he would eventually marry.

Weysh glanced away, fixing his gaze on Prevan's famous bell tower, with its dozen whirring clock faces, rather than on Harth.

"Dragons are Given. She understands that."

Harth snorted, the sound full of skepticism, and Weysh couldn't rightly blame him. As an unmated dragon, Weysh had never lacked for female company. There were always women, curious and hopeful, trying to catch his attention. But Carmenna was different. She had meant more to him than a romantic conquest. They hadn't even slept together, for the blessing of Byen!

She was a friend too. He both regretted and dreaded the inevitable pain he would cause her.

"Look, just leave that up to me. I'll figure it out," Weysh told Harth.

The tower erupted into a tinkling of chimes, signaling the hour.

"Hells, I'm late," Harth cursed. He jogged backward, making for the long, low row of lecture halls. "First class of the year is History of Dragon Diplomacy, so I need to make a good impression, en?" Harth was on track to become a diplomat, like his father. "But I'm glad you've found your Given, Weysh. I suppose you'll be heading home to inform your family?"

Weysh winced. He had been putting off his next visit home for a while now, but it seemed he could put it off her no longer. *His* first class wasn't until later that day. "I suppose I will," said Weysh.

"Good luck," said Harth, seeing the look on Weysh's face. He turned with a wave and sprinted for the lecture buildings.

Weysh sighed heavily. Best to get the family visit over with. He reached deep inside himself for that natural trigger, the one that sent magic rushing through his veins. His skin went numb but smells got sharper, sounds louder, colors bolder, and then he was his dragon self, large and powerful. He stretched his wings, feeling pops along the joints like always when he first switched. A few flaps and he was up and flying, off to face his parents.

Δ

Sylvie came barreling out of the main door, holding up her dress as she skipped down the manor steps. She ran up the cobblestones and Weysh changed back in time to grab her in his arms.

Laughing, he spun her around and plopped her down, breathing in her scent. Though she was a young woman now, she would always smell like a little sister to him—like cherries and flowers and pastries.

"Sylvie, my heart. How are you?"

She hugged him. "Weysh! I missed you."

He ran a hand through her hair, a beautiful mass of brown-blond curls like their maman's, but much shorter than he remembered.

"When did you do this?"

"Over a moonturn ago. It's actually grown out a bit. You'd know if you came by more often." She pouted at him.

He planted a kiss on her forehead. "I'm sorry, lovely. It seems all I'm doing today is making women angry."

"Just today?"

He frowned in jest. "Aren't you funny," he said as he flicked her forehead in the same place he'd just kissed.

"Hey!" She rubbed the spot. "What happened now?"

"The usual, but I have good news as well. Come, let's find Maman."

She was in the sitting room. Weysh smelled the coffee long before he saw the dainty little cup in her hand. He wrinkled his nose at the scent of his mother's husband, Montpierre—it was so different, so other from his maman's and Sylvie's.

"Oh! Weysh!" She smiled but there was a wariness to it. Still, Weysh strode around the plush rug to the wing chair where she sat and draped an arm around her in a loose hug. She turned and pecked him on the cheek. Weysh gave the man across from her a terse nod, which was returned in kind.

"What a surprise!" said his mother. "To what do we owe the pleasure?"

He cleared his throat. "I have good news."

"Oh?" said his mother, her brown eyes wide. "What is it?"

The goofy grin crept onto his face again. "I've met my Given."

Sylvie squealed from behind him, and Montpierre told her to hush.

His mother eyed him over the rim of her cup. "Truly? Is it that beauty with the long black hair? The one from Espanna you brought to dinner? She's quite stunning."

Sylvie laughed and perched on the arm of her father's chair. "You only say that because she looks a lot like you, Maman."

His mother cocked her head to the side. "Does she?"

Weysh brushed aside the bubble of guilt at the mention of Carmenna, the only woman he'd ever introduced to his family. "She doesn't look anything like Maman," he said indignantly, feeling mildly disturbed. "And no, it's not her. You know that's not how mating works for dragons."

"I know no such thing," said his maman, a bit sharply. "Besides, I remember you telling me you intended to choose your own Given."

"Yes, well, things have changed." None of his family were dragonkind. How to explain to them the compulsion his Given had over him, right from the first meeting? The way her scent made strange tingles of bliss radiate from his skull down his spine?

Montpierre coughed. "Hmph. I suppose this means you'll stop terrorizing the women of Imperium Centre?"

"Papa," Sylvie warned, but Weysh only fixed the man with his violet eyes and threw him a lazy smile.

"Yes, Montpierre, I suppose it does."

"Who is she?" asked Sylvie.

"Yenni Ajaya . . . something. Anyway, she's a fiery little thing from the Moonrise Isles."

"Oh! The Sunrise Isles! Like your grandpapa deceased!" cried his mother. "We'll have to take a trip together—it's been too long since I've visited my brother on the Islands."

Weysh shook his head. "Not the Sunrise Isles, Maman. The *Moonrise* Isles."

"Oh. Oh that *is* something. Have you ever met anyone from the Moonrise Isles, my love?" She directed the question at Montpierre.

"Never," he said, and sighed. It turned into a fit of coughs that had Sylvie leaning forward in concern. He waved her off as he brought a kerchief to his mouth, and spoke again once the coughs subsided. "But of course you would match with a woman from the other side of the world. So you're to be married, I take it?" said Montpierre, rubbing the bridge of his nose.

"As soon as possible."

"Just splendid."

Anger flushed the back of Weysh's neck. "Look, Montpierre, I know you were itching to stick another dragon in your family tree, but consider yourself lucky to even have me."

"Yes," Montpierre drawled. "I cannot contain my glee at having to leave my estate to my wife's bastard *dragon* son."

"Stop it now! Both of you!" shouted Sylvie. She looked close to tears. His mother hung her head, silent, as always.

It was time to leave, before Weysh said something he would later regret, but it would be a record-breaking shortest visit home. He hadn't even had a chance to say hello to their housekeeper, Genie. No doubt she was puttering in the cellar and hadn't heard him arrive, or she'd surely have come to greet him. She'd be hurt he'd stopped by without seeking her out, but it was best that he go.

"I just wanted to share the good news," said Weysh, voice clipped. "I'll be going now."

Sylvie rushed over from her place at her father's side. "You won't even stay for dinner?"

He softened at the disappointment on her face. "No. Sorry, lovely. But how about sometime next week I pick you up and we spend the day together?"

"I will not have Sylvie riding dragonback—"

"We'll go by tram," Weysh snapped at Montpierre.

Sylvie clapped. "I love riding the trams!"

Weysh chuckled. "I know." He hugged her. "Until then, en?"

He turned and gave his parents an exaggerated, mocking bow before sweeping out of the room.

Δ

The soft tinkling of the fountain water and *skritching* of crickets didn't do much to ease Weysh's nerves. Shortly after leaving his parents, he'd left a note in Carmenna's residence letter box to meet him that night at the eastern square. The first day of classes was done, the sun descended and the moon aglow, and now Weysh perched like a nervous bird on the edge of the fountain as he waited for Carmenna to arrive.

Her scent reached his nose well before he saw her coming. It had always reminded him of vanilla—well, not exactly vanilla, but something like it: simple, sweet, and comforting. She'd become a soothing presence in his life. He would often seek her out after visiting his parents. She would listen while he ranted about Montpierre, making soft noises of agreement. And when she felt stung by the cold distance of her own papa, he would reassure her that she was a wonderful daughter, that she'd make a world-class healer, and then her father would undoubtedly come around. Her father was all she had, after all—her mother had died giving birth to her.

Carmenna's scent was quite different from his Given's, which had a pleasant sweetness to it as well, but woven into something spicy, almost stinging. Not comforting, per se, but invigorating, like mint, perhaps, or pine, except not.

At last Carmenna stepped out from the night, her dark hair streaming behind her, glossy in the light from the tall lamps ringing the square. The way she smiled as she caught sight of him, happy and warm, made him want to change to dragon and simply take off, but he would not. He would face her.

Gathering her skirts, she plopped down beside him on the fountain's edge. "Hi, Weysh!" she chirped, and moved in to kiss him. Weysh gently put a hand to her shoulder, stopping her. "What is it?" she asked, her brows drawing together. "Weysh, what's wrong?"

He made himself meet her searching brown eyes. "I've met my Given."

She drew in a breath, a short, soft gasp, and jerked back from him. "Oh," she breathed, and paused for a moment. "Oh." She gripped her chest but didn't look away, and even as Weysh watched, her eyes went from pleading to angry to defeated.

"I'm sorry, Carmenna."

"What is there to be sorry for?" she said, and though she smiled, her eyes were wet with tears. "Dragons are Given, after all. Although you said . . ."—and here her voice took on a note of accusation—"I thought you were a severed dragon."

"I know. I assumed—I *believed*—I had no mate. But there's

no mistaking it. I wish I could explain, but she's my Given. I'm sure of it." He hadn't even been in dragon and he'd been able to pick out her scent across the quad. But of all the unlucky timing, he'd been just about to leave on a delivery. He'd only had time to change and smell her up close, to confirm for sure who she was, before taking off.

Carmenna gathered her skirts again and rose. "I see," she said, and dipped in a shallow curtsy to him. "Thank you for letting me know, Weysh. Have a good night."

"What, you're leaving?"

"Yes."

"But shouldn't we talk about this?"

"About what?" she snapped, and then quickly composed herself, standing tall. "Do you intend to forsake your Given to be with me?"

"Of course not!"

She flinched at that, and Weysh grimaced. That was poorly done, but he'd never been good at tact. More often than not his thoughts flew from his mouth before he could stop them.

"That's not how I meant it, Carmenna. But now that I've met my Given, I can't love you . . . ah Byen." He ran a nervous hand across the itchy stubble of his beard as the fountain trickled behind them.

"The way you love her," Carmenna whispered.

"The way you deserve," he said firmly.

"Then we've said all that needs to be said." She nodded to him. "Good-bye, Weysh."

She disappeared into the darkness, heading back toward her residence building. Weysh didn't try to stop her.

Δ

The next morning, just after the sun cleared the horizon, Weysh took off from the rooftop of his townhouse. The air was misty with early spring's chill, and he winged between soaring pastel houses and shops, his wind rustling the flowers in the window boxes. The first trams of the morning trundled and clanged along the tracks beneath him. He was on his way to see one of his professors about an extra-credit course he planned to take.

The night before he'd decided that though he desperately wanted to, he would not yet seek out his Given, partially to give her space and partially out of respect for Carmenna. But as often happened, his dragon mind had dragon plans. As he closed in on the plinths and columns of Prevan Academy the scent of his Given found him, the barest hint of that sharp sweetness teasing his nose. He let out an elated screech and dove after it.

As her aroma grew, so did his excitement. He knew just what to do. He would fly her to one of his favorite spots—a mossy cave sunk into a cliff off Northfall River. And then they would . . . well, he wasn't sure what. Sit together? Enjoy the glint of the sun off the water? All he knew was that her scent called to him as surely as if she shouted his name.

He spotted her: a tiny dark figure marching toward the training sands with a long, metal spear in her hand. Angling low, Weysh swooped in and grabbed her in his arms. She yelled, the spear slipping from her grasp. Weysh let out one more happy screech and, flapping his great wings, shot off for his secret cave.

5

Yenni's stomach dropped. She could withstand no more than a few seconds of the ground falling away beneath her before she had to shut her eyes, turning her head against the leathery warmth of the dragon's chest. His arms wrapped firmly around her waist as his wings beat the air. She did not struggle, but held tighter.

They flew for what seemed like eternity to Yenni, until the dragon finally arced into a mossy hollow carved into a cliff face and touched down with a few quick beats of his wings. He let her go and changed into a man once more, so fast it was as if there had never been a huge dark beast before her, but a man the whole time.

"Lovely, listen," he said and stepped toward her, arms outstretched. She had no weapon, and she'd burned through all her offensive runes, using them up as magic was prohibited during the test, but she was not defenseless. She shuffled back toward the mouth of the cave, letting him get closer.

Father Gu, sacred warrior, lend me your aid.

As the dragon reached for her she yelled, grabbed his arm, and spun up perpendicular to him. She bent over and, using his own forward momentum, rolled him over her hip, clean out of the cave toward the loud river below.

Yenni peeked over the lip of the cave, her heart beating in her chest like a nectar bird. The beast screamed and rose up before her. She scrambled back, cursing herself.

Mothers and Fathers, I forgot he could fly!

He swooped into the cave and once again became a man who stared at her, bewildered.

"I warned you, Dragon," she said, ready to grab and break his arm should he accost her again. "Stay away!"

He blinked at her. "One, how in the name of Byen did you do that? I'm twice your size. Two, did you just try to *kill* me?"

"Yes, and next time I will succeed."

She watched his face twist with outrage and then soften into something pained. He sniffed. "Are . . . are you afraid of me?"

"Of course not!"

"You can't lie to a dragon, lovely, I can smell it," he said softly. "I apologize. I can get carried away when I'm in dragon." He grimaced. "In hindsight, whisking you away unannounced wasn't the best course of action."

"Let me pass," Yenni snarled. "The battle aptitude test is about to begin."

"Byen above, that's today! I'd forgotten admissions were still happening. First-year classes start later than ours," he mused. "Come, I'll take you back."

"Absolutely not," said Yenni. "I will get back on my own."

"En? How?"

She mustered up all her courage and marched past him to

survey the cave entrance. The mouth opened to a sheer drop halted only by the rushing river. Yenni's breathing turned to short, panicked gasps. Curse this ridiculous dragon! If she didn't get back soon, she'd miss the test *and* her chance to enter the academy. The next registration period was in six moonturns, and she didn't have time to waste. Her father's condition was getting worse, and the Sha were watching, judging. She *must* gain entrance now.

Yenni glanced left and right. The cliff face had some good footholds, but even if she made the treacherous climb down, what then? It would take ages to walk back to the academy.

"Let me fly you back, sweet lovely," said the dragon. "It will take less than a minute."

She whirled and faced him. "My name is not 'sweet lovely.' It is Yenni Aja-Nifemi ka Yirba!"

He raised his hands. "All right, lo—I mean, Yenni-Ayi . . . hmm. That doesn't change the fact that we need to get you back."

No, it didn't. She could let the dragon fly her or she could miss the test.

She fixed him with a fierce glare. "When you become a dragon, what is your weakest point?"

He sighed again. "Besides my eyes? My throat, where my neck connects with my shoulder blades, though I suppose you could do some damage if you could get under the scales at the top of my spine. And my wings, of course."

"Are you impervious to fire?"

"In dragon, yes, and as a man if I concentrate."

"If water cannot harm you, what can?"

"So that's what the shower was about," he mumbled. "Well, I'm not partial to ice."

Though it pained her to admit she didn't know the word, she had to ask. "What is ice?"

His brow furrowed. "What's *ice*? Ice is frozen water, lovely."

Yenni gritted her teeth. "What do you mean by frozen?"

"Well . . . frozen. Hard."

"Ice is . . . hard water." What was this dragon going on about? No matter. It was too much to expect he would reveal everything, and she was running out of time.

"Fine, Dragon. Since this is your fault, you will take me straight back to the academy. Know that if I come away with so much as a scratch, you will draw down upon you the full wrath of the Yirba. This I promise you."

"The what?" he said, and shook his head. "No harm will come to you, my heart. On my honor as a dragon. Have you ever ridden dragonback?"

"I have not."

"It's simple. Once I'm in dragon, climb up and settle between the ridges on my back. Hold on and I'll take care of the rest. If I wiggle my right shoulder, I'm about to bank right. If I wiggle my left shoulder, left."

"Shouldn't there be some sort of saddle?"

He scoffed. "A saddle?! What am I, a hire horse?"

"Suppose you drop me?"

His face hardened. "I've never once lost a rider. I'm not about to start with my Given."

"I am not—" Yenni breathed deeply through her nose, calming herself. Now was not the time to debate his ridiculous claim. "Could you not carry me like before?"

"Not that I would ever let you go in a million years, but dragonback is technically safer. More surface area."

Yenni sighed. There was nothing for it. "Very well, change," she said, flicking her hand at him.

"Demanding little thing, aren't you?" he muttered, but he jogged backward to make room, and all at once he was a dragon, huge and steaming. Slowly, he lumbered around so that he faced the shadows of cave's back wall, carefully presenting her with his tail. She climbed up, not particularly worried about hurting him, and settled into a valley near the top of his spine, where she could do the most damage if something went awry. She grabbed the hump in front of her, curling her legs back on either side, the scales smooth and warm against her skin.

"I am ready!" she called.

The beast snorted and turned to face the mouth of the cave, jostling her, and a bout of nerves assailed her courage. She shook her head. *It will be like flying a field sphinx,* she coached herself. *Just like flying Ofa. Nothing I haven't done before.*

The dragon gave a warning cry, ran, and jumped, spreading his wings. Yenni yelped as they dropped slightly, her stomach heaving, and then they were gliding on the air.

Cold wind screamed at her, drawing tears from her eyes and slapping her braids painfully against her face. It was *nothing* like flying a field sphinx. They were much higher up. Worst of all, she had no control. He made no response when, on instinct, she flexed her thighs and called. The dragon simply kept his wings out and rode the air.

She ducked her head and squinted, and through the gap between the dragon's long neck and outstretched wings she caught a dizzying glimpse of the ground below. The world raced by like a living map. There were the towering buildings of Imperium Centre reaching up vainly toward them—the castle, sturdy and

grand at the city's heart; the river running alongside the metropolis; paths carving up the neat fields of barley and maize to the
east; and just ahead, the sprawling academy. It was incredible to
see, and despite herself a wide smile took hold of Yenni's face. She
hardly noticed when the dragon's left shoulder bounced up and
down. He began to turn.

Yenni screamed as she slipped from her perch.

She rolled and tumbled, scrabbling against the smooth scales
for some kind of purchase until she caught herself in the crook of
his wing. The dragon screeched, high and urgent, and leveled out.
Panting, Yenni hastened back to her spot among the ridges of his
spine. "I am fine," she shouted over the singing wind.

He gave a low call that ended in a soft click, and wiggled his
left shoulder dramatically. This time he turned slowly, almost
laboriously, and she held tight as he angled toward the sandy pit
where the test was to take place.

He glided in and touched down on the grass so lightly she barely
felt it, and swiftly ducked low so she could dismount. She slid from
the dragon's back and ran for her spear, glinting in the grass where
she'd dropped it, praise all the Mothers and Fathers.

"Byen, woman! I told you if I wiggle my left shoulder it means
I'm banking left!" He was a man once more. "You almost scared
my heart to a stop!"

Yenni ignored him and snatched up her spear before sprinting
for the training ground.

"You're welcome!" the lackwit dragon shouted after her. "Oh,
and Byen's favor!"

Δ

Yenni slipped through the big wooden doors as two burly Creshen men pulled them shut. She hurried down the short steps, her sandals slapping the stone, and came to stand with the murmuring crowd, corralled like a herd of cattle on the sands of the open-air training ground. They were hemmed in by tall walls of dark lumber, reminding her of a ship's hull. Out of the corner of her eye she caught other students glancing at her but she stared ahead, her chest heaving. She had no time for small talk.

All the leather-clad backs in front of her were depressingly broad shouldered. It seemed most of the applicants were male, the same disturbing trend that had taken over the Sha Islands. Here and there she spotted skin of a darker hue, likely men from the Northern Sha Islands, or the Sunrise Isles, as the Creshens called them.

The din from the group dropped in volume until all was quiet, and Yenni startled when a booming voice shattered the silence. It was louder than she'd ever heard anyone speak before, and it occurred to her the speaker must be amplifying it somehow with ach'e.

"Welcome, young hopefuls! I'm Captain Augustin. Today's test will put you through the paces so we can get a sense of your abilities in melee and with basic weapons."

Yenni stood on her toes but couldn't see anything over the tall, shaggy heads before her.

"Square up!" the voice shouted.

They moved instantly, leaving Yenni looking left and right. Square up? What did this mean? The others were spreading into a wide circle . . . no, a square! Yenni scrambled to fit herself between two of her fellow candidates. At last they were all in place, and in the center of the square stood a squat Creshen man with close-cropped hair. His arms and calves bulged as if he'd stolen them from someone else's body, and his wide smile betrayed more than one missing tooth.

"Nice lot," he said as he paced the square. "But then, the first group of the day is always the most keen." As the captain's eyes fell on Yenni she once again experienced "the look." He came over to her.

"Oho!" he said. "Where are *you* from?"

"I am Yenni Aja-Nifemi ka Yirba and I am from the Moonrise Isles."

"Are you now? Well then, welcome!" he said, and slapped her shoulder. Yenni flinched, unused to being so casually touched by strangers. "Ah-ah, but wait? What is this?" He pointed at the white Masters' rune peeking out from under her wrap shirt. "No magic allowed. Are you trying to cheat?"

"No, not at all," she said, her heart thumping even as she curled her hands to hide the runes on her palms. "It is simply a warning rune. It alerts me to threats on my life. I cannot remove it."

"Does it now," he said thoughtfully, and Yenni's chest clenched with anxiety. *Please! I'm so close!*

"Well, certainly no one should be trying to kill you here, just some friendly sparring is all. And it'd be a shame to send you packing after you came all this way, en? But I'll be watching you closely," he warned.

Yenni exhaled, relieved. "Yes, thank you."

"Can't wait to see you in action," said the captain, and he strode back to the center of the square. He crossed his huge arms. "Right. Prevan Academy of Battle and Magical Arts is the finest tactical school on the continent," he declared. "We select only the fat of the meat, the best of the best, to take part in training here.

To that end, the final challenge in today's test will be something extra special, something I doubt many of you have encountered before." He raised one eyebrow. "But first you'll be sparring in groups of two, according to weight, while I observe."

He began pointing at various candidates. "You and you, and . . . you and you," he called, pairing them off. Yenni ended up opposite a red-cheeked girl with hair like dry grass who refused to meet her eye. She clutched a wooden staff.

In the end about forty pairs were spaced out in the sand. "Now, you're aiming to subdue, not maim," called the captain. "That said, each round will last two minutes, and the one showing the most wear will be removed. Ready yourselves!"

Yenni brought up her spear. "Best of luck," she said.

The girl still wouldn't look at her. "I don't need your luck," she spat. "As if I would let some foreigner from the Isles take my spot."

Yenni was so astonished she laughed, one sharp bark.

"Begin!" the captain boomed.

The girl took the most obvious tack and swung her staff at Yenni's legs. Yenni gave her own spear a practiced twirl and stuck the tip in the sand. Wood struck steel with a clang. While her opponent reeled to the side, Yenni braced herself against her spear and kicked out, hitting the girl in the middle. She grunted and fell to her knees. Yenni waited. The girl stumbled to her feet with all the grace of a newborn goat, but once she was upright Yenni struck, a light rap to the knee that *probably* wouldn't break it. The girl screamed and fell again, and this time she couldn't rise.

"Over already?" Captain Augustin cried as he caught sight of them. "I'll have to keep a closer eye on you, en? Mam'selle Moonrise Isles, you'll move up to the next round."

As the day's trials went on, Yenni bested opponent after

opponent, male and female, until only five prospectives remained on the sand. Yenni flashed Captain Augustin a triumphant smile as he surveyed them.

"Well, well," he said. "Five left. Next we'll see how you work as a team. Ready yourselves."

She brought up her spear, and saw the others, all young men, take up their fighting stances as well. Yenni surveyed Captain Augustin, doing her best to gauge his weaknesses. Five on one seemed like an unfair fight, but he was their instructor, so who knew what surprises hid under his hat.

He burst into a loud laugh that commandeered his whole mouth. "Oh, you won't be fighting me!" he said, and rubbed his hands together. "I just love this part." He shielded his eyes with a meaty hand and squinted into the open cloudless sky. "Right on time, as usual," he said gleefully. "You'll be fighting *her*!"

A star glinted on the horizon, brighter than the day, and as Yenni watched the star grew brighter and bigger, until it turned into a creature flashing silver-blue in the sun, twisting and swirling in the sky like a magnificent giant eel. Yenni's mouth dropped open.

"Byen above!" someone shouted.

"Square up!" Captain Augustin practically sang.

They spread apart as the dragon arced down onto the sand, landing on four clawed feet. Unlike the ill-mannered beast who'd snatched her earlier, this dragon was serpentine and graceful. She glittered like diamonds, but Yenni was not fooled. Some of the most beautiful creatures were also the deadliest. It was futile, but Yenni desperately wished she had her runes.

"Begin!" the captain shouted.

Two of their group rushed the dragon while Yenni and two

others hung back. The dragon's chest heaved and with two darts of her head she shot white jets of water at her assailants, which sent them flying back to thud on the sand. Yenni's eyes went wide. In all the lore of her homeland, she'd never heard of dragons spitting water. The pretty dragon swung her long neck to face Yenni's group.

Water or fire, it mattered not. Yenni's goal remained the same: subdue this dragon and claim her spot at the academy. According to that brute from earlier, a dragon's weak points were the eyes, the area where the neck connected with the shoulder blades, under the scales at the top of the spine, and the wings. But try as she might, she could catch no hint of wings on the smooth length of the creature. It was impossible, but she didn't seem to have wings at all!

"Spread out!" the Creshen beside her shouted, but the dragon screeched and snapped at him as he tried to get behind her. He jumped back, just dodging her sharp teeth. Yenni tried to get around the other side, but the dragon turned and shot a quick stream of water at her. Yenni dove as the stream grazed her arm, making her skin burn. A quick inspection showed a bleeding scrape caused by friction. It was the speed and pressure of the water that caused the damage, not the temperature.

The dragon's attention was on herding the other Creshens back where she could see them. She snapped and spat at the others, and lashed her tail back and forth, keeping Yenni at bay. Instinctively, Yenni tried to pull on her focus rune and spot an opening, but of course the rune was gone. She could find no wings to exploit, and no matter how much she wanted to enter the academy, it would be absurd to blind the dragon during a simple exercise.

She retreated slowly, giving herself some distance while praying the dragon didn't notice and catch on to what she was about to do. By the grace of Father Gu, the other applicants kept her occupied. Yenni twisted her spear, transforming it from long to short. Then she ran, her sandals slapping the sand, and leapt onto the dragon's back. The creature screeched and turned, trying to get at Yenni. As the dragon's great head swung around to face her, Yenni brought the tip of her spear to the tender flesh at the base of the dragon's throat. One wrong move and the creature would be impaled.

Any moment Yenni expected the captain to call a halt to the sparring and declare her team the winners. Instead, the dragon twisted and rolled, sending Yenni tumbling to the sand. Yenni scrambled to her feet and backed away, lest she be crushed. The dragon's screech rent the air and, like a snake shooting venom, she sent five precise jets of water at each of her assailants. Yenni had no time to think before she was hit square in the stomach and thrown back, the wind knocked out of her.

"Enough! Duval takes it," she heard the captain yell. Duval? Zui Duval? As Yenni lay in the mud, unable to do anything but wheeze, she knew the dragon had been toying with them. What manner of test was this?

Yenni was livid. If she'd been allowed to use her runes—but she hadn't, and now she had failed. Even after the pain in her middle had subsided, and she was able to fill her lungs with air, she lay in the mud. It wasn't until Captain Augustin came over and offered her a hand up that she rose, but she couldn't meet his eye. Zui Duval was back on the ground. To Yenni's shame hot tears invaded her sight. Though she wanted nothing more than to run off and cry in private, she was a daughter of the Yirba, so she stood with the rest, muddy and miserable, and waited for the captain to officially dismiss them.

He came to stand beside Zui, clapping thickly. "Well done," he cried, and pointed at Yenni. "*Very* well done. Give us more of the same at the magical aptitude test and I'll see you all on the first day of lessons, en?"

"You mean we passed?" said a Creshen to her right.

"You certainly have, in my estimation." He looked around at their shocked faces, not even trying to hide his glee. "What, you think I expected you newlings to subdue a dragon? With no magic? Especially one as accomplished as Madame Duval here?" He laughed with abandon. "I needed to see your ability to adapt, to handle the unexpected. And I dare say I'm delighted."

Disconcertingly quickly, Zui changed back to a woman. "Congratulations, everyone!" she called, and "Hello, Yenni Ajani! Sorry about that."

The Creshens whooped and Yenni grinned, waving back to her dragon friend without a hint of animosity in her heart. She'd passed! Her final obstacle was the magical exam, and that she would conquer with ease. She was top of her class in runelore, so what could possibly go wrong? A spot at the academy was as good as hers.

"Dismissed!" shouted Captain Augustin. "Go run through your spells. I want to see each one of you standing here bright and eager on the first day of classes."

6

Whenever Weysh stepped out of the city crush into the haven of Sir Lamontanya—commonly known as the dragon district— he felt he could breathe a little easier. Here the buildings didn't crowd so close, there weren't as many people, and the streets were wide enough that he could walk them in dragon form if he wanted, as many others did. The streets ringed a lush mountain, and the green rolling sight of it never grew old. The landscape of Sir Lamontanya defied traditional Creshen architecture. While the townhouses and shops of the rest of the city mimicked the pointed spires of the castle, the rooftops of Sir Lamontanya stayed resolutely flat, and many hosted gardens or even shops of their own.

Once Weysh graduated and took his post in the army, he'd be able to afford a very nice suite here until he ranked up enough to buy a manse. For now, his noisy townhouse on Lor Street was the best he could do on his salary as a delivery and ferry dragon, what with paying for tuition, and Weysh wasn't about to ask Montpierre for a single duvvy. But would his Given be happy there? Surely she would. He recalled his time on the Sunrise Isles as a child, when he would stay with his grandfather. Though he had incredibly fond memories of his time there, compared to the modern structures of Imperium Centre he'd always found the island accommodations to be quaint. Beautiful, but quaint. Besides, they'd only have to live on Lor Street for a year or so.

Weysh walked with a bounce in his step, literally—the streets were made of a soft, springy mixture that was much easier on dragon claws than cobblestone. A deep-blue dragonling scrambled out from the intersection ahead and halted in front of him. Though the little one was only up to Weysh's knees, he spread his wings, roared a squeaky little roar and bared his teeth in a display of dominance. A bigger dragon with the same coloring, his father, presumably, based on their similar scents, lumbered around the corner and nudged his son wearily aside, bowing apologetically to Weysh.

"Think nothing of it," said Weysh, chuckling. He had been the same when he was young; worse because he had no dragon parents. He watched the father and son continue on. In a few years his Given would bear him a little one of his own, and he could pass on everything he'd learned; teach him how to be a dragon. By the Kindly Watcher, his dragonling would suffer none of the slings he'd had to while growing up.

But first, ludicrous as it was, it seemed he had to win his Given over. As much as he'd like to delude himself, Weysh knew he hadn't imagined the sour fear wafting off her at Northfall River. He needed to apologize and make good for his ill-conceived plan, and to that end, he'd decided to pay a trip to Darwish & Darwish Outfitters, known throughout Cresh as the finest purveyors of dragon-riding fashion. As they'd headed back to the academy, he'd caught another scent from her right before she'd begun to slip: a bright, citrusy whiff of excitement, and he clung to the fragrant memory of it, using it to fuel his determination.

The bells above the shop door jingled as he entered.

"Wealth and favor!" the shop clerks shouted. A man in a waistcoat with his dark hair slicked back detached himself from a table of suede gloves. "How can I be of assistance?"

Weysh had the man fetch him a pair of goggles, two pairs of riding pants with the inner thighs and buttocks reinforced (which he suspected his Given would fill out quite nicely), a flying cap, a fine pair of tall black boots, and a pair of the aforementioned gloves, expertly keeping his dismay off his face at the total. When it was all stuffed into his messenger bag, he switched and took to the air.

Once above the city he breathed deeply, sifting through the air for that scent at once new and natural. No one had ever commanded his senses like her, as if she were a beacon on a foggy night. He felt he could sniff her out anywhere, and true to form, within minutes, the barest thread of her drifted teasingly under his nose. He turned sharply, just missing the edge of a decorative balustrade on a shop balcony, and dove after the scent.

He let his nose guide him, shifting on the wind as the fragrance of her strengthened. At last he spied her near the guest housing. She was hidden beneath the swaying tendrils of one of the white willows lining the path to the buildings. As he pulled in she jumped up from her sitting position, accosting him with an acrid plume of anger and panic. He landed on the smooth stone of the path and switched.

"Stay back," she said, and pointed her spear at him. A pot

and brush laid abandoned on the grass beside her and the white markings were back on her skin. Weysh noticed a small group of students who'd stopped on the path a few feet away. Byen above, just what he needed: an audience.

He cleared his throat. "I came to apologize," he said, holding up his hands like he was trying to coax a skittish mare. "I shouldn't—I shouldn't have . . ." The stink of fear coming off her was distracting and maddening. He threw up his hands. "Byen, woman! Do you really think so little of me? That I could harm so much as your baby toe?"

Confusion crossed her face.

"You're my Given," he said firmly. She opened her mouth, no doubt to object, but he rushed on. "I brought you something." He pulled out the goggles and held them up. She frowned at them as they dangled from his hand.

"What is that?"

He patted his bag. "Riding gear, so we can go for longer flights. These goggles will protect your eyes."

Her mouth dropped open and she let out an astonished laugh. "*Longer* flights? Listen to me well, Dragon. If I see so much as your shadow after today I am going right to the authorities."

Weysh was so stung he took a step back. "En? You would report me? Like a criminal?"

She said nothing, only stared him down, the smell of fear ever present. Never in all his fantasies about meeting his Given could he have come up with this. To think that she would treat him this way, with all he had planned for them. All he meant to give her and do for her. It was base. It was *sacrilege*. He felt the heat rising in him, anger flushing the skin behind his ears. It was best to leave now, before he said something crude and somehow made things worse.

"Very well," he said tersely, the only words he trusted himself to say. She clearly needed more time. Once she was better acquainted with Creshen culture, and fully understood the concept of Given, surely she would see reason. His bag still bulging with flight gear, Weysh bowed silently to Yenni, changed, and flew off.

Δ

All night Weysh stayed in dragon, sleeping among the trees of the rooftop garden of his townhouse. But the next morning meant classes, so he had no choice but to switch once he flew back to school. And with the switch came the *feelings*.

His thoughts tormented him during the walk across the quad. Blessed Byen, why did she have to look at him like that, as if she thought he would rip her limb from limb? Cursed Movay, what a mess. He'd never heard of someone being rejected by their own Given.

Telltale wingbeats announced Harth's arrival. He was the only one who flapped at the air like that, quick and frantic, like he was struggling to stay aloft. Sure enough, when Weysh looked over his shoulder he saw a skinny green dragon gliding toward him. Harth switched while still a few feet in the air and hit the ground at a jog, falling into step beside him.

"Look at that face, en? I take it things aren't going so well?"

Weysh grunted. "Can you at least pretend you're not enjoying this?"

"En? Why would I be enjoying it?"

"Because you're like a bedridden old woman with a farscope. You're always looking for a good scandal."

"Come now! That's not true. I just want you to be happy with your Given. You're like the little brother I never wanted."

Weysh shoved him. "I'm bigger than you, you ass."

Harth shoved back. "But not smarter," he retorted.

"I suppose I'm glad to have finally met her. I was worried."

"You sound like some old maid sprouting mole hairs. You're twenty, for the blessing of Byen. The oldest I've heard of someone finding their Given is approaching thirty."

They continued across the quad, ribbing each other until they reached the mouth of the training plain, a green expanse surrounded by rocky, moss-covered cliffs at the far west of campus. General Sol nodded her golden head in greeting as they passed. She always had them walk to the grounds in human form instead of just flying in. She said they needed to learn to observe protocols if they wanted to be leaders in the military someday.

The sight of the bluffs cheered Weysh somewhat. Advanced Aerial Tactics was the class he looked forward to the most this year. The sky overhead was blue, and fluffy clouds lined the horizon like cotton. The air smelled fresh and clean. He grinned at the large, glowing hoops that floated in midair. It looked like they'd be doing precision training today. Some of the others were already there, a colorful array of people lounging on the grass.

"Messer Nolan!" shouted a very familiar, and very unwelcome, voice. "I heard you've met your Given!"

Weysh closed his eyes, letting out a loud breath through his nose. If there was any good to be plucked out of the dung pile of the last two days it was that he'd completely forgotten about Luiz Noriago. He was the only one, other than instructors, who called him Messer Nolan like that, a jab at his adopted parentage. Weysh whipped his head toward Harth and glared, but Harth held up his hands.

"It wasn't me, I swear! I hate him just as much as you, remember?"

No, it was most likely what Weysh liked to call the Dragon Daily—that network of gossip and speculation that plagued dragonkind. He briefly recalled the group that bore witness to his earlier performance with his Given and frowned.

Weysh turned his glare on the man striding up to them. He'd been afflicted with Noriago's presence ever since the dung worm had transferred to Prevan last year. For some nutty reason Noriago had taken an instant dislike to him.

By the end of that year, things had finally devolved into a physical altercation. As the instructor and their classmates pulled them apart, Weysh had shouted at him, "What in the hells is your problem with me?"

"You're exactly like someone else I hate, you shameful excuse for a dragon," Noriago had spat back at him. "You make me sick!"

Noriago never explained further, just continued to look at Weysh with utter contempt. The feeling was mutual—Weysh hated Noriago's stupid beady eyes. He hated his ugly moustache. He hated his annoying Espannian accent. There was a fairly prestigious academy in Espanna, was there not? Why in Movay's name couldn't Noriago simply train in his own country?

Now Noriago ran a hand through his bronze hair. "I also heard she said you can take a swim in stone shoes," he continued and laughed. "She sounds like my kind of girl. I'll have to introduce myself."

"At attention," called General Sol, and Weysh had to bite back his insults, rein in his rage, and fall in line. He stood steaming, the anger festering like it would burn a hole through his stomach. He sent up a silent prayer that he'd be paired against Noriago for whatever training they had that day.

"Today we'll be running paired aerial pursuit through a hoop course. You're all old pros so we're hitting the ground running, folks. Fire is authorized so no holding back. Zui! Make your switch."

"Yes, General!" Zui, who stood back and to the left of General Sol, nodded and switched to her dragon form. The dragons of Minato spat water, not fire, so she worked as General Sol's assistant, putting out blazes during training. Weysh thought Zui made a beautiful dragon. She was long, serpentlike, and flowing, with silvery-blue scales that glinted in the sun. Harth was quite lucky.

"You'll be paired up by surname," said General Sol. "Each pair will run the course while the rest observe. First up, Nicole Allard and Orah Baudin."

Weysh let a smug smile take hold of his face. He was almost sure to be paired up with Luiz Noriago. It was like they were fated to be enemies. He watched each match, making mental notes and criticisms, fidgeting with anticipation until sure enough, General Sol called them forward.

"Weysh Nolan and Luiz Noriago."

They stepped forward together.

"I should offer the poor thing some comfort," said Noriago, so low only Weysh could hear and still staring ahead at General Sol. "Stuck as she is with you."

"Shut up, you stinking, wrinkled monkey's scrotum," hissed Weysh, also staring ahead. "If I smell you on her, I'll rip that shit stain you call a moustache off your face and feed it to you."

"Messer Nolan, you'll be in pursuit," said the general.

Perfect.

"Switch!"

Weysh tugged on the trigger inside, and a moment later his wings rested, wide and reassuring, against the muscles of his broad dragon back. General Sol now craned her head to look up at him.

"Noriago, take off!"

Noriago turned, smacking Weysh with his tail, and took off for the hoops.

"Nolan, take off!"

Weysh roared, spread his wings and pushed off with his incredible leg muscles, taking to the sky. He pulled his legs in as tightly as possible and leaned forward, pushing through the air with long, powerful wingbeats. Everything fell away and in that moment he had only one purpose in life: to take down Noriago.

Wind whistled in his ears and hot fire churned in his chest. Weysh opened his mouth and released his flame in a glorious jet, hoping to distract the other dragon more than anything, but Noriago darted down and it passed over him, the light of it flickering in his bronze scales. Noriago put on a burst of speed and soared ahead.

Weysh growled and shot after Noriago, but Weysh's fire breathing had only served to steal focus from his *own* flying and he dropped too low, causing an instant, icy burn that seared his stomach. Hissing, he pulled up. The hoops were floating rings of ice magic, and a bright patch of frost now stung his underside. Ignoring the pain he sped on, chasing Noriago's skinny hide through the hoops. But the little snake was fast. If he could just catch him he would knock him into the rings and send him spinning to the ground below. Then he'd land on him and push him into the grass, maybe tear one of his wings and put him out of commission for a while. Show him his place.

But the distance between them was increasing, and they were quickly approaching the end of the flight course. He couldn't let that jackass get away. Weysh drew in a deep, gurgling breath and shot off another frustrated jet of flame, but when the plume of fire cleared Noriago was gone.

Something slammed into Weysh from below, shoving him up into the top of one of the ice hoops. He caught a glimpse of the bronze-scaled dragon underneath him before pain zipped through his wings and they went numb. He roared, deep yet screeching, as he fell through the hoop and hurtled to the ground. He hit the grass hard, pushing all the air from his lungs, and lay there in dragon, dizzy and moaning. Noriago switched to human and stood over him laughing, and if Weysh could have moved he would have snapped him in half between his jaws, murder charges be damned.

"All right, Noriago, take your place," called General Sol, and then it was her standing over Weysh, disapproval all over her face.

"Do you need to go to the infirmary?"

Weysh changed to human, still on the ground.

"I'm fine," he wheezed.

"Hmph. Sit out for five minutes, then rejoin the line."

"Yes, General," he groaned.

Weysh stumbled off behind the line and plopped down on the grass, head bent, fantasizing about ways he could kill Noriago and get away with it.

Δ

Once class was ended and General Sol dismissed them, Weysh took off without waiting for Harth, begging Byen to keep Noriago away from him. He was in his last year; he didn't want to get kicked out and throw away everything he'd worked for over that pig's dung-hole. He took to the white footpath that ran along and between the academy's many buildings, absently following it to the lecture halls as he'd done a million times before, letting his feet lead the way.

Harth rushed up next to him. "Weysh, what was that? I have a reputation to maintain. You can't be my unofficial brother if you're going to be falling for basic tricks."

"Shut up, Harth. I can't focus today."

Zui glided up and took Harth's arm, falling into step with them. "Are you still having trouble with your Given?"

Weysh grunted.

"Well, have you spoken to her since?" she asked.

"Yes."

"Oho! And how did that go?" asked Harth.

"Badly," Weysh said.

"What happened?" asked Zui.

Reluctantly, Weysh recounted all that had passed between them.

"Weysh," said Harth once when Weysh was done. "Are you *trying* to make her hate you?"

"I was in dragon! One minute I caught her scent and the next she was in my arms."

"I can't believe she actually threw you out of that cave. By Byen! I like her more and more. I think you've literally met your match, Weysh," said Harth.

"I hope you apologized for snatching her off the ground like that. She must have been terrified!" cried Zui.

"I tried! But she wouldn't have it. I can't afford this nonsense right now! This year is pivotal. I need the highest marks I can get to achieve the highest rank possible in the army, more so now that I have a Given to take care of. Perhaps if I explain that to her—"

"No, no, no. If she's two seconds away from putting up Wanted posters you should leave her be," said Harth.

"This is all so ridiculous. She would go to the peacekeepers and charge me with what, exactly? Loving her too much?"

"Then you love her?" asked Zui.

"Of course!"

Zui paused and squinted at him. "What was her name again?"

Weysh and Harth stopped with Zui. "Yena, Ajaya . . . something like that," said Weysh.

"You don't even know her name?"

"I, well, we have the rest of our lives to learn each other's names!"

"Even so, if you're trying to win her over, that's where I would start," Zui said dryly. "I believe her name is Yenni Ajani, though I admit I've forgotten the rest. But I could ask her."

Weysh sighed. "Would you talk to her for me, Zui? Explain the concept of Given? It might help to hear it from another woman."

Zui crossed her arms and raised an eyebrow at him. "What exactly would you have me say?"

Weysh shrugged. "Tell her the truth, that as Given we have a responsibility to each other and to the Kindly Watcher. She has to give birth to my dragonling."

Zui exchanged a slow glance with Harth, who put a heavy hand on Weysh's shoulder.

"Let's do the math on this one, my friend. What happened the first time you told her you were to be married?"

How could he forget? "She attacked me with a spear," Weysh said, scowling.

"And your second encounter?"

"She somehow threw me out of a cave."

"Your third?"

Weysh simply glared at Harth. "Very well, I see your point," he snapped. "Clearly I haven't made the best impression. But I'm working to fix that. I mean, look at how happy the two of you are. How could she not want the same?"

"Weysh," said Zui patiently. "Would you like to know my advice, as a woman? Right from the source of the wellspring?"

"En? Oh yes, that would probably be helpful. What do you think, Zui?" he asked hopefully. "How do I make her see reason?"

"You don't," Zui said with finality. "She'll decide on her own if she wants to be with you. Not everything can be fixed and solved, especially when it comes to love. And Given or not, if you continue to push her, you may just push her forever out of reach."

Weysh furrowed his brow, confused. "So I should simply leave her be?"

"If that's what she wants."

"But *why*? How would that endear me to her?"

Zui threw a quick, fond glance at Harth. "Because respecting a woman's wishes is one of the most seductive things a man can do."

Weysh shook his head. It seemed incredibly counterproductive, but everything else he'd tried so far had been nothing short of disaster. "All right, Zui," he said, resigned. "I'll try it your way. For the time being at least."

7

Yenni frowned, bit her lip, and stared again at the interesting writing instrument they'd given her: a slim stick of something like charcoal wrapped in wood, so different from the slim reed brushes and black scribe ink she used at home.

What sort of test was this? How did one pull ach'e by answering absurd questions on a piece of paper? Not only was everything written in Creshen, but half of it made absolutely no sense. *Define the theory of otherspace.* Other what? *Name a negative effect of the Law of Self-Preservation.* Law of *what*? With each passing minute, punctuated by the echoing *tick, tick, tick* of a large mechanical timepiece, Yenni's confidence waned. She glanced around at the other students. So many. And they all had their heads down, scribbling furiously. She stared, brows furrowed, at her own nearly blank sheet.

"And pencils down!"

Yenni jumped at the professor's trilling voice. He stood at the front of the lecture hall beside a podium with his hands behind his back, eyes squinted as he stared into the rows of students to see who continued to write. Two tufts of gray hair stood up on either side of his head as if trying to make up for the lack of hair in the center. Yenni let her stick fall from her fingers onto the knotty wood of the table. It wasn't as if extra time would have made a difference. She simply had no idea what to write.

"The magical aptitude test is over," said the professor. Two aides in long navy coats went around collecting the tests. "You will wait in this room as your scores are tallied, and we will call you individually to let you know your results."

As a young woman took her paper Yenni let out a heavy sigh. This test should have been easy, but there hadn't been a single question pertaining to runelore, nor any chance for a demonstration.

As the minutes ticked by and the room slowly emptied, Yenni's anxiety grew. If she failed to gain entrance what was she to do with herself? How could she help her father? Yenni breathed deeply, bowed her head, and prayed.

Father Ri, divine purveyor of destiny, I would not be here if it were not your will. Please receive my worries and calm my restless mind.

After a few moments of reflection she felt the tightness leave her, felt more resolute in the certainty that admission was her course—her *only* course. She turned her attention to her surroundings. Though now mostly empty, the seats had held over a hundred students, she believed. Astounding. Back home education was largely left up to each compound. Only children of the chiefclan bloodline gathered daily to be tutored.

And then there was this . . . what did they call it? *Lecture theater.* Her schoolroom back home was a wooden structure, open and airy, but this room was stony and closed, with only a few small windows high up on the wall to let in light.

Time passed by, and Yenni focused on her breathing as name after name was called. She fidgeted, worried at her hair, hummed the hymn to the strength rune, until finally she was the only one left in the room.

"Yenni . . . Ajana Femmy. Kayirba."

The man butchered her name, but who else could he mean? She stood and followed him through a door at the front of the room to the left of the podium. Inside was a little office taken up almost entirely by a large, dark desk, behind which sat the administrator of the test. She was surprised to see Captain Augustin standing by one of those colored-glass windows. He turned from it and ran a hand over his short hair while nodding at her. "Please have a seat," he said, gesturing to a cushioned bench in front of the desk.

The magical instructor—Professor Mainard, as he'd introduced himself at the start of the test—scowled at her. "I will be blunt. It's as if you know nothing of magical principles whatsoever."

Her cheeks stung with a sudden flush. "I am accomplished at runelore," she said. "If you will give me the chance to show you—"

"Runelore? That primitive rubbish? Here there are theories, laws, principles! Have you studied any of this on the, ah,"—he waved a hand as he read from a sheet of paper—"Moonrise Isles?" His bushy, gray eyebrows rose and he scoffed.

Yenni frowned, not accustomed to being addressed in such a way. Didn't this man know that she was—no, of course he didn't.

"Yes, I am from the Moonrise Isles. We do things differently there." She glared at him, and he matched her with a simmering glower of his own.

"We're offering you a spot at the academy," Captain Augustin cut in, interrupting their staring contest, "on the strength of your battle aptitude test." He smiled slightly. "That was, well, full marks there. Combined with what little you could achieve on the magical exam, it's enough to get in."

"Just barely," Professor Mainard spat. "You have taken, quite literally, the last open spot. We'll have fewer true-or-false questions on next year's exam, you mark my words," he grumbled. "You'll be expected to pass all four sets of yearly exams, both battle and magical, like any other student, or, believe me, we won't hesitate to cut you loose."

Yenni burst into a smile and stood. "Thank you very much," she said to Captain Augustin. "I'm very grateful!"

The captain handed her a sheet of rolled paper. "Take this to admissions to sort out your student identification. They'll also be able to help you with housing. Oh, and they can set you up with a tutor." His eyes shifted to Professor Mainard and back before he whispered, "You wouldn't be the first talented fighter to struggle with magic, en? But it would be a shame to lose you."

She took the paper, her smile now brittle. "I see," she said as she put it in her satchel. "Well, thank you for your advice and your advocacy, Captain Augustin. I will do as you suggest."

"Splendid!" he said, and clapped her hard on the back, making her stumble. *What a curious habit*, she thought, but at the moment she didn't care. As she made her way through the echoing lecture theater and out to the cool morning air, her heart swelled until it was all she could do to keep from jumping up and down. She was in!

But moments later her excitement waned. See a tutor? Back home it was *she* who tutored her younger cousins. Yet, in the end, this was just why she'd come, was it not? To learn something new? What was newer than pulling ach'e through words and theories? She sighed and took out her map, then took off for the building marked *Student Services*.

Δ

This time the student services building was much less crowded, and Yenni simply made her way to the long counter at the back of the room. She ran a finger along the edge of the wood, tracing the leaves etched there. Students sat on long, cushioned benches that ringed the room, reading or talking, and tall shelves stretched from floor to ceiling, full of books. There was a little silver bell perched on the smooth wooden countertop. Yenni picked it up and gave it a ring, high and tinkling.

A silver-haired Creshen woman rushed out from a door behind the counter. "Hello-oh!" She brought a spotted hand to her bosom. "And what can I do for you today?"

After over an hour discussing her options, and her runes, with the woman, Yenni paid her fees and received her identification chit—a flat oval slab the size of her palm carved with the school's crest of a river running beside a castle.

"Only students and staff can make the river flow," the woman said, and recited something. The water etched at the bottom of the crest seemed to shiver and undulate before her eyes.

"Oh!"

"You try," said the woman.

"Oh yes, I will, later," Yenni said, and shoved the chit into her shoulder bag.

They also sorted out her schedule. The woman said the average student took eight classes a year, so Yenni signed up for ten. Among them were Foundations of Magical Theory, Defensive Strategies for Dragon Combat, An Introduction to Dragon Psychology, Dragons in Religion and History, and Basics of Runelore. But the classes she really wanted, the ones pertaining to healing, she was not yet allowed to access. She had to pass something called prerequisites before she could be admitted to those. So she pushed down her frustration and took the classes available to her. She was here, a student of the academy—by the Sha she would find a way to heal her father, one way or another.

The woman left and returned with several sheets of paper. "You've got some shopping to do, young lady. These are the texts required for each course and"—she looked Yenni up and down—"you'll need a uniform as well. You can find everything at the academy shop. It's just on the west side of the campus." She shuffled and arranged the papers. "Interested in dragons, I take it?" she said, then leaned in, scratching at her spotted nose. "You know, my cousin's wife is dragonkind."

"Uh, yes. There are no dragons where I am from, so I am very curious about them." That was an understatement. Clearly, Yenni knew nothing about dragons, and she would need all the information she could get to deal with the one who now stalked her.

"There is one more thing," Yenni began, a warm flush of embarrassment creeping up the back of her neck. "I've been advised to seek a tutor."

"A tutor you say? And you're interested in dragonkind? Hmmm," she frowned, lost in thought. "I believe . . . yes. I think I know someone who would be a good fit." She scribbled something down and put it into a letter box behind her. "Be back here at around four strikes of the bell tower. I'll introduce you to someone who can help you."

Yenni went off to purchase her class materials and secure her lodging, and when the bell tower struck four times she was already back at student services. She took a seat on one of the cushioned benches, wondering just who this tutor who knew so much about dragons could be.

"Hello?"

It was a feminine voice. Yenni looked up and found a young woman with dark hair standing over her.

"I heard you're looking for a tutor?"

Yenni stood. "Yes, that's right."

"A pleasure to meet you. My name is Carmenna."

She held up a hand and Yenni touched palms with her. "I am happy to meet you, Carmenna. My name is Yenni Ajani."

"And what can I help you with, Yenni . . ."

"Ajani. Yenni Ajani." She eased back on her seat and patted the spot beside her. Carmenna followed her lead. Yenni noticed her eyes were a little red, tired.

"I need help learning Creshen magic."

"Oh? I was told you were interested in, erm, dragonkind."

Yenni made a face. "I am not so much interested in dragon-kind as in deterring one dragon in particular. He has told me I am given to him, or some such nonsense."

Carmenna's face went slack with shock. "Oh Watcher above, you can't be serious."

"Yes! Have you ever heard of anything so brazen?"

"What's—" Carmenna swallowed. "What's his name?"

"Washi? Ah no. It is Weh-sheh."

"You—you don't by chance mean *Weysh* do you?"

"Yes, that is what I said. Weh-sheh."

Carmenna seemed to deflate before her eyes, like a flag that had lost the wind. "So he left me for you," she said, and Yenni was not at all fond of the assessing way Carmenna's gaze flitted over her. "And you don't even want him." She turned away and laughed bitterly. "Oh, Weysh, you buffoon."

Sudden understanding lit up the crevices of Yenni's mind. This woman must be the lover, or former lover, of the dragon. It seemed that tricky Father Esh was hard at work.

"Carmenna," Yenni said firmly. "It seems to me that we both want the same thing, which is for the dragon Weh-sheh to leave me be. Help me learn about Creshen magic and I will drive him back in your direction, though I must say I think you can do much better."

Carmenna gave her a hopeless look. "You clearly don't know much about being Given, and even less about Weysh. When he wants something he puts his everything into achieving it. He's incredibly hard working and resilient. It's one of the things I love—*loved*—most about him."

"I am not some*thing*, I am some*one*," said Yenni. "And I am much the same. I will set everything right. You will see."

Carmenna bit her lip. "I highly doubt this will work, but if you're willing to try—"

Yenni sighed. She was not one to put things off for long. Now that she had secured her place at the academy, and would be here for the next year, it was time to deal with the dragon once and for all.

"Where can I find him?" she asked Carmenna.

"He likely just finished a class," Carmenna said, her voice firmer. "It's a new year, so I'm not sure of his schedule anymore, but there's a solid chance he's at the Rearwood. I think now is about the time he meets up with his tracking group."

"The Rearwood? And where is that?"

Carmenna held out a hand. "Your map," she said wearily. Yenni handed it to her and Carmenna reached into the folds of her long skirt, pulling out another of those gray writing sticks.

"Here," she said, and drew an *X* at the cluster of trees to the north. "Dragons often go there to practice tracking each other by scent through the forest."

"I see," said Yenni, retrieving her map. "Then I will go speak with him now. Once I have convinced him to see reason will you consent to tutor me?"

"Yes?" said Carmenna uncertainly.

"Good. My first day of classes is tomorrow. Let us meet back here the day after that. Until then, Carmenna."

Yenni stood, resolute. The prospect of going back to the counter and explaining why she needed a new tutor made her head ache, so once and for all she must deal with Weysh.

Δ

Student services was at the north end of the academy grounds, and it took her only a quarter of an hour to reach the Rearwood. Just as Carmenna had said, a few dragons arced back and forth over the trees like giant birds of prey: about three green ones, a rusty red one, and, yes, the violet-black dragon Weysh. Yenni stood for a moment, mesmerized by the grace of them weaving in and around each other, the sunlight flickering off their scales. Such creatures—people—had truly once existed on the Islands?

Suddenly Weysh swiveled in the air, as if jerked by an invisible string, and came zooming toward her. The other dragons continued to circle, but craned their necks in Weysh's direction. He landed lightly, pulled back his wings, and curved his long neck toward her, clicking softly. To her surprise, Yenni felt no fear. In fact, she had the strangest urge to reach out and stroke the scales of his face. Instead, she balled her fists at her side and cleared her throat.

"Weh-sheh, I have come to speak with you."

The dragon bent his knees and sat, curling his long tail to his side. He turned one eye on her and regarded her expectantly, with all the assured confidence of every prince she'd ever met.

"I am here to study, and I have no time for you and your distractions. I am not your Given and never will be, is that clear?"

Yenni held his gaze, steeling herself against his response.

8

Weysh drew deeply of her scent, savoring it. Not a hint of fear. He caught the sharp, steely tang of determination, but to his delight that sour fear was missing. He touched his nose gently to her shoulder. She let it rest there for the barest moment before stumbling back.

"Are you listening, Dragon?"

He let out a soft, clipped screech. *Yes.*

She looked confused. "Is that a yes? Change into a man."

Weysh hesitated. She was so much more receptive to him in dragon.

"Change," she said again. "I don't have time to waste."

Resigned, Weysh reached within for that inexplicable trigger, right at the core of his chest, and switched forms. The world became dull, except for Yenni, who seemed to rise up toward him. Her skin was painted all over with white Island runes. Rumor was that the Moonrise Islanders used the blood of small animals, even infants, some said, to make their runepaint. But that couldn't be true. He wouldn't believe it of his Given.

89

"You're used to telling people what to do, en?" he said.

She ignored his comment. "Did you hear what I said? We cannot be together, and I expect you to leave me to my peace."

The first flickering embers of anger stirred within Weysh. "One, that's exactly what I've been doing—*you* came and disturbed *my* tracking practice. Two, that's not for you to decide. Our union is the will of Byen."

"Who?"

"Byen. The Kindly Watcher. Ruler of the worldly domain."

Yenni waved a hand at him. "I do not bend to the will of your Creshen gods."

A flush crept up the back of Weysh's scalp and he took a deep breath, focusing on a pigeon's low cooing in the tree above. "I'm beginning to question what he's up to as well. Nevertheless, you have no choice. Neither of us does."

"Lunacy. There is always a choice. I choose to complete my year here and return to my tribe."

"Like hell you will," Weysh growled. "We'll be married and you'll stay here with me in Imperium Centre."

She gave him a shocked laugh. "And do *what*?"

"Run the household. Raise our dragonling. Women's duties."

Her mouth fell open, and she slowly pulled it closed, put one hand on her hip, and tilted her head up to him, glaring into his eyes. "No," she said, pursing her plush lips. He couldn't decide whether he wanted to kiss her or shake her, never mind that he could do neither.

"Enough, Yenni Ajani!" Weysh barked. Her large eyes went even larger. "You are my Given, and you will do as I say. We are—"

Something wet slapped the side of his face, dripping onto

his lower lip. He blinked. Looked up. A pigeon sat on a branch directly above him.

"Ah!" he screamed and wiped frantically at his mouth. "Aaaaaahh!"

Yenni burst out laughing and doubled over. "Oh!" she gasped. "Oh Father Esh, you trickster. Thank you!" She stumbled away with tears in her eyes, holding her stomach and chuckling.

Weysh spat on the grass. His Given was still laughing and struggling to breathe. Weysh teetered on the brink of letting out a bellowing roar of rage and bursting into his own bout of raucous chuckles. As he took in his Given almost crying in mirth, the utter random ridiculousness of the situation hit him and the laughter won out.

"Well played, brother pigeon," he said between chuckles. He scrubbed his face with his shirt, and noticed her eying him cautiously. "It seems your gods have spoken," he said.

She nodded, wary, but he smelled no fear from her. "Look, lovely—"

"My *name* is Yenni Ajani."

"Yenni Ajani. I'm not a bad person. All I want is to know more about you."

She stayed silent.

"How were the admissions tests?"

"I passed," she said slowly.

"Congratulations!" And praises to Byen. That meant she would be sticking around. "Will you focus on battle or magic?"

"Magic. I already know much about battle."

"Clearly. You never did explain how you threw me out of the cave."

"Jabdanu wrestling."

"En?"

"It is a fighting technique used only by women where I'm from. We use the weight of an opponent against him."

Weysh shook his head. "Will wonders never cease."

"Weh-sheh," she said, and the strange way she pronounced his name made him smile. "You have told me that you are not a bad person. Prove it. I want your word that you will not interfere with my ambitions here at the academy. I must learn as much as I can."

"I'll do you one better," he said. "Am I wrong to guess that while you excel at battle, you struggled with the magical test? That's often how these things go."

"Creshen magic is very different from runelore," she admitted.

"Then allow me to be your tutor." Brilliant. He would be giving her what she wanted while giving himself ample opportunity to change her mind.

"Oh Father Esh, not this," she muttered.

"Come now, there has to be a thing or two I can teach you. If I'm still here it means I'm passing my classes, en? In fact, go ahead, ask me anything."

She pursed her lips, thinking. "Well, firstly, what happens to your clothes?"

"My clothes?"

"Yes, when you switch between human and dragon. I would think they would rip to shreds, but when you change from dragon to human, there are your clothes, intact."

"*That's* your first burning question?" said Weysh, and then he smiled a half smile. "If you want to see me with my clothes off, lovely, just say the word."

"Dragon!"

He raised his hands. "Sorry, forgive me. Basically, we wear spelled clothes that make use of the theory of otherspace."

"The theory of . . ."

"The theory of *otherspace*. Objects exist in, and can be sent to, another plane of existence. And then there's the principle of—" He scratched his head. "Watcher, what is it? Inversion! Yes, just as we pull things from otherspace, we can send things there as well. So the instant my clothes touch dragon flesh they disappear to otherspace, and when I switch to human they return."

"I see," she said, but he could tell she didn't. He didn't understand it all that well himself, to be honest. No one did; that was why it was only a theory. "Go on, ask me another. Something from the test."

"Very well. What is the Law of Self-Preservation?"

"Easy, I learned that in first school. It's what keeps us from destroying ourselves when we use magic. Why you don't incinerate your own hands when casting a fire spell, for example."

"Oh, is that all?"

"Yes. That's also why we can't use healing spells on ourselves."

"So that would be the negative effect," she mused.

Weysh pointed to a dainty wrought-iron bench nestled among the trees at the entrance to the Rearwood. "Why don't we sit over there, and today can be your first session. You ask, I'll answer."

She looked up at his classmates, intently scouring the trees from above. "Are you not occupied?"

"Hmm, wait right here." Weysh changed and pushed off. The wind whistled in his ears as he made a quick, gliding circle over the forest. He let out a sharp screech: *Carry on without me.*

He touched down before her, his dragon nostrils getting a good dose of her irresistible scent before he changed back. "There, I'm all yours."

The war within her showed plain on her face. At last she touched a hand to her stomach through the thin material of her wrap shirt and nodded. "You have told me some useful information so far. Should I agree to this, I do not want to hear anything about us being Given. Is that clear, Dragon? You are my tutor only."

He hesitated. How was he to convince her if he couldn't even bring up their union?

"I see. Well, if you cannot agree, I must be going." She turned.

"No! Yes. Agreed," said Weysh.

Without another word, she strode past him toward the bench, and once they were seated under the cool shadows of the trees, he began.

"What else would you like to know? Go on."

"Why is it that dragons like Harth Duval and Zui Duval are colorful in their human form, but you are normal, even though as a dragon you are that deep shade of violet?"

"Well, first of all, it's perfectly normal for dragons to be all sorts of colors. It's how Byen marks us. Second, I *am* violet. See?" He made a fist in front of her face, showing her his knuckles, where the purple tinge was most prominent.

"Ah!" she said. "I hadn't even noticed."

He nodded. "It's a bit difficult to see because of my Island ancestry, but the color is there."

Yenni's eyes went wide. "You're an Islander?"

"My grandfather was, on my mother's side, but he died when I was ten."

He frowned. Ah Movay, he didn't like to think about it. He missed the man. When he was a child, Weysh's mother would send him off to the Sunrise Isles every winter, where he would spend time with his grandfather, uncle, and cousins. His grandfather had been a stark contrast to Montpierre, always warm and kind. Then again, he'd been the type of person who could make anyone feel like they were the most important person in the room. Weysh always thought that was where he got his charm with women—well, most women. He'd visited the Sunrise Isles a few more times after his grandfather passed, but it wasn't the same. His memories of the Islands brought him more sorrow than comfort, and so he stopped going.

"Ah," Yenni mused, invading his thoughts. "The Songs of the Sha say this as well, that the dragons of old had skin of multiple colors. Dragon people were the descendants of *true* dragons, beasts as tall as mountains that protected the divine realm of the Sha from the shadows at the edges of the world."

Weysh nodded. "Exactly! We may call ourselves dragons now, but really we're dragonkind. True dragons are as tall as mountains and have no human form, just as you say."

"Have you met a true dragon?" Yenni asked, her pretty eyes wide.

"No, praise Byen. That would mean Movay's demons had returned."

"Who?"

"Movay. In the beginning, Byen, the Kindly Watcher, was at war with Movay, Mistress of Demons. She sent her hell minions to destroy the world but was defeated by Byen and his true dragons. After that, Byen gave ten percent of humanity the ability to transform into a lesser version of his sacred warriors, to defend the world should Movay's demons return."

She cocked her head. "Do you really believe you are a divine warrior in the service of your god?"

"Huh. Maybe, maybe not, but if Movay's demons return in my lifetime I'll cross that bridge then, I suppose."

"I see. Well then, how is this ten percent maintained?"

"Dragons can have only one child. And what I mean by that is literally every dragon rears one child, so a pair of mated dragons could have two children, but a couple like you and me will have only one."

"We are not . . . hmph." She closed her eyes, huffed out a breath, and opened them again. "What is to stop you from having more children?"

"The will of Byen."

"Interesting," she said. "Your history sounds similar to the Songs of the Sha."

"Who is the Sha?"

"Who *are* the Sha. They are the creators of all. They made this world together, and sprang from Mother-Father Ool, the creator of all other Sha, who is both male and female."

Weysh laughed incredulously. "What? Both male and—that's the silliest thing I've ever heard! How can someone be both male and female?"

Yenni jerked back like he'd slapped her, then narrowed her eyes at him. "Well, how can you be a sacred warrior? That is the silliest thing *I* have ever heard." She jumped up from the bench and began to march away.

"Lovely, no! Wait!" He instinctively reached for her arm, but on second thought pulled back. The last thing he wanted was to be on the receiving end of another of her attacks, and Harth's comment about him manhandling women bothered him more than he cared to admit.

"Yenni Ajani, I'm sorry!" he said, throwing up his hands help-lessly. "That was rude of me."

Through Byen's mercy she stopped and turned back to him, her arms crossed. "Yes, it was."

"Forgive me?"

"I have to be going. I must sort out my accommodation for the year."

"Well, then let's meet again," Weysh said quickly. "How about at the library tomorrow evening? Six o'clock?"

"Perhaps," she said, then suddenly the markings on her legs glowed a brilliant blue-white and she took off, darting away with all the speed of a startled fawn. Weysh hung his head and sighed; things had been going so well! But not all was lost. She didn't say she *wouldn't* meet him tomorrow.

He grunted in irritation. Why was he doing this? He was a dragon; there was no shortage of women vying for his attention. And what of Carmenna? He loved her well enough, and she didn't put him through these humiliating paces. She was sweet and kind, and didn't deserve the pain he was causing her. Besides, it was clear Yenni Ajani was thoroughly unimpressed by him, so he should have some dignity and leave her be, Given or no.

But he knew he wouldn't, not with the scent of her still clinging to the bench, making his head swim. He let out a bitter chuckle. Byen knew him well. He'd always had a soft spot for the darker-skinned women of the Islands. The ones who had given him his first kiss and more.

So he knew he would find himself at the library tomorrow evening, waiting until the lanterns ran low.

9

Yenni made a slow circle, assessing herself in her long looking glass. She was dressed in the academy's special school clothes, a uniform it was called. *Mothers and Fathers but these Creshens like to drown themselves in clothing.* On her legs she wore tight, uncomfortable gray leggings, and over that a long white shirt that went almost to her knees called a tunic, and over that a thick green shirt with no arms called a vest, and then tall shoes like fisherwomen wore, though admittedly much nicer. The Creshens called them boots, and hers were made of some kind of animal hide and dyed a forest green to match the vest. Finally, over everything else, she wore a long green contraption the Creshens called a mage's coat. It had a big, loose hood and a belt at the waist. Her braids had gone fuzzy so she freed her hair from them and it made a halo around her head.

She glanced around her suite, her home for the next year. After a cramped and noisy night in the academy's guest lodging, she'd firmly decided it was worth the money to have the best rooms she could get, so along with her tuition she had paid for accommodation at a women's residence called Riverbank Chambers.

It was all very Creshen. She couldn't rightfully call the suite small, but the way it was sealed, with no gap between the wall and ceiling, made it feel stifling. Thankfully, it had a little balcony, so she could open the doors. She also had a big Creshen bed, which was soft and fluffy and fun to bounce on, but made for a hot and fitful sleep. Off the bed chamber was another small room—a nook, really—with a big window; a dark, sturdy desk; and a padded chair.

Yenni looked in the mirror and smoothed her vest one last time. No more dallying. This morning she would attend her first class: Foundations of Magical Theory. She didn't want to be late, especially since the class was taught by that irritating Professor Mainard. As she exited her suite Yenni took one last look at the desk, where she'd left her runepaint and brushes. She was no longer as concerned about the dragon: not once had the Masters' protection rune reacted to him. And she needed to conserve her runepaint, so today she sported just a few small, quick speed and strength runes.

And, of course, the runes on her hands. She ran her thumb along the swirling white rune on her left palm, offered up a prayer to Father Ri for guidance and wisdom, and set out for her first class at Prevan Academy.

$$\Delta$$

The other students' excited chatter echoed all the way up to the schoolroom's high ceilings, but as soon as the big double doors at the front creaked open and Professor Mainard strode in, their voices faded like a wave leaving the shore.

"Good morning, class."

"Good morning, Professor," a few voices said back.

Professor Mainard slammed a hand down on his podium. "I said *good morning*, class!"

"Good morning, Professor Mainard!" the class replied, much louder this time.

"Very good," he said. "Welcome to Foundations of Magical Theory. Here you will refine and in some cases relearn the theories, principles, and best practices of spellcasting. Strong magic requires a strong foundation, and it is my intention that every student of this academy have such a thorough understanding of magical theory that they can recite Uhad's sixty-seven laws of casting"—he snapped his fingers—"*on command*. Now, now, I know this must all sound intimidating, but remember that only the best and brightest are permitted entry to Prevan Academy. Though I expect excellence, that should be no trouble for the likes of . . ." He paused, and his eyes landed on Yenni. "The majority of you."

Yenni stiffened and glared at him. Just what did this man have against her? Whatever it was, it didn't matter. She had come to the academy at the instruction of the Sha and it was their judgment alone that concerned her.

"Since this is our first lesson together, let us start with something I fear most of you will find insultingly simple. Nevertheless." He pointed at Yenni. "Explain the Law of Self-Preservation." He crossed his arms and smiled a smug smile, waiting.

Ah! The dragon had explained that one. "The Law of Self-Preservation means that magic cannot affect the person who casts it," Yenni said.

Mainard squinted at her. "Correct," he said. "Therefore, what is the law's negative?"

"One cannot heal themselves," Yenni answered without missing a beat. Now the smile took hold of *her* face. This was more like it. She was used to having all the answers back home.

"Also correct," Mainard said, his voice flat.

He went around the room, his shoes making muffled thuds on the deep green carpet of the rows separating the desks. He pointed out students, demanding they answer his questions.

"What is the principle of spatial maneuvering?"

"Objects can be physically moved through space with source energy," replied one young woman.

"What is the principle of stasis?"

"Through source an object, or with advanced casting a living being, may be commanded to remain still," a serious young man intoned.

On and on Mainard went, and Yenni did her best to keep up with her charcoal stick—a *pencil*, she now knew. She scribbled awkwardly with the strange writing tool, noting what she could.

"The principle of energy to light?" she heard Mainard demand.

"Source energy may be transformed into illumination," a high female voice replied.

"Very good. Well then, perhaps a practical demonstration. Mam'selle Kayerba!"

Yenni glanced up, surprised to find Mainard right in front of her desk.

"Give us your best magic lantern," he said.

Yenni stared at him. "I-I am unfamiliar with this magic," she said, the admission burning like bile in her chest.

Mainard let out one sharp bark of incredulous laughter. "Queyor's Magic Lantern? But this is elementary, Mam'selle Kayerba. Come, class, what is the incantation for Queyor's Magic Lantern?"

"*Source to light and here remain*," her classmates chorused.

Mainard nodded and held out a hand. "*Source to light and here remain*," he said. Yenni felt a spike of ach'e and a gentle, white-blue light, like runelight, glowed in the professor's hand.

"Please stand, Mam'selle Kayerba."

Yenni stood warily.

"There now. You have the incantation. Show us your lantern."

Yenni held out her hand and carefully pulled ach'e, feeling the energy tickle and tingle down her spine and to her palm. "*Source to light and here remain*," she said softly. A hint of light glimmered across her palm.

Mainard chuckled. "Oh yes, that lantern would come in quite handy. On a pleasant stroll on the surface of the sun, perhaps."

The entire class laughed. At her. Hot humiliation and rage zoomed up the back of Yenni's skull, and her breathing quickened. How dare they? She was a princess of the Yirba, and she refused to accept such disrespect. Yenni pulled ach'e hard, like a child first learning her runes.

"*Source to light and here remain!*" she shouted angrily. Ach'e rushed through her, making her shiver, and brilliant light burst from her palm, so bright she had to turn her head. She heard Professor Mainard and the students around her cry out.

"Enough!" Professor Mainard yelled. "Are you trying to blind us all?"

Yenni closed her palm but the light continued to leak out between her fingers.

"*Source's light by source undone*," Mainard said, irritation plain in his voice. Foreign ach'e smothered her hand, wet and clammy, and the light in Yenni's palm went out.

"Oh, by all that is holy," Mainard grumbled. "Do sit down, Mam'selle Kayerba."

Yenni sat, seething.

Mainard shook his head. "I'd expect nothing less," he said. "Give up, Mam'selle Kayerba, you're in over your head."

He walked off to terrorize some other student and left Yenni clenching the edges of her desk.

"Never," she growled through her teeth. She would not give up. She was Yenni Aja-Nifemi ka Yirba. She was the equal of any one of these Creshens, and she would master their strange magic, learn a way to save her father, and return to her tribe triumphant. Giving up was simply *not* an option.

$$\Delta$$

By the grace of the Sha, the rest of the day's classes were far less traumatizing. Neither of her professors in Basics of Offensive Spellcasting or Basics of Defensive Spellcasting had required demonstrations. She was free to simply listen, make notes, and absorb their lessons.

Her best class was her last: An Introduction to Dragon Psychology. Perhaps the most interesting thing about it was Professor Rosé. She was dragonkind, and had skin that was pale pink, like the wild daisies that grew in the fields back home. Waves of thick, deep-pink hair spilled from her head down to the middle of her back, and her eyes were a disconcerting almost red. Still, she was friendly and enthusiastic, the opposite of Professor Mainard. And it was amusing to watch the silly, lovestruck expressions on most of the men in the room.

"In conclusion," she said as she sat at the edge of one of the tables and flipped her long hair over her shoulder, "we drag-onkind are still people. Now, yes, I know today's lesson has been an examination of differences in personality when we're in human and when we're in dragon forms, but you'll find that even in dragon we're not so different from you. To that end, you have some homework."

A few people groaned.

"Oh, boo, hoo, hoo," said Professor Rosé as she jumped up from the table. "Trust me, you'll be thanking me later," she said and winked. "Your task is to find someone dragonkind, ask them to switch to dragon, and observe the dragon personality. I want a page, just one measly page, of notes by next week. And if any-one gives you trouble, tell them Professor Rosé sent you. That's it! Class dismissed."

The bell tower tolled in the distance over the scraping and the din of her classmates' chatter. *One, two, three, four, five, six.* Creshens marked time by hours. Six peals of the bell meant it was six in the evening.

Yenni bit the inside of her lip as she collected her things. Perhaps she could ask Zui Duval for her help with Professor Rosé's assignment. Or perhaps Zui's husband Harth? But where to find them?

Then again, there was always Weysh.

I really shouldn't encourage him.

Even if she'd wanted it, there could never be anything between them. At the end of the year she would go back to the Northern Sha Islands, heal her father, and more than likely begin prepara-tions to marry Prince Natahi ka Gunzu.

But how likely was it that she would bump into Zui or Harth Duval within the week? Weysh, on the other hand, she knew exactly where to find. And she had much studying to do to arm herself for her next encounter with Professor Mainard. It would be wise to get Professor Rosé's assignment out of the way.

With a sigh, Yenni hitched her back-satchel up on her shoulders and headed for the library.

Δ

The dragon leaned against one of the carved white pillars along the library's entrance, arms crossed, with a satisfied smile on his face. Despite the chill in the air his shirt was mostly open, his long braid trailing down the muscles of his chest.

"Hello, lovely," he said as she approached. "Our uniform suits you, but then I suppose you'd look alluring in just about anything, en?"

"I didn't come here to listen to your nonsensical ramblings," said Yenni.

He cocked his head to the side. "Oh? Then why did you come?"

"You said you would help me study."

Weysh nodded. "That I did."

"I require your help with an assignment."

She explained Professor Rosé's homework assignment to him, then pointed to the wide grass lawn before the library. "Go and change over there," she said.

Instead the dragon sauntered up to her until he was about an inch away and bent over. He looked into her eyes, smiling slightly. Yenni glared back at him, refusing to be intimidated.

"You know," he said slowly, "it's customary in Cresh to say please when asking a favor of someone."

"I do not have time for this," she ground out, but he simply stood smiling at her, waiting. "Please," she finally said through her teeth.

"Sorry? I didn't—"

"Please help me with my assignment," she said, cutting him off.

He took a long stride back and bowed to her, sweeping one hand to the side. "Anything for you, my heart."

He jogged to the lawn and changed.

At least now he can no longer talk, Yenni thought as she made her way down the steps to meet him. And she wouldn't have to worry about any unwelcome advances. According to Professor Rosé, dragonkind felt no romantic feelings toward human beings while in their beast form. As she reached him, the dragon stuck out a clawed arm and bent over it in an elegant bow, a low clicking noise coming from his throat. Yenni couldn't help but smile. He truly was a magnificent creature to behold.

"Right," she said, hands on her hips as she stared up at him. How exactly was she supposed to go about observing the dragon personality? She tried to make a circle around him, but he followed her, turning so he was always facing her.

"Let me get behind you, Dragon," she said, but he made a low soft moan and shook his head.

"Why not?" said Yenni. "Are you afraid you'll sit on me?"

He huffed and stood up straight, and Yenni had the distinct impression she'd offended him. *As if I'd sit on my own Given*, his posture seemed to say. He turned his head and looked down at her from one huge, jewel-like eye, and the expression so reminded her of her brother Dayo it made her heart ache.

"My apologies," she said to him. "I suppose it is only good manners to keep someone in front of you when you're so big, isn't it?"

He bowed his head slowly, a nod.

"I think I *do* see the difference in personality, Dragon," said Yenni. "As a beast you seem somewhat more regal."

He bent down and surged forward, so that his big head touched her neck and shoulder. The action was so similar to how her field sphinx, Ofa, would nuzzle her in affection that before she knew it she was stroking his scaly face, and she planted a light kiss on his hot, dry nose.

He shuddered, spread his wings, and let out a sharp, happy cry. Yenni laughed. Dragon turned slowly, keeping an eye on her, and sank low, presenting his tail. He wanted her to mount him.

"No, Dragon."

He thumped his tail on the ground impatiently, looked back at her, and snorted.

"I said no."

He stretched his neck up tall and let out one sharp, indignant click. *You don't trust me?*

"The last time we went flying was because you snatched me up and whisked me away to a cave."

He sank low to the ground, head bent at an angle to watch her, and made a low, mournful noise.

"Yes, I'm sure you *are* sorry," said Yenni. "Especially as I have no intention of flying with you." No matter how exhilarating it had been. No matter that once she was home she would never get the chance to fly like that again.

He made that low gurgling noise once more, and though he was a beast, a very human sadness was plain in his eyes. "Oh Mothers and Fathers," Yenni sighed. She touched her stomach: not a hint of reaction from the Masters' protection rune. Still, she didn't quite trust him.

"No," she said with finality.

Dragon stood and bobbed his head sadly, then swung it to the side as if to say, *This way*. He turned and started away.

"What is this, Dragon?" said Yenni jogging to keep up with his great, stalking strides. He led her around the tall gray columns of the library to a wide dirt path dappled by the evening shadows of the trees. "Where are you taking—oh!" They emerged and Yenni found herself facing an expanse of white among a field of wildflowers. Dragon sank back on his haunches and waited, expectant.

"You wanted to show me this place?" she asked him. He nodded, one slow bow of his great head. Then he motioned to the sea of white ahead and grunted as if to say, *Well, go on, then*.

Yenni moved forward to inspect the strange scene before her, and gasped softly as realization dawned. It was a pond covered in gigantic white water flowers, each one as big as her middle. Yenni stopped at the pond's edge and stared, amazed, while the dragon slunk up next to her and drank, disturbing the water flowers and sending them spinning away.

"Dragon, it's beautiful!"

He turned and bowed to her again, and Yenni clenched her fist behind her to keep from stroking his face.

He sank to a sitting position, watching her. Yenni sat cross-legged beside him, and sighed as a light breeze caressed her face and ruffled the grass around her. The dragon responded with a low, contented rumble and flattened his head to the ground next to her, facing the pond. A few other students sat scattered on the grass around the pond, many of them couples.

"There is much and more to learn about Cresh," said Yenni. They sat in comfortable silence for a while. Birds twittered as the evening sun painted the sky in shades of amber, and Dragon's slow breathing soothed her, made her eyes heavy. It was the most peace she'd had since coming to Cresh. A part of her wanted to lean against him, as she would have with her field sphinx, but that would not have been wise. He was not Ofa, and he was not some gentle beast. He was a man. A brash, rude, presumptuous man. And yet . . .

"You're less beastly as a beast," Yenni said at last. He made a short huffing noise she interpreted as a laugh. If Yenni was honest with herself, Dragon's presence was more than tolerable; it was enjoyable. After the day she'd had it was nice to sit and recuperate with someone who expected nothing of her. Amazingly, in his beast form Weysh was *more* civilized, when he wasn't licking her or grabbing her up off the ground, of course. She glanced sidelong at him. It seemed she would have quite a lot to write for her report.

And then that would be that. This sort of idling together was not something she, or he, should get used to. She was there to learn Creshen magic, please the Sha, and save her n'baba, not become some dragon's plaything. And with Creshen magic being so much more difficult than she anticipated—

Yenni sat up straight, gasping softly. Her magic tutoring! She was meant to be meeting with Carmenna that very moment! She sprang to her feet, and Dragon lifted his head, watching her curiously. Mothers and Fathers but he was a distraction. She'd all but forgotten about her pact with the other woman. Yenni composed herself and stood tall.

"Dragon, there is something we must discuss. I cannot be your Given, but there is a woman named Carmenna who is quite fond of you. She would make a more suitable match. You should turn your attentions to her."

Dragon slowly rose to his feet, and in the span of a blink he changed back to the man, Weysh. He gave her a look full of skepticism.

"En?"

"She is my tutor, and I told her I would steer your attention to her in exchange for her help."

"What?" said Weysh, and it came out laced with incredulous laughter. "Surely you're joking—*Carmenna* is your tutor?"

"Yes, and your efforts are best spent on her, not me."

"Sweet," Weysh said patiently, "I'm not some breeding stud you can cajole into plowing a mare. Carmenna is not my match." He held her eyes with his own. "*You* are."

Yenni paused at that, at the strange anxiousness his frank gaze stirred in her. No man had ever dared look at her like that before, his thoughts so plain on his face. It made her angry, but there was something else too. A nervous adrenaline, like when on a hunt.

"Well, I do not want you."

He threw up his hands in frustration. "Then what on Byen's hallowed soil *do* you want, if a thrice-damned *dragon* isn't good enough for you, en? What must I do to prove my sincerity to you?"

"What I want is to study the magic of Cresh, *only*." She pulled on her back-satchel. "I must go." Carmenna was waiting.

"Yenni Ajani!" he called after her, but it seemed he was capable of good sense after all, as he wisely did not follow.

10

Lights—what Yenni now knew were Queyor's Magic Lanterns—hung suspended in bowls of glass on poles lining the walkways. She hurried along until she was back at student services. Carmenna waited on one of the leather sofas against the walls, her chin in her hands and her dark hair tumbling like a horse's mane over one shoulder.

"There you are!" she said as she caught sight of Yenni. She stood and they touched palms, Yenni once again holding back a grimace at the awkward intimacy of the gesture.

"I'm sorry to have kept you waiting," she said. "There is much I want to discuss with you today—" Yenni cut off as her stomach let out a loud, embarrassing grumble.

Carmenna raised an eyebrow. "I'm starving too. Why don't we take this conversation to the dining hall?"

And so they made the short trip there. The dining hall was a long, corridor-like building made of stone pillars that curved up to arches high overhead, and large windows let in the night sky while more magic lanterns floated above them like stars. Yenni and Carmenna sat across from each other, surrounded by laughter and chatter and clicking utensils. The rich and meaty smell of Yenni's Creshen stew made her mouth water, and it was an effort to wait as the crusty bread sopped up the broth, softening it. She took a bite and held back a moan. It could simply be that she was hungrier than a plague of locusts, but the savory stew and crunchy bread were like a rare and luxurious delicacy.

Carmenna spoke around a mouthful of her own stew.

"Mmm. Now then, what are you struggling with? What should we focus on?"

"Magic," said Yenni.

"Could you perhaps be a bit more"—Carmenna waved her bread for emphasis—"specific?"

"Creshen magic."

Carmenna watched her helplessly. "Are you having trouble with specific incantations? Anchoring? Battle magic? Healing magic? Domestic spells—"

"Ah! Healing magic! I want to know about Creshen healing magic," Yenni said excitedly.

Carmenna swallowed another spoonful of stew. "Well that's lucky. I'm in studies to become a general physiology mage myself."

Lucky indeed! *Praises to Mother Ib and Father Ji*, thought Yenni, even though by tradition, they weren't supposed to intervene.

"What is it about healing magic that has you so intrigued?" asked Carmenna.

Yenni hesitated—should she tell? This woman may be able to help her, and wasn't that why Yenni had come? She bit her lip and glanced at the rune on her left palm. "My father is very sick," she said softly.

"I'm so sorry," said Carmenna, and there was real sympathy in her eyes.

"None of the healers back home have been able to cure his illness, only slow it, but he is getting worse."

"What are his symptoms?"

Yenni found herself holding back tears as she explained the way her father's body refused to obey him, how difficult it was for him to get out of bed each day, his constant pain. A knot of guilt formed in her stomach at not being with him, not having to see him suffer.

"That *is* difficult," Carmenna said. "With symptoms like that it could be anything. I'll do my best to help you, but I'm still studying. Why not have a physician look at him?"

"I doubt he could make the journey to Cresh," said Yenni.

"Well, couldn't you have a healer go to him then? Or is that too costly?"

"Exactly that," said Yenni, latching on to Carmenna's explanation. It would be troublesome to tell her the real reason they couldn't simply import a Creshen healer—no Creshen had visited the Yirba in hundreds of years. Think of the insult to the Healers' Guild! If the first Creshen to set foot on Yirba soil in centuries was brought in to save the chieftain, it would be politically devastating, especially when there was no guarantee that a Creshen healer *would* be any more knowledgeable. Even Yenni's journey would cause grumbles, but as she was on Orire N'jem, who could argue with the Sha?

"I have heard that there have been instances of a similar illness in Cresh recently," said Yenni.

Carmenna tore of a hunk of bread and chewed, lost in thought. "There has been something going on, yes. My professor brought it up just today, in fact, in *Advances in Magical Physicry.* To be honest, it has the medicinal community, both magical and not, somewhat at a loss. The onset is sudden, and leaves the patient weak and gaunt, no matter how much they eat. They seem especially prone to respiratory issues. Has your father been coughing up blood?"

"Yes," Yenni all but whispered.

Carmenna clicked her tongue. "That's not good."

"Is there no cure? No treatment?"

"Well, that's the thing. Apparently, the first case of this illness was reported more than a year ago, and no one has been able to determine what causes it or the best course of treatment. The only good thing is it doesn't seem to be contagious. Still, it's somewhat alarming, especially the name." She dunked her bread in her stew and glanced up at Yenni. "They call it the wither-rot."

"I see," said Yenni. She stirred her stew dejectedly, her appetite having fled. So the Creshens knew no more than she did.

"I'm sorry, Yenniajeni. I do wish I could be of more help."

"It's Yenni *Ajani*."

"Ah," said Carmenna, wincing. "Sorry."

"That's all right," said Yenni, waving absently. Where was she to go from here? Why would the Sha tell her to seek magic if magic could not help her? "Is there no one else who would know more about this?" Yenni asked Carmenna. "Your professor, perhaps?"

"The most likely person would be the head of the magical department here at Prevan."

"Oh? Who is that?"

"Professor Claudieux Mainard, Magus Grande, First Class."

Yenni sighed. *Oh Father Esh, why him?*

"Yes, good luck there," said Carmenna. "I've always found that man to be like a snappish crab. His hairstyle even resembles one."

She made two crab hands above her head and the two burst into laughter. As their chuckles died down Carmenna cleared her throat.

"Did—were you able to speak to Weysh?"

The dragon. Hot, buzzing annoyance tingled under her skin at the thought of him, but then she recalled sitting peacefully by the water with him as a beast, and her emotions cooled into something warm and fond.

"I did," she told Carmenna. "He is as stubborn as you say, but I will get through to him."

Carmenna hummed as she stirred her own stew, the sound full of disbelief. Yenni watched her, utterly confused. Here was a woman who was smart and driven. She wasn't promised to anyone, and could have any man she chose. So why by all that was holy did she pine for the affections of that arrogant dragon?

Yenni squinted at her. "What is it that you see in him? Ah! I know. You like to fly together."

"Byen above, no! I can't stand flying." Carmenna shuddered. "I suppose what attracts me to Weysh is his honesty. It's a rare trait, especially among men." She gave Yenni a knowing look. "But what you see is what you get with him. There's no trying to decide if he's manipulating you—he simply lacks the guile." Carmenna laughed. "And he can be quite considerate. Once when I was in the middle of an exam, a torrential rain pour started up suddenly, and I had a good walk to my residence. I was dreading it, but when I came out I found Weysh waiting on the steps. He'd been there since the last clock chime, and he shielded me with his wing all the way back."

Yenni considered this. She supposed that fit with what she'd

seen of his character, but what of his brashness? His presumptive-
ness? His hardheaded nature?

*It matters not in the end. I will almost certainly be married off
when I return.*

Yenni nodded to Carmenna. "I will do what I can to steer him
in your direction."

Carmenna leaned back in her chair and studied Yenni. "You
don't have to do this, you know. It's a little strange, don't you
think? I mean, you're his *Given*. Suppose you start to develop
feelings for him?"

Yenni shook her head. "That will not happen. It *cannot* happen. I must return home at the end of the school year whereas
he would have me stay and tend his home. Don't worry, I will fix
this."

Carmenna crossed her arms, skeptical. "So you're saying
you're positive you won't fall for Weysh?"

Yenni opened her mouth to confirm it, but the memory of her
and Dragon sitting by the water's edge, the sun setting, and the
smell of wildflowers soft on the breeze halted the words in her
throat, and she saw the skepticism on Carmenna's face harden
into pain.

"I'm positive," Yenni forced out, resolute. Carmenna could be
a great help to her, and she must not let this silly dragon interfere
with her plans. "You have my word, Carmenna."

11

Weysh would have laughed at the dainty white cups of hot cocoa before himself and Sylvie if he hadn't just paid four duvvies for them. *Each.* He scanned the decor of the café—the lacy white curtains, pink walls, and the flimsy white tables—with open disdain. He was actually afraid to put his full weight on his spindly little chair, but it was Sylvie's favorite café, so what could he do?

Still, he rolled his eyes as he grabbed the tiny cup handle between his thumb and two fingers. At least the cocoa smelled good—rich and chocolaty. "Byen, Sylvie, I feel like I'm back at one of your tea parties from when we were children." He looked around. "I hope no one I know catches me in here," he muttered.

Sylvie just laughed, her face still flushed and pretty from the tram ride. "Their cocoa is the best in the city, Weysh. They import the beans all the way from Sainte Gregine. Go on, taste it and tell me I'm wrong."

Weysh squinted at his cup. "You're assuming I'll be able to taste anything. It'll be gone before it even hits my tongue."

"You're supposed to sip it, Weysh, not gulp it down like a barbarian. Normal people can't finish a hot drink in one swig, you know."

Weysh made a mocking face at her; she mimicked him, and they both laughed. But as their laughter died a chorus of feminine giggles took its place. Weysh noticed a group of young girls standing shyly behind Sylvie. The one with blond twin-tails tapped Sylvie on the shoulder.

"Hello, Sylvie," she said as his sister turned.

"Oh. Hello, Gabrielle," said Sylvie cautiously.

"Who is your friend?" Gabrielle's eyes were glued to Weysh.

"Oh, erm, this is my brother."

The girls gasped as one. "The one who's dragonkind?" asked Gabrielle.

"The very same," Weysh said, and smiled cheerfully. "Hello, lovelies."

They tittered at him and drowned him in hellos, each watching him coyly from beneath their eyelashes.

The main girl, Gabrielle, fanned herself with a piece of paper, pushing her scent in Weysh's direction. "I'm having a soiree at my manse to celebrate the start of the new school year. I'd love for you to come." She handed Sylvie the paper.

"Of course. Thank you for the invite, Gabrielle," said Sylvie quietly.

"Your brother is more than welcome as well."

"I'll do my best to make it," said Weysh, and winked at her.

Her face went red and she smiled wide. "Wonderful! Well then, see you at school tomorrow, Sylvie!"

The girls said their good-byes and exited the café, setting the bell at the door tinkling. When Weysh looked back at Sylvie, her face was dark.

"What's wrong?"

"Why do you always have to do that?" she grumped.

"En? Do what?"

"Flirt like that."

"I was being friendly!"

She glared at him. "You have a Given now, you shouldn't be flirting with other girls."

"One, I wasn't flirting," said Weysh. "And two, I haven't seen my Given in days."

"Oh? Why not?"

"It seems I haven't made the best impression." He recounted all that had happened between them in the past week and a half. "She seems to respond much better to me when I'm in dragon, though." He took a sip of the cocoa. "This is incredible, by the way."

"I told you," said Sylvie. "And Weysh, I say this with love, but you can be a bit much for people who don't know you very well."

He was aware of that. This wasn't the first time his mouth had gotten him into trouble and it wouldn't be the last.

"Yes, but she's my Given."

"Well," Sylvie said slowly, "if she's not receptive to you, maybe you should leave her be."

"Sylvie!"

"What?"

"She's my Given! I can't just 'leave her be.'"

"Well, what would you do if a boy was bothering me like that?"

"I would sit the young man down and have a civilized conversation with him." Sylvie let out a sharp peal of laughter that made Weysh scowl. "And anyway, this is different. We're Given! I'm not bothering her . . . am I?"

Sylvie took a sip of her cocoa and glanced at him over the rim of her cup, saying nothing.

"Well, how am I supposed to win her over if I can't even speak with her?" said Weysh.

Sylvie shrugged. "I'm sure she'll come around."

Weysh frowned at her. Something was wrong. A hint of bitter resentment wafted from her and stung his nose. "How was your first week of second school?" he asked.

"Fine."

"Are you making friends?"

Sylvie gestured back at the door. "You saw."

"I saw you get invited to a party."

"Yes, because of you."

"Nonsense. They invited *you*, Sylvie. I was an afterthought."

She dropped her head down on her crossed arms, sending up a plume of bitter annoyance. "By Byen, but you can be dense, Weysh." She looked up at him bleakly. "It's hard to make friends, *real* friends, when your brother is dragonkind." She dropped her eyes. "And now even you're leaving me."

"Sylvie, what are you taking about?"

"I barely see you now, and I'll never see you again once you move to the Moonrise Isles with your Given." A cloud of heartbreaking sadness emanated from her like cloying perfume.

He took her small hand in his. "Listen," he said softly. "I'm not going anywhere."

She looked up at him with tears in her eyes. "You promise?" she whispered, and sniffled. Where had she gotten such an idea? Weysh already had everything planned out. He would join the army, rank up, build a manse, and live there peacefully with his

Given and dragonling. He would be the father he'd never had, and have the harmonious family he'd always wanted.

He nodded, resolute. "You have my word, Sylvie."

$$\Delta$$

Weysh breathed deeply and let out a contented grumble. His Given was here.

For two weeks he'd occupied himself with work, ferrying packages and people across the Empire. He'd occupied himself with classes, pushing himself to his physical limits so that he would be too tired to think about his Given at night. And he'd even taken up cartography again, creating his own maps featuring all his favorite interesting spots outside the city. But in two weeks Yenni Ajani had made no effort to see him or contact him.

He had taken everyone's advice, leaving her to her own devices and trusting in the Watcher. Today he'd flown to the training sands, and was waiting nearby in dragon for the current class to let out. He planned to change and get in some melee practice, as it was important to get sufficient training as a man as well. Dragons were often tempted to rely on their dragon form and neglected training their human muscles. But catching his Given's spicy-sweet scent from inside the wide open doors was a welcome surprise.

Weysh lay on the grass hill to the right of the training sands, eyes closed as the noonday sun warmed his scales. At last the class let out, her scent getting stronger as he saw her exit. She wore the battle uniform: tight leather pants dyed green, knee-high boots, gloves, and arm bracers. Very suitable for flying. She spotted him and frowned, marching up to him amid curious glances from her classmates.

"What are you doing here, Dragon?" she demanded. He rose, then sank into a respectful bow and her scent changed, the eggy wariness fading to something mild and sweet, like toffee. It wasn't his imagination: she was definitely more receptive to him in dragon. His chest went warm inside and a low purr escaped him at the thought of how she'd stroked his face and kissed him the last time they'd met.

I missed you.

"What?" she said, uncertain. "Change to a man."

Weysh switched. "Hello, Yenni Ajani. It's been too long."

"What are you doing here?" she asked again, and the smelly wariness began creeping into her scent again.

"I simply came to get in some melee training," Weysh said quickly. "How have your first couple of weeks been at Prevan?"

"I have been very busy," she said.

"No doubt. First year is usually the most demanding. How go your magic classes?"

She sighed, and he caught a quick, metallic hint of frustration. "Difficult, to be honest. I need to speak with Professor Mainard about something, but he refuses to meet with me until I can produce a perfect magic lantern."

"Well, that's not right," Weysh said, sensing an opening. "It sounds like you could use some help. You have an hour or two free now, en? I usually did around this time as a first year."

"Yes," she said slowly.

"Then let's head to the library. You can practice with me."

He could see the wheels turning in her head.

"It's true that Carmenna could not meet with me today,"

she said, more to herself than him. Weysh wasn't thrilled about Carmenna being her tutor at all, but he couldn't very well forbid Yenni to see her. He knew exactly how that would turn out, so he pressed his lips firmly shut and awaited her decision.

"All right, Dragon. You will show me what you know about creating a magic lantern."

"Excellent," he said. He put out his arm, intending to escort her, but she sighed, shook her head, and went on ahead of him.

$$\Delta$$

Magus Helene Duvictoire Memorial Library was a masterpiece of architectural achievement. Domed ceilings painted with famous scenes from Creshen history reigned over tall stained-glass windows, which spilled colorful patches of light on the bowed heads of students and the cold, marbled stone of the tables below. But most notably, here and there white trees curved up and out, spreading branches of green leaves overhead and giving the place the feel of a forest. It was mostly quiet, except for the steady hushed whispers of the other students.

"Now, what's giving you trouble?" asked Weysh. He sat across from Yenni at a small, marbled table.

"I have a practical exam tomorrow in Foundations of Magical Theory. I know that Mainard will call on me to create and house a magic lantern, but I still haven't mastered it."

"En? Queyor's Magic Lantern? But that's easy. *Source to light and here remain,*" he said, pulling on source energy. A blue orb of mage light sprang to life in his hand.

"Yes, but then how to get it off your hand? To make it stay in one place?"

"*Source's light by source attached*," said Weysh, focusing on the tabletop. He moved his hand and the light stayed behind, hovering above the table.

"I just don't understand," said Yenni, and Weysh once again caught the rusty tang of frustration. "I've memorized the spells inside and out, exactly as Professor Mainard says them, and still my spells fail."

"Well, there's your problem. It's not just about memorizing the spells, you have to *believe*, en? Have faith in the laws and principles. And then you *anchor* source energy with spells."

"This is very different from runelore," she said.

"Yes, runelore is . . . something else." He tried not to think about the rumors around runelore, but Yenni squinted at him.

"What? What is that?" she said pointing at his face. "Why do people act so strange when I mention runelore?"

"Well," Weysh began.

"Well, what?"

"There are some who believe Moonrise Islanders use the blood of animals or . . . or infants to make runepaint," he said, and cringed as he waited for her response. But at her crestfallen look of horror he spluttered. "Of course, I know that can't be true—"

"People really think that about us?" she whispered.

"It's just an ignorant rumor," he said soothingly. "I never once believed it."

She stared off in the distance, her eyebrows drawn together in distress. "In ancient times, Masters would use some of their own blood in runepaint, but we no longer do that," she said.

"Of course not," Weysh said softly. "Show me a rune," he said, desperate to clear the air of that terrible, rotten-sweet scent of despair. "Do you have your paint?"

"Yes, I do," said Yenni.

"What *does* go into runepaint then?" asked Weysh as she pulled her jar and brush out of her back-satchel.

"A special type of flower, crushed and dried, sap from a certain tree, a crushed mineral that we mine, a certain powdered root, and dragon eyes."

"I see . . . wait, what?"

She grinned at him. "Just kidding."

He blinked and grinned back. She'd never smiled at him like that before. It made him want to drag her across the table and kiss her breathless. "Aren't you funny," he said instead.

"Put out your hand," she said. He did, and she dipped her brush in her paint, then began to paint his palm. Weysh suppressed a shiver at the tickle of the brush across his skin. She sang as she worked, low and wordless. Her voice was beautiful—trilling and smooth, and thick with magic. Something about her song reminded him of the comforting heat of an open fire.

"There," she said. "Now pull ac—pull source to that spot, and it should become fire. You might not be able to do it, but—"

Weysh concentrated, drawing on source, and a small flame flickered to life in his palm, without any incantation at all. "Look at that!" he cried.

"Very good!" Yenni said happily. "Many of the students in my runelore class have trouble. It must be easier for you due to your Island blood."

"How do I stop it?"

"Just stop pulling ach'e, of course."

"Ah-chey?"

"Ah, magic. Source."

He stopped and the flame went away, leaving a faded rune. He wiped at it. "It's not coming off."

"No, the rune won't disappear until it's used up."

Weysh started as a sudden thought occurred to him. "Runelore requires no spellcasting," he said. "Theoretically, I could use runelore while in dragon."

"I suppose so," said Yenni.

"So why aren't we doing this?" he said, incredulous. Imagine being able to use magic in dragon—he'd be practically unstoppable!

"Your people don't seem to put much stock in runelore," said Yenni.

Weysh frowned. "Well, we should," he said.

"Weh-sheh, please show me again how to attach a magic lantern to one spot."

"Of course. Give me your hand, lovely."

She hesitated, but held a hand out palm up, and he cupped it in his own.

"Good. Now, you remember what I told you? Do you *believe* it can be done? You just saw me do it."

She glanced at the orb, still floating beside them. "Yes."

"Good, keep the principles fixed firmly in your mind, and repeat after me: *Source to light and here remain.*"

She furrowed her brow. "*Source to light and here remain,*" she said. A nice-sized lantern formed in her palm.

"Good, now the next spell?"

"*Source's light by source attached,*" she said, glaring at the table. She slowly moved her hand, then he moved his, and the lantern stayed in place. She let out a happy gasp.

"Well done, my heart," Weysh said, and smiled at her.

"Why did you hold my hand? Are you able to somehow pass energy to me to make it easier?"

He half smiled. "No. Consider it moral support."

She scowled.

"My heart—" Weysh began, but she cut him off.

"You cannot continue to pursue me, Weh-sheh. You should turn your attention back to Carmenna."

Why did she keep trying to match him with Carmenna? He scowled. "Did she tell you to say that?"

"No one tells me to say anything," she said simply, and Weysh believed her. "I'm to be married when I return home and—"

"You WHAT?" Weysh's loud voice echoed throughout the quiet library, and the students around them whipped their heads in his direction, startled.

"Weh-sheh!" Yenni hissed. "You're making a scene!"

"Married? What married? You're *my* Given! You'll marry no one but me!"

Yenni stood and thrust her chin at him. "I am not your anything!" She put a hand on her hip and looked up her nose at him. "Honestly, Weh-sheh, what reason would I have to marry you, other than being your Given, as you say?"

"What other reason is there?" he exclaimed, utterly perplexed. "I—"

I love you, he went to say. But the words shriveled and turned to dust in his mouth. He stared at her in horror.

She angrily snatched up her back-satchel. "Presumptuous ass!" she hissed at him, and marched out of the library.

I love you, he tried to call after her.

But he couldn't.

12

Yenni paused with her charcoal-and-wood stick over the paper, gazing off into the sunrise through the little window above her desk. To say it had been an eventful few weeks would be like describing the ocean as vast. What should she include in her latest letter home?

She refused to mention the dragon. He would only give her family cause for concern, and once she left Cresh she would never have to worry about him again. In the end she settled for writing about what she had learned so far, explaining the confusing Creshen magic as best she could, and soon it was time to get ready for her first class of the day.

Today she was off to the only magical class she actually enjoyed: Basics of Runelore. At her first lesson the week prior she'd been relieved to see concepts she understood, and the professor had been delighted with her, excited to have a student from the Moonrise Isles.

In fact, when she walked into the small classroom for her second lesson his face lit up at the sight of her.

"Yenni Ajani! A pleasure to see you again."

He met her at the door and took her hands in his, his smile twinkling in his blue eyes. Yenni glanced around at the smattering of students seated at the wooden benches, wondering if they had received the same enthusiastic reception. Based on the interested looks she was getting, they hadn't. She slid her hands from his.

"Thank you, Professor Devon. I enjoy your class."

He cleared his throat and looked slightly embarrassed, perhaps realizing he was being a bit overzealous. But he had likely never met anyone Yirba before, and he was young as far as professors went—not more than a few years older than she was, surely, so she could forgive his zeal.

"Take a seat and we'll get started in just a few minutes," he said.

Yenni took stock of the small, windowless room. There were more Islanders than usual in her runelore class, but Creshens still made up the majority. She locked eyes with a friend she'd made in class last week, smiled, and sat beside her. She was a lighter-skinned Island girl with long, fat braids. She touched her palm to Yenni's.

"Hello, Diedre," said Yenni.

"Welcome back, mams," she said and grinned. Island women in Cresh often called each other this word, *mams*.

"Look at this," she said. She showed Yenni her palm, where she had drawn a passable wind rune. She pulled on it, and blew a slight breeze in Yenni's face.

"Impressive," said Yenni. "But Professor Devon hasn't introduced the wind rune yet. Where did you learn that?"

"Mams, I studyin' runelore since second school. I had a book

I used to hide away, an' I would sneak and practice runes in the night."

Yenni frowned. "But why would you have to sneak?"

She shook her head. "If meh folks only knew. They are good, loyal Byenists, Yenni Ajani. They would tear out their hair if they knew I was practicin' 'godless' runelore. An' probably my hair too."

"Godless? Runelore is the opposite of godless!" said Yenni. "It's the ultimate communion with the Sha! What do you think the rune hymns are? They're the language of the Sha made manifest!"

Diedre put a hand on Yenni's shoulder. "You don't have to tell me," she said. "I love rune hymns, they're beautiful."

Just then Professor Devon called for their attention. "We'll continue our work with the water rune today," he said.

With a brush and teaching paint, he drew the rune on a slate board at the front of the room as he sang the wordless water hymn. In truth, his voice was quite nice.

"Like so," he said when he was done. "If you have any questions or need another demonstration, come see me."

Yenni drew a quick water rune on the back of each of her hands to be a good sport. At least she was able to use Professor Devon's paint instead of her own. It was serviceable, but if she was to describe it in cooking terms, she would have said his paint was somewhat bland. The scent wasn't quite as robust as it should be, the consistency not quite as thick, the color lacking depth.

She spent the rest of the time helping Diedre until Professor Devon called out to the class. "It seems a good number of you are having trouble infusing the runepaint, so try adding a word here and there to the hymns."

Yenni froze. Add words to the rune hymns? The hymns were too sacred to be contained by mere human words!

Yenni stood up. "Professor!"

She was suddenly aware of everyone's eyes on her.

"Yes?"

"The rune hymns should be wordless," she said firmly. "It is an insult to the Sha to try to contain their magic with our inadequate words."

He smiled sheepishly. "Ah yes, I've read that, but we Creshens are used to spells, you see, so it's helpful to add a word or two . . ." He trailed off, likely at the dismay on her face. "You know what? You're right. If we're going to use runes, we should do it properly. Forget what I said, everyone."

The class continued, with the students doing their best to make water runes, but despite Professor Devon's retraction, Yenni could swear she heard a whispered word here and there. She said a silent prayer to the Sha, begging them to forgive the ignorance of the Creshens. As the class went on, a few other Islanders sought out her help. The native Creshens kept their distance, however.

When class was over and they gathered their things to leave, Devon called to her.

"Yenni Ajani, could I have just a minute or two of your time?"

"Oh, of course, Professor."

Diedre turned her back to Professor Devon and rolled her eyes before leaving. Guilt fluttered in Yenni's chest as she made her way to the front of the room. She'd needed to speak up, but she liked Professor Devon. He'd been kind to her, and she worried that she'd made him look incompetent in front of his class, and that he would now be annoyed.

But as she approached his podium he looked embarrassed. "I

must confess myself mortified." He laughed nervously. "I meant no offense. You know, I've always been drawn to runelore because of the rune hymns. They're much more organic, closer to source than the unwieldy spells we Creshens use, en?"

"That's all right, Professor. Apology accepted," said Yenni, relieved.

"You were a great help in class today."

Yenni smiled. "I am happy to help, thank you."

"You know, I would love the chance to talk more intimately about the best practices and culture behind runelore. Feel free to stop by my office anytime, anytime at all."

"Oh! Then I will, thank you."

"Anytime!" he said again. "I look forward to seeing you, Yenni Ajani."

$$\Delta$$

A jet of water slammed Yenni in the side and sent her sprawling to the mud, drenched and winded. She held her spear but her shield went flying and hit the mud with a slap.

"Roll, Kayirba!" yelled Captain Augustin. "You'd be on fire if this was a real battle. You should be working Yoben's Rainfall!"

She gritted her teeth, gazed up at the blue sky, and ground out the spell. "*Source-drawn rain here come and fall.*"

A spattering of raindrops sparkled in the sunlight above her and fell on her body and face, barely wetting her further.

"That wouldn't put out a candle, Kayirba," said Captain Augustin, and he moved into Yenni's field of vision. "You may be good with a spear, but you need to work on your spellcraft, en?"

He held out a hand and helped Yenni to her feet. "Did you get a tutor?" he asked under his breath.

"Yes, I did," Yenni replied.

"Good. First quarter exams are coming up. You don't need to make Magus, but you need to at least pass all your magic classes, or Mainard will send you packing."

"Yes, Captain," said Yenni, her stomach sinking. She slunk back with the others to watch the next student face off against Zui, who volunteered as a sparring partner for the Defensive Strategies for Dragon Combat class. Since she spit water, it made practice marginally less dangerous. As Yenni retreated, Zui gave her an apologetic bow, and though Zui had just given her a thrashing, Yenni couldn't help marveling at how stunning she was, with her silvery-blue scales glinting like steel in the sun.

For the hundredth time Yenni wondered at the needless complexity of Creshen magic. Who had time to remember spells and theories in the heat of battle? If she'd been allowed to use runes she could have drawn down a torrent. Or she could have pulled on speed, and Zui's jets wouldn't even have touched her.

But she had to admit that the young man after her fought Zui expertly—using some spell that seemed to give him short bursts of quickness, he weaved and blocked and evaded Zui's jets and got past her defense, bringing the point of his spear to the soft spot under her chin.

Captain Augustin nodded in approval. "Very nice, Moreau, but make sure to keep your shield up. You let it drop a few times."

And so class went on. When the hour was up, Yenni hung back and waited for Zui.

"Yenni Ajani!" she said once she'd changed forms. "Sorry about earlier."

Yenni waved a hand. "Never be sorry for defeating a foe," she said. "I wanted to ask—if you have some time, could you help me with Yoben's Rainfall?"

"Sure! I have somewhere to be soon, but I have a few minutes. Now, this might sound strange, but it always helps me to imagine the smell of the rain."

"The *smell* of the rain?"

"Exactly—the way the world around smells fresher, cleaner, after a rainfall. Do you know what I mean? Try it."

Yenni shook her head but she closed her eyes and tried to remember the way the jungles smelled during a rainfall, and the sound of the water pattering on the leaves. "*Source-drawn rain here come and fall,*" she said softly. A small shower started above their heads. Yenni looked at Zui and they both laughed.

"Nice job!" Zui said. They tipped their faces up to the rain and let it wash some of the mud off until the shower dried up a minute later.

"So, how are things with Weysh?" Zui asked cautiously. Yenni frowned. "Oh dear," said Zui. "Well, I can't say I blame you."

"I can't stand how he treats me like his property," Yenni fumed.

Zui sighed. "Weysh is—his upbringing was difficult. I think he's so eager because he thinks now that he's found you he can erase the past. He can start a new, better family."

"That's no excuse," Yenni said.

"No, it isn't," Zui agreed. "But it *is* an explanation. I know Weysh has a long way to go, but with time he could make you a wonderful Given, if he ever learns to get over himself."

Yenni crossed her arms. "I doubt that," she said.

Zui opened her mouth to speak again, but the bells of the tower pealed out.

"Oh!" she cried. "I'll be late!" She turned and ran. "Take care,

Yenni Ajani!" she said over her shoulder as she waved, then she switched to dragon and took off, disappearing into the sky like a glittering ribbon.

Yenni stood with her arms crossed, thoughtful. At least now she knew the reasoning behind Weysh's obsessive behavior, but his issues were not her concern. Her most pressing task was to find help so that she could pass her classes. Carmenna had her own classes, and many other students to tutor, so she was available to Yenni only an hour or two a week. Zui was much the same, acting as assistant for too many classes to count. Was Weysh really her only option?

Feel free to stop by my office anytime, Professor Devon had said. She started for the professors' offices, hoping to find him between classes.

When she arrived, Yenni wasn't quite convinced that Professor Devon's office wasn't just a repurposed storage room of some kind. It had no windows and was just wide enough for his desk and the chair across from it. He sat behind that desk now, and for the life of her Yenni couldn't figure out how he'd gotten there. Did he have to climb over it?

"Good evening, Professor," Yenni said.

He looked up at her and beamed. "Yenni Ajani! I never dreamed I'd see you again so soon! Have a seat, have a—wait! What by Byen is that?!"

He jumped up, eyes wide, and he pointed at her stomach.

Yenni looked down at herself. "What? What is it?"

"That *rune*," he breathed. "I've never seen anything like that before." He was referring to the Masters' rune on her stomach. The shirt of the battle uniform covered only the top half of her midriff, and the rune was visible beneath it.

"Lift up your shirt," he said, gesturing as he gazed greedily at her stomach.

Yenni jerked back. "Excuse me?"

He met her eyes, and his mouth opened in horror. "Oh blessed Byen, did I just ask a woman to lift her shirt?" His whole face went alarmingly red. "A thousand apologies! I don't know what's come over me! Please forgive me."

"That's all right," she said, perhaps a bit sharper than she meant to.

"But I'm making the worst impression," said Devon, and he sighed. "Let's start over. Would you be so kind as to explain the nature of that exquisite rune on your torso?"

"It is a rune for protection," Yenni said, even as Devon felt around his desk—his eyes never leaving her middle—for paper and something to write with. "It alerts me to threats against my life."

"Extraordinary," he muttered as he wrote. "How so?"

"Theoretically, if my life is threatened it will burn."

"Really," he murmured, and looked up. "Theoretically? You've never used it?"

"No. It was given to me for the first time by the Masters before I left my island."

"What is the hymn? Which strokes are drawn first? Is it native to the Yirba tribe?"

"I don't know," Yenni said, slightly overwhelmed. "It took three Masters to draw it. Only they know the way to create it."

Devon hummed his disappointment. Looking sheepish, he made a lifting gesture with his hand. "Would you mind terribly . . ."

"Not at all," Yenni said. She lifted her shirt to the top of her stomach, exposing the rune. It was so nice to finally find people in Cresh who shared her enthusiasm for runelore. Besides, he would never be able to replicate it. Not without the rune hymn, the stroke order, and the sheer wisdom and instinct of the Masters.

Professor Devon made a quick frantic sketch and told her she could lower her shirt.

"Professor," Yenni said, before he could ask any more questions. "I actually came to ask you about Creshen magic."

"En? Creshen magic?"

"Yes, I've been struggling in my other classes. My spells don't come out as strong as they should, or too strong, or sometimes not at all."

"Hmm, well that usually points to a lack of conviction when it comes to the rules and principles."

They spent a few minutes going over the spells that gave her the most trouble until he said, "Forgive me, but I have one more question about the protection rune. The paint is still quite vivid. I take it you haven't had any threats to your life?"

"No, none."

"Byen be praised. But if you did, would the rune fade or disappear entirely? How many attempts on your life would it take to use it up?"

"I don't know."

"Ah, of course not. And with any luck you never will, en?"

This led them on a tangent about runelore until Yenni steered the conversation back to Creshen magic. Professor Devon gave her a few more tips, nothing she hadn't already heard, before he said again, "Just one more question: You said three Masters together created the rune. Did they sing together, or one after the other? Oh, and how long is the hymn, longer than most?"

Yenni answered his questions and they continued on, with Devon interrupting again and again to ask questions about runelore, until finally Yenni realized she would get very little help from him.

She rose. "I'm sorry, Professor, but I have to be going."

"Oh, so soon?"

She shuffled toward the exit, claiming she had some assignment to complete, then slipped out the door, escaping his office.

"Come back anytime!" Devon called after her.

Δ

In the weeks that followed, Yenni spent all her free time studying and practicing, gritting her teeth through frustration and futility. The evening before first quarter exams she met Zui and Harth in the library, though Weysh was nowhere in sight. She hadn't seen him in over a moonturn, since his outburst when they'd studied together, and she was grateful. True, it would have been useful to have him as a tutor, but not at the price of his harassment.

At the moment she was focusing her attention on Harth's quill, a bird feather that the Creshens used to write, of all things.

"*Here to me by source compelled*," she said as she pulled ach'e. The quill wobbled, but didn't move.

"No, no," said Harth. "Uhad's Retrieving is *There to me by source compelled*. You're mixing it up with Meyor's Repulsion: *Here from me by source repelled*."

She looked at Harth helplessly.

"She's not getting this at all, en?" Harth said to Zui. "You know, when I was in first year, I remember there was a book that was great at giving tips for distinguishing the spells that are similar to each other. What was it . . . oho! *Perry's Spell Compass*."

"I think you mean *Perrone's Incantation Compendium*?" asked Zui.

"No, no, I'm sure it was *Perry's Spell Compass*. I'll go find it." He stood.

"Then it was definitely *Perrone's Incantation Compendium*. I'm going with you," said Zui. The two of them disappeared into the stacks, arguing in whispers.

Yenni would have laughed at them if she wasn't so frazzled. Her exams were *tomorrow*. She needed to have simple spells like this mastered.

The two of them came back with a dark-covered book. *Perrone's Incantation Compendium* gleamed in gold writing on the front and Zui threw Harth a smug grin. Harth and Zui went over the spells with her as Yenni's head ached and ached, until at last she stopped them.

"I cannot even read the words on the page anymore," she admitted. "They're swimming before my eyes."

"Then we should call it a night," Harth said. "All the studying in the world won't do any good if you're too tired to recall what you've learned. Do you think you'll be ready for tomorrow?"

"I must be," she said. "I *must* pass."

Zui squeezed her hand. "I believe in you, Yenni Ajani. You can do this."

And so the next day Yenni sat her exams, sweating and struggling through every answer and demonstration. But she gave each test her best effort, using all the time allotted.

Two days later, with her heart in her throat, Yenni stepped up to the front of the lecture building. In the foyer, professors' aides were still spelling the grades into slabs of marble, and though the sun had just risen, there was already a big crowd of students gathered.

Her chest constricted when she spotted her name chiseled into the stone. As she skimmed, and read, and reread her results, a cold sweat broke out on her forehead, and her hands went clammy wet.

She had failed every magical exam except Basics of Runelore.

13

Weysh flopped on his bed, sighing in relief. For the past moon-turn he had thrown everything into his classes, determined to achieve top marks, and when he checked the grade tablets that afternoon, his chest had swelled with satisfaction. His battle stats were the highest they had ever been, and he was even doing well in his one remaining magic class: Advanced Offensive Spells for Combat. Truth be told, the constant drilling helped distract him from the Given bond tugging relentlessly at him, demanding he claim Yenni Ajani as his. Her scent was everywhere: he could tell which halls she'd passed through, where she'd sat in the library or the dining hall—day in and day out small reminders of her tormented him. But after their disastrous last meeting, he was at a loss as to how to approach her, how to win her over. And so he'd studied, but now he had no more exams, no more distractions, and far too much time to think.

What reason would I have to marry you? Yenni Ajani had asked him. Weysh shoved his hands behind his head on his pillow and growled his frustration at the ceiling. Being dragonkind had always been enough before, but now, with his Given of all women, it wasn't. Very well, he would show her. As a top-ranking officer in the Imperial Army he would be able to provide for her every want and comfort, and she would forget all about this other man she was supposed to marry, whomever he was.

Certainly her lifestyle with Weysh would be more luxurious than on the Islands. If she lived anything like his cousins did, she might reside in a modest house built on stilts, open to the air. She might have a room of her own perhaps, if her father was a successful merchant or owned a business, like his uncle. Her family must have some reasonable bank if they could afford to send her to Prevan Academy. Maybe she . . .

Weysh froze. *Was* her father a merchant? Did she have any brothers or sisters? Byen above, two turns of the moon and he'd learned next to nothing about his Given other than her name. He'd heard all of Carmenna's deepest wishes and fears, but he knew so little about Yenni Ajani that he could only make guesses and assumptions about her life back home. No wonder he couldn't tell her he loved her—he hardly knew her. Had she even passed her classes? He was so caught up in his own efforts he'd forgotten to check. Weysh groaned and knocked himself in the forehead with his palm. Stupid, stupid, stupid. He resolved to check the results first thing tomorrow.

However, that turned out to be unnecessary. Harth came over that night with a bottle of Ritter's cognac—the good stuff. The two of them sat in Weysh's den, puzzling over a game of kings and castles.

"Not that I mind the silence," said Harth as he snatched another one of Weysh's pieces, "but since when am I able to get through a game of kings and castles without a never-ending stream of shite talk from you? I'd say you're focused on the game, except you're losing so badly that can't be it . . . or maybe it can. This is *you* we're talking about, after all."

Weysh just grunted and moved one of his pieces, hoping to steal one of Harth's the next round.

Harth took the piece Weysh just moved with one of his own, and gave him a sympathetic look. "Byen, Weysh, I know you probably don't want to talk about it, but what's your plan?"

"En? Plan for what?"

"Your Given!"

Weysh stared at him blankly.

"She didn't pass her magic classes. By the Kindly Watcher, did you really not know?"

Weysh felt his stomach dive. "She didn't pass?"

"No, my friend, she didn't."

"She's leaving?" Weysh rasped.

"I don't see how she can stay. Weysh, I'm sorry, en? I mean, maybe you can convince her to stay with you but . . ." His voice trailed off as Weysh put his head in his hands, gazing down at the whorled wood of the table without seeing it.

"This is my fault," Weysh said, more to himself than Harth. He got like this with too much cognac—moody and introspective. "I should have been there to help her but I pushed her away. Some Given I am." Harth said nothing, and Weysh looked up at him. "What, no comment? That's rare," he said bitterly.

Harth shrugged. "You're doing a fine job of summing things up on your own."

"Byen, I have to help her. She's *smart*, Harth, she just needed more time. Oho! Your father could talk to the head of the magical department. Your family has donated a small fortune to this school, en?"

But Harth shook his head. "He's away for the next half moon-turn," he said.

Weysh sighed. "Of course he is. I have to find some way to help her. I can't let her leave now, not when I've finally real-ized . . ." He trailed off, not exactly sure how to articulate his thoughts from earlier.

"What?" prompted Harth. "I can practically see the gears turning in your head. Don't strain yourself."

"Being Given and being married are two different things," said Weysh.

"So close," said Harth.

"Being Given and being *in love* are two different things."

Harth reached across the table and punched him playfully in the shoulder. "Give the man a prize!"

"Why didn't you tell me?"

Harth snorted. "Would you have listened?"

Weysh stayed quiet.

"Hey, some things you've just got to learn the hard way, en? But if you didn't know about Yenni Ajani failing her classes, what had you so quiet?"

"I was thinking about how I know so much more about Carmenna than I do about my own Given." He glanced up at Harth. "I do feel bad about how things ended with Carmenna, en? I think I shouldn't have strung her along as I did, but since we weren't sharing a bed I thought . . ." He paused and laughed roughly. "With the others, the transaction was simple: I got to have fun and they got to bed an unmated dragon. But maybe I was using Carmenna in a different way."

"And maybe she was using you, too, in a different way. Well, Weysh, I must say, this has been a day of vigorous thinking for you. You're going to have one demon of a headache tomorrow, and not from the cognac."

"Go kiss a pig's ass, Harth."

Harth only laughed.

"I tried the same thing with Yenni Ajani, didn't I? But she wouldn't have it."

"Seriously, Weysh, how has your head not exploded yet?"

Weysh closed his eyes and pinched his nose bridge. "I want to know more about my Given, Harth—*really* get to know her. I'll find her first thing tomorrow. I need to apologize, and I need to make this right."

14

Yenni lay with her eyes wide open as the sun slowly rose, lighting up her chamber in oranges and golds. Three days they had given her to vacate the school. Three days—now two.

For the fiftieth, maybe sixtieth time, she checked the rune on her left palm, the tightness in her chest releasing at the sight of it—just as strong as the day her father had drawn it there. "I haven't failed you yet," she whispered to it. There was still time. She swallowed, fighting back the constant lump that had formed in her throat, that ever-present despair that threatened to strangle her. The Sha still watched, there was still time.

She closed her eyes and breathed deeply. *Father Ri, once more I throw myself upon the mercy of your divine wisdom*, she prayed. *Lend me your insight, show me how I can stay, how to release my father from the illness that weakens and pains him, how I may please you and avoid drawing your wrath.* For two moonturns she'd poured everything into her studies, both for her classes and with Carmenna, learning about healing magic and the body. But not only was she no closer to finding something that might help her father, she had proven herself unworthy to attend the academy. She'd never felt like such a failure.

The room suddenly seemed too small, the walls too encroaching, and her bed a soft prison. The sun was up on her second day, and she had work to do. Yesterday she'd looked for Captain Augustin, though it made her skin seem to crawl with shame to do so. She dreaded admitting her failure to him, but he had been her advocate before, perhaps he could help her again. However, there were no classes for five days after examinations, and the professors were given time off as well. She hadn't been able to find him anywhere on campus, and after a few hours of looking she'd given up and spent the day in the library, studying and practicing the spells that gave her the most trouble until her head ached.

Today she would seek him again, starting with the training sands. By the grace of lucky Ib-e-ji, he would decide to run through some battle exercises during his vacation. Yenni decided she would spend a few hours doing so as well. If nothing else, it would help her work off the nervous, panicky energy just under the surface of her careful calm. She washed and dressed in her hunting clothes from home—short pants and a simple green top that wrapped around her middle and over each shoulder, crossing on her back. Then she set out for the training sands.

The campus was peacefully silent with the students taking a well-deserved break after examinations. The towers and spires of the academy rose like tall, gray sentinels over the pristine green lawns and snaking white paths of the grounds. Yenni's sandals crunched on the grass, wet with morning dew, until she reached the wide swath of the training sands. She hadn't expected Captain Augustin to be there right away, but her heart sank just the same to see the place deserted. Her lonely steps crunched on the sand as she approached one of the training dummies—a vaguely broad-shouldered torso shape that stuck out of the sand on a thin pole. She'd just begun to stretch when the she caught the *whoosh, whoosh* of wingbeats above.

She whipped her head up, and her heart thudded at the sight of Dragon. His scales glimmered violet in the morning light. It had been so long since she'd seen him, and she marveled at how pretty a figure he cut against the pink and orange of the morning sky, even as wary irritation crept into her muscles. He touched down in front of her and surged his head forward, a low, comforting gurgle coming from his throat. He put the warm side of his face to hers, and Yenni found herself closing her eyes, leaning into his touch, as if her tired brain couldn't remember that the beast and the man were one.

"Stay in dragon form," she murmured. "Please. Just for a while."

He silently sank down and curled around her, his warmth warding off the morning chill. Yenni sighed and sat on the wet grass, leaning against him. "So you've heard," she said.

Another low, soothing noise.

"I should have studied more," she said, stroking the scales of his side, drawing comfort from the warm, rough feeling of them under her fingers. "During meals maybe, or at night until I fainted from exhaustion. I tried hard, Dragon, but I should have tried harder. And now—" Her breath hitched. She hardly wanted to contemplate it, but the Sha were watching, judging her, finding her lacking. She *must* find a way to stay, or . . .

She yipped as the dragon's warm bulk disappeared and she fell back, but strong hands caught her by the shoulders.

"Byen, woman," a deep voice rumbled behind her. "You reek of terror. What are you so afraid of?"

Yenni shook his hands off and scrambled to her feet, but Weysh simply stayed seated on the sand, his violet eyes full of concern.

She looked away. "Failure," she whispered. Failure and the consequences for her father, for her tribe, for herself.

"I'm so sorry, sweet lovely. This is my fault."

She squinted down him. "What are you talking about?"

Weysh pushed himself to his feet, dusting off his loose, black trousers. He ran a hand through his hair, which now spilled long and free down his back. "I should have—" His eyes darted away and back, full of turmoil. "I should have been more focused on helping you. This never would have happened if I had been."

To her surprise, Yenni found herself wanting to laugh. There was such sincerity in his eyes, such arrogant sincerity, as if he truly believed he was all that stood between her and ruin.

She put a hand on her hip and smirked at him. "So if I understand correctly, with you as my tutor, I would have been guaranteed to pass?"

He nodded firmly. "Yes. I would have devoted every free moment to helping you. There's no way I would have—*should* have let you fail. As your Given I've let you down. I'm sorry."

Yenni took one more look at his anguished face and burst into giggles. *Oh Mother Shu, deliver this poor fool from the clutches of heedless love*, she thought. When she looked up, he was scowling at her.

"Well, at least you're laughing," he muttered.

"You are certainly passionate, I will allow you that much," said Yenni. "And confident as well."

"Yenni Ajani," he began, and moved a step forward as if he meant to reach for her, but instead he shoved his hands into the pockets of his pants. "You don't have to leave. Stay in the city with me. I'd give you the bedroom and sleep on the sofa or the roof. And I swear on my honor as a dragon I would never put so much as a finger on you. I'll stay in dragon when we're alone if that helps, but don't leave. Please. There's so much more I want to know about you."

Yenni turned her head to the side, studying him. "Stay with you, the man who grabbed me like a mauling bear? The man who insists I must marry him?"

He winced as if in pain. "I see now that I acted somewhat beastly toward you in my, erm, enthusiasm to have met you."

"I could not go outside without constantly checking the skies for days after you whisked me away," she told him.

Remorse twisted his features. "I'm so sorry, lovely. Truly. I hate the thought that you might fear me." He sighed and ran his fingers through his loose hair. "How about this—let's start over, en?" He stuck his arm. "Weysh Nolan."

Yenni hesitated, then slowly reached out and grasped it. They shook.

"Yenni Aja-Nifemi ka Yirba," she said.

"Yenni Ajani Femi Kayirba. Yenni Ajani Femi Kayirba." The dragon repeated her name under his breath.

"No talk of marriage," Yenni told him.

He nodded. "No talk of marriage. I simply want to help you."

"Why?" asked Yenni, wary.

"Because—" He crossed his arms and bowed his head, thinking. At last he met her eyes. "Because I like you, Yenni Ajani. I like your confidence and I like your tenacity. I feel we're two of a kind."

She studied him. What was it Carmenna has said? He lacked the guile for manipulation? "I believe you," she said at last. "And I don't want to. Leave, that is."

But could she really stay with him? It was a bad, bad, *bad* idea. Because leave she would, eventually, and when the time came, he would not let her go easily. But what were her other options?

"Is that a yes? You'll stay with me?"

But Yenni shook her head. "No. I need to speak to Captain Augustin. Perhaps he can help me."

She tensed, waiting for another of his outbursts, but he simply nodded, his face grim. "I see. Well, I guess I have no choice but to respect your wishes, en? But my offer is always there. You only have to say the word."

"Thank you, Weh-sheh," she said, and bowed her head to him. "By the way, do you know where I can find Captain Augustin? I am hoping he will want to train today and he will show up at the sands, but if not . . ." she trailed off uselessly.

Weysh looked thoughtful. "He might. And there's a good chance he'll be in town tonight, at one of the pubs." He cleared his throat. "So, speaking of pubs, what are your plans for the day?" he asked, far too casually.

She kept her head down as she smiled, but made sure to wipe it from her face before she straightened. "Figuring out a way to stay. I will train at the sands and wait for Captain Augustin."

"Perfect! I'll train with you," he said.

But Yenni wasn't in the mood for company. She shook her head. "I need some time alone. To think."

"I see," he said again, clearly disappointed.

The smile tugged at Yenni's lips again. "I have no intention of leaving, Weh-sheh. You'll see me again."

"Count on it," he said softly, a promise. "Farewell, Yenni Ajani."

Yenni smiled. "Good-bye, Weh-sheh." He changed and took off, and as Yenni watched him soar away she found, for some strange reason, her spirits were just a little lighter.

Yenni ran through her old, familiar spear drills—the ones she'd practiced during many a sunrise back home. First, swift gazelle, where she darted and spun to keep an enemy at bay, then wise tortoise, using her spear to block and parry, and finally fierce lion, where she struck hard with the blunt end of her spear and stabbed harder with the tip.

She alternated between training and resting, and as dawn lightened to noon the training sands stayed resolutely empty, with no sign of the other students and no sign of Captain Augustin. Once the bell tower rang the midday hour she switched strategies and practiced battle spells, doing her best to incorporate them into the smooth, flowing dance of her spear forms. But it was difficult to shift from fighting to reciting spells. As she panted through incantations she lost focus and her spear form went sloppy. *Curse these Creshens and their needlessly complicated magic!*

As the bells rang one past midday, Yenni's frustration reached its peak. She yelled, threw her spear down, and plopped onto the sand, resting her head between her knees.

"Small wonder they don't want me here," she muttered to herself. Perhaps she should give up, as Professor Mainard suggested. Perhaps this was the work of the Sha—their way of punishing her for her arrogance. With her affinity for runes, she had been sure she'd master Creshen magic, too, but this was beyond anything she could have predicted.

Perhaps she should give up, but . . . she opened her palms, staring at the twin runes painted there. "I can't," she whispered and gritted her teeth against her tears. "I can't," she ground out again.

Yenni jumped to her feet. She could stay there all day, wasting her second last day at the academy, and still never find Captain Augustin. She hated this feeling, this waiting around. She needed to *do* something. Where was it Weysh said she might find Captain Augustin? Ah, in town at the pubs.

What was a "pubs"?

Yenni snatched her spear up from the sand. She was about to find out, because she was going into the city to locate Captain Augustin.

15

First, Yenni went back to her suite and studied for a few hours, as according to Weysh she wouldn't find Captain Augustin at the pubs until nightfall. Besides, she must be fully prepared to start her next semester's classes, as start them she would.

The sun made its descent and one of the residence maids came and used some Creshen spell to fill her bathtub with warm water. Yenni took a quick bath and changed into her lecture uniform. Not only were the leggings and mage's coat her best defense against the chill in the air, she'd learned that students often wore their uniforms into town as a sign of prestige. Her stomach rumbled as she slid on her long mage's coat, reminding her that she hadn't eaten all day. She grabbed her back-satchel, where she kept all her remaining Creshen money, and slid it on. She might as well buy something to eat while she was out.

She was nervous about using up her stock of runepaint, but under her uniform she'd painted some small runes for speed, strength, and even pain ward, though she didn't anticipate needing them—it was more a precaution than anything. She eyed her spear leaning against the wall beside her bed. Once, in her Basics of Battle Strategy class, General Sol had told them to avoid carrying weapons into town, or to do so discreetly if they did. It wasn't illegal, but it was frowned upon, as it tended to make people nervous. Yenni could think of no way to carry her spear into town discreetly, so her knife would have to do. She strapped it to her thigh rather than her arm in order to hide it under the flaps of her mage's coat.

As she was checking herself over a knock sounded on her door. Yenni opened it to find Diedre, who lived one floor down in the same residence. Yenni held up her hand to give Diedre the Creshen palm touch, but instead Diedre wrapped her in a crushing hug.

"Wha—" cried Yenni.

"Oh, how are you holdin' up, mams?" said Diedre, resting her chin on Yenni's head. She let Yenni go and held her loosely by the wrists. "I came to ask if you feel to go for dinner with me in town before, you know . . ."

"Before I leave the academy?" Yenni finished for her. "I am not going anywhere, Diedre, you will see. In fact, I was planning to go to the pubs to find Captain Augustin and yes, I would very much love your company."

Diedre looked confused. "Augustin? But what he could do about this?"

"He has helped me before, perhaps he can help me again."

Diedre shrugged. "If you say so, mams. Come, if we run we could catch the next tram."

Diedre led her at a steady jog to a road at the north of the campus where two long, silvery tracks, stretching off toward a copse of trees, divided the dirt. Beside them was a row of stone benches covered with wooden awnings where a few students sat in their uniforms, likely waiting for the tram-cart too. As they approached the tracks glowed blue with ach'e.

"Oh!" cried Yenni. Her skin tingled with the energy coming off the ground. As the other students stood from the benches Yenni heard a rumbling noise, then the ting of a bell, and a strange contraption came trundling along the tracks toward them. It looked something like a pleasure boat, with a red roof and rows of seats, but on land. It shuddered to a stop and students streamed off.

"Incredible!" Yenni breathed.

The other students filed onto the tram and Diedre and Yenni hurried to follow, but when it came Yenni's turn to board the operator put out a white-gloved hand and stopped her.

"Just a minute, where's your fare, en?"

"Pardon?"

"Your fare for the tram, mam'selle. It's a quarter duvvy."

Comprehension dawned on Yenni: she must pay to ride.

"I see," she said, and reached into her back-satchel. She pulled out a hundred duvvy note. "Will this do?"

The man's eyes went wide. "My dear, that's far too much."

"But what . . ." said Diedre from behind her. She trailed off incredulous and, shaking her head, reached into her own hip bag and pulled out a duvvy note about half the size of any of the notes Yenni had.

"Here you are, sir. Come on, mams," she said, and linked her arm through Yenni's. She guided Yenni over to one of the hard benches inside and down they sat. The interior echoed with the clop of shoes on the wooden floor as everyone else settled. Finally the bell dinged again and the tram was off. Yenni wobbled and clenched the underside of the bench.

Diedre put a hand on her shoulder to steady her. "And jus' what you tryin' to do, Mam'selle Yenni Ajani? Pay the man's salary for the year?"

"What? Oh, oh yes. I must have reached for the wrong type of duvvy note. Thank you."

"Mmm-hmm," said Diedre, watching her shrewdly.

Yenni averted her gaze. It wasn't exactly that she didn't trust Diedre, but she didn't want anyone to know she was of the Yirba chiefclan. It would raise too many questions.

"Oh! Look at that view!" she said, drawing Diedre's attention instead to the window on their right. The tram moved even faster than she did with speed runes, though not as fast as she did on her field sphinx, and certainly not as fast as Dragon. She could clearly see everything as they traveled from the greenery surrounding the academy to the city center, trundling between buildings taller than she could have imagined possible, like an ant among giants. Who could climb all those stairs? Some even had bridges overhead connecting one building to the other.

And like on Sainte Ventas, the buildings came in every color imaginable—blues and pinks and oranges; rainbow-like structures surrounded them, blocking out the sky. In fact, a few made a bright barricade dead ahead. Yenni gasped as the tram quickly closed in, but as they crested a hill she saw that the track curved to the right, and they carried along without harm. People walked along the stone-paved streets on either side, paying no mind to the tram even though it passed by close enough that she could reach out and touch them if she wanted.

Periodically the driver called out districts of the city. "Marshay Street" or "West Castle West" and the tram would stop, letting off a stream of riders. At last the driver called out "Pub Street."

"That's us," said Diedre. The tram slowed to stop and they made their exit. Once again Yenni marveled at how different Cresh was from home. Tall metal lamps that curved like drooping flower stems lined the streets, and strong, meaty smells wafted on the mild breeze. The tram dinged, voices chatted everywhere in musical Creshen, and even the way people's shoes hit the stone ground was foreign, a hard *clip, clip*.

Yenni put her hands on her hips as she surveyed the area. "Where is the pubs?"

"Well, take your pick," said Diedre. She waved her hand to encompass the rows of buildings lining the streets, flush with light and vibrating with energy. Creshen music, high, quick, and cheerful, danced on the air.

"Oh! Of course. Now, where can I find Captain Augustin?"

Diedre bit her lip. "Is only magic I does study, you know— runelore and theory of spellcraft mostly, but—" Abruptly, she put two fingers in her mouth and blew a high, piercing whistle that had everyone looking in their direction, including a group of young Creshen men across the street who were wearing their school uniforms.

"Hello!" Diedre called waving to them. She jogged over and Yenni had no choice but to follow. "Do you fine fellows know Captain Augustin?"

"Augustin? What about him?" This was from a young man who wore his dark hair in a short tail, like Harth Duval's.

"Could you tell us where to find him?"

Another student, this one with shaggy hair like wheat that fell into his eyes, spoke up. "I'd try Les Canards." He pointed to a building with wooden cutout of three ducks hanging in front. The boys exchanged a knowing glance.

"Thank you," Diedre said sweetly, drawing Yenni away. They hurried toward the building with the hanging ducks. Stepping under a bright-green awning, they faced a door with peeling green paint. Diedre pushed it open and a dull roar of conversation assailed them. The place was dim and a bit run down in Yenni's opinion, but there were quite a few people inside, filling almost all of the wooden tables and chairs. On closer inspection, she even recognized a few students from her classes. Serving men and women carrying trays full of food scurried between the tables, like at feasts back home. She supposed a pubs was something like a big feast where all the people were strangers.

One of the servers in particular seemed to stand out like a very bright star in the night sky. Men constantly called out to her, and even reached for her. She tossed back her yellow hair and laughed along with the men at one table, and lightly slapped away the reaching fingers of a drunkard at another, wagging her finger at him. Yenni felt for the poor woman, but she seemed to know how to handle herself. Eventually she breezed past them, enveloping them in a flowery scent. "Just sit wherever there's room, ladies, be with you in a moment."

Yenni stood on her toes, scanning the room for Captain Augustin, but she didn't see anyone who looked remotely like him. She even led Diedre on an impromptu tour of the cramped pub, dodging pointy table ends and harried servers, but he was nowhere to be found.

"If Augustin is not here now, is a good chance he will be," said Diedre as her eyes trailed the woman who'd greeted them. "Is a reason this place is so popular, an' is not the beef pie." She smiled slightly, a similar smile to those of the boys they'd met outside. "I always did want to come here."

Before Yenni could ask why, Diedre had already taken her gently by the wrist. Yenni let her friend direct her to one of the very few tables left at the back of the pub, and eventually the pretty woman who'd greeted them glided up to their table, her face aglow with a warm smile.

"All right, loves, sorry for the wait," she said as she tucked stray strands of hair behind her ear. "My name is Celeste and it's my pleasure to serve you. Today's special is our famous beef and potato pie, with a pint of *paradis blond* and a strawberry tart for dessert. Will that do for you?"

"Ah yes, that will be fine, thank you," said Yenni. She liked the beef and potato pie at the academy well enough. She wasn't sure what the other two things were, though *strawberry* sounded familiar.

Diedre ordered the same. As they waited for their food, Yenni kept jumping up every time someone entered the pub to see if it was Captain Augustin. Eventually, her eyes fell on two Creshen men at the table across from her, who watched her with interest. She glared at them until they laughed and went back to their own conversation.

"You have *got* to relax yourself, Yenni Ajani," said Diedre.

"I can't, Diedre. I don't have much time. Tomorrow is my last day here. I *must* find a way to stay."

"I know, I know, mams. An' believe me, I want you to stay, but you're ridin' yourself to hell and takin' me along with you. Come. Relax. Fill your belly, an' if is no sign of Augustin by the time we finish, we'll check every pub in the district until we find him. Good?"

Yenni sighed. "All right."

Soon Celeste was back and placed their meals on their table. "Five duvvies each," she said.

"Oh, of course." Yenni took off her satchel and reached inside, finding the same one-hundred duvvy note from before. *This is likely too much*, she thought, remembering the comments of the tram operator. She pulled out all her money and started going through it, trying to find something smaller.

"Oh my," breathed Celeste, blinking her large blue eyes.

Diedre glanced up from her own bag and her mouth fell open. "Watch'Ahmighty! Mams!" she hissed, and gestured frantically at the money. "But why it is you have all that bank on you at once? Put it away!"

"Bank? I don't understand."

"Money," she clarified and leaned in to stuff the duvvies back into Yenni's satchel. She paid for both of them with a note of her own. "I don't know how you all do on the Moonrise Isles, but is not smart to be traipsin' around the city with all that. Suppose someone decides to help themselves to what you have?"

"Oh!" That had not even occurred to Yenni. Back home she didn't have much use for money. If she needed something she asked her mother for it, and more often than not things were gifted to her. Yenni shook her head and focused on her tray. The beef and potato pie looked delicious, the top crispy and brown. Beside that was a small, bowl-shaped crust with a red and sticky filling. Yenni took the smallest of bites. It was very sweet, but a bit sour, too, and salty besides. Altogether she found it pleasing. In a heavy metal cup with a handle was something foamy and white. She took a sip and made a face—some kind of Creshen beer. She'd never been a fan of beer, but it would have to do. She took up her Creshen fork and took a bite of the beef and potato pie. Maybe it was hunger, but it was far better than the pie at the academy. Despite the ravenous hunger in her belly she ate slowly, the result of years of ingrained etiquette lessons from her mother and stewards.

Even so, by the time she'd finished everything, even the bitter beer, there was still no sign of Captain Augustin, and no matter what Diedre said, the panicky flutter in Yenni's chest continued to grow, until at last she jumped up.

"Let's go."

Diedre stood slowly after her. "Listen, mams. I know you need to find Augustin, but do you really feel is wise to be prancin' around with a small fortune on you? Maybe we should go back—"

"There is no time," said Yenni, shaking her head. She'd already lost so much, and she might well miss Augustin completely if she left the city. She had no idea if he could even do anything to help her, but right now the friendly captain was her only lead. "That's all right, Diedre. I would not want you to be uncomfortable. I can continue on my own."

"Absolutely not!" cried Diedre. She threw up her hands. "Fine, let the hunt begin."

Stepping outside, Yenni saw the sky had gone dark, and the tall metal pole lanterns lining the streets glowed bright and blue-white. The city was transformed by sundown. The windows of the buildings glowed from within, and way up above, the tallest buildings were surrounded by rings of colored light. She craned her neck upward, her mouth open slightly as she regarded the twinkling illumination of the city. A tram rumbled past, bringing her back to reality. She had work to do.

Mother and Father Ib-e-ji, watch over me.

Yenni and Diedre spent the next two tolls of the clock ducking in and out of pubs, dodging servers and the grabbing hands of men with stale breath and staler compliments. Despite Diedre's constant reassurances Yenni found herself getting more and more frustrated and panicked, until at last she rushed out of the latest pub like a rabbit smoked from its den, heedless of her friend.

She gulped the night air as a deep bell somewhere in the heart of the city chimed the hour. Nine reverberating peals later she realized how little time she had left, but the thought of shoving her way through another noisy, sweaty crowd set her teeth on edge. Fighting back tears, she dragged herself to the alley beside the pub she'd just left, desperate for a few quiet seconds alone to think and regroup. She made her way to a pile of big wooden boxes at the back and sat down, grateful for the quiet and the shadows, soothing to her stressed and overstimulated nerves.

"Yenni Ajani!" Diedre's worried voice echoed on the night air.

"Over here," she called wearily. She sat with her head tipped back against the cool stone, listening to the screechy Creshen music leaking mutedly from the pub. Eventually the *clip, clip* of Creshen shoes echoed off the walls of the alley—two sets of footsteps.

Yenni glanced up and saw two men coming toward her, side by side, blocking the alley entrance. They stopped about ten paces from her.

"Hello, darling," said the one on the right. He had limp hair and small cruel eyes, and Yenni recognized them as the two men who had been watching her at Les Canards.

Yenni sprang to her feet. "What do you want?"

"Now, now, no need for things to get messy, en? Give us your bag and you'll be free to go."

Her bag? Her bag with all her money? Icy comprehension crept down her spine: these two were thieves, and she had given them quite a show. She slid her hand to the knife at her thigh. "No."

"Yenni! Yenni Ajani!" Diedre's frantic voice was fainter than before, farther away. Yenni debated calling out to her again, but it was Yenni's own silly fault she was in this mess, and she was loathe to drag Diedre into danger too.

"Suit yourself," said the thief. He took his hand out from behind his back and made a fist in front of his chest. Metal gleamed faintly in the weak light of the lamppost across the street. He wore some kind of weapon that had wicked spikes jutting out from his knuckles. Yenni gasped as a hot, sharp pain seized her stomach.

The rune . . . Mothers and Fathers, these men mean to kill me!

If only she had her spear! It would have been perfect for keeping them at bay in such a narrow space. But, alas, she did not, so she pulled her knife free and flipped it up, backing up against the wall. Though her instincts screamed to avoid being cornered, her logic told her not to let one of them get behind her.

"Careful, Felix," said the other thief, who now leaned against the wall on her right. "Seems the little mageling has some skill with that knife."

Someone dropped from the roof of the pub on her left, landing in the alley with a thud. Another Creshen man with limp hair and a cold smile crouched behind the one advancing on her. "Is that right, Louis?" said the newcomer, rising. He flipped a knife into his palm. "Maybe she can teach me a thing or two, en?" They laughed, and Yenni started when she realized another voice had joined the three in the alley. She darted her eyes upward and caught a fourth thief crouched among the shadows of the roof to her right. Four of them against one of her. If she gave them her money, would they let her go?

As if in answer, the rune on her stomach blazed again, sending another sharp, burning sensation through her skin. No, she had seen their faces and knew their names. They would not let her leave this alley alive.

"Diedre!" she finally shouted, praying her friend would hear. The men with the weapons advanced slowly, cruelly, toying with her.

Good.

If they were underestimating her, she had the element of surprise. Still, her shaking as they closed in was not feigned. She had one chance, one shot to get free. She could not die here, fail here, in this alley leagues away from home.

Father Gu, lend me your warrior's heart.

Their weapons glinted dully in the dimness of the alley, and their steps were slow and echoing, louder than the muted twang of the Creshen music coming from the pubs, louder than her thudding pulse.

"What do you plan to do with that knife, en?" said the one with the bladed knuckles. "Clean a chicken?"

Closer, just let them get a little closer.

She squeezed her eyes shut, and they laughed. She pulled ach'e, feeling it rush through her veins and tingle on her skin.

"Source to light and here remain!"

Light exploded into the alley, bright against her closed eyelids, and the thieves screamed. Yenni pulled on the speed runes on her legs, then her arms. She ducked and dodged around two of the thieves, then slashed at the tendons behind their knees.

The two of them hollered and the steely stink of blood filled the air. Before they could hit the ground Yenni was rushing for the third thief, the one who stood blinking against the left wall. Pulling on her strength rune, she put her hand to his face and slammed his head against the brick. He slumped to the pavement.

She spun, ignoring the groans and curses flying at her. Where was the fourth man? Nowhere she could see, and the way out of the alley was clear. She dashed for the exit.

"*Source as twine to bind my foe!*"

Yenni stumbled. Her legs tried to stick together while her arms felt as if they were being pushed against her body. Oh, unholy shadows, even a petty Creshen thief could cast Fenton's Body Bind? She'd been struggling for *weeks* with that spell!

He couldn't cast it well, apparently, as she could still move, albeit very slowly, as if walking through mud. She flared her strength runes and speed runes, desperately staggering toward the mouth of the alley. She glanced back at a noise from behind and found the first thief on his hands and knees, crawling after her with his teeth bared in pain, growling like a wild dog.

"Jean, you rat prick!" shouted the other thief as he stumbled to his feet. "Get down here!"

"He's long gone," growled the first through his teeth. "I told you this would happen. I never trusted him, not from day one."

Yenni could feel her runes fading, but the mouth of the alley was straight ahead. She just needed to get inside one of the pubs, where there were crowds of people—so close but so oblivious to her plight.

Her speed and strength runes gave out, and the sluggish weight of her body seemed to double. Yenni gritted her teeth, throwing all her will into each dragging step, sweat sliding down her back even as the sounds of the thieves behind her grew closer. But the street was right there, right there!

"Someone! Diedre!" she screamed, knowing deep down it would do no good. No one had heard all the commotion so far, not with the two pubs' music competing. And poor Diedre had disappeared in the other direction. A hand clamped around her leg and pulled. Yenni stumbled but managed to keep her feet. She looked down into the hateful eyes of the first thief she'd maimed. "Island bitch," he spat, and pulled again. Yenni's arm burned with exertion as she struggled and failed to raise her knife.

Something thudded into the alley in front of her.

Yenni whipped her head around in time to see another Creshen man rushing at her with a blade.

"Get her, Jean!" shouted the thief farther down the alley. He hobbled toward them using the wall for support.

Yenni tried to think of some spell, any spell that would help her, but too soon the thief Jean was on her, grabbing her by the front of her mage's coat. His blue eyes burned into hers from above a kerchief wrapped around his face.

Mothers and Fathers, forgive my failure and receive my spirit.

She yelped as his knife nicked her left shoulder, then her right one, so sharp it cut right through her coat. Two more quick slashes on the left and right side of her torso and her satchel fell free. He grabbed it.

"*Source-fueled leap to mimic flight!*" he shouted and then jumped clean up into the air. His ratty coat flapped around him as he disappeared onto the roof with her bag.

"Jean!" bellowed the thief back in the alley, but the other one gave Yenni's leg one great yank and she tumbled. She couldn't put out her arms to break her fall, and her shoulder smacked painfully into the pavement. The thief dragged himself over her, grabbed her hair, and slammed her head into the ground. Pain bloomed from the back of her skull, spreading into her teeth and jaw. By instinct she pulled on her pain wards otherwise she may well have fainted.

"How should I repay you, en?" said the thief. The stale stink of his breath made Yenni want to gag. Her head ached, and her pulse made a loud thudding in her ears. The thief held the blades of his knuckle weapon in front of her eyes. "You like blinding people? Maybe I'll blind you, bitch."

"There from me by source repelled!"

Yenni saw the thief's eyes go wide and a split moment later he went flying toward the back of the alley, pushed by an incredible force.

"Yenni!"

Diedre's beautiful face hovered above hers. "Come on!" She pulled Yenni to her feet, supporting her as she swayed and blinked back white lights at the edges of her vision.

"Diedre," Yenni groaned.

"Yenni! What—ah!" Diedre screamed and jerked against Yenni. Cruel laughter rose above the muffled pub music. One last thief continued to hobble toward them, hugging the alley wall. Diedre breathed heavily, her braids falling across her face and a knife sticking out of her shoulder. She turned back to face the thug, rage in her eyes.

"Sleep by source, wake no time soon," she snarled.

A thick, heavy blanket of ache coated the air. The thief on the wall slumped to the ground in a dead faint, as did his friend, whom Diedre had sent flying. Yenni's own eyes went heavy, her legs weak.

"No, no, no, not you, mams!" said Diedre, her voice hoarse with pain. She shook Yenni. "Fight it! The spell is not that strong, it only worked on those guys because they lost so much blood already!"

Yenni clung to Diedre and did her best to shake off the grogginess, but it was so hard to move, to think.

"Come on, Yenni!" Diedre pleaded. "I can't carry you on my own an' I don't want to leave you! Gohad's Forced Sleep is an advanced spell and I'm not the best at it. They could wake up any time!"

"I am trying," Yenni slurred, and she wasn't sure if she was speaking Creshen or Yirba. Her pulse fluttered in her ears.

"Yenni—oh! Watch'Ahmighty!"

Dimly, Yenni was aware of another body dropping into the alley ahead of them. Her stomach plunged and she felt sick with dread—more members of the thieves' gang?

A deep, rage-filled roar, like nothing she'd ever heard before, dwarfed the alley. Yenni snapped her head up, the loud noise blasting away her sleepiness. At the sight at the mouth of the alley she let out a sob of relief. He crouched with steam hissing from his nostrils and fire sparking behind his bared teeth, dark and deadly, like some demon beast from the shadows.

Dragon.

16

Kill, kill, kill.

The instinct gripped him, commanded him from the moment he'd caught Yenni's scent below, rancid with fright. It may as well have been an alarm.

He'd arced right in the sky, shooting after it, his friends screeching after him. Now the scent stung his nose, along with the unclean stink of what looked to be a band of street thugs, and the only thing keeping him from blasting the whole alley with fire was his Given. She stood embracing another woman, the two of them watching him, wide eyed. Movement at the back of the alley drew Weysh's attention. He stalked past the women, who pressed up against the alley wall to let him pass. Weysh crouched, growling, over the weakly thrashing body of a greasy thug and held him down with one sharp claw. The man opened his eyes.

"Oh shit," he whimpered. "Oh *hells!*"

A strong whiff of urine accosted Weysh's nose. He longed to run his talons down the goon's body. Just one swipe, through his clothes, through his skin and fat and muscle, and all his useless guts would come tumbling out.

"No, Weysh. You can't kill him. You'll be charged."

Zui's voice, as if she knew what he was thinking. He hadn't even noticed when she and Harth had landed.

"Yeah! You can't kill us!" This from another thug, slumped in a sitting position in the right corner of the alley among empty crates.

"Oh shut up," Zui snapped at him. "*Source as twine to bind my foe.*"

Zui handily incapacitated all the thieves with magic. Legal, but nowhere near as satisfying as ripping them apart.

Weysh changed and brought his face close to the thug's, even though he smelled like an outhouse. He didn't say a word as he punched the man hard in the stomach, but smiled as he curled up, moaning and wheezing.

"Weysh," Zui said without conviction. She shook her head as she and Harth helped the women to the ground.

"If he didn't do it, I would have," Harth said behind him. "Shit eater," he spat at the thug. "Are you two ladies—there's a dagger protruding from your shoulder, mam'selle!"

"Yes, I know," Yenni's friend groaned.

"Harth, find the peacekeepers. These two need to get to a healing hospice."

"Right," said Harth. He changed and took off.

"And stop struggling!" Zui shouted suddenly at thieves. "If you break my body bind I'll have no choice but to eat you."

The thieves went still. Weysh loped over to Yenni's side and took her hand in both of his. "Lovely?" He felt as helpless as a child. Byen, he could smell her blood! Had she been stabbed?

"I'm fine," she said and attempted to push herself upright, but Zui gently held her down. "How is Diedre?" Yenni asked, and Weysh clenched his teeth at the weak breathiness of her voice.

"I'll live," her friend replied from on the ground beside her, but her eyes were closed and she was breathing hard through her pain.

"Thank you, Diedre, for saving me," said Yenni.

Weysh glanced between the two of them. Looked back at the thieves and the blood-soaked alley. "What on Byen's hallowed soil happened here?" he cried.

Yenni briefly recounted how she'd ended up in a dark and secluded alley in the pub district and been attacked.

"Four against one and you did this much damage?" A bubble of pride swelled through the haze of Weysh's rage, fear, and disgust. "That's my girl."

"I'm not your anything," she muttered, but to Weysh it seemed quite halfhearted.

"But, lovely, if you needed to find Augustin that badly, why didn't you simply ask me to sniff him out for you?"

"I did not think of that," she admitted. A sinking feeling took hold of Weysh's insides. She didn't ask him because she didn't trust him. It didn't even occur to her that he could help her.

Suddenly Yenni attempted to sit up again.

"You should rest, Yenni Ajani. Relax until the peacekeepers arrive and take you to a healer," said Zui.

"I have no time to visit a healer," she replied, fighting off Zui's gentle hand. "One of the thieves escaped with all my money. I have to find him!"

"En? What do you mean someone has all your money?" Weysh asked Yenni.

"I had it in my back-satchel. He cut it right from my shoulders and used some spell to jump onto the roof and get away. I have nothing left," she whispered.

"Movay's name, woman! What were you doing walking around the city with all your bank?"

"Thank you!" her friend beside her exclaimed weakly, her eyes still closed tight.

Yenni shot Weysh a hard look. "I needed to eat. How was I to know how much I would need?"

"Well, how much did you lose?" asked Zui.

"More than a thousand duvvies. I'm not exactly sure."

Zui and Weysh were flabbergasted. "A thousand—Watcher above! You came out to buy dinner with over a thousand duvvies?" Weysh studied her closely. "Your father must be a very rich merchant, en?"

"Oh . . . yes," she said.

Weysh got to his feet and stalked over to the thug who lay slumped against the back corner of the alley. His long, greasy hair was stuck to his face with sour sweat. Weysh crouched down before the man, unsmiling. "Where is he?" he said simply.

Weysh could tell the man would have been shaking if he wasn't so thoroughly constricted by Zui's body bind spell. "I don't know," said the thug. "By Byen I don't know. He double-crossed us. Please, I don't want to die here."

Weysh curled his lip up at the cretin. "The only reason you're not a smoking pile of ash right now," he said, and pointed back at Yenni, "is because of her. You *will* tell the peacekeepers everything you know."

The thug nodded weakly. "Yeah. I want to see Jean get what's coming to him as bad as you, en?"

Weysh scoffed as he got to his feet, and it was an effort to hold back from kicking the weasel. He went back to the women.

"I doubt they'll be much help," he said, pinching the bridge of his nose.

"What if you track him?" asked Yenni.

"I'm so sorry, lovely, but it's not that simple. His scent will be incredibly difficult to follow."

"And yet you're always able to find me," she said, her tone slightly accusatory.

"One, you're my Given." Her friend Diedre made a shocked little noise at that. "Your scent is like a beacon, stronger than anyone's. Two, I'm not a bloodhound. Tracking a stranger's scent through the muck of the city when they've already gotten a head start? It's basically impossible but—you said he has your bag?"

"Yes."

Weysh nodded. "I might be able to work with that. It's not the same as tracking *you*, but it's something."

"Thank you, Weh-sheh."

Weysh's chest went tight at how small and tired her voice came out. It was very lucky indeed that he'd found her. In fact, he had planned to visit his parents that night. After spending the day thinking, and planning, and combing his brain, he could only come up with one possible way to help Yenni stay at Prevan. Something he deeply, desperately did not want to do. But for her, he would swallow his pride. And so, after tracking practice, he'd planned to stop briefly at pub street with the other dragons for some liquid courage before doing what he must. And good thing he had.

"I hate to leave you, but the longer I wait, the colder the trail, so I'd better get started. I trust you have things under control, Zui. Once everything settles down could you or Harth find Augustin?"

"Absolutely."

"Then I'm off." Weysh exited the alley and changed. Then he took to the skies, in search of the unlucky rat prick who'd robbed his Given.

Δ

Once the peacekeepers apprehended the thieves they took Yenni and Diedre to a healing hospice, where Creshen women in blue, wide-brimmed bonnets ushered them into a cozy room with two beds, one lantern, and one window. A Creshen healer checked Yenni's hearing and vision and pronounced her fit, explaining her exhaustion as the result of extended use of magic and trauma from the night's events. They patched Diedre up as well, and then a peacekeeper returned to ask them question upon question, making sketches of the thieves based on their answers. It turned out the band of thugs were fairly notorious for attacking people in the pub district of late, and so Yenni's and Diedre's actions were ruled self-defense on the spot, and they faced no charges.

Not long after their interrogation Zui returned with a harried Captain Augustin in tow.

"Captain Augustin!" Yenni called weakly.

He crouched beside her bed, tsking his tongue. "What mess have you gotten yourself into here, Kayirba?"

Now that Augustin was before her, his face inquisitive and expectant, the slow burn of shame heated Yenni's cheeks, but she pushed past it. After everything she had been through, with everything that was riding on her staying in Cresh, she must follow through and seek his aid.

"I failed my magic exams, Captain."

"Un!" he grunted. He crossed his arms, shaking his head. "Ah, curses, a shame that. A damn shame."

"Yes, I've been told I must leave the academy the day after tomorrow, but I had hoped you could help me find a way to stay."

He gave her hand an affectionate squeeze. "Would that I could, Mam'selle Kayirba. Truly, I mean it. But that's not a ruling one such as myself can overturn, en? That's the way of things at the illustrious Prevan Academy. But a damn shame, truly. You've a rare talent, you know."

All at once Yenni found she just didn't have the strength to hold her head up any longer. She let it fall back against the scratchy pillow.

"I see," she all but whispered.

Augustin put his hands on his knees and rose to his feet, tsking his tongue again. "I can tell you two have been on a glorious tour of the hells tonight. I'll let you get some rest then. A damn shame," he muttered to himself again as he exited their hospice room.

"I'm sorry, Yenni," Diedre said once Augustin had left. Yenni did not correct her about her name. Her friend had saved her from her own foolishness, after all. She could call her whatever she wanted, as far as Yenni was concerned.

"I'm the one who's sorry," she told her. "You were injured because of me."

"Don't act as if you wouldn't do the same if our places were reversed. Is not long I know you for, Yenni, but I can tell you're not one to leave back a friend."

Yenni turned her head to look at Diedre, who lay beside her on another small cot. "Thank you," she said. "I'm very glad we met."

Diedre lay on her front, her head cradled on her arms, and she turned it to face Yenni. "Same."

"I really need to find a way to stay at Prevan," Yenni said sadly.

"But why? Write your folks for more funds and stay in the city."

"No, I must do this on my own. My father . . . I do not want to disappoint him."

"Ah," said Diedre. "I know all about that. Typical Island parents, en? So easily disappointed. If mines only knew about me, Watch'Ahmighty."

"You mean about your study of runelore?" Yenni asked sleepily.

"Oh. Yes, exactly."

"Hmm, if they really knew runelore they would come around." Yenni yawned. "I'm going to rest now. Sleep well, Diedre."

"Call me Deedee. And good night, Yenni."

17

Weysh's mother kept up a stream of light, happy chatter, a valiant onslaught against the looming silence threatening to engulf the breakfast table. After a frustrating night of cruising the city, fairly straining his nostrils trying to sniff out Yenni's robber, Weysh was able to locate Yenni's stolen bag—discarded and empty on a quiet back street. Having failed Yenni once, he was determined to help her in whatever way he could, so he'd paid his family a morning visit. Now he took up his spot in their awkward milieu.

Weysh was used to all of it—used to the careful dance they all did around the long, oak table to make sure he and Montpierre weren't seated too closely; used to all the curtains being open to let in as much sunlight as possible (the sunlight is good for your condition, my heart, his maman would tell Montpierre); used to the strong, medicinal sting of cam-cam incense. His mother often burned it because it was known to open the passages of the body. Even so, Montpierre periodically held a handkerchief to his mouth and coughed into it, the sound hacking and dreadful.

Whenever he did, both Sylvie and his maman leaned uncon-
sciously toward him, even as they gave their quiche and croissants
more attention than necessary.

"It's warming up," Weysh offered after a particularly echoing
bout of coughing. "The doctors say that should help the cough,
en, Montpierre?"

Montpierre grunted.

"Why don't we sit in the back garden for a while after breakfast, Papa?" said Sylvie. "The fresh air would be nice."

"In this morning chill? No, child, I plan to retire to my study.
I'll leave the gallivanting to you three."

"Actually, Montpierre, I'd like to have a word with you, if I
could," said Weysh. He chanced a quick look at his mother and
saw her eyebrows raise. Weysh had debated going to her, having
her act as intermediary on his behalf, but in the end he decided
he must face Montpierre man to man.

Montpierre's fork paused on the way to his mouth, the piece
of melon there dangling dangerously. "You'd like to have a word
with me," he said flatly.

Weysh met his eyes steadily. Gone were the days when he was
a child and Montpierre could quell him with a look. "I would."

"Love," said his mother softly. He wasn't sure who she was
talking to exactly, but Montpierre closed his eyes, tilted his head
back, and shook it resignedly. "So be it. You'll join me in the study
after breakfast."

Weysh nodded. "Much appreciated."

Montpierre grunted again. "Well, at least you're learning some
manners at Prevan."

Weysh froze. *I don't see what it matters to you, en? It's not
like you're paying*, Weysh wanted to retort aloud, but he held his

tongue. It was an effort, but for Yenni Ajani he held his tongue, simply giving Montpierre a tight smile. Sylvie caught his eye and shot him a quizzical look. Weysh shook his head in a gesture that said *I'll explain later.*

She gave a small shrug. "Oh! Speaking of Prevan, Weysh, how is your Given? Is she coming around?"

His mother made small noise of concern. "Yes, Sylvie told me the two of you had not gotten off to the best of starts. I hope things have improved, I do want to meet her."

Weysh cleared his throat, embarrassed. "Yes, she's . . . things are getting better. So, Sylvie, how is second school?" he asked, deflecting. "Did you ever go to the party?" That started his mother on another stream of cooing and gushing over Sylvie.

No matter what Weysh told himself about his supposed immunity to Montpierre, a nervous energy ran through him for the duration of the meal until they were down to the final sips of their coffee. Weysh wasn't sure if he wanted Montpierre to hurry up and finish or pour himself another cup.

But Montpierre put his cup down with a clink against its saucer, and as if that was a cue their housekeeper, Genevieve, came humming into the dining room to collect the dishes.

Weysh rose and wrapped an arm around her shoulders. "Wonderful as usual, Genie," he said and pecked her on the cheek.

She laughed and patted his shoulder as the rest of the family heaped her with praise. "You always did like my cooking. Maybe a taste of what you've been missing will tempt you to come around more often," she said.

Genevieve had been with their family for more than a decade. Tight guilt gripped Weysh's chest as he remembered how sometimes, in his bed late at night as a child, he'd wish that Genevieve were his mother instead.

Montpierre rose with a groan from the table and slid his eyes in Weysh's direction. "All right, let's get on with it."

Weysh nodded to Sylvie and his maman, pasting on a reassuring smile to combat the wariness in their eyes.

Montpierre's study was on the first floor, right under the twin curved staircases that led to the upper den and bedrooms. Weysh felt a small thrill as they approached the door. As a child it was always *Stay out of Montpierre's study*, and *Don't bother Montpierre in his study*, and now here he was, about to enter Montpierre's precious study. Montpierre opened the door and waved him inside. Mild disappointment hit Weysh as he surveyed the room. It was so ordinary. It wasn't as if he expected an alchemists' laboratory or some such, but the place had always been so mysterious and forbidden. Yet all it held was a large oak desk, two high-backed wing chairs, a dark carpet, and some shelves with books and ledgers. On the walls were portraits of Montpierre's family—his parents, his siblings, Maman, Sylvie.

Montpierre took a seat behind his desk and directed Weysh to one of the chairs.

"Now then, what is all this about?"

"Well, I find myself in need of your help."

Montpierre did not respond; he simply squinted at Weysh until he was forced to continue.

Weysh took a fortifying breath. "Yenni Ajani—my Given— has been having some trouble with her magic classes. Despite her best, most valiant efforts, she's failed her first quarter magic exams and as a result, she's been asked to leave Prevan Academy tomorrow."

Montpierre let out a long-suffering sigh. "And you are bringing this to my attention because . . . ?"

Another fortifying breath to cool the anger rising within him at Montpierre's tone. "Because, I know that your aunt is *rectrice* of Prevan Academy, which is how you received the contract to supply and repair some of the windows for the school. Clearly you have her ear, and if anyone can reverse this ruling, it's the school's director."

Montpierre chuckled bitterly. "Let me make sure I understand. You would like me to contact my aunt Mathilde, who is busy running the best martial and magical academy on the continent, to have her reverse her faculty's decision to rightfully expel a student who failed her exams?"

Weysh gripped the armrests on his chair and literally swallowed his frustration before answering. "Would you not do the same for Maman? Sylvie?"

"I am not about to disturb Mathilde with something so trivial."

"This is not trivial," Weysh said, letting a slight growl slip into his voice. It was the wrong thing to do, as Montpierre tensed and frowned at him.

"If the school has decided she doesn't belong, then she doesn't belong." He stood. "I will hear no more of this."

Weysh stood as well. "Montpierre, please—"

Montpierre sighed loudly, cutting him off. "Do you know what I think? This woman may have failed her studies, but she's smart enough to avoid you and your womanizing ways, and your pride will not allow you to let her go. Have some self-respect and leave her be. Let her find someone more suitable."

Montpierre's words hit a nerve, and Weysh's lips were moving before he could stop them.

"I suppose you'd be just as willing to step aside if Maman were to find someone more suitable, en?"

"You ungrateful bastard!" Montpierre thundered.

Weysh jerked back, shocked. The man's face was the red of king crab, and he shook.

"I have gritted my teeth and tolerated you for twenty years," Montpierre said through teeth that were even at that moment clenched in rage. "To think you would have the audacity to ask me for a single thing. I have been forced to raise another man's son, clothe and feed you, bequeath you my estate, and this is what I get for my trouble. A disrespectful, womanizing beast of a stepson who plans to abandon his family and run off to the Islands." He fell into a fit of coughing just as Weysh's maman, Sylvie, and Genevieve ran into the study. Weysh hadn't noticed, but Montpierre had left the door wide open.

Weysh could only stare, wide eyed, as his maman crouched down next to her husband. He'd always felt a dull resentment radiating from Montpierre, but never had he experienced this kind of passionate disgust.

Montpierre regained control of himself and stood, his dark eyes hard. "Who says dragonkind are Byen's most noble creatures, en? You are living proof that mating is just for show, so pick a more suitable woman and settle with her. You never seemed to have any qualms about who you dallied with before." Montpierre shook his head. "Just like your sire."

Weysh took a menacing step forward. "Take that back," he said, his voice low and warning.

"Weysh!" cried Maman.

"No!" snapped Montpierre. "You will not intimidate me in my own house! It's no wonder this woman wants nothing to do with you. You are an animal who knows only how to eat and fornicate. Better she run long and far than end up abused and cast aside like your father's Given, Dominique Pain."

He didn't know how he got there, but suddenly Weysh had lifted Montpierre clean off the ground by his shirt lapels. He stared into Montpierre's wide, white eyes.

"Take. That. *Back*," Weysh snarled.

Genevieve and Sylvie tugged at his arms, screaming. "Weysh! Stop, Weysh!"

"Weysh, lovely, *please*," his mother begged.

He turned to her, his face contorted in anger. "Do you agree? Am I just like Guste Pain?"

She backed away, almost tripping over the hem of her dress, tears making tracks in the powder on her face, and the terror in her eyes made Weysh's heart ache.

He let go of Montpierre, who collapsed in another fit of coughs.

"Maman," said Weysh, his voice practically a growl. "Why do you always TAKE HIS SIDE?"

His voice had risen to a roar against his will.

"I'm sorry," she said, shaking. "I'm sorry."

Montpierre collected himself and scrambled over to his wife, taking her in his arms. She held his face in her hands, checking him over while Montpierre glared at Weysh, defiant, a trickle of blood staining his brown beard and flecks of blood dotting his white cravat.

Weysh turned to find Sylvie crying behind him, clutching Genevieve, who held a hand to her chest and stared at him in horror.

Byen divine, they were right. He *was* an animal.

"You should go, Weysh," said Genevieve, her voice breathy.

"I'm sorry—"

"Just go!" Sylvie shouted.

Weysh looked at Sylvie and Genevieve pleadingly. "Not you too. Please."

"GO, Weysh!" Sylvie yelled again, and then, softer, "How could you *do* this?"

Cursed Movay, he couldn't face her. Them. Weysh stumbled out of the study and through the house like a drunk, the horror and terror on the faces of the people he loved most burned into his mind's eye. He let himself out, his steps turned to a jog, and then he took off into the sky.

18

When Weysh first took off he flew aimlessly, with no goal other than to let the wind and open sky cleanse the images of his mother's frightened gaze, Genie's shock, and Sylvie's tear-stained face from his mind. Eventually he ended up circling the streets of West Castle West, where all the jewelers and goldsmiths took up shop. Notwithstanding that morning's disaster, he would eventually have to face Yenni Ajani and tell her he'd failed her. Not once, but twice. He'd let the thief who'd wronged her get away, and he'd let his temper get the best of him, dashing any hope of help from Montpierre. For once, he was not eager to see his Given.

He swooped in and changed before touching down on the white cobbled streets of West Castle West. There was Beaumont's Fine Timepieces, with its large gold-plated gear clock ticking over the door, the iconic sky-blue awning of Olivier's Appraisers, and the slim white mannequins bedecked in glittering gems in the window of Dame Dubois. Across the street, a large, tacky ring with a giant diamond made of glass marked Nicolas & Nicolas.

Weysh had never been inside. It was known that while their prices were cheaper, so were their wares, with gems that were cloudy and cuts that were basic.

Weysh crossed his arms and nodded to himself.

Presents.

They wouldn't make everything right, or erase what he'd said and done, and failed to do, but that had always been his instinct. Dragons were known for their penchant for giving presents— the shinier the better. In fact, the streets of West Castle West were just as wide as those in Sir Lamontanya, in anticipation of all the dragon traffic.

It wouldn't fix everything, but jewelry was something tangible, something concrete to demonstrate his remorse. Byen, this was turning out to be an expensive year. Nothing less than Dame Dubois would do. He started for the shop, already eying an ivy-stone necklace dripping from the neck of one of the mannequins. Perhaps Yenni Ajani would like that one. The glittering veins of green in the pearly stone would suit her, and match her uniform besides. He could get earrings for Maman, some charms for Sylvie's bracelets, perhaps a bejeweled comb for Genie, and a box of dried pig shit for Montpierre.

He ducked in and perused the impressive displays. His pockets, as well as his credit balance with the bank, were much heavier once he set the door tinkling with his exit. As he stepped into the street again, someone called his name.

"Weysh?"

Carmenna stood across the street, right outside Nicolas & Nicolas, with one hand covering her mouth, as if she'd spoken without thinking, and the other hand wrapped around the arm of Luiz Noriago.

Weysh wanted to groan aloud. This was the absolute last thing he needed, but Carmenna was looking right at him—it would be rude to ignore her. And besides, what was she doing with Noriago of all people?

He crossed over to them. "Hello, Carmenna, you're looking well."

"Weysh." Carmenna nodded at him and stood straighter, the picture of civility. She clung tighter to Noriago, who smirked at him, a strange, eager glint in his eyes.

"Messer Nolan, fancy meeting you here."

"Erm, yes," said Weysh, glancing between Noriago and Carmenna. He suspected it wasn't his place to say anything, but he'd never been good at keeping his mouth shut. "Carmenna, could I have a word?"

"What for?" Noriago challenged him.

"I was talking to Carmenna," said Weysh.

"What would you have to talk to her about? She's not your Given. She doesn't want to talk to you, Nolan."

"Carmenna can speak for herself," Weysh snapped, his already frayed nerves fraying further.

"What is it, Weysh? Say what you have to say," said Carmenna.

"Look, we may not be Given, Carmenna, but I still care what happens to you. *He*," Weysh said, and jabbed his finger in Noriago's direction, "is not someone you want to associate with."

Carmenna's eyes went soft, uncertain. "You care about me?"

Noriago rolled his eyes. "Enough," he said. "You can't have every woman in Imperium Centre, Nolan. Let's go," he said to Carmenna, and took her wrist, pulling her away.

"Wait," she cried, and pulled back.

"Let her go," snarled Weysh. He took a step after them. Noriago did, in fact, let Carmenna go, but only to whirl around and shove Weysh hard enough to make him stumble back.

"Or *what*, rat prick?"

Gasps and murmurs rose from the shoppers around them. Weysh closed his eyes, breathing deeply. *Can't touch him. I'll go to jail. Can't touch him. I'll get expelled.*

He opened his eyes and looked pointedly past Noriago at Carmenna. "Let's get you back to campus."

Noriago pushed up close to Weysh's face and let a bunch of curses fly in Espannic. "You think you're better than me? Change, let's settle this right here."

Weysh gave him an incredulous look. "You want to fight. In dragon. On the streets of West Castle West." The place was usually crawling with peacekeepers, though he couldn't see any in the immediate area. But there was a guardhouse the next street over.

"I just can't understand what makes you think you're above me, Nolan, you know?" Noriago said, and shoved him again. Weysh curled his hands into two fists at his sides.

Can't touch him. Can't touch him. Cursed Movay, he should have just kept his big mouth shut. He had to leave before he got himself into even more trouble.

"Carmenna," he said again. Urgent. Pleading.

Noriago thrust his face in front of Weysh's, breaking his eye contact with Carmenna. "She's with *me* now, and I say she doesn't want to talk to you. You have a Given—unless you plan to keep a stable of reluctant women like your real father. At least *my* parents are properly mated, you know?"

Weysh's fist flew.

He connected with Noriago's jaw and felt blazing satisfaction right in his gut as Noriago's head snapped to the side.

"Weysh!" Carmenna screeched, and her voice shuddered through him like nails on a slate, far too similar to the way his mother and sister had screamed at him only an hour ago. It doused the fire of his rage and he backed off.

But Noriago snapped his eyes up to Weysh, a line of blood trailing down the side of his mouth, and smiled, savage and hateful. He jogged back into the middle of the street and changed into dragon. A dame in a ridiculous feathered hat cried out and dove to the left to avoid his swinging tail and her bags went flying, the contents spilling out all over the ground. Weysh rushed to help her up and gather her things.

"We can't fight out in the open street, Noriago," Weysh yelled up at him as the woman leaned against him, moaning in distress and patting her precious hat. But Noriago ignored him and lunged, jaws wide.

"By source make my movement quick!"

Weysh recited Harquette's Speed Burst to launch them both out of the way. He stood and turned to Noriago, astonished by the sheer audacity of him. "Are you insane?!" he shouted. The older woman fled, screaming, to the safety of the street side. Weysh took a hurried glance around to make sure no one would be underfoot, and changed.

Noriago roared and rushed him. He slammed his bulk into Weysh, who stood firm as the other dragon snapped at him like a raving hound. Weysh strained and heaved him off, and though it was unwise to open his wings to an enemy, Weysh spread them and tried to fly, hoping to at least lure Noriago away from town.

He only got a few feet off the ground before Noriago screeched, and Weysh could hear the mockery in it. *Running?* He grabbed

Weysh by the tail and yanked him down again. Weysh howled, spikes of pain running along his tail and spine.

Weysh turned back and snapped at Noriago, desperate to sink his teeth into whatever he could, but Noriago darted back. Weysh roared. Fire crackled painfully in his chest, and all his dragon instincts screamed at him to unleash it, but his man-mind held him back. Instead, he charged and stopped short at the last second, sweeping his tail around in an attempt to knock the other dragon off his feet. But Noriago leapt over it and slammed into Weysh. He clawed at Weysh's shoulder, trying to pull him down and wrap his jaws around his neck. Weysh bucked, frantic. If Noriago got him by the neck he'd be finished.

He beat at Noriago with his tail, using it like a whip, but Noriago wouldn't let up. So Weysh rolled, praying everyone in the street had the sense to have gotten far clear of them. He slammed Noriago into the ground and scrambled to his feet. Weysh wanted more than anything in that moment to turn around and rip into Noriago with his teeth or melt his eyes with fire, but not here, where people could get caught in the blaze. He tried to take off again, but agony zipped up his left leg, ripping a piercing screech from him. Noriago held Weysh's leg between his jaws, and the only way Weysh would fly off would be missing a limb. He swiped at Noriago with the claws of his other leg, aiming for his eyes, until at last Noriago let go.

Weysh dropped clumsily to the ground. The two of them bent low on all fours and circled each other, growling and snapping. Noriago roared and charged for him again. Weysh roared back and charged to meet him, heedless of his injured leg.

A piercing whistle sent pain lancing through his eardrums and he stumbled, his claws skidding on the stone.

"Change back immediately or we will use whatever force necessary to restrain you," said a female voice, magically amplified.

Weysh's anger diminished, leaving behind only a cold stone of dread in his stomach. He changed and slowly put his hands over his mouth, facing the contingent of peacekeepers fanned out around them, swords drawn.

Noriago changed a second later and put his hands over his mouth as well, but Weysh could have sworn he saw something like triumph flash in his eyes.

The woman at the center of the officers stared out from the shadow of her metal helmet. "You are both under arrest for reckless endangerment," she said.

Noriago ripped his hands from his mouth. "I would like to formally charge—"

A spark crackled through the air and hit Noriago right in the chest. He fell to the ground, convulsing.

The woman turned to Weysh. He pressed his hands tighter against his mouth.

"You will come with us," she said. "Resist, and as I said, you will be subdued using whatever force is necessary. You may not speak until you are in official custody, and then you will be interrogated to determine first strike."

She gestured and a couple of her officers moved forward. They held gag cloths, manacles, and dragon collars that would keep the two dragons from changing. The restraints all glowed with the strength of their magical wards.

The cold stone in Weysh's stomach turned to a block of ice. He'd punched Noriago first, and he'd be charged with first strike. And once the powers that be at Prevan heard what happened, they would expel him for sure. Five years of hard work, his shot at a high-paying post in the military, all of it gone right as he'd found his Given. Damned, thrice-cursed Movay.

"Wait!" someone cried. The gathered crowd seemed to shiver as someone pushed their way through. It was the woman from before, the one Noriago had almost hit with his tail. Her pudgy face was red. "It was all him," she said, stabbing a finger at Noriago. "He nearly sent me flying! That man was just trying to defend himself," she said, and held out a hand in Weysh's direction. "He even tried to get away." She pointed at Carmenna. "The fight had something to do with that young woman there. She can tell you, the weaselly one there started everything!"

Others in the crowd murmured their agreement. The high peacekeeper turned to Carmenna. "Is this true? Who had first strike?" she demanded.

"It . . . I mean, that is . . ."

"I will remind you it is against the law to lie to a high officer."

Carmenna lowered her eyes and pointed to Noriago. "Luiz had first strike. He shoved Weysh. Twice."

Luiz snapped his head up from where he knelt on the ground and fired off an explosion of rapid Espannic, earning him another zap from the peacekeepers. Carmenna cringed.

The high peacekeeper took off her helmet, revealing a green face and shiny green hair cut in a short bob to her chin. She sighed. "Very well, you're free to go," she said to Weysh.

Weysh dropped his hands and exhaled. "Thank you," he said to the high officer, and then again to the woman who'd come to his defense, "Thank you."

She straightened up and beamed at him. "Oh, you're very welcome, young man."

And then to Carmenna. "Thank you."

"All I did was tell the truth," she said.

Noriago shook as they pulled him upright, gagged, and bound him. He glared at Weysh as if he could kill him with his eyes alone, and Weysh knew somewhere, somehow, Noriago would exact his revenge.

As the crowd dispersed, helped along by the peacekeepers, Weysh felt a light touch on his arm.

"Are you all right?" Carmenna asked.

"I've been better." Weysh winced and rubbed at his sore leg. The pain from dragon injuries often transferred over to human bodies, if not the actual damage. It was just one of the many mysteries regarding the link between dragon and human. "Carmenna, I know it's not my place, but Noriago—"

"How is Yenni Ajani?" she asked sharply.

Weysh sighed. "Well, if you must know, she failed all of her magic exams. Unless she can find some way to stay, she has to leave Prevan tomorrow."

"What? That's awful! I had no idea!" Carmenna frowned, lost in thought. "What if . . . has she been doing any extracurricular activities? Working as a teaching assistant, for example? I know as a tutor I get some reprieve. There may be something there."

"En? Then we have to tell her! Come on! I'll fly us, there's no time to waste."

But she shook her head, backing away. "You know I'm not one for flying. Go on without me. I'll speak with her later."

"Very well." Weysh jogged backward into the wide main street where he had room to change. "Be well, Carmenna, and thank you."

He changed to dragon, ignoring the pain in his leg as it intensified. It was a minor injury, and his dragon body would heal it on its own. Weysh spread his wings, flapped, and took off to find Yenni.

19

The letter box beside Yenni's sitting room door had papers of all colors peeking out. She'd been so distracted she hadn't checked it for days, but it was not the time to be sifting through her messages. She'd already lost half the day, her last day, sleeping off her injuries from last night's assault. Today she must put aside all her pride and appeal to that horrible Professor Mainard as soon as possible.

But something about that mess of papers nagged at her. She raised the creaky lid of the metal letter box and sighed in dismay. Grabbing a handful of papers, she quickly skimmed through them: A reminder to vacate her residence by the end of the day. An official transcript of her shameful grades and—what was this? A missive from Professor Devon?

> *Yenni Ajani,*
> *Come find me in my office as soon as you get this. I*
> *saw your exam scores. I know things must seem bleak,*
> *but there is a way you can remain at Prevan.*

Yours,
Emmanuel Devon

Yenni gasped and jumped to her feet, the other messages abandoned as she yanked the door open and dashed down the hallway, her sandals slapping on the marble tile.

She came barreling down the stairs, and the foyer attendant made a small noise of shocked surprise as Yenni zipped past her. Yenni had just cleared the black, wrought-iron gate that marked the entrance to the residence when someone called out to her.

"Yenni! Yenni Ajani!"

She skidded to a stop and turned to see Professor Devon jogging up to her, his robe fluttering around him.

"Professor!" she cried, and very nearly hugged him out of relief. "Praise the Mothers and Fathers!"

"Where on Byen's hallowed soil have you been? I've been trying to find you for the last two days! I promised myself I would camp here all day until you showed up. Did you get my message?"

"Just now," Yenni said breathlessly. "Is there really a way I can stay?"

"Yes, but we have to act quickly. We can register you as my teaching assistant. Due to the increased workload you're permitted one failed exam in each class without being expelled. With all the help you've been giving in my runelore lessons, you're practically my assistant anyway. Not to mention there's a nice little stipend that comes with the position as well."

Yenni grinned wide and let out a whoop of sheer joy. And then, unable to help herself, she threw her arms around him.

"Thank you!" she cried. She pulled away, and at the sight of the strange, embarrassed half smile on Devon's crimson face she felt her own cheeks start to burn as well.

"Please excuse me, Professor, but I'm just so relieved!"

"Quite all right," he said and cleared his throat. "Completely understandable. I'm happy to help. Now, there is one thing—"

He cut off as a high screech split the air. Yenni whipped her head up.

Dragon!

Her traitorous heart went light and happy at the sight of him, sleek and beautiful against the blue sky. He arced in toward them, and Yenni reached out to him, longing to feel the smooth, warm scales of his face against her fingers. But before he'd even hit the ground he changed, hitting the ground at a jog in that way he did. He hurried up to her.

"Yenni Ajani," he said, slightly breathless. "I think I may have a way you can stay at Prevan!"

"Oh? I was just discussing the matter with Professor Devon here."

Weysh turned to Professor Devon. "Weysh Nolan," he said and held out his hand.

Devon clasped his arm firmly. "Professor Emmanuel Devon," he replied, and it may have been Yenni's imagination, but his voice seemed deeper than before.

"Weh-sheh, Professor Devon is my runelore professor. He says that if I become his teaching assistant I can stay at the academy!"

Weysh's eyebrows rose. "Carmenna told me just the same. Is it true?" he asked Devon.

"Absolutely," Devon confirmed, and turned to Yenni. "But we have to act now. I need to make a case to the head of the magical department. We'll need him to sign off on this even though you weren't officially my assistant at the time of exams. But I'll emphasize all the help you've given in class. I'm sure it will be fine."

"The head of . . . not . . . Professor Mainard?" Yenni asked hesitantly.

"The very same."

Yenni sighed, slumping her shoulders. "For whatever reason, he's not fond of me. I doubt he would be willing to grant me any favors."

"But that can't be right. What could he possibly have against *you*, en?"

"I'm not sure, but I assure you, he is not a fan of me."

Devon waved a hand dismissively. "Then we'll give him a demonstration of runelore the likes of which he's never seen. Whatever it takes. I don't want to lose you, Yenni."

Weysh cleared his throat. "Yes, Yenni *Ajani* certainly is something special, isn't she?"

"Yenni Ajani is my preferred name," she told Devon. "And thank you for your advocacy Professor Devon. I'll do my best."

"Ah, I do apologize, Yenni Ajani." His eyes flicked between her and Weysh. "If I may ask, how are the two of you acquainted?"

"Weh-sheh is a friend of mine." She turned to Weysh. "Isn't that right?"

He gave her a rueful smile. "That I am."

"I see. Well then, I'll need to go finalize the paperwork. Yenni Ajani, put on your most impressive runes and meet me outside the administrative building by next chime."

"Yes, Professor, I'll see you there."

"Then I'm off!" He dipped his head in a shallow nod to Weysh. "Messer Nolan," he said, and hurried down the whitestone path.

Weysh shoved his hands into the pockets of his pants. "Well, I can't say I care one ass boil for that professor."

"Weh-sheh!"

"I only speak the truth, lovely."

"But why? He's helping me stay."

"I have my reasons. But, and it's like searing my own skin to say this, he can help you where I failed you, so I suppose that's that, en?"

There was real shame in his eyes. Dragon's eyes. Against her better judgment Yenni touched him on the arm. "Thank you for trying, Weh-sheh. And thank you for coming to my aid last night."

He stared at her hand on his bicep, and then his eyes slid slowly to hers, full of that same intensity from the first time they'd met. She let her fingers fall away.

"You act like I had a choice," he said. "When I caught your scent laced with terror as it was, and your *blood*." He shook his head. "I've never wanted to kill—rip and tear and *kill*—someone the way I did last night." His face was anguished. "But I couldn't find the man who stole from you. All I found was your empty bag. I'm sorry."

"There's no need to apologize," said Yenni. "It was my own lack of foresight that got me into this mess. And Professor Devon said I can earn a stipend as a teaching assistant. Furthermore, my tuition and lodging are already paid. I will be fine."

Weysh smiled. "I have no doubt you will, which is one of the reasons why I like you so much."

To her shock, Yenni felt her cheeks heat. What? Oh, what by all the Mothers and Fathers was *this*?

Weysh was nowhere near the first man to pursue her, and certainly not the most prestigious. She'd flirted with kings and princes cool as you please. So why, Oh wise Father Ri, was she reacting to the simpering flattery of Weysh, of all men? Was her affection for the dragon bleeding over to the man?

No time to worry about that. One disaster at a time.

She was a princess of the Yirba, and had years of practice at political bluffing. So though her heart fluttered in her chest, she simply nodded her head and said, "And please thank Carmenna for me as well."

"En? Oh yes. That I will. Oho! I brought you something, to apologize for failing you and for scaring you."

"That's not necessary," Yenni began, but he handed her a dark box lined in a soft, fernlike material, and the look in his eyes, the contrition there, strangely reminded her of Ofa when he brought her dead birds and rodents after she'd reprimanded him. Yenni smiled at the thought and opened the box. Then she gasped.

This was no dead rodent.

"What type of jewel is this?" she said wonderingly. A drop-shaped pendant fell suspended from a delicate silver chain. The stone was iridescent white with shimmering forks of green, like emerald lightning, running through it. It would make even her sisters jealous, and they had the most extensive jewelry collections on all the Islands.

"It's ivystone," Weysh said. "Do you like it?"

"Yes," Yenni breathed, "But this is too much! I cannot keep it."

"You can and you will," Weysh insisted. "Or I'll take it as a grave personal insult."

"Oh. All right," Yenni conceded. It truly was beautiful, and she would hate to insult him when he was going to so much effort to make amends. "Thank you." She stepped back. "I need to prepare for the demonstration now," she said softly.

Weysh nodded. "Byen's favor," he said. "If anyone can pull this off, it's you. I'll be back in an hour or so, en? We can take a celebratory flight once you undoubtedly convince Mainard to keep you on."

"All right," Yenni said again.

"See you soon, Yenni Ajani," he said, and winked. As she turned to head back into her residence, Yenni heard wings beating the air. She smiled to herself.

If anyone can pull this off, it's you.

It was lunacy, but for some shadowy reason his praise made her feel stronger. Yenni breathed deeply and squared her shoulders.

She was ready to face Professor Mainard.

20

Yenni was covered in runes. Her heart fluttered in her throat like a trapped moth as she trailed behind Professor Devon. Professor Mainard's office was on the very top of what Devon called the Watcher's tower—a tall structure in the center of the administrative building that soared up some twenty stories high. She looked up at the peak, capped with an iron balustrade bookended by sculptures of resting dragons. True to the name, she could imagine Mainard up there with his tufts of hair glaring down at their approach.

"I thought the professors were off during the study break," Yenni mused.

"Not Mainard," muttered Devon. "I'm willing to bet he hasn't taken a break since Prevan was founded three hundred years ago."

"What? He's that old?" Yenni said. "Do Creshens live so long? How? By magic?" And could this longevity of life, she wondered, help her father in some way?

Devon stopped and turned back to her, giving her a sheepish look. "It was a joke, and not a very good one, it would seem."

"Oh! Oh I see," said Yenni, disappointed.

He took her through a corridor with high ceilings and tall windows that let in beams of dusty sunlight. Finally they reached a small room closed off by a black, iron gate that squealed as he pushed it aside.

"After you," he said. Yenni had no idea why he wanted her to step into the little room, but not wanting to appear ignorant, she did as he directed. He stepped in after her and there was another grating screech as he closed the gate.

"Through source rise, floor number ten."

Suddenly the ground rumbled under her feet and began to rise. Yenni gasped and stumbled into Devon, who put an arm around her.

"Are you all right? This isn't your first time in a lift, is it?"

She felt her cheeks flush. "Well, yes, to be honest."

"Ah. It must be somewhat uncomfortable for you, en? You can hold on to me if you'd like."

She cleared her throat and straightened, sliding away from him. She was not some uninformed savage who needed to be coddled when confronted with "civilized" technology. "Thank you, Professor, but I'm fine."

The lift deposited them on the tenth floor, which was much more elegant than the main halls below. Here wide windows draped with gauzy white curtains let in muted sunlight and the floor was covered in a rich red carpet that muffled her footsteps.

"Professor Mainard's office is just ahead; he's expecting us," said Devon, and Yenni's heart redoubled its effort to escape through her mouth. "Just show him what you can do. We'll give him such a demonstration he'll no doubt see the myriad benefits of keeping you on. I'm sure of it."

Yenni wished she could share Devon's confidence. When they reached the dark and imposing door barring entrance to the office, each rap of Devon's knuckles on the wood sent little jolts of anxiety zipping through her.

Mainard answered the door unsmiling. "Yes, yes, come in," he said. Yenni glanced around wide eyed. Books rose in piles and stacks from tall side tables, round end tables, low coffee tables, and his own large desk. Oh, there were shelves, but those were taken up with various devices and knickknacks she couldn't hope to name. In fact, his desk was built right into a cubbied wall packed with wooden and metal boxes, some of which leaned haphazardly out of their sections, and it was apparent the shelves were stuffed to capacity. Did the man never throw anything away?

He sat at his desk and twisted his chair around to the side so he was somewhat facing them. "Have a seat," he said.

Where?

Every chair was piled with junk.

Devon gestured toward a stack of books on a small sofa on the other side of a coffee table. "Ah, may I?"

Mainard's only response was a grunt that must have meant yes, because he didn't object when Devon cleared a space for both himself and Yenni. Once they were seated, Devon began.

"Now, Professor Mainard, I come to you as a fellow scholar. There is much to be gained in analyzing the magic of other cultures, and—"

"Just get on with the demonstration, please," said Mainard. "I haven't got all day."

"Ahem. Yes. Yenni Ajani, could you start by drawing a rune for us?"

"Absolutely, Professor," she said.

Which to use? The quick, high hymn of the speed rune had always been a favorite of hers. She sang the hymn and drew the rune on the inside of her wrist, doing her best to keep her voice and hand from shaking, trying not to think about this being her last chance to impress the professor and remain at the academy. She tied off the rune with a final note, and its glow dulled as it set.

Devon came to stand beside her. "Here we see how the drawing of the rune and the singing of the hymn act in tandem as both anchor and shaping mechanism. Fascinating, wouldn't you say?"

Mainard wouldn't, if his unimpressed glowering was any indication.

"Right. Well, how about a demonstration of strength runes? Yenni Ajani?"

She stood. "What would you have me do, Professor?"

He looked around. "Ah, pick up that end table there, the one piled with books."

She did as he asked, the runes blazing on her calves, thighs, arms, and back.

"You see that?" said Devon excitedly. "Now that's a strange sight isn't it? Such a tiny person holding up such a load as if it weighed nothing at all."

"Nothing that couldn't be achieved with Melichor's Muscular Fortification," said Mainard.

"Ah, I thought you might say that," said Devon. "However, Melichor's Muscular Fortification is something of an advanced spell. We wouldn't expect a student to master that until they were well into post-secondary education. When did you first learn the strength rune, Yenni Ajani?"

"I must have just passed nine rains," she replied and set the table down with a thud.

Devon nodded. "Yes. And furthermore, the strength rune, as well as others, can be applied to inanimate objects and controlled remotely, though admittedly this is a more complex procedure."

"None of this changes the fact that Mam'selle . . . Kayerba has failed all her magical examinations," said Mainard, frowning at Devon.

"All except runelore," Devon clarified, and his voice took on a sharper tone she'd never heard from him before. "As I said, she was working as my teaching assistant at the time—"

"Not according to any official records, Professor Devon. You know the rules. I can't break them merely because you've taken an interest in this Island woman."

Devon's face went red. "Now see here! Mam'selle Kayirba is a credit to this academy and I'd think that as a man of magical science you would see the benefit in having her around. It won't do—"

Professor Mainard pounded his desk with his fist, his face just as red as Devon's. "What won't do, Devon, is having a young upstart marching into my office and trying to tell *me* how to run *my* division!"

Devon glanced up and Yenni followed his eyes. A pointed metal instrument teetered just on the edge of a shelf right over Mainard's head.

"Professor Mainard—" she began.

"Be quiet! Nothing you say will persuade me. I've heard enough."

"How dare you speak to me in that way?" shouted Yenni, even as Devon mumbled nervously beside her. "I am trying to—"

"Exit my office this instant!" He slammed his fist on the desk again, and Yenni could have sworn she felt the slightest tremor of ache. Was Mainard readying some spell to attack them?

The pointy thing tipped over the edge, shooting arrow-like for the gleaming crown of Mainard's head.

"Professor Mainard! Above!" shouted Devon. Even as Mainard was looking up Yenni was dragging on all her speed runes, sending warmth through her arms and legs. She hurtled over the coffee table and snatched at the blade-like device, catching it a mere inch from Mainard's forehead. It cut into her skin but she flared the pain ward painted down her spine and held it. She threw the thing, whatever it was, on the desk and held her bleeding hand to her chest. Mainard gaped at her.

"Byen!" cried Devon and hurried over. "Yenni—you're bleeding!" He took off his professor's stole and wrapped it clumsily around her hand.

"Are you all right?" Yenni demanded of Mainard, even though it was clear he wasn't.

He shook, and brought trembling fingers up to his forehead. "I could have been killed," he said wonderingly, still staring at Yenni. "You saved me."

She frowned. "Of course I did. Why wouldn't I?"

He stared at her for a few more moments. "Why indeed. But how in all creation could you simply catch a falling blade like that and hold it?"

Devon piped up. "Speed runes to catch the blade, pain ward runes to hold on to it as it cut into her skin, isn't that right, Yenni Ajani?"

"Yes," said Yenni, still pulling on pain ward.

Mainard shook himself as if coming out of a trance, and took in her bleeding hand. "Byen above! Get yourself to the infirmary posthaste before you faint from blood loss."

"I'm not sure I can," said Yenni, still pulling on pain ward. "I'm no longer a student here."

Mainard squinted his eyes at her, rubbed his balding head. "Devon!" he barked. "Have you got the teaching assistant application with you?"

"Why, yes, Professor Mainard."

"Give it here, I'll sign it."

Yenni gasped. "Truly?"

"Yes, yes," he said, motioning for Devon to hurry.

Devon scrambled to fish the application out of his robe pocket and Mainard scribbled his name on it without even looking at it.

"Now go! Show that to the attendants if they give you any trouble."

"Thank you, Professor," said Yenni, even as she cradled her dripping hand to her chest.

"GO!" he thundered.

Devon grabbed her by the shoulder and pulled her out of the office, and the two of them dashed for the infirmary.

$$\Delta$$

Yenni sat on the edge of a narrow white bed. With no classes in session, all the other beds in the row were empty, the room quiet. Once Devon had concluded that she would be fine, he hurried off to file the application, ensuring no security would show up to escort her from her residence tomorrow. It was lucky indeed, praise Ib-e-ji, that she had noticed that dagger-like instrument, and that she had been able to use her runes to protect Mainard. Nothing less than saving the man's life would have been enough to convince him of her worthiness to stay.

But as useful as her runes had been, her pain ward lasted only so long, and now the row of stitches along Yenni's palm itched and burned, and the slices through each of her fingers stung. An ugly red pucker split her father's rune, but it remained. Once a rune was set, it was set. Nothing short of cutting it out of her skin would destroy it, and even then, her people had accounts of captured warriors miraculously using runes their enemies had already carved from their flesh.

Still, she hated the sight of it. It seemed like an ill omen. She looked at the rune on her right hand, her mother's rune, the loops and swirls of it unmarred. Compared to her father's rune . . .

Yenni froze. Was it . . . no. She stared hard, willing it not to be, but it was plain in front of her eyes, and as her gaze flitted between her palms she let out a small noise of distress.

Her father's rune had faded.

21

It was almost imperceptible, and she may not have noticed had she not been comparing it against her mother's rune, but she couldn't deny that the swirling white lines on her palm were not as vibrant as they had once been. She wasn't sure if her light-headedness was due to her injury or the terrible truth painted right in front of her. A wild panic took hold of her mind, sending her thoughts racing. What was he doing? Could he walk? Speak? Why was she here, leagues away when she should be by his side? What had possessed her to come here to Cresh on this fool's mission? Was it truly the will of the Sha? Was it truly to help her father? Or . . .

For the first time she acknowledged it, that guilty selfish feeling deep down. Was it because, just for a while, she had wanted to escape? She had wanted to be someone, some*thing* other than Princess Yenni Aja-Nifemi ka Yirba? Chieftain's daughter? Future prince's wife?

Yenni bowed her head and closed her eyes. "Almighty Sha," she whispered in her native tongue. "If this is your reprimand for my selfishness, then I throw myself on your mercy. Do not punish my father for my mistakes."

Someone cleared their throat. Yenni's eyes snapped open, and her eyebrows flew up when she saw who stood in the doorway.

"Professor Mainard?"

He came in, his boots clicking on the tile floor of the infirmary.

"They've stitched you up I see. Good, that."

"What are you doing here, Professor?"

He had the audacity to look affronted. "What do you mean, 'what am I doing here'? I came to inquire as to your well being of course."

"My being is well, thank you."

He grunted. "As it should be. Nothing but the best at Prevan, and that includes our healing practitioners. Yes, the pinnacle of magical science."

A sudden thought occurred to Yenni. "Professor," she said. "What was the nature of the blade that cut me? Was it something that can"—oh, what was the word she was looking for?—"something that can cancel magic?"

Perhaps the fading of the rune was not due to her father's health, but whatever magical device had injured her.

But Mainard shook his head. "It was a tool, part of an experimental device it would take far too long to explain. But in and of itself it has no magical properties."

"Oh," Yenni said, feeling herself deflate.

"Why do you ask?"

Yenni paused. Finally, here was her chance to glean more information about this wither-rot disease, straight from the head of the magical department at the most prestigious magical school in Cresh. A man who by his own admission was versed in the latest advances in Creshen magic, including healing magic. But he would undoubtedly want to know why she was so interested. Dare she trust him?

Dare she *not* trust him? Yenni was desperate, having already spent two moonturns in Cresh and learning only the barest details regarding the wither-rot from Carmenna. And the rune on her palm was a sobering reminder that time was running out.

"Professor Mainard," she said softly. "Do you know the reason I came to study magic at Prevan?"

"Because it's the best school on the continent, of course."

A chuckle bubbled its way to the surface of Yenni's despair at how self-assured he was. "Yes," she admitted. "I'd heard Prevan was the best. And I need the best, because there is a sickness that has recently appeared on my Island. The symptoms are the same as what you have named the wither-rot. I need to find a way to cure it because my father is dying." She swallowed against the admission.

Mainard stayed quiet for a long time, his wrinkled brow more wrinkled than usual. "What is the nature of this illness?" he said finally. Yenni explained her father's symptoms—the way his muscles would suddenly give out and his constant pain.

"I confess, I am not a healing professional but yes, that does sound like the wither-rot."

"What can you tell me about this disease, Professor? Please, anything you know will help."

Mainard clucked his tongue. "I can appreciate how difficult this must be for you. After all, the medicine of the Islands is not quite up to the task of such a debilitating disease, hmm?"

"This is a sickness we have never seen before. Our healers are doing their best," said Yenni, sharper than perhaps was wise. She bit back her retort that Creshen healers seemed to be just as clueless about the disease as anyone.

"Yes, well, the wither-rot is just as terrible as it sounds. It involves the cannibalization of the body's muscular system by its own magical energy system."

"But what causes it? Where did it come from? How can it be treated?"

"The cause of the disease remains elusive," he said grudgingly. "There is no consensus on where it originated, merely half-cooked theories it would be irresponsible of me to disseminate. All I will tell you for certain is that it seems to be triggered by excessive spellcraft, and further exacerbated by too much casting, and we've only recently been able to confirm this."

Yenni frowned, confused. "So this is a disease that enters the body through ach—through source energy?"

"I have said no such thing!" Mainard blustered, suddenly and inexplicably agitated. "The only conclusive and peer-reviewed information I have given you about this disease is that spellcraft quickens the patient's deterioration. That is all."

So the best treatment for the disease was to avoid pulling achè, but the healers back home were doing exactly the opposite, having her father draw on purification runes every day to remove the toxins from his body. She would need to write home with these new insights right away. Yenni exhaled, feeling her chest release as she expelled all the tension of the last few days.

"I see. Thank you, Professor."

Professor Mainard waved a dismissive hand. "I doubt we're dealing with the wither-rot in your case—I can't imagine your papa has much affinity for spellcraft. But you've come to the right place. With a superior base of medicinal and magical knowledge to draw on, I'm sure your papa will be well in no time."

And just like that, she wanted to throw something at him again. Not least of all because she couldn't argue. She had come to Cresh for a solution that hadn't yet been found back home. Still, that pitying smile, that condescending tone, the pleasure she knew he took in helping the little Island savage save her father— it was enough to make her want to scream. But for her father, and *only* for her father, she hung her head to hide her disgust, knowing Professor Mainard would see in the gesture grief and gratitude.

"I'm off," he said. "I'll give your account to my Head of Healers and have an official diagnosis for you as soon as possible."

Yenni simply nodded, unable to suspend her dignity long enough to thank him, and wondering what she had done to that trickster Father Esh to deserve this.

Δ

Once she was cleared to leave the infirmary Yenni rushed back to her residence, took out some paper and a Creshen pencil, and imme- diately wrote home about what she had learned from Professor Mainard, urging her mother to write back as soon as she could.

Such a strange disease. Whoever heard of ach'e, the divine energy of the Sha, causing sickness? But perhaps that was why they hadn't been able to find a cure. The idea that ach'e might be the source, well, it was beyond belief to her, and it would certainly be the same for the healers back home. Still, she would send her letter. The rest would fall to her mother, her older brother, and her charming, charming sisters. It would be up to them not only to bring the concept to the attention of the healers, but to con- vince them the cure had been their idea to begin with.

Weysh would be back soon to see ho⸍
had gone. She could get him to fly her ⸍
could send the letter by what the Cres⸍
According to Professor Rosé, some young ⸍
flew mail and packages back and forth between C⸍
Northern Sha Islands, the ones Cresh had claimed as con⸍
From there her letter would be ferried to her home by ship.

She bit the edge of her lip. Even express post would take about ten days, and it would cost—Mothers and Fathers! She had no money!

Yenni groaned and rubbed her temples. One thing after another after another.

Maybe Dragon could fly her home. Would that anger the Sha? Ah, but Dragon was not a ship. He couldn't fly nonstop straight across the ocean. He would need to stick to the coast, and rest at night. He might take just as long or longer. Besides, Mainard was still looking into the matter. What if the sickness wasn't the wither-rot after all, but something else? She needed to remain at the academy so she could send any and all information back to her parents.

She could sell the necklace Weysh had given her.

No. No, she did not want to do that.

Very well, though it shamed her, she would instead ask his help to pay her postage and she'd return the money as soon as she received her stipend from Professor Devon. She nodded to herself. Surely the Sha could take no issue with that. She would mail the letter that day, and pray with everything she had that her father held on.

Yenni swiveled around to her writing nook and caught sight of the mess of letters and messages piled in front of her door, abandoned

e she'd discovered Devon's note. Sighing, she went over to gather
em up, and froze when she noticed a roll of familiar deep-brown
paper, made from the innards of the papua tree native to the Islands.
A message from home? Grabbing the roll, she slipped free the fine
golden thread that held it together.

She undid the roll and frowned in confusion. Instead of the
familiar field sphinx with the wings spread wide that represented
her home, the corner of the page was emblazoned with the Gunzu
crest: a long shield crossed by a spear.

Bright and Sha-blessed Yenni Aja-Nifemi,

*I must confess, it is with great concern that I write
to you, knowing you are so far from civilization. It
pained me greatly to hear that you had departed to live
among the barbarians of Cresh, to learn of their ach'e
of all things. But I understand that you have been so
instructed by the Sha, and one cannot question their
mysterious ways. In truth, I suppose it is best to know
one's enemy, but I pray that the Sha guide you true on
your Orire N'jem, and your pure spirit is not subverted
by the godless ways of the Creshens. Please remember
our last conversation. They are not to be trusted. Used,
perhaps, but never trusted.*

*I assume you have been in contact with your family,
but I feel it is my duty to let you know the Yirba's
standing with the other tribes weakens along with your
father's condition. To be truthful, I was surprised to
hear you had left at such a volatile time. What machi-
nations could the Sha be up to, sending you away?*

I apologize that I am not writing to you with happier tidings. That said, I look forward to meeting with you upon your return, as there is something very important I must ask you. Something that I think will have a positive outcome for both our tribes.

May the Mothers and Fathers smile upon you,
Natahi N'lanla Olashawela ka Gunzu

Yenni took the letter over to her little desk and slumped into the chair, feeling utterly drained. Everything was going wrong. Well, the Gunzu were still open to a union between their tribes, so there was that at least. However, the prospect of marriage to Natahi did not bring her the relief it should. Fears and worries continued to tumble around and around in her head, slowly driving her mad.

She put her head in her hands. "Mothers and Fathers guide me," she said wearily. She would need to write back with a diplomatic response. Yenni took out another sheet of paper and simply stared. Long minutes passed and still she stared, with no idea where to start, until a sharp familiar cry invaded her mind's haze.

Dragon.

She'd completely forgotten he was coming to see her. A strange, nervous energy vibrated through her limbs. Yenni rose and went to her Creshen vanity to check her hair. She'd recently taken an evening to redo her braids, and they hung in her usual neat fall just past her chin. Satisfied, she made her way down.

Dragon stood on the path to the main gate of Riverbank Chambers, and as she approached he pulled his wings close, stuck one leg out front, and bent over it in a bow. Yenni balled her hands into fists and put them behind her back against the urge to stroke his face.

"Hello, Dragon."

Quick as a blink he changed to a man and came up to her, his eyes clouded with sympathy.

"You've had a rough few days, en? You smell stressed," he said.

Yenni crossed her arms and raised an eyebrow. "And what exactly does that smell like?"

Weysh furrowed his brow in thought. "Something like burnt bread mixed with sweat."

Yenni jerked back. "Are you trying to tell me I need a bath?"

Weysh put his hands up, as if in surrender. "No, no! Not a bath, well, not unless you think it would relax you. And perhaps after . . ."—he gave her a mischievous grin—"when you're all warm and soft, and your muscles are more pliable, I could give you a soothing back rub. I'm told I give *very* good back rubs."

"Oh, I see," said Yenni. "And who gave you that glowing review? Carmenna?"

He cringed and scratched the back of his head. "I suppose I walked right into that one. Erm, how did your demonstration go?"

"Mainard has agreed to let me stay." Yenni detailed all that had happened in the last few hours.

"I never had a single doubt," said Weysh, smiling fondly at her. "Still it's lucky you were there to stop that . . . whatever it was from braining the man, en? Byen be praised."

"Yes," Yenni said slowly. In truth it *was* quite lucky, and something about that nagged at her, but now was not the time to dwell on it. She had more pressing matters to attend to. "Listen, Weh-sheh. I need your help."

She explained what she needed and he readily agreed.

"And after that I'll take you to a good height where you can take in the city and we'll just cruise for a bit," he said. "That always does wonders for me. And then—oho!" He snapped his fingers. "I know just where to take you. You'll forget all your worries when you see this place, trust me."

That sounded absolutely wonderful. The chance to get free, even for a little while, of the worrisome thoughts that had been plaguing her for days was a powerful temptation. And yet she had made a promise to Carmenna, and then there was the letter from Prince Natahi.

"I'll stay in dragon if that puts you at ease," said Weysh. "But please let me do this for you—as a friend. I know you like flying with me, lovely. And I hate to see you upset."

At Yenni's hesitation he backed up and changed again to dragon, then bent low so she could mount.

She sighed and climbed onto his back.

Δ

Yenni would never, ever get tired of flying. The sky was full of fat white clouds. After sending her letter Weysh and Yenni had left the academy and the city center behind, and now they flew over green fields dotted with grazing animals and divided by yellow roads. Here and there were Creshen houses of stone and brick. Yenni closed her eyes, listening to the steady song of the wind and the occasional leathery snap of Dragon's wings. He was right; this was exactly what she needed.

Dragon seemed to be headed for a chain of mountains in the distance. As they flew Yenni marveled at the quaint Creshen scenery below, enjoying the way the shadows lengthened as the sun began its descent. The mountains loomed bigger and bigger, until at last Dragon shrugged his shoulders, tilted his head back, and let out a quick, clipped cry, signaling a sharp ascent. Yenni gripped tighter with her thighs and wrapped her arms around the ridge of his spine.

"Ready!" she shouted.

Up they went, Yenni grinning with excitement and surrounded by the *whoosh* of Dragon's wings. The ascents and descents were the most fun parts of flying. She pressed her face against the hump in front of her to shield herself from the wind, until finally Dragon crested the mountain. As he leveled out he gave a high, urgent screech, as if to say, *Look!*

So Yenni looked.

And gasped.

Oh divine Mothers and Fathers!

The mountains gave way to a plateau pool that perfectly reflected the scenery around them. The amber sunset and glowing clouds were doubled, as were the mountains, so that it felt as if they were encircled by the sky. The sheer beauty of it struck Yenni so suddenly that it drew tears from her eyes. Dragon wiggled his shoulders and made a low, clicking noise, and it took Yenni's awestruck mind a moment to register that he wanted to descend.

"Oh! Yes, I'm holding on," she called. To Yenni's shock he headed straight for the pool, but before she could protest, he landed so smoothly she barely felt it, and Yenni realized that while it looked like they were walking on water, it was as shallow as a puddle, and as reflective as a highly polished mirror. She looked down and caught Dragon's eye in the reflection. He made a soft huffing noise that went up at the end, and she could practically hear Weysh's voice: *What do you think? It's pretty, en?*

"Gorgeous," she whispered.

Dragon did not let her down, but instead took her on a slow walking tour, right across the center of the plateau. It was wonderfully empty and quiet, except for Dragon's claws crunching on something under the water. With each passing second Yenni felt the knots within her loosen, and the anxiousness of the past week fade. Here, enclosed in the mountains, with the sun glowing gold above and below, and the rosy clouds seeming to go off into infinity, Yenni could easily pretend this was all there ever was and ever would be. Her, Dragon, and heaven.

"Thank you," she whispered as she stroked Dragon's neck, then she leaned forward, wrapping her arms around it as best she could in a hug. "Thank you," she said again.

The noise he made was soft and rumbling, with a smug contentedness that made Yenni laugh. His swaying steps soothed her and the heat of his scales warmed her, making her feel something similar to drunkenness, reckless and unguarded. After a while she looked down at their reflection. Her cheek was pressed against his neck as she leaned casually across his back. She smiled sleepily at herself. It both looked right and felt right.

"It has been hard," Yenni found herself murmuring to him. "Cresh is nothing like I could have predicted. I'm used to being good at things, considered competent, but here I am not. I keep making mistakes, terrible mistakes."

Dragon made a low groan that ended in a hissing sigh, and Yenni imagined he was trying to comfort her, telling her *Everyone makes mistakes.*

"Perhaps," she said, stroking his neck. "But I'm making mistakes

I cannot afford to. I need to be here, Dragon. My father is ailing, and I came here to find a way to help him. It's all up to me to save him."

Dragon grunted. *That's too much pressure.*

Yenni ran her hand lazily across the scales of his spine. "Would you not do the same?"

Dragon didn't answer, and after a time Yenni must have dozed, because the next thing she knew Dragon was jostling her slightly, wiggling his great bulk. He let out a soft screech, again beckoning. *Look.*

The mirrored plane before them had turned from burnished gold to a diamond-dusted sky, a thousand stars surrounding them, reflected in the water. "Incredible," she breathed. It was perhaps the most beautiful thing she had ever seen, and the sight of it, the majesty, calmed the restless anxiety within her, dissolving it like a house made of sand before the ocean.

"I want to thank you, Dragon—Weh-sheh. Face to face. Please let me down and change," she said. But Dragon snuffled and shook his head.

"Why not?" Yenni asked, confused. He let out a low growl that sounded to Yenni not angry, but concerned.

"Is there something wrong with the water? Will it harm me in some way?"

He growled again and dipped his head.

"Oh, but what about you? Does it hurt?"

He shook his head.

"Good. Still, I would speak with you, as Weh-sheh. Could we not sit at the edge of the plateau over there?"

Dragon made a series of soft clicking sounds. *As you wish.*

He spread his wings with a familiar flutter and snap, and Yenni held tight in anticipation. Dragon made a soft, high screech. *Ready?*

"Let's go!" said Yenni.

Dragon ran, splashing as he galloped across the water, then he spread his wings and took off.

Yenni whooped as they took to the air, but the flight was only a few seconds, and then they were on the rocky sand at the edge of the mountain peak. Dragon lay flat and Yenni slid free. She sat, pulling her knees to her chest as Weysh changed and sat beside her.

"You smell much better," he said.

"Quiet," said Yenni, and she pushed him lightly by the shoulder. He laughed.

Yenni took a deep breath of the mountain air, as if she could breathe in the beauty around her. "Thank you, Weh-sheh," she said. "Truly. This helps."

"Anytime, my heart." He gazed out at the water with a satisfied smile. "I'll admit this is one of my best finds, but I have a lot more to show you."

More to show you. His words plucked a chord of guilt in her chest. She wanted him to show her more. She'd love to fly off with him to other enchanting places such as this, but she shouldn't. Couldn't.

"Why would you not let me down on the water?" asked Yenni, changing the subject. "Is it poisonous?"

"Lovely, why would I bring my Given somewhere poisonous?"

Yenni shrugged. "Who can say what goes on inside that strange mind of yours?"

Weysh grunted his annoyance. "It's a salt flat," he said. "The salt and minerals are what give the water that mirror sheen. I didn't think you'd want to ruin your uniform boots."

"Oh," Yenni said, sheepish. "Thank you."

"You're welcome," sighed Weysh.

They fell into silence again until at last Weysh said, "You're the only person I've shown this place to."

"Oh?"

Weysh nodded. "I was very much into cartography in first and second years. Whenever I'd fight with my—uh, I mean, whenever I had free time I would fly around looking for interesting places to map. If I found somewhere nice I'd take people back there. Harth and Zui, or . . ."—he cleared his throat—"women I wanted to impress. But I never took anyone to the best spots. Those I saved for my Given." He turned to her. "For you."

Yenni had no good retort for that, so she simply turned back to the sparkling salt flat. After a moment she felt his big, warm hand close around her own, where she pressed it against the ground, leaning back to support herself.

I should pull away, she thought. *I must put a stop to this.*

But she didn't.

"What's your family like?" asked Weysh at last, breaking the silence. "Do you get along?"

"Yes," said Yenni, not wanting to go into more detail.

"That's good," he said, still looking out over the plane. "Family is important."

"Yes," she said again, and then to her horror tears formed in her eyes. It was as if at that moment some dam within her had finally burst, and all the worry of the last week came pouring free.

"En? What is it?" Weysh took her gently by the shoulders, his face alarmed. "Byen, what did I do now?" He cringed. "Your father."

"I worry for him," Yenni admitted.

He ran his thumbs in soothing circles over her shoulders. "I'm sorry," he said, and looked away, troubled. "I suppose this is what it's been like for Sylvie."

Yenni wiped her tears. "Who?"

"My sister. Her papa is sick too."

"What do you mean 'her papa'? Is he not your father as well?"

Weysh dropped his hands. "No," he said, and didn't go into further detail than that. "But I'm truly sorry to hear about your father. Montpierre—my stepfather—is also sick. A mysterious illness called the wither-rot. It's nasty business."

Yenni leaned back and stared at him. She would have laughed if she wasn't already crying. All this time, these moonturns past, *Weysh* of all people was her connection to the illness killing her father? Somewhere in the realm of the Sha, Father Esh sat cackling at her, she was sure.

"But this is the same illness that could be affecting my father! How is your stepfather treating it? Please, Weh-sheh, anything you can tell me will help."

"Fresh air, incense, and plenty of rest, for all the good it does. Forgive me, Yenni Ajani. I can't say I know much about the wither-rot, no one does. But the moment I learn anything, you'll be the first to know."

"I see." So many frustrating false trails and only the barest hints of direction. It was a sobering reminder that she had much more work to do. The Sha were not appeased yet.

"Please take me back to the academy now," she told Weysh. She saw the disappointment cross his face but he only nodded.

"Very well."

Δ

The night seemed more vibrant than usual.

Weysh reveled in the warm air currents gliding across his wings. Yenni was perched firmly on his back, her presence a comforting heaviness. The clean, sweet, spice of her teased his nostrils from time to time. In that moment his dragon heart was swollen with contentment. As long as Yenni was near, he was happy.

The flight back took them over the lights of Imperium Centre. Weysh ducked and weaved, avoiding the tallest towers with the help of the signal rings, halos of multicolored light that warned of the towers' presence. At one point two other dragons came cutting through the air from the other direction—Rosh and Sween, by the scent of them. They were brothers from the province of Ouet, just to the west, and like all the dragons out there, their green scales were tinged with blue. They had been in pretty much all of Weysh's classes growing up. They let out sharp cries of greeting as they approached, which Weysh returned.

"Hello!" he heard Yenni yell from atop his back, and he could picture her waving frantically. Weysh wiggled his shoulders to warn her, and then angled his wings to let them descend, so the draft from the brothers wouldn't buffet her.

"Good-bye!" his sweet Yenni called after them as they passed overhead. He made a small moan of disappointment as the spires of the academy crested the horizon. He didn't want to let her down. Would she object if he took one more turn around the city?

In the end he decided against it. She'd asked him to take her back, so he would do so. Too soon he was angling for the walkway to her residence, lined with lush green trees backlit by magic lamps. He let her off and changed.

"There you are, lovely. Safe and sound."

"Thank you," she said. She gave him a strange little bow where she touched her fingers under her chin and nodded to him. Some gesture from her homeland no doubt. "Good night, Weh-sheh." She started for the gate.

"Wait!" said Weysh. She turned, expectant.

"I just wanted to say that . . . you're . . . incredible," he finished lamely. Ah Movay, what was *wrong* with him lately? When had it ever been this difficult to woo a woman? He should tell her how bright and pretty her eyes were, how beautiful and smooth her skin. How her competence and confidence made him want to kiss her and touch her until she forgot her own name. Yenni turned back to him. The gate creaked in the distance as a soft breeze rustled the trees, and that was when he caught it: a familiar scent that Weysh knew well. Sweet, musky, and rich like cocoa—desire.

Emboldened, he stepped close to her, trapped her eyes with his. "You're incredible," he murmured again, stroking her silky cheek with his thumb. He leaned in and finally, *finally* claimed those enticing lips of hers.

Watcher above, her kiss was so warm and soft. Her mouth on his sent lightning tingling up to the top of his head, to his fingertips, sparking through his chest. She clutched his shirt, arching into him. Weysh broke off the kiss, but only to bury his nose against her neck and breathe deeply of the maddening scent of her. It went straight to the base of his brain, stirring something primal and possessive.

"You. Are. *Mine*," he said, punctuating each word with a kiss along the column of her throat. He moved in for another taste of her mouth only to be shoved back. Hard.

He blinked, stunned. "What—"

"No," Yenni said firmly.

"But your scent—"

"*No*," she said again.

"All right. I apologize." He'd never been more confused. He knew he was not mistaken about her scent, and yet she clearly told him no, so how could he argue?

"I am meant to marry, Weh-sheh."

"So you've told me," said Weysh, annoyed. "But do you even want to—"

"There you . . . are?"

Yenni whipped her head to the gate and then quickly skipped back, widening the gap between them. Weysh followed her gaze and saw Carmenna standing on the lantern-lit path, her eyes darting from Yenni to him. Weysh let out a whooshing breath. Apparently a demon of mischief was plaguing him. Of all the awful timing.

"I heard the news. About your exams," she said to Yenni.

"Oh," said Yenni. Her chest heaved up and down with heavy breaths.

"Yes," said Carmenna, though she came no closer. "I came by to see you earlier, but you were out."

Yenni swallowed. "Thank you for your concern."

"Good evening, Carmenna," said Weysh. Things were awkward enough without them pretending they didn't exist to each other.

"Weysh," she said, nodding back politely. She rubbed her upper arm. "Were you able to find a way to stay, Yenni Ajani?"

"I was. I'm to be a teaching assistant."

"Oh! That's wonderful! I'm so happy for you!" And Weysh

could tell by the soapy, clean scent of relief that she was—but also a little not if that quick, sour whiff of disappointment, like milk gone off, was any indication.

"Well, I simply came by to see how you were. I have a lot do, so I'll be on my way." She curtsied to them. "Good night."

"Good night, Carmenna," said Yenni.

"Be well," Weysh called after her as she hurried down the path so fast she was practically running.

"Thank you for a beautiful evening, Weh-sheh, but I must go." Yenni bowed and hurried away almost as fast as Carmenna, slipping through the gate and into her residence. Weysh sighed, tipping his head back to the night sky. He'd been so close! What, by all that was holy, could he do convince her, his own Given, that they were meant to be?

"Kindly Watcher, why have you done this to me?" he muttered.

22

Four days had passed and second-term classes were in session, but Weysh hadn't seen Yenni since the night they'd kissed. Part of him wanted to seek her out—he was sure of what he'd caught in her scent, tasted on her lips—but there was only so much rejection his bruised ego could take at once, especially after the fiasco with his family.

He still hadn't been to see his maman and Sylvie either. The presents he'd bought languished in his townhouse. He told himself it was because he was busy and tired from the start of the semester. Harth told him otherwise.

"You're stalling," he said. The two of them lounged on the low roof of the lecture hall annex, the rough wall of the main lecture hall against their backs. It was one of their favorite spots to sit and people watch. The sun was setting on the campus below, the buildings making long shadows across the paths and lawns.

Harth tossed an almond into the air and caught it in his

mouth. "You know it's not you Montpierre hates, right? It's the *idea* of you," he said around his chewing.

"Thank you, Harth, that makes everything better."

Harth shrugged. "It's the truth," he said, and then he frowned. "And it's not right."

"I could give a dog fart about Montpierre," Weysh grumbled. "But Maman, Genie, and Sylvie, the way they looked at me—" Weysh sighed. "It was like they didn't know who I was anymore." He slammed his thigh with his fist. "Byen! I shouldn't have let my temper get the better of me."

"Who wouldn't?" asked Harth, incredulous. "Quite frankly I don't think you're the one who should have to apologize. It was foul, what Montpierre said, and low."

Now Weysh shrugged. "It's not the worst."

Harth shook his head, and the two of them sat in amicable silence for a while, watching people pass by below. Weysh tossed a handful of almonds into his mouth, crunching away. "You're right, though," he said with his mouth full. "I need to see them soon—I think I'm starting to lose my mind. I could swear I see Sylvie down there right now."

Harth sat forward. "Weysh, I think that *is* Sylvie."

Weysh sat forward as well, dusting his hands on his pants. "En? What's she doing here?"

Weysh and Harth shared a worried glance, then jumped off the roof, changing to dragon in midair to glide to the ground below.

"Sylvie!" Weysh called once he changed back. She started and turned around, then ran to him, throwing herself in his arms and enveloping him in the cloud of her scent, friendly and familiar. Weysh *umphed* as he caught her.

Harth bent over and waved. "Um, hello, Sylvie."

"Hi, Harth." Her reply was muffled by Weysh's chest.

"Sylvie, what is going on?" asked Weysh.

She pulled back and fixed her ruffled brown-blond curls, her cheeks flushed. "Nothing, nothing, it's just . . ."

Weysh raised his eyebrows at her expectantly.

"I thought I'd never see you again," she said sheepishly. "It sounds silly when I say it now, doesn't it? But after what happened—"

"You're not angry with me?" Weysh said softly.

She sighed. "I was . . . am, maybe. But I'm also angry at Papa. It wasn't right, what he said. You shouldn't have grabbed him like a thug, but it wasn't right—hey! Weysh!"

Weysh had lifted her right off the ground in a crushing hug, spinning her around before setting her down. "I can make amends with Montpierre as long as you and Maman can forgive me."

"Oh," Harth said, wiping a fake tear from his eye. "That's just beautiful."

Weysh and Sylvie turned to him. "Shut up, Harth," they said in unison.

"Hmph!" said Harth. "I take offense to this familial bonding at my expense. Shouldn't you be out shopping for hair ribbons and petticoats and whatnot with your second-school friends?"

Sylvie rolled her eyes. "Do you not know me at all?"

Harth crossed his arms and smiled. "Better than you realize, which is why it's so easy to get under your skin," he said and winked.

"Harth has a point," Weysh said. "How did you get here?"

"The tram, of course."

"This late?" The image and the sickly scent of Yenni lying in the alley accosted him. That had been enough to drive him half mad, but Sylvie in her place . . .

"The sun hasn't even set yet, Weysh."

"I'm taking you home," Weysh said. "I'll likely take the blame for this, too, but that's life I suppose. And it's probably time I faced Montpierre, en?"

"Actually"—Sylvie's shoulders slumped—"I doubt he's there. He and Maman had a big fight about you, and now he's always out surveying his warehouses or in meetings when he should be resting at home."

Weysh froze. "They fought about me?"

Sylvie nodded sadly. "Yes."

"Oh. And, erm, what did Maman have to say?"

"You can ask her yourself when you take me home," she said and smiled sweetly.

Weysh narrowed his eyes at her. "This was your plan all along, wasn't it?"

She bit her lip and looked away. "If you're busy I'm happy to take the tram home. You know how I love the tram. And the walk from the stop is only about twenty minutes, and reasonably well lit. Except that one stretch where—"

"I should hire a carriage and charge it to the house," Weysh said sternly.

Her face fell.

"But I miss you, conductor," said Weysh.

"You know I hate that nickname," she groaned. He'd given it to her due to her strange enthusiasm for riding the trams. He often asked why she was wasting time in school when she was just going to end up as a tram conductor someday.

"Yup," Weysh agreed and tweaked her nose while Harth

laughed in the background. "Besides, you riding dragonback will annoy Montpierre. I'll fly you home. Do you remember the signals?"

She clapped her hands together and squealed. "Yes!"

"Good."

"And you'll talk to Maman? She hasn't said it, but I can tell she wants to see you."

Weysh flicked his eyes to Harth, who gave him a shallow nod.

He sighed a soul-deep sigh. "All right, I'll talk to Maman."

Δ

After a quick stop at his townhouse to grab the presents (*I love it!* Sylvie had exclaimed at the dragon charm with amethysts for eyes), Weysh was now bearing down on his family's red-bricked manse with Sylvie perched on his back.

As always, Weysh gave a screeching cry to let everyone know he was there, then he jerked his shoulders to let Sylvie know he was planning to descend.

"Got it! I'm holding on!" she yelled. As Weysh dove in Sylvie whooped in glee. He touched down a little rougher than usual, just enough so the bump would give Sylvie a jolt. "Whoa!" she exclaimed excitedly.

He bent to let her down, and she surrounded him in endless excited chatter. "That was so much fun! I missed flying with you, Weysh—I wish we could do this more often! Maybe I can convince Papa. Byen, the world looks so different from above! We need to—"

"Weysh? Sylvie?"

Their mother stood at the door with Genevieve, frowning with confusion. "What is going on?"

Weysh changed and hastened over to her. "I picked Sylvie up from school, Maman," he said quickly. "I bought her a present from Dame Dubois. You and Genie as well."

Weysh reached into his hip bag for his mother's earrings. They were beautiful cascading diamond drops, the kind of thing she loved. He held his breath as she studied the earrings, turning them this way and that to make them sparkle in the light of the lantern by the door. Her expression was curiously sad.

"Come inside, Weysh," she said at last, and turned to lead him in.

As Weysh passed Genevieve in the hallway he slipped her an ivory comb studded with pearls. She gasped, her pale cheeks went rosy, and she pulled him into a tight embrace.

"Welcome home, Weysh."

He threw his other arm around her neck in a one-armed hug.

"Thank you, Genie," he said by her ear. "I'm sorry if I upset you the other day."

She simply patted his back. "I know you didn't mean anything by it, love. You've always been a good boy. A bit of a handful growing up, but good. I do wish my Martin was more like you."

Weysh frowned at the scent of bitter regret and the sickly stink of shame, like something dying. Genevieve's son Martin had a bad gambling habit, and hadn't been able to shrug free of it in all the years she'd been with them. Weysh gave her one final squeeze. "Be well, Genie," he said before following his mother to the sitting room. The fire was already blazing cheerily, but his mother went to work lighting the candelabras on the walls.

"Have a seat, Weysh," she said as she worked. "Sylvie, my heart, leave us be for a moment. I'm sure you have studying to do."

"That's not fair!" Sylvie cried. "I'm part of this family, too, Maman. Stop keeping secrets from me."

"Sylvie!" she snapped, and then closed her eyes, inhaling deeply. "This is not about keeping secrets. This will be hard enough for me as it is."

Weysh squinted at his mother. Something was wrong. It was rare that she let her mask of propriety slip, even with him. Perhaps especially with him.

"Go, Sylvie," he said softly. "We'll catch up later, en?"

"All right," she said uncertainly, finally reading the mood in the room. She slipped out, closing the door behind her. Weysh's mother folded herself gracefully into the armchair across from him, without even offering him cake or biscuits or coffee. She truly must have been distraught.

She rubbed her temple and let out a bitter chuckle through her nose. "She's too young," she said. "Too young to be burdened with all of this. Perhaps you are, too, but you seem to have met the woman you want to marry"—she sighed—"and marriage is no easy thing."

"I'm twenty, Maman, I'm a man grown." Weysh forced a firmness into his voice that he didn't feel.

"And was it a man grown who attacked Montpierre last week? Were those the actions of a man grown, Weysh?"

Weysh cringed. "I'm sorry, Maman."

"Then be quiet and listen."

A cold, unsettling feeling tingled down Weysh's spine. Something seemed strange and off about his maman. Grave, and yet more real. Perhaps as real as she had ever been with him. The air about them loomed heavy and ominous, and Weysh could sense that the thing, that dark, shadowy *thing* hidden under her charming laughs and her impeccable skills as a hostess and model wife, was dangerously close to the surface.

"At first, I went to Guste willingly," she began.

Weysh's insides went icy, as if he'd inhaled a frigid breath from the realm of demons at the edge of the world. Oh, Kindly Watcher, not this. He had never been good at hiding his emotions, and by the tight set of his mother's mouth, he knew his dismay was plain on his face. He could have happily gone his whole life in ignorant bliss, unaware of the sordid details of his mother's communion with Guste Pain.

But another, morbid part of him wanted to know everything. What had she seen in him? What had he done to her? What was so horrible that she couldn't quite bring herself to fully love their offspring, her own son?

Him?

"Montpierre was not a particularly rich man when we met," she began. "But he was ambitious. He got along well with your grandfather, you know. Both of them are self-made men, cut from the same cloth. Montpierre had just started his window-outfitting business with an old school friend as his partner. Through his wheelings and dealings and constant searching for investors, he eventually crossed paths with Guste Pain.

"Guste was charming and enthusiastic about the business, and as with most dragon families, his was quite wealthy. He gave Montpierre a modest initial investment, which helped his business take off. After that the two of them became fast friends, and he was always visiting with us. For a while the business went well, but the death of the emperor and the succession of his son had a negative effect on the Creshen economy, and Montpierre's contracts dwindled. What's worse is we were also preparing for our wedding at the time.

"With the economy as it was, no one was willing to invest in a fledgling window company headed by an untested young businessman. Believe me, Montpierre tried. Guste was all we had—your grandpapa's delivery business was not the thriving enterprise it is today, barely breaking even. An infusion of funds from Guste would allow Montpierre to keep his company going, weather the storm until things improved. And Guste knew this. So he came to me and said he would give Montpierre the money, if in return I gave him myself."

"No, Maman," said Weysh, sounding as breathless as if he'd just flown across the ocean.

"I did say no, at first. And then for two moonturns I watched Montpierre's business fail, watched him become sunken, sallow, and irritable, and watched our plans for a future shrivel like kindling in a fire. Eventually Montpierre was able to suspend his pride long enough to ask Guste for a loan, but Guste refused, of course, and their friendship faded. Then one day Montpierre took me out on a romantic moonlit stroll by the castle moat and gardens, and told me we couldn't be married.

"He had nothing to offer me, he said. I told him he was overreacting, I loved him no matter what the circumstances may be. I told him I had faith in him. But Montpierre said that by the following week, at the end of the moonturn, his business would fold. He had no more money to pay the rent on his manufacturing workshop. He said he would not make me his wife until he could give me the life I deserved, and that I should find a man worthy of my beauty and kind soul."

She paused to wipe at two tears trailing down her cheeks. "So the next day I sought out Guste Pain."

Weysh let out a long exhale. "I see," he said. It was a terrible situation, and his maman did the only thing she believed she could at the time.

"Foolishly, I thought it would be a one-time thing," she continued. "It was not. He gave Montpierre his loan, but he also said that if I didn't continue with him he would tell Montpierre I had thrown myself at him. He even kept one of my underthings as his so-called proof."

Weysh shivered. Sometimes just knowing that psychopath's blood ran through his veins made his skin crawl. "But, Maman, why didn't you say something before he had the chance?"

She laughed, the sound bitter. "Weysh, you lovely thing. Who would you expect people would have believed? The golden son of a wealthy dragon family or the wife of a fledging businessman? The *half-Islander* wife of a fledgling business man? Even after your birth, when it was clear Guste must have participated willingly, there were those who disbelieved me, who grumbled that I had somehow sought to entrap him. They said I should have been happy with the Creshen I'd already managed to catch, but I was a greedy harlot who'd hoped for bigger game." Her eyes glistened with angry tears. "I thought it would never end. Even when I became pregnant it didn't occur to me that it could be Guste's."

Whether fact or folklore, it was thought to be practically impossible for a man who was dragonkind to impregnate any woman but his Given. Some scholars went so far as to say that dragonkind men could not impregnate anyone before they had found their Given, that her scent alone gave him that capability. Clearly, Weysh was proof of the contrary.

"Some days I relish that your birth beat the odds. It forced everyone to finally see Guste for what he is. Other days I wonder why it had to be me."

Weysh's heart sank. "I'm sorry, Maman." His mouth twisted like he'd bitten into something sour. Every time she looked at him she saw the man who had kept her hostage. Every time Montpierre looked at him he saw his failure as a provider, the lengths to which he had driven the love of his life.

"Oh, lovely, no," she soothed. "It was my mistake. I was young and I believed—" She sighed. "My grandmother who raised me was never warm or kind, but she did drive home one piece of wisdom: a woman's beauty is her power. Again and again, as she critiqued my posture, my complexion, my hair, and my smile. 'A woman's beauty is her power.'"

"Do I look like him?"

"There is a resemblance," his mother said truthfully.

"En? Even with my hair so long?"

"What does that have to do with anything?"

"The picture you showed me." As a child of about six, Weysh had no real understanding of the nature of his parentage. He only knew Montpierre wasn't his father. He had begged and pleaded for close to a year before his mother finally relented and showed him a portrait of Guste Pain in the newspaper. In hindsight, that must have been an article about him being disgraced and disowned by his family—for a dragon, a sacred warrior of Byen, to commit *any* sort of crime was a menacing scare to polite society, much less something as terrible as adultery or rape.

The man she'd shown him looked severe, with an aristocratic nose, a sharp and angular face, and Weysh's violet eyes. He'd also worn his purple hair cut quite close to his head.

"His hair was very short," said Weysh, as if that explained everything. His mother got up from her chair and came over to him. She placed a delicate hand on his cheek, and smiled.

"Oh, Weysh," she said softly. "I'm your maman, lovely, and I can see what you're thinking. I'm glad you were born, and not merely because your birth forced Guste Pain into the light. You've made your mistakes," she said, stroking her thumb along the side of his face. "As have we all. I regret deeply my decision to succumb to Guste Pain, but I do not regret you, my heart. You are not Guste. You're simply Weysh. My Weysh."

Relief spread through him like warm brandy at that, melting something icy and hard in the pit of his stomach that he hadn't even realized was there. He stood and enveloped her in a squeezing hug.

"I love you, Maman, always."

"And I you, lovely." She didn't attempt to pull away, but Weysh noticed her voice sounded a bit strained, so he let her go. She took his hands.

"Leave Montpierre to me," she said. "I think it would be best if you gave him some time to cool off before attempting to reconcile."

Reconcile was an optimistic word. How did one reconcile something that had never been in the first place? "Maman, what is it you see in him?"

"Montpierre is not one to suffer fools," she said, "but he has always been fiercely loyal to me, whether I deserved it or not. The Pain family wanted to take you away, ship you off somewhere you could be forgotten, wherever they sent Guste perhaps, but I wouldn't allow it. You were, are, my child, and I would raise you as my own. And because it was vitally important to me, Montpierre adopted you, knowing full well that everything he is able to earn in this life will go to you as his first male heir."

"I don't want it," Weysh grumbled. "I plan to turn everything over to you and Sylvie. I can make my own fortune."

"Don't be so quick to dismiss it," she said a bit sharply.

"Montpierre has toiled for years to build his business, and you will be starting a family of your own soon, will you not?"

"I, well, that is . . . probably."

"Yes. So think long and hard before you cast aside everything Montpierre has worked so hard to provide us."

Us, she said, as if she truly believed Montpierre cared one rat shit about him. Still, he didn't want to argue with her. "All right, Maman, I will," he said.

"And do bring your Given by soon. I'm very eager to meet her."

Weysh hesitated. That would take some time. First and foremost, he had to get Yenni to admit she was his Given. But to explain it all to his mother would be complicated, not to mention embarrassing.

"All right, Maman, I will," he said again.

Δ

An aggressive summer wind whipped stray strands of Weysh's hair from his braid back. He closed in on the bank of the River Noureer, which ran along the eastern side of the campus. Here the grass was charred and brown, and tall, metal poles stuck up from the ground. This was where Prevan held fire-breathing class, in which dragons worked on the longevity and accuracy of their flame.

Weysh was early. His conversation with his mother the day before had put him in a mood, and even changed to dragon he'd been restless and unable to sleep. Spitting fire at targets for an hour or two would make for a good distraction. But as he approached the riverbank he saw a few of his classmates were early as well. They sat hunched on the river's edge in human, their backs to him. One was a woman with shining green hair cut short—his classmate Feiy. And—he wanted to groan aloud—another woman with long green twin-tails, that rumor-monger Clairette. His classmate Sween, whose blue hair burst from his head in its usual mess, as though it was permanently wind-swept, sat between them. They couldn't hear or smell him coming against the wind, if their topic of conversation was any indication.

". . . in West Castle West of all places. It makes us *all* look bad!" said Feiy.

"Well, Weysh isn't a bad sort, though," said Sween.

Feiy made a noise of disapproval. "No, I know but—well, you know, about his father. Either way, dragons shouldn't be fighting in the streets like that."

Weysh stopped, letting the wind blow his scent downwind, and blow their words back to him.

"Forget about Weysh," said Clairette, waving a hand. "Wait until you hear what my cousin had to say about Luiz."

"Your cousin with the peacekeepers?" asked Sween.

"Obviously, Sween. Who else would know about all this? He told me that back in Espanna, Luiz's father was charged with adultery, *and* he was *ministralto* for the whole of the Church of the Sacred Vigil."

"No!" cried Feiy.

"Yes! It was *quite* the fall from grace. And—oh, this is the sad-dest part—the shame of it was so great that his mother took her own life."

Weysh jerked back, stunned.

"Oh, Watcher above!" cried Feiy. Sween shook his head.

"Tragic, isn't it? No wonder he left Espanna. *That's* why he transferred to Prevan last year. Well, that and what I just told you, about . . ." Clairette had lowered her voice and Weysh couldn't catch the last part of what she said.

"I wonder why those two are so constantly at odds when they have such similar grim backgrounds," mused Feiy.

Weysh rubbed at his temples: not this again. No matter what he did, his father's legacy plagued him. A classmate to whom he'd perhaps said five words to all year seemed to think she knew all about his background. Weysh was long used to the gossip and the whispers, but he never would have guessed that Noriago was subject to the same treatment, not with all the high and mighty airs he put on.

Weysh marched up to his classmates. "Windy today, isn't it?" Watching them startle was so incredibly satisfying. "It will make practice difficult," he continued. "Everything is blowing back west, en?" He grinned and pointed the way he'd come.

"Oh! Weysh! Hello!" said Feiy. Sween simply cringed, not even trying to hide the fact that they had been talking about him. Weysh nodded to Sween and ignored the others, making for the practice targets at the back of the building.

"Well that was rude," said Clairette.

Weysh changed to dragon and made some circles around the training field, putting them from his mind and instead doing his best to judge how the wind would affect his shots.

In due time Lieutenant Duval—Harth's cousin on his mother's side—took to the field. He was gangly and sallow, but in dragon could he ever control a flame. More of Weysh's classmates joined them on the riverbank including, to Weysh's shock, Noriago. Weysh was sure starting fights in the streets would have been grounds for expulsion.

He wondered what connections Noriago had back home, or if it was simply that Prevan's powers that be had decided they didn't want to make a minor ripple into something more and cast negative attention on the school. Or perhaps Noriago was simply benefiting from being dragonkind. Whatever the reason, it looked like Weysh would be stuck with Noriago until the bitter end.

Noriago, for his part, ignored Weysh all class, and Weysh didn't feel much like talking to anyone. Thankfully there was no partnering in fire-breathing training. Lieutenant Duval had them sail over the targets one by one, blasting them with fire and critiquing their performance in front of the others. Weysh was glad to change to dragon and simply focus on the class, pushing himself to melt the metal poles as quickly and cleanly as possible. But after a time, when he was back on the riverbank watching another of his classmates take their turn, someone settled in beside him.

"Erm, sorry about earlier, Weysh," said Sween.

"It's nothing new," Weysh replied.

"I told them you're not a bad guy. But listen, Clairette told us some things about Noriago, things he did in Espanna. If they're true, I'd stay clear of him, Weysh."

"En? Such as?"

"Well, he already has a record. There was a house fire and a woman was badly burned and disfigured. Noriago was suspected in connection to it—largely because the woman was his father's mistress. There was no proof he did it or anything, but it seems that's the only reason he got off."

Weysh frowned; that *was* serious. And yet Noriago had been cleared. Weysh couldn't believe he was about to advocate for Noriago of all people, but more than once in second school

Weysh had been pinned with the blame for crimes he hadn't committed—petty thefts, vandalism, starting fights when he was only defending himself—simply because he fit the profile of a criminal and the teachers and administration were too lazy to investigate further. And he certainly couldn't have turned to Montpierre for help.

"But if there was no proof that he did it, that's that. Why are we talking about this?" asked Weysh, suddenly irritated.

"It's true there's no proof but it's suspicious. Just watch yourself with him, en?"

"I'm not afraid of Noriago," said Weysh, and turned back to the lesson, ending the conversation.

Still, once class was over and Weysh saw Noriago trudging across the burned plain toward the spires of the campus proper, the sudden urge to confront the other dragon took him over. Weysh never was one to leave well enough alone, after all.

"Noriago!" he called, and jogged up to him.

Noriago put his head down and walked faster, his steps crunching on the dead grass. "Sweet Sienta Marin, what in all hells do you want, Nolan?"

"I heard about what happened in Espanna with your father. The others were talking about you."

He stopped and whirled around to face Weysh, ready for a fight. "And?"

"I know what it's like to be fodder for gossip and ridicule."

"As if I care what any of those rat pricks think."

"Then why did you leave home?"

"I . . . that's . . ." Noriago sputtered, then laughed, disbelieving. "So what, you think we're the same? What could you possibly know about it, Nolan?"

"I know more than you think. As a child I had classmates spit at me, and make signs of warding, like I was some sort of demon—at least until I threatened to roast them if they didn't stop."

Noriago scowled at him. "Spare me your whining. That's a day at the seashore compared to what I've been through. Someone like you couldn't begin to understand how much I've lost."

His maman, for one. To his surprise, Weysh actually felt sympathy for Noriago.

"I'm sorry," Weysh told him, and meant it. "Listen, this is the last year of schooling for both of us. We have a lot to accomplish and this fighting is an unnecessary distraction. I say we call a truce." Weysh stuck out his arm.

Noriago watched him for a long time, his bronze eyes hard and his hair fluttering in the wind.

Weysh sighed. "I'm not trying to be your best friend, Noriago—I simply need to concentrate and get the best scores possible this year, especially now that I have a Given to support." He thrust his hand at Noriago again. "Truce?"

Noriago finally smirked at him. "I'll think about it."

"That's better than no, I suppose. And one more thing—when it comes to Carmenna . . . she's not your Given, is she?"

Noriago scoffed. "That dragon hunter? Not on your life."

Weysh frowned. *Dragon hunter* was a derogatory term for women who sought out dragons for dalliances. "She's not like that," Weysh said firmly. "We were something of an item once—"

"You think I don't know that? I only sought her out to get under your skin."

"En? Why would that get under my skin? I have a Given now."

"That never seems to bother men like you, Nolan."

Weysh bristled. "You don't know anything about me," he said, a low warning growl lacing his voice. He wanted to make amends, but his patience was wearing thin.

"Likewise. You know nothing about *me*, Nolan. We are *not* the same, but you're not wrong. I expect this"—he waved his hand to encompass the school, his face twisted in disgust—"is all that's left to me now." His face changed so fast Weysh thought he might have imagined it, except that the wind blew the quick scent of something bitingly bitter, rotting, rank, and *wrong* his way, an emotion he had no words for, and Noriago looked positively crazed for a moment. But when he turned to Weysh he fixed him with his characteristic sneer. "You stay out of my way, and I'll stay out of yours."

Without another word Noriago changed to dragon, looming over Weysh. He let out a couple of puffs of steam from his nostrils, then took off, blasting Weysh with warm air from his wings.

23

Yenni worried her lip between her teeth as she stared at her palms: worse. Her father's health was definitely getting worse. The rune had faded steadily over the last week, and was now half as strong as her mother's rune on her other palm. Her stomach had been in knots for days.

I need to go home, she thought for the hundredth time. *How will I live with myself if N'baba dies while I'm away?*

But I cannot! I pledged a year abroad to the Sha on this Orire N'jem. If I anger the holy ones by breaking my vow the whole tribe will suffer, including N'baba. My best chance to save him is here.

"What exactly are you looking at, Yenni Ajani?"

Yenni blinked and looked up into Carmenna's confused brown eyes.

"Oh. It's nothing."

She stared past Carmenna's shoulders at the soft light filtering between the trees of the library, illuminating the dust motes. *I must focus*, she told herself. *I can't fail again. It may be that my first failure angered the Sha, and that's why N'baba's health is in further decline.*

This was her first tutoring session with Carmenna since the new semester had begun, and the first time Yenni had seen her since the encounter in front of Yenni's residence. She planned to make the most of her time with the older girl.

But Carmenna took a deep breath and expelled it on a sigh. "I'm so sorry, Yenni Ajani. I wanted to tell you in person. I don't think I can tutor you anymore."

Yenni blinked. "What? But why?"

Carmenna closed her eyes. "I didn't want to fall for Weysh. I knew it was foolish, but it didn't seem to matter. I fell anyway and now . . . now this hurts."

Yenni fought to hide her alarm—she needed Carmenna's help now more than ever!

"Carmenna," she said patiently, "the other night was a mistake. Weysh was only trying to comfort me after—"

"That horrible attack. I know. I was sorry to hear about it. I'm very glad that you're all right," said Carmenna.

Yenni touched her hand to her chest. "Thank you, and whatever Weysh says, I cannot be with him. I'm already promised to another." Well, almost promised, but Carmenna didn't need to know that. "Please, Carmenna, I need your help."

But Carmenna shook her head. "You ask too much of me. Think, imagine our positions were reversed. Picture Weysh holding my face in his hands, smiling down at me, kissing my lips like he used to."

Yenni did, and a terrible cold feeling stole through her whole body. It was suddenly hard to breathe.

"I . . . no . . ." Yenni stammered.

"Yes," Carmenna said sadly. "That feeling right there, that's why I can no longer tutor you, Yenni Ajani. I'd be doing you a disservice if I did."

Yenni looked away. *Mother Shu who tends the fires of the heart, stand with me against the trickery of Father Esh, who now tries to sow within me a false and unobtainable love. Help me douse this false feeling, and instead stoke the flames of something true.*

Life would be better for everyone if she could just fall in love with Prince Natahi.

"I gave you my word that I wouldn't fall for him," said Yenni, her own voice disbelieving.

Carmenna shook her head. "It wasn't your word to give."

"But I don't want to marry him!" Yenni hissed desperately, trying to keep her voice down in the quiet library.

"As long as your scent calls to him, and as long as he senses the smallest chance you return his feelings, he'll never want to let you go." Carmenna stood, and Yenni saw her eyes were wet with tears. "Farewell, Yenni Ajani. I wish you all the best. Sincerely."

There was nothing more Yenni could say. She watched helplessly as Carmenna exited the library.

$$\Delta$$

Weysh waited until the end of that week to seek Yenni out, in dragon of course. He called to her from outside her residence, and waited close to an hour, but she refused to appear. All the next day he tried to speak with her, but she dodged him, taking her meals at home and avoiding the library. Finally Weysh camped outside her Practical Application of Magic for Battle class and waited for her to come out. When she did, she took one look at him and marched the other way.

"I never took you for a coward, Yenni Ajani," he called after her. It hit the mark, as she paused, though she kept her back to him.

"I am not a coward," she snarled.

"Truly? Because you certainly run like a coward."

She whirled around and marched up to him, hitting him with a plume of peppery irritation. "I am not a coward!" she shouted.

"Then why do you refuse to face me?"

She threw up her hands. "What is there to say that has not already been said?"

"Well, to start, you could admit your feelings for me."

She took one short, sharp intake of breath, and that terrible scent of sadness, like algae, swam past his nostrils. He was about to reach for her when her scent changed, alarmingly quick, to acrid, smoky rage. Yenni darted her eyes left and right, taking in the nosy crowd forming around them from the dismissed class.

"Come with me," she said, and marched off. Weysh jogged to catch up with her.

"Where are we going, lovely? If you give me a moment to change I can get us there much faster—"

"No," she snapped.

Weysh clenched his teeth to keep from snapping back. She certainly wasn't easy to deal with when she got this way, but he used the memory of her upturned face, her long lashes brushing her cheeks, her velvety lips against his, to help him hold his tongue.

She led him to the rows of outdoor study nooks on the lawn east of the training sands. They were comprised of stone tables and benches enclosed by matching stone partitions covered in creeping ivory. Yenni stomped under the archway to one of the benches and slid roughly onto the seat while Weysh smoothly took the seat across from her. Yenni placed her palms on the table and her eyes flashed at him. Weysh had never seen her so undone.

"We. Cannot. Be," she said through her teeth, as if it was all she trusted herself to say.

Weysh met her glare unflinchingly. "We already are," he said. "Honestly! Do you really plan to spend the rest of your life like this, in longing, denying what you feel? Why torture yourself?" *And me*, he added silently. "Do you feel for this other man the way you feel for me?"

He wrestled back his climbing panic at her hesitation, staring her down as he waited for her answer. No matter what Yenni said, nothing could change that she'd let him hold her and kiss her. Nothing could erase from his mind the rich, intoxicating scent of her desire. She wanted him, he *knew* she did. *De woman is a confusion*, his grandfather would have said. On the one hand, she was a rebel who very much disliked being told what to do. On the other she was fiercely loyal to the idea of this marriage, if not the man she was intended to marry. What would it take to get her to shift that loyalty to him? Was the decree of the almighty not motivation enough? What could this other man provide her that he, a dragon, could not?

Yenni glanced away. "No," she admitted, answering his question.

Triumph bloomed in Weysh's chest, but instead of lunging across the table to embrace her as he wanted to do, he simply nodded. "And you never will. No man will match you as well as I will. We are Given."

"Carmenna will no longer tutor me because of you," she said angrily.

"En? Byen, I'm sorry about that, lovely. Truly. But I'm always available to help you. And I'm sure Harth and Zui will pitch in as well. And what of your friend Diedre? And you can always get another tutor."

But her face was long with sorrow, and she stared at her palm.

"Why are you always looking at your hand?" Weysh asked her. "You do it all the time, even before you were injured."

Suddenly she thrust both her palms in his face. "This is my mother," she said, waving her right palm. "And this is my father." She waved her left palm.

"En?" What was she talking about?

"Do you see these runes?" she asked him. Indeed, two white runes twisted along her palms. The one on her right hand was solid, the one on the left quite faint, split by an ugly red welt. "These runes represent the lives of my parents. The one on the right is my mother's, the one on the left my father's." She stared at her left palm again. "Every day my father's rune fades a bit more," she said softly.

Ah, poor thing. "I'm sorry, my heart. What can I do? Should I fly you to see him? I can make arrangements to leave as soon as possible—"

"Stop!" Yenni said, and it came out strangled, pained even. "Stop being kind. You cannot help me. My father's death will affect not only my family and me, but the entire Yirba tribe, as he is our chieftain. And my marriage will affect not only me, but the entire Yirba tribe, as I am their princess."

Weysh sat back, positively blown away. He looked Yenni up and down and slowly pointed at her.

"This explains so much," he said, punctuating each word with a slight jab of his finger. In his world princesses were delicate, fluffy things meant to be protected and cooed over. They were not warriors who could disarm three thugs in a dark alley or throw around men twice their size. And yet, of course Yenni was a princess, and not simply because she was clueless about the value of money. It was in that irresistible confidence of hers, the way she unthinkingly commanded respect. The way she assumed she would be obeyed.

Yenni turned her head to the side and squinted at him. "Do you see now why we cannot be together?"

"Nope," said Weysh, and he smiled at her. "Princess or not, we're still Given."

"This is not a laughing matter!"

"Who's laughing?" he said. "I've never been more serious about anything in my life. We'll work this out together."

"Dragon—"

"Of course your intended will be disappointed to lose you, but surely he'll see reason. A Given bond trumps any other union."

"Dragon—"

"And if not, well, I'll just have to *make* him see reason, en? By whatever means possible—"

"WEH-SHEH!" Yenni shouted. It was a voice he had never heard her use before, high and desperate. "How?" she continued in that same tortured tone. "How am I supposed to take you, a man of no political standing, and a Creshen no less, back to my family, my tribe? My intended is a prince, the second son of our most powerful ally and you, Weh-sheh Nolan, are nobody."

Nobody? Did his Given, the woman he was bonded with, the one he was meant to build a life with, the one person in this world who was supposed to unconditionally accept and love and support him, just call him *nobody*?

As he took in her glare, cold fury rose within him. He closed his mouth with a click of his teeth and stared down his nose at her. "Apologize."

"No! It is true."

Weysh felt even his dragon-mind stir from slumber at the back of his consciousness to growl in righteous anger. Perhaps that was why he placed his hands on the table, leaned forward until their faces were inches apart, and snarled at her. "You will apologize to me, Yenni. I would never treat you with such disrespect."

"It is Yenni *Ajani*!" she fired back. "And haven't you already? Assuming I would fall at your feet simply because you are a dragon and because you say I am your Given. What was it you said you had in store for me? 'Women's duties'? How are you different from any other man? Why should I spurn a prince, risk *war*, for you?"

Weysh's breath was coming in ragged pants by now. The dizzying scope of his anger alarmed him. Not even Montpierre could get him this riled. Only this woman, his Given, could cut him so deep. Emotion rumbled and built inside his chest until it spewed forth like a plume of flame.

"APOLOGIZE!" he roared at her. "This instant! Or I swear by all that is holy you will never hear from me again!"

She was shaking, and he caught a trace of sickly-sweet dismay among the smoky heat of her anger, but all she said was, "Good."

Weysh gawked at her, and something inside him seemed to snap and crumble. She couldn't possibly be serious, but her face was hard and unyielding. Why? Why was it always so easy for her to dismiss him? Weysh rose, weak and weary like a man three times his age.

"So be it. Good-bye, Yenni Ajani," he said, and stormed away, ignoring the salty, brackish scent of her tears on the air.

$$\Delta$$

Later that evening, Yenni ran a finger along the plush velvet of the armrest of her common room armchair, lost in thought.

"You seem distracted," said Diedre. She gently took Yenni's left hand across the low tea table between them, tracing a finger along the welt left by her cut. She *tsked* her tongue at it. "How are you holdin' up, mams?"

Yenni sighed. She knew Diedre was referring not only to her injury, but to how she was coping since the attack in town. Over the last couple of weeks, people Yenni barely knew had been coming up to her in all her classes to ask for the gory details, and also to ask if she was truly a dragon's Given. Her nerves were already stretched thin with worry about her father, and she had snapped at her classmates more than once for their intrusive and idiotic questions. She knew she was making a terrible impression, but she couldn't bring herself to care.

"I'm doing my best to stay focused. I must pass the next set of exams," said Yenni. "And you? Your shoulder?"

Diedre waved dismissively. "Is all patched up. An' don't fret yourself over exams, they're not for over a moonturn, an' from what I see of your study sessions with me you'll be jus' fine. Watch, is only a couple weeks pass an' already you're better at almost all the spells was givin' you a hard time. Uhad's Retrievin', Fenton's Body Bind—"

"Yes, I definitely wanted to master that one. But I need to master Mereena's Unbinding," said Yenni. She gestured to the knotted piece of rope on the table before them. "I'm almost certain it will be on Mainard's next examination."

"Ah, well, you know magical theory is my thing. I'd say the problem is you still strugglin' to connect the spell and the outcome. How are you comin' along with Uhad's sixty-seven laws?"

"I've memorized them all," Yenni said with pride. "Uhad's First Law: the Law of Source and Seven. All incantations must contain the word *source* and have exactly seven syllables. Uhad's Second Law—"

"All right! I believe you, mams. Is no need to recite every las' one. Hmm, then try this: imagine the sound of the rope slidin' out of the knot."

"Oh! All right." Yenni breathed deep, doing her best to clear her mind of all worries about her father and all thoughts of Weysh. She concentrated on hearing in her mind the hiss and scrub of the rope sliding against itself. And then she pulled ach'e, focusing on the short, knotted rope on the table between them.

"*Through source tangled come undone.*"

The rope moved slow and snakelike until it freed itself of the large knot in its center.

"Nice one!" said Diedre.

"You know," said Yenni, "my friend Zoo-ee told me something similar about Yoben's Rainfall. She advised me to imagine the smell of the rain."

Diedre nodded. "Is a well-documented phenomenon. Focusin' on a smell or sound or even the feelin' of something can really help with spellcraft. Zui is one of your dragon friends, yes? The beautiful one from Minato? She helped us in the alley."

"Yes."

"Ah. She's as smart as she is stunnin', it would seem."

The mention of the alley brought back the memory of Dragon, steaming and vengeful like her own guardian beast.

"Oh, what is *this*?" asked Diedre. "You should see your face, Yenni. Who is it who makes you smile that secret smile, hmm?" Diedre squinted at Yenni, flashing a knowing smile of her own. "Is the other dragon, your Given."

The smile left Yenni's face. "He is not my Given simply because he says he is."

"But, Yenni, why you don't like he? Is a *dragon*, mams. A pretty one too."

"He is Creshen, my parents would never approve."

Diedre gave her a skeptical look. "Even though you two are Given?"

"We are not—" Yenni paused, taking a deep breath to swallow her frustration. "Yes, even so, Deedee. There is no concept of Given on the Moonrise Isles."

"Oh. Well, that seems sad."

Very sad, if the sinking feeling in Yenni's gut was any indication. "What about you, Deedee," said Yenni, attempting to turn the conversation around. "Is there anyone special to you?"

"Ah." Diedre glanced away, uncharacteristically nervous. "There is someone, yes."

"Oh?" Yenni leaned forward.

"Yes, but is the same situation. My family would never accept it."

"Really? Why?"

"Um, well . . . tradition. Is not the type of person they would want me to marry."

Yenni hummed knowingly. "But if your family did approve, do you think you could marry him?"

Diedre sighed. "In a perfect world, I think so."

"Oh, Deedee. Still, you'll have to point him out to me sometime."

"Erm, yes. An' you? In a perfect world, do you think you could marry your dragon?"

Yenni paused. "This is not a perfect world," she said at last. "So there's no use thinking about it. Now come, I need to practice Meyor's Repulsion."

24

He was cursed. He had to be. It was the only way to explain how his Given could look him in the eye and tell him he was nobody, *nobody* to her.

A bird trilled overhead in one of the pine trees. Weysh had hoped to find some peace here on the mountain, but the quiet only made his thoughts louder. A little over a moonturn had passed since he'd last spoken to Yenni. True to his word, he hadn't sought her out, or wanted to seek her out. Half-year exams were approaching, and when he should have been concerned with helping her pass, the thought of her only filled him with empty hollowness.

"We're not speaking," he'd told Harth and Zui when they'd innocently asked after her. He didn't go into detail, even when they pressed him. It was simply too embarrassing. "Just make sure she passes her exams," he'd begged them. "Take care of her for me."

He hoped this horrible numbness was not how the women he'd left in the past felt. How Carmenna felt.

Weysh shook his head and focused on moving forward on the mountain trail. Before him twin dragons stretched high enough to rival the pine trees surrounding them, their stony wings forever spread back and their onyx eyes shining. Long necks curved toward one another, creating an archway before an incline of stairs so steep they could lead straight to heaven itself. Weysh considered flying up to the top, but he was here to pray for guidance from Byen, and somehow taking the stairs seemed like it should be part of that effort. He'd already flown up the mountain to reach this chapelle, after all.

So he took to the cracked, white steps, and when the burn of exertion spread through his legs he relished it, considering it penance. He shouldn't have unleashed his anger on Yenni as he did, but he doubted she would take kindly to his attempts to make amends. She likely didn't want to see him any more than he wanted to face her. He breathed deeply of the pine-scented air and kept going.

When he reached the top, the scenery at last stirred something in his murky soul. If Mount Eglise was a king, then the chapelle was his gleaming white crown. It consisted of columns carved with curving dragons arranged in an arc, with delicate, trellis-like woodwork stretching across them to make a roof that still let in patches of cerulean sky. The altar to Byen stood beneath.

Weysh's footsteps echoed on the stone, and the shadows from the roof fell over him like black lace. He knelt before the altar and prayed. First he renewed his vow to Byen to serve as his divine warrior. Then he entreated Byen to lift the curse upon him.

Kindly Watcher and ruler of the worldly domain, I seek forgiveness for my sins and the sins of my father now visited upon me. Help me understand the woman you have seen fit to bless me with as Given.

Weysh frowned. Why did his words feel so empty? Perhaps because Yenni did not feel like a blessing. She was pain, and frustration, and endless humiliation. Suddenly his townhouse on Lor Street seemed impossibly small. How was he supposed to convince her to leave a palace to live there? He wasn't even sure what compelled him to keep going, *praying* to the almighty for her acceptance. Was it simply the Given bond? Well then, perhaps he should be praying to be released from it instead.

Weysh sighed and continued. *If I am not yet the man who can be Yenni's perfect match, then help me to become him. Byen watch over me.*

He ended his prayer and stayed at the chapelle for a while in solitude. It was usually only dragonkind who visited here. Few were willing to make the hike up the mountain, especially when there was a larger chapelle at the base. This place was perhaps the closest thing he'd seen to heaven. From the summit the world seemed suspended between twin voids of azure sky and navy sea, and it was easy to pretend, even for just a while, that there was nothing else.

He had been enjoying the quiet for near an hour when he heard wingbeats and a familiar rusty scent hit his nose. He forced himself to stand slowly, turn calmly, and nod his greeting. "Noriago."

Noriago stood at the top of the steps, his hands jammed into his pockets. He gave off the scent of triumph—sunny, sweet, and rich, like the juice of an orange. It clashed unpleasantly with his natural metallic sharpness. "You look like you've been living on the streets, Nolan."

Weysh scowled. He hadn't been paying as much attention to his appearance of late, it was true, but he'd had more pressing matters on his mind.

"What do you want?" he snapped.

"I've been hoping to catch you alone like this for a while. I want to talk, dragon to dragon."

"What about?"

Noriago started toward him. "What you said about how we've been through similar hardships."

"So you've come to accept the truce?"

Noriago kept coming closer. "When my father was disgraced we lost everything, my brother and me. We lost our mother."

And here his scent changed—vinegar and algae. "We lost our standing, and we lost our father, the man we looked up to more than anyone. My brother is young, he decided to stay in Espanna. He thinks with time we can bounce back."

He stopped in front of Weysh.

"But I know better. Even after I graduate from Prevan I'll never have the life I could have. The Church of the Sacred Vigil has shunned us entirely. Even if I meet my Given, her name will simply be dragged through the mud with mine."

Weysh shook his head. "That's not true, Noriago. You owe it to yourself to fight. If you give up, they win." It was a mantra Weysh had repeated to himself hundreds, thousands of times.

Noriago laughed, and it was not a pleasant sound. "I was supposed to be head of the whole Espannian chapter of the Church of the Sacred Vigil one day, practically as powerful as the king of Espanna himself. What's left for me now—delivering packages, like you?"

"There's no shame in making an honest living," Weysh said stiffly.

"Either way, it doesn't matter anymore. You showed me the truth of it, the future in store for me. What I wanted to tell you is this: *Source-drawn wind blow forth with force!*"

Wind whipped at Weysh, and a cloud of something red burst in front of him. Instantly his face was on fire.

"We are not the same!" Noriago shouted, even as Weysh coughed and sneezed, and tears streamed from his closed eyes. It seemed like grains of sand were stuck under his eyelids, and his nose and lips burned, inflamed.

"I have always walked the righteous path, while you have strayed, debauched, put pleasure before service," Noriago prattled. Weysh lashed out, trying to hit him, and met empty air. "And yet I am rewarded with ruin, while you are given a woman you could never hope to deserve! The only thing that brings me even the slightest solace now is watching sinners like you suffer."

Weysh crouched, still sneezing, blinded not only by his tears. He also couldn't smell. "Poison, you coward?" he yelled between burning sneezes.

"Not quite." Noriago's voice came from the left, and Weysh jerked to face it. "But this is the next best thing. Good luck smelling anything ever again, including your ill-gotten Given."

"Thrice-damned lunatic!" Weysh shouted, lashing out again, longing to dig his fingers into Noriago's scrawny neck. "They'll lock you away for this!"

"They didn't the first time. And anyway, I have nothing left to lose."

"I'LL KILL YOU!" Weysh roared.

Noriago laughed, and a moment later Weysh heard wingbeats on the air. No way in hell was he about to let that festering *ass boil* escape! Weysh changed to dragon, and instantly regretted it. His sensitive dragon nose amplified the pain unbearably. He screeched and changed back to a man.

It felt as if his face was melting. He needed water, but couldn't even open his eyes to find it, much less smell through his inflamed sinuses to sniff it out. So he lay on the chapelle floor, sneezing and moaning until slowly, *terribly* slowly, the agony subsided to painful yet bearable tingling. He opened his swollen eyes.

Thank Byen, he could see. And yet something seemed to be missing. He stared down the steps at the trees below. The color was off or . . . no. He sniffed. Sniffed again. Inhaled a deep searching breath. He couldn't smell the trees, or anything else. Noriago was right: his sense of smell was gone.

Δ

Yenni sat rigid as a rod in bed, staring in numb disbelief at the runes on her palms. Was she awake? Or was this a dream?

Her father's rune was almost as strong as the day he had drawn it there.

Yenni traced a finger over the rune, registering the sensation. As her shock wore off bright joy built within her until she sprang up with a whoop, jumping and dancing on her mattress. Oh praises upon praises to those most holy! The week prior she had at last received a letter updating her on life at home. And though her mother found the concept of the wither-rot highly strange, she assured Yenni she would find a delicate way to pass the information on to the Healers' Guild.. Since then, nothing.

Until this.

Yenni didn't question the suddenness of her father's healing. She only cared that he was well, that she would see him again. Surely all would be explained in her next correspondence from home.

It was with a bounce in her step that she dressed and prepared for her first class of the day, runelore. That morning she decided to leave the front half of her hair in its relatively neat row of braids, which she had done curving on a slight angle. She let out the back, tying it into a high puff, which she moisturized with the coconut and shi-shi root oil from Diedre. Yenni turned this way and that, frowning at her reflection. She couldn't seem to get the shape of her puff right through finger-combing alone. She opened the drawer of her vanity to get her long pick comb, another present from Diedre. It was very useful for working out the tangles in her hair. But as she opened the drawer she froze. In the corner, sparkling in the light of sunrise, was the necklace from Weysh.

Yenni picked it up and sighed, her mood dampened. It was a hurtful thing she'd said to him, she knew, and untrue besides. The sensory memory of his lips whispered across hers. He was not nobody. Not to her.

Which was all the more reason why she had to drive him away. So she should be glad that he'd made no attempt to see or contact her in over a moonturn. It was what she had told him to do. She should be glad.

So why wasn't she glad?

Why did she keep picturing Dragon, beautiful and terrible as he dwarfed the mouth of the alley? Dragon, curled up and letting out low moans of mourning as she departed for the Islands? The images never failed to send darts of guilt and longing right into her heart.

Yenni shook herself and placed the necklace back in the drawer. She missed Dragon desperately, that she could not deny. But Weysh was arrogant and presumptuous, crass and overconfident. And fearless. And honest. And friendly, generous, kind.

Yenni slammed the drawer shut. There was no use in dwelling on it. The most important thing was that her father's condition had improved, praise all the Mothers and Fathers.

She kept lifting her uniform glove to peek at her rune as she hurried down the red-carpeted steps of Riverbank Chambers. Diedre lived on the second floor, and they would often walk to class together. Yenni made her way down the corridor until she reached the familiar *Suite 2-5* etched in gold on the dark, whorled wood of Diedre's door.

Yenni knocked sharply. "Good morning!" she sang.

A few moments later the door opened and Diedre loomed over her. The gold clasps adorning her braids glinted in the light of the wall sconces.

"Is far too early for you to be this cheery, mams," she muttered. Yenni simply laughed.

It was a decent walk to Professor Devon's class from where they lived. His classroom was relegated to a previously abandoned outbuilding on the southeast outskirts of campus. As Devon's teaching assistant, Yenni arrived early to help him set up—and to answer his exhaustive and never-ending questions about runelore. Diedre, blessed soul that she was, had taken to arriving early with her. She acted as a nice buffer, as with other students present Devon tended to rein in his zeal for the sake of propriety.

Yenni could easily run to class in a few minutes using her speed runes, but Diedre wasn't as skilled in them yet and couldn't keep up. Besides, Yenni enjoyed these morning walks with her friend. Diedre was funny, and her impressions of their professors, especially Devon and Mainard, had helped to keep Yenni's gloom at bay.

They stuck to the white, interlocking path down to the main

quad of the campus, chatting amicably about nothing of consequence. The elegant white willow trees shading the walkway were now alive with little yellow blossoms, and their sweet scent drifted down to them on a happy breeze. Yenni breathed deeply, her heart at ease.

Until the sound of quick wingbeats reached her ears, followed by a sharp, screeching cry.

Yenni snapped her eyes upward, her heart fluttering in nervous anticipation as she squinted desperately through the willowy tendrils above.

Something thumped to the grass beside her. The shadows of the willows made such gorgeous patterns on him, sliding like water across his gleaming green scales as he stalked toward her. Those eyes, like brightest jade, slid first from her to Diedre, lingering and unreadable. Mysterious. So at odds with who she knew him to be as a man.

"Ahh," Diedre began.

"Hello, Har-tha," said Yenni. He had seemed to take mild offense to her calling him by his full name, finding it too formal, so she had taken to drawing out his first name.

He changed, and his green face looked troubled. "Good morning, Yenni Ajani," he said, and turned to Diedre. "I don't believe I've had the pleasure of an official introduction."

"This is my friend, Diedre," said Yenni, and the two of them clasped hands.

"Yenni Ajani, a word?" Harth said to her. Yenni took in the clouds across his normally sunny countenance and her chest tightened.

"Diedre, apologize to Professor Devon for me and let him know I'll be late," she said, still frowning at Harth.

"But how is this? I'm your messenger now?"

Yenni blinked and turned to her. "I'm sorry, Deedee. I didn't mean—"

Diedre laughed. "Relax! All is well and good, mams. Is joke, I joke. I'll tell him."

Yenni let out a relieved breath. "Thank you."

"See you in class!" said Diedre, and she shot Yenni a look that she knew meant she would have explaining to do later on. With a wave, Diedre took off, still chuckling.

"I like her," Harth said with a gravity that was almost comical, then turned back to Yenni. "Look, something's happened to Weysh. He told me not to tell you but, Byen above, I can't stand to see him like this. Two days ago he was up at the chapelle on Mount Eglise, and he was attacked."

Yenni gasped despite herself and listened, first unbearably anxious and finally furious when Harth concluded how Weysh had been maimed.

"What's more, you could be in danger, too, as Weysh's Given. Movay, he must really be out of it not to have even realized that. It's true Noriago would have to be brainless to show up at the academy with the peacekeepers all searching for him, but clearly he's unstable."

Yenni gnawed on her bottom lip, more concerned for Weysh than herself. "So now Weh-sheh cannot smell?"

"No. Not now, and possibly never again."

Yenni ached for him, and at the same time she wanted to find that other dragon, Noriago, and drive a spear through his wings. "That . . . that . . ." She launched into a tirade about Noriago in Yirba, cursing him to the depthless shadows at the edges of the world, cursing his stones to shrivel up and fall off, so he could never bear children as horrible as him.

"Whatever you said, I agree completely," said Harth. "So you'll visit Weysh?"

Yenni paused "Har-tha, I cannot . . ."

"All right, I don't know what went on between you two, but"—Harth blew out a breath and ran his fingers through his green hair—"I've seen Weysh bounce back from a lot of things, but losing his sense of smell, as a dragon . . . this broke him."

Yenni put a hand to her chest, trying and failing to shake that image of Dragon flat to the earth, scales dull, deflated and depressed.

"Beat him and berate him when he gets out of line—in fact, I recommend it regularly just to keep him in check—but don't abandon him."

"Abandon him?" she repeated, her voice small.

"He needs you. Even just the sound of your voice might, I don't know, bring him back to *life*," said Harth, throwing up his hands. "He's like the living dead."

The ache within her grew and grew, until she had to swallow against the swell of it before she could speak. "He won't want to see me. Not after what I said."

"He will," Harth insisted.

Yenni took a step back. "I'll only make it worse."

"You won't!"

Another step back. "I must get to my class." She pulled on her speed runes.

"Yenni Ajani!" Harth shouted, as angry as she'd ever heard him. But how much angrier would he be if she led on his friend only to abandon him for the good of her tribe? How much worse would the pain be for Dragon? For Weysh?

For her?

"Good-bye, Har-tha," she said and took off for runelore class.

Δ

In attempting to forget about Weysh, Yenni focused on her father's healing and what it meant for her Orire N'jem. She was ecstatic that her father had made a recovery; she just hadn't expected it to be so sudden. She'd been abroad fewer than four moonturns—not even halfway into the complete year she'd promised the Sha. If her father was healed, could she return? Or did she need to stay the full year? Did she even want to leave yet? True, she missed home and wanted very much to see her family again, but she'd be returning to a marriage to a man she barely knew. And no matter what Natahi said, she'd be expected to give up the things she loved—hunting and sparring and possibly even heavy study of runelore—for propriety's sake. Was it selfish to want just a few more months of exploration and study? Of excitement and novelty? Of *freedom*?

"You seem quite distracted today, Yenni Ajani. Is everything all right?"

Yenni glanced up from her seat at the chipped, rectangular table that served as Devon's work desk. Both he and Diedre, who was sprawled out across from her on a chair at the front of the classroom, stared at her with expressions of mild concern.

Her hand had stilled in whisking up the runepaint for the day. She must have been staring, lost in her thoughts.

"I . . . oh! Yes. I'm fine, Professor."

Devon's brow furrowed and he shot a quick glance at Diedre. He looked like he wanted to say more but held his tongue.

Shortly after, students started to file into the room, greeting

Yenni just as deferentially as Professor Devon. Once everyone was seated, Devon took his place behind his table and leaned forward, hands spread wide. He had the most curious, conspiratorial look on his face.

"Now, class, we're not far from midyear exams. I'm willing to bet you're well and truly sick of all the review, en?"

A number of students voiced their agreement, Diedre included.

"Very well, why don't I show you something new?"

The smug smile spread along his face, and he even went so far as to wink at Yenni. Yenni blinked back at him, nonplussed. Just what could he be up to? He'd given her no indication they'd be introducing new material to the class.

"What I'm about to show you today is something few people have seen. A rune I've been working to perfect all year. And I know I claimed you need a break from exam review, but in truth I'm so excited to demonstrate this new rune that I simply cannot wait until next term.

"Here in Cresh, we've unfairly labeled Moonrise Islanders as being warlike and primitive. But today I'll be showing you a rune native to the Watatzi, a small but engineering group confined to an island just southwest of the border of the Sunrise Isles."

The majority of the students around them gave Devon the awed and intrigued reaction he was looking for, but faint apprehension churned in Yenni's stomach.

"This rune was only recently discovered by a mentor of mine, Magus Gilles Desroches!"

He paused, allowing for some of the class to react with noises of surprise. Yenni knew of this Magus Gilles Desroches, if only because when Devon wasn't peppering her with questions about runelore, he was singing the praises of this man, who was apparently something of a rebel and an eccentric within Creshen magical society. He was the foremost Creshen expert on runelore, often taking research trips to the Northern Sha Islands—the ones like hers that had not succumbed to Cresh's campaign of colonization three hundred years ago. And though Yenni had come to understand how little the average Creshen respected runelore, Desroches's books were still incredibly popular. She attributed his success to the vivid pictures his works painted of life on the Islands, which Yenni had to admit were engaging.

Or perhaps it was something more. Desroches's most popular work, *Runerise*, was meant to be a manual on the basics of runelore, and the history of runes on the Islands. She'd noticed how her fellow students, Creshen and Islander alike, carried the book openly, like a badge. Perhaps reading the works of Desroches, and being labeled a radical by association, gave them some sort of thrill.

But what did Devon mean when he said Desroches had discovered a rune? Expert or no, from what Yenni had read of *Runerise*, Desroches's understanding of runelore was still quite basic. He might understand the forms and songs, but he didn't grasp how runes were integrated into the very fabric of Island society, so she highly doubted the Sha had seen fit to bless him with their divine inspiration, thus allowing him to create a new rune.

"Without further ado, I give you the deception rune!" Devon boomed.

Yenni's frown deepened. She had never heard of such a rune before. Perhaps this was a Creshen translation she didn't understand.

Devon lifted the shaggy, wheat-like hair that fell in waves to his ears, and Yenni gasped. On each of his temples he had painted a rune she had never seen.

He pulled ach'e, and the runes on his temples blazed, but curiously his eyes blazed as well, like a Master infused with runelight.

And then the room erupted into birds.

Shouts and screams broke the tense silence as big, colorful jungle birds appeared all over the classroom—perching, flying, ruffling their feathers. But strangely, they made no sound. Yenni reached out to touch the large, bright blue bird that now blinked at her from on top of her desk, and her mouth dropped open as her hand passed right through it. Slowly, the bird faded. She glanced up at Devon. The runelight had left his eyes.

The class jumped to their feet, clapping and cheering, and Devon gave a bow.

"Teach us!"

"Show us how to draw the rune!"

"Come on, Professor!"

As the rest of the class begged Devon to teach them the rune, a sinking feeling invaded Yenni's stomach. *No, no, this isn't right.*

Devon held up his hands for silence. "Brilliant, isn't it?" he said. "The Masters among the Watatzi can create sound, smell, even the sensation of touch! It's a step above Ibeena's Sensory Illusion, wouldn't you say? I've always found that having to speak a spell aloud to create an illusion took away from the overall effect. It removes that element of surprise. No matter how powerful the illusion, the intended target will always know they are in fact in the grip of something false. But this, walking into an illusion unawares . . ." He shook his head. "This rune alone may explain why the Watatzi, while so close to Cresh, escaped the worst atrocities of the Colonial War.

"But regretfully, this particular rune is not a part of the curriculum, so legally I can't teach you how to draw it yet. Even today's demonstration might get me into some trouble. But I am, first and foremost, a proponent of knowledge, and I believe you, the bright minds of the future, have a right to know what's on the horizon, magically speaking."

The others groaned their disappointment, but Yenni stood. "Professor Devon," she said slowly, "how did your mentor come to learn this rune?"

"Ah, well." Devon suddenly looked uncomfortable. "He's spent the last three years visiting the Watatzi, you see, practically living among them, learning their ways, until finally he was able to get close enough to observe their Masters in action as they painted their royalty."

"Able to . . ." Yenni stared at him, horrified. "Are you saying he spied on the Watatzi Masters and stole one of their hidden runes?"

"Knowledge cannot be stolen, Yenni Ajani. It should be available to all."

Yenni simply stared at him. Professor Devon had always seemed so amicable—overzealous, yes, but he was one of the few Creshens who seemed to appreciate her culture. But perhaps it was because he was Creshen that he couldn't understand the gravity of what his mentor had done. Very well, she would have to explain it to him.

"Professor this—this is not how things are done! Each tribe has runes that are sacred, secret. They give economic leverage against the other tribes in times of peace, and protection in times of war. The Watatzi may well have been hiding that rune for thousands of years! It's not right for your mentor to come along and steal it!"

"I see. Well, you are, of course, entitled to your opinion."

"What? But, this is not my opinion, this is truth! There are things that are right and things that are wrong! I—" Her tirade spluttered out, and for once she was completely at a loss for words.

"We'll speak about this after class," Devon said and turned his attention to the room. "For now, let's continue our work with the life rune. Yenni Ajani?"

As Yenni moved, trancelike, to attend Professor Devon, Diedre touched her on the wrist. "All right, mams?" she whispered.

"Yes," she said softly.

"I'm with you on this one. I did like Desroches, but this is just sneaky."

"Thank you," Yenni whispered back and Diedre squeezed her hand before letting it go.

Yenni helped hand out pots of dying flowers. Using the life rune, as it was translated in Creshen, the class would work on bringing the plants back to health. It was a useful rune, especially in times of bad harvest, and it was the base rune for many other runes as well, including healing runes.

They spent the rest of the class working on the plants. Yenni somehow found the strength to push back her horror and disappointment. She flitted from student to student, giving advice on how to draw the life rune—the correct pressure with the brush, where to strengthen and soften the voice—until at last the hour was up, and they were left with flowers in varying states of health.

Soon everyone was filing out of class, and a few threw Yenni guilty looks. Diedre was the last to file out, and she gave Yenni a glance heavy with meaning. *Let him have it*, her eyes seemed to say. Once everyone was gone Yenni rounded on Devon, but he spoke before she could.

"I understand why you might be upset," he said, moving around picking up plants. "Truly. But can't you see that what Gilles has done is for the good of all mankind? Now the High Magus Council will *have* to take runelore seriously."

"What Desroches had done will be perceived as an act of betrayal, perhaps even an act of war," said Yenni as she brushed up the remnants of the herbs used for runepaint.

Devon paused, his eyes going wide. "But that's a bit extreme, wouldn't you say?"

"No. Most of our wars have been fought over runes. That rune likely gave the Watatzi leverage and prestige with the other tribes in a way neither you nor your mentor understand."

"Oh. Well, suppose you were right, and the worst were to happen, the Watatzi tribe is tiny compared to the might of Cresh, and have no dragons besides."

Yenni threw down the brush she'd been using to sweep the table clean and put her hands on her hips. "And that makes it acceptable to steal from them?!"

Devon cringed. "No, of course not. I'm only saying they would likely think twice before attacking. Listen," he said in what he must have assumed was a soothing tone, "what about you, en? You're here learning all about the magic and culture of Cresh. You have that right, as does anyone who visits our Empire. Why should runelore not be the same? The world grows smaller every day, and I predict that one day there will no longer be hidden runes, just as there are no hidden spells. Magic belongs to everyone, Yenni Ajani. Rich and poor. Islander or Creshen."

Yenni suddenly remembered what Natahi had said before she left. *It is their nature to take what does not belong to them.*

"That is not the same," Yenni insisted. "Creshen knowledge is given freely, even forcefully, in some cases. And while spells may not be technically hidden, there are nonetheless advanced spells that it would take years of study, and many Creshen duvvies to access. It should be up to the Watatzi if and when they want to reveal their hidden runes."

Devon touched his finger to his chin and studied her. "You know, I wonder if perhaps you aren't feeling some frustration that a Creshen has discovered a rune you knew nothing about."

Yenni's eyebrows flew up. "One, your Desroches did not *discover* anything. The Watatzi have likely been using that rune for millennia. Two, my frustration is because you either cannot understand or do not care how awful a thing your mentor has done. What of the Watatzi? Once this rune is publicized they will lose much leverage with the other tribes."

"That is unfortunate," Devon admitted.

"Or suppose your emperor decides to try to claim the Islands again? The deception rune, as you put it, kept the Watatzi safe once, but they will have no protection in the event of a second attack."

"That will never happen," Devon said with finality. "I speak for most Creshens when I say we reject and are deeply ashamed of our past as bloody conquerors."

"Well, perhaps your next campaign will be not to acquire more land. Perhaps it will be to acquire something more—the very soul of a people."

Devon's mouth opened and closed, until he finally said. "There's nothing to be done. Desroches presented the rune to the High Magus Council not two days ago. It's up to them to decide what to do with it now."

Yenni closed her eyes and sighed.

"Yenni Ajani," Devon said, his voice pleading. "This is a good thing. I promise you."

Unbelievable. Here was, in his own way, a man more stubborn than Weysh. Clearly she was not getting through to him, and she was tired of wasting her breath. Yenni snatched her back-satchel up from her seat and shrugged it on.

"I appreciate everything you have done for me, Professor Devon, but wrong is wrong." She shook her head and left him spluttering after her.

25

Diedre was waiting for Yenni on the stone steps to Devon's classroom.

"Well?" she said as she stood.

Yenni put her head in her hand. "Like trying to reason with a ram, as we say. Come, I need to get away from here for now."

They set off for the campus proper, abandoning the scrubby, dry grass and dingy outbuildings for the whitestone path, manicured lawns, and distinguished spires of the academy.

"Was only a matter of time, yes?" said Diedre. "Watch, in five years runes will be the latest fashion here."

"It's just so infuriating!" Yenni cried. "What is wrong with Creshen men? It's like I say one thing and they hear another!"

"The women same way," said Diedre. "But they have their charms."

"I'm so disappointed, Diedre. I have always thought of Devon as the opposite of Mainard, open headed instead of closed, but now I am not sure. A part of me wants to give up the class completely, but who knows what other sacrilege Devon will spread without me there to correct him? And I suppose I need the teaching stipend besides."

Yenni sighed and fell into a brooding silence as they walked. Coupled with her betrayal was a nagging sense of unease and guilt. Should she make the existence of this rune known to her family? The Creshens were about to expose it to the world anyway. But to do so would make her no better than that unscrupulous Gilles Desroches, would it not?

"Well, if you go, I go. You're the only reason I still take this class, mams. Devon does try, but he can't teach me much I don't already know or can't learn in books. I know some of the others will feel the same." Then, as if reading her mind, Diedre added, "You plan to tell your people about the rune?"

Yenni bit her lip. "I don't know. I am loyal to them, but if I tell them does that make me as bad as these two? Would you do it?"

"I . . . am glad is not my problem, mams," said Diedre.

Yenni cut Diedre a glance from the side of her eye. "You are so *incredibly* helpful," she said.

The taller girl laughed and squeezed Yenni around the shoulder. "Ugh, this is depressing, yes? Let's change the topic." Her face turned sly. "Tell me why you have dragons droppin' from the sky at your feet."

Yenni groaned. "Deedee . . ."

"No, no, no, mams. You know this was comin'. Is a friend of that big dark one, en? Your Given."

"Weh-sheh is not my Given," Yenni snapped. Diedre held up her hands and gave Yenni a look like she thought she had lost her mind. "Very well, my mistake."

Yenni felt terrible for yelling at her friend. "I am sorry, Deedee. I shouldn't have yelled at you. It's just that Weh-sheh—"

Diedre nodded. "You don't want to want him, but you do."

Yenni stared helplessly at her.

"Ah, I know exactly what's goin' on here. Is because you're an Island princess and the king say you mus' marry another man."

Yenni stopped short and jerked her gaze up to Diedre, shocked.

"But how . . . I didn't ever . . . how could you—"

Diedre's eyes bulged. "Is true?! Was joke I jokin' to lighten the mood, but you're really a princess?"

"I, well . . ."

"Oh my goodness!" Diedre squealed, and then narrowed her eyes. "But wait, you told me your folks is big rune mages, like magi here."

"They are," Yenni said. "It is expected of them as the chieftain and chieftainess of our tribe."

Diedre blew out a breath. "But this makes perfect sense," she said, reminding Yenni uncomfortably of Weysh.

"You cannot tell anyone," Yenni said firmly.

Diedre looked hurt. "I would never. How I could put my friend in danger so? You came alone, right?"

"Yes."

"But why? Was me, I'd march right up to the castle an' demand a room."

"I have my reasons," said Yenni.

"Hmm. An' the rest is true too? You mus' marry another man?"

Yenni simply nodded.

"An' you want him instead of the dragon?"

Yenni paused for a moment, then shook her head.

"Oh, mams."

They walked in silence for a while. "What's the worst thing could happen if you follow your heart?" said Diedre musingly, almost as if to herself.

"War, perhaps," Yenni replied softly.

"Watch'Ahmighty that *is* bad. Well, what's the worst thing could happen if you *don't* follow your heart?"

The worst thing? She would never see Weysh or Dragon again. The sadness of it hit her like a sudden, crashing wave—an intense, longing ache that surprised her. Her sisters, either through luck or their own clever maneuvering, were both quite happy with their matches, so why couldn't she be as well? But would Weysh make her happy? He wasn't perfect, but he was . . . something. Something to her. The way he constantly went out of his way for her was touching, difficult to resist. And no matter what she told herself, the notion of never seeing him again was painful.

"Mams, you look like someone died."

Sighing, Yenni shook her head.

"I can't say I know much about Moonrise politics, but I know livin' your life for someone else is a good way to live no life at all," said Diedre.

It was strange. Yenni had always thought of herself as independent. She'd resented Weysh's making plans for her, but Diedre was right. She was living her life for others, following obediently along the inevitable road of propriety. Why? Was she truly afraid of war, especially now that her father was well? Or was her fear something deeper, older?

And then the thought of Dragon—of Weysh, injured and mourning, bothered her deeply, no matter how she tried to ignore it. *Oh sweet Mother Shu, when did I come to care for him so?*

"Say something, mams."

"I miss him," Yenni admitted.

"Then go to him!"

"And tell him what?"

"Whatever you like. Whatever you feel."

Yenni stopped. At the very least she should apologize for calling him nobody. And in truth, she wanted to see him, to know he was well and to know if he still felt the same way about her.

"I will," she whispered.

"What's that?"

"I will see him." She hugged her friend. "Thank you, Deedee!"

"My pleasure, Your Highness," Diedre said and bowed before Yenni. And the gesture was so strange, as if one of her sisters was teasing her, that Yenni burst into giggles. Her heart pounded with nervous excitement, and she felt as if a heaviness had at last been lifted from her chest and shoulders. For something that would most definitely bring trouble, it certainly felt like the right decision. She would be meeting Zui that evening for a final study session before exams, so she would decide when and where to meet, and have Zui get the message to Weysh. She just prayed that he would agree.

"Oh, but the same goes for you as well!" Yenni told Diedre

"What's that?"

"The man who has your heart. You should try for him too!"

"Oh, oh yes. I will. Hey, look! How pretty!" said Diedre, pointing. A group of delicate yellow butterflies flitted across the path, five in total. Yenni grinned. Mother Shu's number was five, and her color gold.

Guide me.

Δ

Yenni found Zui leaning back against the railing outside the library. She faced away from Yenni, toward the building, and her straight, pale-blue hair trailed over one shoulder. She already wore the summer uniform: no tunic but instead a flowing green dress cinched by a large belt with the school's crest. And no leggings, only short and sturdy brown boots. Against the backdrop of the setting sun, she looked as pretty as a painting. "Zoo-ee!"

Yenni met her at the top of the steps and they touched palms. It was clear that Zui had something on her mind, but Yenni spoke before Zui could get in a word.

"I want to see Weh-sheh."

Zui gasped. "Truly? Oh blessed Byen, that's wonderful! It's just awful what's happened to him! And none of us dragons have been able to sniff out that rat Luiz Noriago. Every dragon at the academy has been keeping their nostrils clear, so to speak, but he probably took off back to Espanna. Poor Weysh. Losing your sense of smell as a dragon—I can hardly describe it. It might be like losing your ability to see colors. Does that make sense?"

"Yes, I think so," Yenni said softly.

"Well then, he's probably at home. Give me a moment to change and I'll fly you to see him right now."

"Now? But we should study!"

"Oh nonsense, you'll pass no problem. You've been flying through the practice exams. This is more important!"

"I had intended for you to take a message."

"Why wait? I'll do one better and take you to him instead," Zui said with a wink.

"I . . . but . . . what if he doesn't want to see me?"

Zui gave her a secretive smile.

"What is it?"

"I like this side of you. It's charming to see you so vulnerable. He'll want to see you, I'm sure of it. Now not another word, I'm changing." She skipped down the steps to the lawn and switched to dragon, then stood long and glittering in the waning twilight, one silvery eye turned expectantly on Yenni.

Δ

Yenni had never flown with Zui, and it was quite the amazing experience. Incredibly, the dragons of Minato had no wings. Instead, Zui flew by instinctively drawing on ach'e, similar to the gorgeously patterned sky snakes of the Fuboli Islands.

Zui curved and dipped through the night sky, her flight as graceful as a dance, scales glimmering in the moonlight. For a while Yenni could simply sit back and enjoy the ride and the night view of Imperium Centre, with its hundreds of lit windows like a never-ending festival. At last Zui descended on a row of colorful, conjoined buildings. Was this where Weysh lived?

Zui landed near a gate fronting a long path that led to the buildings—houses. She hunched down on her claws and gave a little impatient shake, indicating that she wanted Yenni to dismount. Dragon Zui was more aggressive than human Zui, it would seem.

Once changed, Zui moved quickly, tossing a greeting to a guard at the gate's entrance. Yenni was practically running to keep up with her. She led Yenni up a long path lined with bushes, up a couple of flights of steps until they stood in front of a white door surrounded by a pale orange façade. Twin lamps on each side of the door held blue-white magic lanterns. Zui raised the knocker ring and gave the door three smart raps.

Yenni's heart galloped as they stood for long seconds waiting. Nothing.

The women glanced at each other, and Zui rapped the door again, four knocks this time. Again nothing. Zui *humphed* and banged the knocker forcefully against the door as she shouted, "Weysh! I know you're in there!"

Something inside hit the floor and heavy footsteps approached them. The door flew open.

"What! I'm studying," Weysh grumped, and then paused when he noticed Yenni.

"Weh-sheh?" said Yenni uncertainly. Since the day of their fight he'd grown out a scruffy, unkempt beard, his hair now hung free in ratty tangles, and his violet eyes were dull, with none of that usual sparkle. He wore his green mage's uniform trousers but no shoes, and his white undershirt was rumpled and unbuttoned. She wanted to reach out and stroke his face the same way she'd often stroked Dragon's, but she resisted. He filled his doorway, staring blankly at her and saying nothing. Finally his eyes flicked back to Zui. "My house is a mess, you couldn't have given me a warning?"

"Nope," Zui said simply. "It was best to get her here before she changed her mind. Now I have somewhere very important to be. Weysh will see you home, Yenni Ajani."

"What? Zoo-ee, wait!" cried Yenni.

But Zui was already off, hurrying down the path, and a moment later she changed, taking to the sky. Yenni turned back to Weysh.

"Oh. May I come in?"

"I can't very well leave you standing out there," said Weysh. He stepped aside, allowing Yenni to enter a small foyer. She had never been inside a Creshen home before, but Weysh's house reminded her of her suite at Riverbank Chambers. Bigger, of course, but just as closed in, and with the same dark wood walls. The tiled foyer branched off in three directions, each with an engraved archway. The one on the right led to a cooking area, the one on the left to an eating area, and the one straight ahead to a sitting area. Weysh closed the door behind her.

"This way," he said, and led her forward into the sitting room. Two plush armchairs were arranged around a small round table that held a glass bottle of something dark brown—some kind of Creshen wine no doubt—and a half-empty glass. Other empty, unwashed glasses littered the room as well as books, some strewn open. Clothes sat piled and crumpled in the left armchair. He grabbed them and threw them carelessly into a corner.

"Have a seat," he said, gesturing to the now empty chair.

"Thank you," said Yenni as she slowly sank down into her seat. Weysh plopped into the chair across from her and held up the bottle. "Whisky?"

"Oh . . . no."

He shrugged and set the bottle down, then picked up his glass. Yenni watched him drink with a hard lump of fear in her throat. Zui and Harth were right. She had never seen Weysh like this.

"Weh-sheh, I heard what happened to you, and I am so sorry. You didn't deserve it."

Weysh examined his empty glass, tipped it back to drain the remains, and reached for his bottle to pour another.

"And I'm sorry I said you were nobody."

Weysh saluted her with his glass and took a swig.

"Please say something," said Yenni. "You—I have never seen you like this. I don't like it. It scares me."

Weysh leaned back in his chair and inhaled deeply through his nose, then shook his head, frowning. "How's your papa?" he said, though his voice was flat.

"Better," Yenni said, she took off her uniform glove to show him the rune. "See?"

He took her hand, and Yenni's heart fluttered at the warmth of his large palm. He squinted at the rune, and traced his finger along the red line of the injury to her palm, causing her to suppress a shiver. "Good, I'm happy to hear that." He let her hand go, and Yenni frowned at the twinge of disappointment, how cold her hand felt without his.

"And your studies? Are you confident you'll pass?"

"Yes, I'm doing well on my practice exams."

"Very good," he said. A cold silence settled between them, and Yenni let out a small noise of distress.

Weysh propped his face in his palm, looking moodily out the sitting-room window. "Are you even my Given anymore if I can't smell you?"

Yenni's stomach dropped but she threw on her royal poker face. "So your feelings are gone, then?"

He chuckled bitterly. "At the very least your scent is no longer driving me to distraction. Perhaps I'm a severed dragon after all."

"Severed dragon? What does this mean?"

"A dragon with no Given."

Yenni's stomach dropped further. "I see," she all but whispered. "Har-tha told me you might never be able to smell again. Is this true?"

Poor Weysh sighed right from his core. "It's possible. According to the healers at the hospice, that sizzling rat shit hit me with *pimentel*."

"What is pimentel?"

"Illegal is what it is. It's a concoction of poisonous minerals and spices used in the Colonial War to knock out a dragon's sense of smell. How he even came by it the Watcher only knows. I wonder if it wasn't some sick poetic justice on his part, since I'm part Islander."

"I am so, so, sorry Weh-sheh."

Suddenly his eyes snapped to hers. "Why did you come?"

She opened her mouth to tell him something, *anything* other than the truth. Some merciful fib that would let him go peacefully, if not happily on his way. But something had finally flickered in his dead eyes. The faintest flash of hope, and just like that she couldn't bring herself to lie.

"I care about you."

He sat back and crossed his muscular arms, raising an eyebrow at her. "Did Harth tell you to say that?"

"Think about what you just said, Weh-sheh."

A smile tugged at the corners of his mouth, tugged harder, and then he was laughing, and the strength of the relief that flooded through Yenni, that threatened to wring tears from her eyes, both soothed and panicked her.

He smiled softly at her. "Never change, Yenni Ajani," he said, and then cringed.

"What is it?" Yenni asked.

"I apologize for"—his brow furrowed as he searched for the words—"for planning your life for you, and for saying you would have women's duties." He looked her up and down and shook his head. "I've said some idiotic things in my time, Harth will attest, but I think that one will go down as a classic. I'm sorry that I disrespected you."

Yenni's heart fluttered harder in her chest as she met his mes-
merizing, jewel-toned eyes. As her gaze flitted down to those
sensual lips, his strong jaw, she was glad Weysh could not smell her.
Only through years of practice was she able to keep her face a mask.

"Thank you, Weh-sheh," she said, and dipped her head in that
queenly, magnanimous way her mother often did.

"Please don't take this the wrong way, but I have some experience with parental expectations. It's not right for someone to
dictate how another's life should be lived, especially someone as
extraordinary as you. You're so much more than simply someone's wife, mine or otherwise."

Yenni couldn't help it—the mask slipped, and she knew Weysh
saw her shock.

"You truly mean that?"

He nodded solemnly. "I do."

"You would leave me free to choose my own life, even if it
doesn't include you?"

"I've come to realize that there is no other alternative, short
of locking you away and keeping you miserable, and what's the
point of that, en? I would have you with me happily and willingly
or not at all," he said softly. "But I meant what I said. I will never
give up on you. And if you choose to leave, I'll be waiting until my
dying breath for you to return."

"But why?"

He held her gaze. "Why do you think?"

Dangerous, this was so very, very dangerous. Still, Yenni
could not stop herself. "But you can no longer smell my scent,"
she whispered.

He nodded again. "Indeed. I suppose that's how I know this
feeling is real."

Yenni stood and slowly went over to Weysh, taking his hands. "I cannot promise you anything, Weh-sheh. All I know is that it does not make me happy to be apart from you."

"Truly?" Oh the sweet hope on his face.

"Yes."

He beamed at her and gently pulled her to sit in his lap, placing a soft kiss on her cheek. He nuzzled her neck as his arms came around her, and Yenni let out an indignant cry at the feel of his bristly beard on her skin. Still, he felt warm and wonderful and Yenni didn't want to let him go, even though . . .

"Weh-sheh, how long has it been since your last bath?"

Weysh stopped nuzzling and groaned. "Never one to mince words, en? At least not with me. A while, I suppose. Apologies, my heart, it's one of the unfortunate side effects of having no sense of smell, and being mired in a depressive funk . . . *literally*, it would seem." He guided her to stand. "Give me some time to get ready and let's go somewhere."

"But shouldn't you rest?"

Weysh shook his head. "I've been cooped up in this very sitting room for the last two days. I even slept in this chair. I need to get out. You can study while you wait. I should have all the books you need here somewhere. I know my home is no palace but—"

"It's wonderful," said Yenni.

"En? Really?"

"Yes. It reminds me of you."

The boyish grin he gave her all but stopped her heart. "Well, great! I'm glad you like it. Maybe that means you'll want to spend more time here." His smile slipped into a smirk. "Perhaps even spend the night . . ."

"Go bathe, stinky dragon."

Weysh laughed that beautiful, honest laugh of his, and she had never been so happy to hear it. He started for the stairs at the back of the sitting room. "I won't be long," he said, clomping up the stairs. "And we can take off from the roof once I'm done. Happy studying!"

"Welcome back," Yenni whispered after him.

26

Weysh frowned his displeasure at the mirror. Had he really been going out in public like this? His beard was an itchy, wiry tangle, and he'd been getting by most days with his hair pulled back in a dark, messy knot that he now realized didn't do as much to hide its state of disarray as he'd thought. He sorely needed the services of a barber, but for now he'd do what he could.

At the moment his hair was wet from his shower, courtesy of Yoben's Rainfall. Typical dragon that he was, he had never been particularly adept at spellcraft, but he sure as hell did his best now.

"By source make my movement quick."

There was that familiar rush as source tingled and flowed through his limbs down to his fingers and toes, and he felt light, zippy. He reached for his comb, on the ledge above the sink basin, and it was in his hand in an instant. With the help of Harquette's Speed Burst Weysh combed through his matted locks, grunting through the pain. His beard he trimmed as best he could. By the time he was done his bathroom was a hairy mess, but the man in the mirror was far more recognizable. He dropped the spell, and with source no longer flowing through the channels of his magical nervous system, the strain on his body eased.

Weysh wrangled his hair into its usual loose braid and changed into a pair of dark trousers, a good linen shirt, and a long brown leather coat, the kind with the stiff collar that never went out of style. He thudded down the stairs like an exuberant schoolboy, a maelstrom of emotion fueling his adrenaline. He was still anxious about the damage to his sense of smell, and could still recall, with terrible detail, the suffocating pain of the pimentel if he thought too closely about it. And if he only let his mind stray to the barest thoughts of Noriago a blazing rage flared up in his gut. But Yenni was here, in his home. She'd come to see him.

She cared for him.

He clung to that, letting the warmth of it suffuse his heart, chasing away all else.

Weysh landed with a thud at the bottom of the stairs and Yenni glanced up from some textbook, startled.

"What—"

"Are you hungry?"

"Yes," she said warily.

"I know just where to take you. Come on!" He grabbed the wooden banister with one hand and held out the other to Yenni. She shook her head, smiling, but stood up and took it, following him to the second floor.

"I bet you miss Island food, en?" he said, glancing back as he led her down the hallway.

"Ah, you cannot imagine how much!"

"Then you'll love this place." Weysh took her past his bedroom and the bathroom across from it, to the end of the hall, where two glass-paned doors opened to a wide balcony. He led her up the wrought-iron steps to his building's rooftop garden.

"Pretty!" she exclaimed.

"Yes, I spend a lot of time here," said Weysh. It was walled by a perimeter of potted trees, and at the moment lanterns illuminated the wicker benches and trellises creeping with ivy and flowers. But the best part was the large open space in the middle, where he could lie during the day and sun himself in dragon.

Weysh pulled Yenni close, sliding his arms around her lower back. "It's romantic, wouldn't you say?"

Yenni snaked her arms around his neck. "You're looking and"—she sniffed him—"*smelling* much better."

Weysh groaned in shame but she only laughed. "Cruel little thing," he murmured. "And here I am about to take you to the best restaurant in Imperium Centre. You know what? I do believe I've given you enough free rides. From now on you have to pay a fare."

Her doe-like eyes went even bigger with mock concern. "A fare? But, Weh-sheh, I have no money! How can I possibly pay?"

Weysh put his forehead to hers and smiled down at those enticing, full lips. "How indeed," he said, and gently claimed her mouth with his. No other woman's kiss had ever been as soft and as warm, he was sure of it. He could taste the barest hint of her scent, and joy filled him at that. He pulled in her bottom lip, craving more. Her fingers threaded their way into his hair, their grip slightly painful, but not at all in a bad way. He relinquished her lips to plant soft kisses all over her face, savoring her delighted giggles. Then he hugged her close.

"I missed you, Yenni Ajani," he whispered in her ear.

"Call me Yenni, and I missed you too," she replied, and it sent a fresh surge of warmth straight to his heart.

Reluctantly he let her go. "Come, Yenni, we'd better get going or we might never make it to dinner, en?" He winked at her and she rolled her eyes.

He got some distance from her and changed to dragon, and Yenni's cry of delight was like the sweetest note of a symphony. She rushed to him and hugged his head against her, kissing him and running her hands over his scales and horns, and Weysh closed his eyes and hummed low in his throat at her petting. But as heavenly as it was, after a time he noticed that something was off. Yes, it was his Yenni, but he couldn't smell her, and it was like a part of her was missing. Weysh let out a hissing, disappointed sigh.

"What is it?" asked Yenni. "Weh-sheh, what's wrong?"

He sighed again.

"It is because you can't smell, isn't it?" She hugged his head again. "I'm so sorry, Weh-sheh. Mothers and Fathers!" she suddenly exploded. "I want to hunt down that worthless dragon and make him pay for hurting you! Do you want me to? In fact we could do it together. Just let me know."

Weysh nuzzled his face against hers and let out a soft growl. *No, I don't want to worry about Noriago right now. I just want to fly with you.*

"Yes, you're right," Yenni said. "We shouldn't let him ruin our time together."

He turned around and sank flat to the ground to let her mount, and once he felt her reassuring weight on his back, he took off for the lights of the city.

Δ

Weysh fluttered his wings, making a tight landing on the southern boardwalk. If you were looking for Island food, there was no place better than the docks, and *especially* no place better than Suli's.

"Hey! A dragon!"

"Perfect landing!"

A group of drunk young men, a mix of Creshens and Islanders, hooted and cheered at him on their way. Weysh let Yenni down and changed.

"Byen, I love the docks. It's the next best thing to Sainte Ventas," he said.

He took Yenni's hand as they walked beside the water. Various shacks and restaurants lined the boardwalk.

"Is that where your family is from?" Yenni asked over the cries of a fruit seller.

"It is," said Weysh. "My uncle and cousins live there. I'll take you to meet them sometime. Oho! Suli's is right up here."

As they closed in on the confection of colorful umbrellas out front, the music of the Islands wafted out to meet them.

"*Ko'ra!*" Yenni cried.

"En?"

"That stringed instrument! You call it maybe . . . a harp, or a guitar, but we call it a ko'ra. Oh, it sounds like home," Yenni said wistfully. Weysh smiled down at her.

Inside was busy as usual, but the conversation was set at a low hum, just under the romantic plucking and soft drums of the music.

"Aye! Is trouble come?" Weysh's friend Isaac weaved through the packed tables toward them. He worked as a host for Suli, sending money back to his maman in Sainte Ventas. Weysh sometimes took things back to Isaac's family for free when he was making a trip there to retrieve supplies for Suli.

Weysh gripped his arm. "Good man, Isaac."

"Is a long time from ah see you, brudda. Where you been, en?"

"Ah, well, you know. Here and there," said Weysh evasively.

"An' who is *dis*?" he said, flashing a gap-toothed grin at Yenni.

"I am Yenni Aja-Nifemi ka Yirba," said Yenni. She held out her hand in greeting but Isaac took it and placed a kiss on the back. To Weysh's surprise, it didn't concern him at all. Strange. Just a few weeks ago another man even looking at Yenni might have sent him into a jealous fit. Was it because he couldn't smell her scent?

"Welcome to Suli's," said Isaac.

"Tell me you have a table free," said Weysh.

"For you man, I'll build a table. I'll tell ol' man Suli you come, en? He gon wan' say hi. You wan' de patio?"

Weysh looked to Yenni.

"What is a 'de patio'?" she asked.

"Outside, lovely."

"Oh! Yes, that sounds nice."

"The patio it is," Weysh told Isaac.

"All right, brudda. Gimme half a secon', en?"

As he left them waiting by the entrance Weysh squeezed Yenni's hand. "Well?"

"Perfect," she said happily. "Your friend Isaac is very nice. His accent reminds me of my friend Diedre's, but it is much thicker."

At last Isaac took them to a prime table for two right by the water.

"I have never been to a restaurant like this before," said Yenni. "It's nicer than a pubs."

Isaac laughed. "But Weysh, where you find she?"

"She's from the Moonrise Isles," said Weysh, smiling fondly at Yenni.

"Is so? If ah known is women so pretty out dey I'da visit long time." Isaac grinned at Yenni, then pointed at Weysh. "If dis one step outta line you know where to find me, en?"

"No, thank you," said Yenni. "If this one steps out of line, I know exactly how to put him back in his place."

Isaac laughed. "Weysh, brudda, hang on to she, en?"

"I intend to." After everything they'd been through, he'd be a thrice-damned fool not to do everything in his power to make her want to stick around.

Isaac gave them menus. "Ah comin' back jus' now," he said, and left them.

Yenni studied the menu, occasionally piping up excitedly. "Oh, fish and dumpling soup! And fried plantains with sweet pepper sauce! And . . . oh! Curry goat!"

"We're definitely getting the curry goat," said Weysh. "It's likely the only thing I'll be able to taste. Order whatever you like, lovely. Get the whole damned menu if you want."

She very nearly took him up on his offer. When all was said and done their table was piled with various dishes that hung precariously close to the edge.

"Bon appetit," said Weysh. It was a testament to Suli's skill that even with his diminished sense of taste the famous curry goat still hit the spot. But he got far more enjoyment out of watching Yenni. She sampled each dish like a child let loose in a sweet shop, moaning in delight with each bite.

"Mmm," she said, swallowing a piece of plantain. "The food is not quite the same as what we have on the Yirba islands, but it is familiar, and all very delicious. Thank you, Weh-sheh. I needed this," she said, gesturing around. "Island music, Island food, Island people . . . something recognizable."

"Oh? And why is that?"

Yenni told him what had happened in her class with that weaselly professor.

Oho! I knew it! Weysh wanted to shout. He had *known* something was off about that phony professor, but he held back. The last thing he wanted to do was push his luck.

"I can't say I'm surprised," he said instead.

"Really?"

Weysh nodded. She was bound to bump up against this sooner or later.

"I sometimes feel torn between three different worlds: Islander, Creshen, Dragon. The emperor presents us to the world as a sophisticated metropolis, repentant of our past mistakes, now home to any and all. But make no mistake—deep down many Creshens still consider themselves superior to everyone else, and it will come out in their actions if not their words."

He'd experienced that firsthand himself when growing up. In the first year of second school he'd fallen in with a group of three other Creshen boys, and for a good half year they were inseparable, bonded by their love of pranks and mischief. That winter break Weysh introduced his friends to Harth—who went to a different, more exclusive and expensive school—and they instantly absorbed him into their gang. And despite what came after, Weysh still fondly remembered that era as one of the most entertaining periods of his childhood.

This friendship continued into the next year as well, even though their classes changed and they were no longer constantly together. However, in one of his upper-year classes Weysh met a new friend—Isaac.

He introduced Isaac to his gang with the same enthusiasm he had Harth, but he noticed something was different. They weren't as receptive. When one day, confused, Weysh asked why they weren't as welcoming to Isaac, his friend Philippe spelled it out for him.

"Isaac is great, Weysh, he's funny and all, but do you think he can keep up? What if he can't afford to go to Pascal's with us after school?"

"En? So what?" said Weysh. "We'll go somewhere else. Pascal's is overpriced anyway. And if worse comes to worst, I can pay for him."

By then Weysh's uncle had taken him on to expand the delivery company from sea to air, and paid him handsomely for it. In fact, Weysh and Isaac had bonded over the fact that they were both working to put themselves through school. Weysh for his uncle; Isaac at Suli's.

"You shouldn't have to do that," said Philippe. "Besides, it would just embarrass him. Look, Weysh, he's a nice enough fellow, but he just doesn't fit in with our crowd. It's probably best you do your own thing with him when you're not with us, for his sake."

But after that, Weysh found it just wasn't as fun hanging around with Philippe and the rest anymore.

And, ah Movay, he wasn't immune. He'd assumed the same thing about Yenni, expecting that his modern Creshen townhouse would impress her when she lived in a thrice-damned palace.

"Weh-sheh? Are you all right?"

Weysh shook himself, focusing on the present. "Yes, sorry,

lovely." He broke off a piece of flat bake to scoop up some salted snapper. "I guess we're no longer killing and pillaging, so there's that. Still, no matter what pretty words the emperor and the powers that be may spout, it will be a long time before the colonies are perceived as equal. They're like the bastard children of the Empire, as it were. Perhaps that's why I'm so close to my maman's Island side of the family. That and she would ship me off there every school break to get me away from my stepfather."

He popped the bake and snapper into his mouth, only to choke at the peppery sting of it. He had such a visceral reaction he was forced to spit it out lest he empty his stomach. It brought him right back to when he was on the ground of the chapelle, his eyes swollen and streaming tears. Thrice-damned Movay, he'd always loved spicy food. So Noriago had ruined that for him as well. Rat prick.

Yenni didn't seem to notice. She frowned into space, lost in her own thoughts. "But I have met kindhearted Creshens in my time here. Captain Augustin, the woman at the pubs, Har-tha."

"Oh, indeed," said Weysh, pulling a plate of sweet, *non*-spicy plantains to his side. "I have many Creshen friends as well. I *am* Creshen, for the blessing of Byen. I'm not saying to write us off entirely, but curb your expectations, en? Sometimes just when you let your guard down someone will pull something shady, like this professor. It's disappointing, but as a society we still have a long way to go."

"I see. I hope—I hope my family is not like that. I have considered telling them about the rune, but it seems wrong somehow."

"I think anyone with power is bound to abuse it at least a little. There have certainly been times when I've thrown my weight around as a dragon. You've just got to do your best to treat people fairly, en?" Yenni rested her hand on her fist and watched him. "What?" he asked, wondering what could be going through her head.

"That was a more thoughtful answer than I expected." She smiled at him. "How did you do it, Weh-sheh Nolan?"

"Do what?"

She shook her head. "I can't think of anyone I disliked more than you on first meeting."

Weysh cleared his throat. "Ah, well, that is . . . perhaps I did come on a bit strong."

Yenni gave him a flat look, and a flush of embarrassment crept up the back of Weysh's neck, which he rubbed self-consciously.

"Fine, I was an ass. And I *am* sorry, truly. But it's been half a year and I've already learned so much and grown so much thanks to you. You make me better, Yenni."

Yenni's eyebrows raised. "*I* cannot make you better. I have neither the power nor the will to do so." She poked him in the chest. "You are *choosing* to change. Furthermore, I am not perfect either."

"You are," Weysh murmured, bringing her hand to his lips.

She smiled. "Weh-sheh?"

"Yes, my heart?"

"I am glad I did not kill you that day when you flew me into the cave."

Weysh chuckled. Coming from Yenni that was as good as a declaration of undying love.

"Me too, lovely, me too."

Isaac came around a few more times to chat with Weysh and see to their needs, and eventually Suli tore himself away from the kitchen to visit. It didn't seem to matter to the old cook that he owned one of the most popular restaurants in the city; he said his place was in front of the stove and that would never change. He left the business end of things to his eldest daughter and her husband.

Weysh grinned from ear to ear at the sight of the older Island man. He was light skinned with a slight paunch in his belly and a ring of close-cropped, salt-and-pepper hair that refused to grow past the middle of his skull. He'd always reminded Weysh of his grandfather. The minute Weysh saw Suli coming, he stood: nothing less than a bear hug in greeting would satisfy the old man.

"Weysh!" he said in his gravelly voice. "Is you come to eat out meh whole kitchen, en?"

He gave Weysh a couple of affectionate thumps on the back and let him go.

Then he turned to Yenni. "Good evening," she said. "I am Yenni Aja-Nifemi ka Yirba." She stood and held out her arm like a proper lady, then gasped as Suli swept her up in a hug as well. Her shocked eyes met Weysh's, and he had to bite down on his lips to keep from laughing.

"Welcome, welcome!" said Suli.

He stayed and chatted as well, expressing similar shock that Yenni was from the Moonrise Isles. "Imagine," he said. "Is tree hundred years dis war done, an' Sunrise Isles an' Moonrise Isles stay like oil an' water. You know who is to blame for dat, en?"

As with Isaac, Weysh did not tell Suli that Yenni was his Given. Things were going remarkably well, and he didn't want to put Yenni on the spot and upset her.

"What a pair, de first woman of the Moonrise Isles to study in Cresh, an' de world's only Island dragon."

"Oh!" Yenni exclaimed, as if the thought had just occurred to her. But Weysh sighed. Suli was fond of telling everyone Weysh was the world's only Island dragon.

"For the Blessing of Byen, Suli. I keep telling you my dragon side is Creshen. The creature that sired me is certainly not an Islander."

"You is a dragon?" Suli asked.

"Yes."

"An' you is an Islander?"

"Of course."

"Den you is an Island dragon."

Weysh knew this was an argument he would never win, and he couldn't help but enjoy the way Yenni was looking at him, as if she were seeing him for the first time again, so he simply nodded. "As you say, Suli."

At last they finished up, and Weysh spent a good five minutes arguing with Suli, trying to pay, but the old cook wouldn't take his money, so Weysh insisted he would make a free run for him sometime in the future.

Weysh and Yenni headed back onto the boardwalk, strolling aimlessly. For someone with no sense of smell, Weysh was inconceivably content. His stomach was full, the night was warm and vibrant, and he walked hand in hand with his Given. Hard to believe that only hours ago he was sulking in his den, surrounded by empty whiskey glasses.

"Weh-sheh, there's something I want to ask you," said Yenni cautiously.

"What is it, lovely?"

"Before, you said that your sister's father is not your own, and today you said your mother wanted to get you away from him. Why is that?"

Weysh sighed. "Well, Yenni, that's a long story, but I suppose it's time I told you."

As they navigated the boardwalk, awash with the light of gas lamps lining the way, he explained the circumstances of his birth, what his mother had done and what was done to his mother. Every time he glanced at Yenni her pretty eyes were a little wider, a little sadder.

"The man who sired me is a rapist," Weysh finished, struggling to say the words. "Does that disgust you?"

Yenni squinted at him. "Have you ever forced a woman against her will?"

"Never!" he hissed.

"Then why should this disgust me?"

"Ah, my heart, you don't understand. They don't teach you this in class, but being a dragon is a twice-pointed sword. As Byen's divine warriors, we're expected to be model citizens. Rape, violence, these things aren't unheard of here, but for a dragon—a *mated* dragon—to commit such a crime is inconceivable. Guste is known as one of the most terrifying psychopaths in decades. I believe if it had been any another man of high standing, my maman would have taken the brunt of the blame. But Guste underestimated our society's reverence—and fear—of dragons. He was disowned by his family and exiled once everything came out. Rightly, too, demon that he is. He's likely on one of the smaller islands somewhere. So thank the Watcher the man who raped my mother was dragonkind, en?" Weysh muttered, bitter.

Yenni squeezed his hand, her only response.

"There are those who feel that somehow his madness has been passed on to me," Weysh continued. "I can't say I've done much to dissuade the notion. I probably shouldn't have bounced from woman to woman as I did but"—he sighed—"it was comforting."

"Those people are wrong," said Yenni with all the finality of a princess making a royal proclamation. Weysh squeezed her hand back and bent to touch his forehead to hers.

"Thank you, Yenni."

He wanted the night to go on forever, but as they reached the edge of the boardwalk and the planks yielded to the black ocean, Yenni stopped and turned to him. "This has been such a wonderful night, Weh-sheh, the best I've had since coming to Cresh, but we should get home. We still have exams to pass."

"I don't suppose you'd like to come back with me?" he asked hopefully, but Yenni shook her head.

"Not tonight. Please take me back to my suite."

Weysh nodded. "So be it. But you must pay the fare regardless. It's doubled, by the way."

"What? Doubled? But why?"

Weysh shrugged. "Supply and demand, lovely. There's nothing I can do."

"This is, how do you say it, *extortion*!" she said in mock outrage.

"You're royalty, you can more than afford it. Now come here and stop being cheap."

He took her soft face in his hands and kissed her. The dings of the buoys, the music, and the lapping of the ocean against the boardwalk all fell away. For long moments there was nothing but warm, sweet Yenni.

"I collect the first half on setting out and the second half on delivery," he murmured once they broke apart.

"That was at least ten fares in one!" Yenni cried.

"Nope," said Weysh, grinning at her. "As long as we remain

unbroken it counts as one. You really should have studied up on Creshen economics before leaving the palace, Your Highness."

"Oh shut up, Dragon," she said and lightly slapped his arm. "Well, tell me this: what happens if I refuse to pay when we reach my destination?"

"I'll simply fly around with you on my back until you do. Forever, if need be. That, or I might eat you."

Yenni's mouth dropped open. "Weh-sheh," she whispered. "Have you ever . . ."

"Oh, Kindly Watcher! *Really*, Yenni? Now who's being ignorant?"

"Well, I mean to say . . . so the answer is no?"

Weysh rolled his eyes and shook his head. "No, Yenni, I have never *eaten* someone, but there's a first time for everything, and you're looking particularly delicious right now, so don't tempt me."

"If you do, I will give you the worst stomachache you have ever had in your life."

Weysh threw his head back and laughed, loud and free. "Come, let me get you home before I get myself in trouble."

27

It wasn't until a week later, when they had both finished all their exams, that Yenni consented to go out with Weysh again. Aside from agreeing to study with him, she insisted on putting off any outings until they were done.

"It's important that I pass these exams and remain here," she told him, and he couldn't exactly argue. So when not with Yenni, and not running through drills, he'd spent the majority of his time with Harth and Zui, who were both happy and relieved to see him somewhat back to himself.

Yenni had finally accepted the riding gear he'd bought her all those moonturns ago, so to celebrate the end of exams Weysh took her for a long nighttime flight. They went past the city, and even past the surrounding farms, and Yenni never once asked where they were going. But after perhaps an hour he felt her began to shift and squirm, even despite the riding pants. Weysh gave her the signal and swooped down onto a grassy plain where one giant tree stretched its thick branches skyward, as if reaching for the full moon.

She dismounted and sat cross-legged, and he lay down and put his large dragon head in her lap. They sat listening to the cool breeze rustle the grass and the cricket's lilting serenade. White lantern flies rose up from the grass, glowing silently around them and tingeing the air with magic.

"Look at that moon," Yenni said as she stroked the scales of his face. "It's so big, it makes me want to dance."

He made a high moan she correctly interpreted as *Why?* She was very good at understanding his communication in dragon.

"Right now on my island it is the Big Moon Festival. Every year I danced on the beach with the other girls of my tribe."

He made another sound, a low grunt, and she laughed.

"All right, I'll show you."

She got up and moved away, then she began to dance, skipping and jumping and swinging her arms and rolling her hips as the lantern flies bobbed around her. She was lost in a rhythm only she could hear, and didn't seem to notice when he changed to a man. Byen, she was so graceful and strong, her movements sensual in an effortless way. She probably wasn't even trying to seduce him, but at that moment Weysh wanted nothing more than to throw her down on the grass and slowly tease her the way she was now torturing him.

"You are so *achingly* beautiful," he said.

She stopped and faced him, and as the crickets chirped and the leaves and grasses whispered, they simply stared at each other.

Weysh sat on the grass with one knee up, and he opened his arms to her. "Come here, my heart."

Yenni smiled shyly and shook her head as she took a step back.

Weysh raised an eyebrow. "What's this?"

"You will have to catch me," she said, taking another step backward.

Weysh narrowed his eyes, and as he surged to his feet Yenni shot off, laughing. The two of them pounded through the grass. He was fast, but she was *quick*, even without her runes. Her lithe form darted like a doe ahead of him, and he couldn't catch her. She reached the tree and scrambled up, and sat taunting him as he stood huffing below.

"You can't reach me up here, Dragon."

"And what makes you so sure?"

"Because your hand is the size of my head, you big brute. By the time you haul yourself through these tight branches I will be halfway back to Imperium Centre."

He surveyed the tangled network of tree limbs. This was true. And it wasn't as if he could fly up in dragon and perch like a crow.

But she had never seen him half-change. Even as she sat swinging her legs and sing-songing at him he reached for his inner trigger. He felt the horns stretch from his head, felt the cool air on his bare torso once his shirt whisked away to otherspace at the touch of his wings. But thanks to the Law of Self-Preservation there was no pain. His nails became talons, but he stopped himself from changing fully, though it was a challenge to maintain, like walking on one's hands.

With a few strong pushes of his wings he rose, coming to land in a crouch beside her on the thick branch. She gasped.

"Don't be afraid," he said. His voice had always been deep, but now it was not much more than bass, closer to his dragon's rumble.

"Weh-sheh?"

"Yes, it's me," he said and moved toward her, pleased when she didn't scoot away. "This is called half-change."

"Oh."

"We don't do it often, because it's difficult and tends to make people uncomfortable. It scared the piss out of my maman the first time I did it as a child."

"Your eyes are quite something."

"They're my dragon eyes."

"Oh," she said, mesmerized. She touched his horns, then cupped his cheek.

"You're not bothered?" asked Weysh.

"No," said Yenni. "It's like seeing both you and Dragon at the same time. Amazing."

"Yenni, I *am* Dragon. We are one and the same," said Weysh, and he covered her hand where it rested on his face. "Whatever you feel for Dragon you feel for me."

"Not quite," Yenni whispered, and smiled at him.

Weysh stood up on the massive branch, digging his claws in for balance, and reached a hand out to Yenni.

"Come, let's get down."

She went to him and he wrapped her in his arms, then jumped, gliding them safely to the grass. He kept his arms around her as he slid out of half-change back to a man.

"My fare?" he asked.

"What? For that little hop?"

"A man has to make his living somehow, lovely."

"So if I am understanding correctly, you will starve and die without my kisses?"

Weysh put his forehead to hers. "Precisely."

"Oh, I would not want that," she said. Weysh laughed softly, took her chin in his hand, and gently brushed her lips with his, teasing. He did it again, and again, with slightly more pressure each time until finally Yenni grunted in frustration and threw her arms around his neck. She kissed him with such searing passion that by the time she was done his head spun like he'd polished off a whole bottle of cheap wine.

"Wha—" He squinted at her. "Where did you learn to kiss like that?"

"Instinct," she said.

"Is that right," he said dryly, but he could hardly fault her for having kissed or even slept with other men in the past. Byen knew he hadn't exactly been celibate. He tuned out the insecure whispers trying to stoke the embers of his jealousy. It was *him* she was kissing now. "Well, I don't care how you learned to kiss like that, as long as you promise to do it again," he told her.

In response she embraced him and put her head against his chest.

"Yenni," he said, running his fingers through her braids. "I want to introduce you to my family. As my Given."

She was silent, too silent. In the quiet the whispers of insecurity grew louder.

"Yenni?"

She looked down at the grass. "If I meet your family then this becomes real."

Weysh let her go, frowning. "It's already real, at least to me it is. But if you'd rather not meet them yet, then I won't force you."

Yenni stepped back and wrapped her arms around herself, chewing on her bottom lip. "Weh-sheh, when I first met you, you were just like everyone else who has ever told me who to be, how to act, how to live. But now you listen to me, and respect my freedom to choose. Why?"

"Because I love you," he said. It came out easily, like singing in the bath, like the truest truth in the world. He was no longer in love with the idea of her, but *her*: Yenni Aja-Nifemi ka Yirba, the Moonrise princess who beat up thugs, mastered complex spells in a matter of weeks, and always spoke her mind.

"I know you can't say it back yet, but you will," said Weysh, to himself as much as to her.

Yenni opened her mouth, closed it, then nodded. "Take me to see them."

28

A few days later, near the end of their midyear break and after Yenni had confirmed—with great relief—that she had passed all her midyear exams, Weysh flew her to his family's manse. Now he stood in front of the familiar white double doors with their engraved borders, his stomach a knot of nerves. He wished he could smell what Yenni was thinking.

At Yenni's request, he didn't reveal her royal lineage to his family, and just as well. His maman had gone into a fit over Yenni, sending him multiple notes a day through the hourly post, based on the assumption that his Given was simply a wealthy international student. Watcher only knew what it would have done to her if she realized she was entertaining a princess.

Montpierre would be dining with them as well, which was the main source of Weysh's apprehension. But he couldn't keep running from his problems, and he refused to let Montpierre keep him cowed. It was important to him that his family meet Yenni. As his Given, she was his family too. He would simply have to do

NANDI TAYLOR

his best to maintain his composure. It was Weysh's first meeting with Montpierre since his outburst, and he wasn't sure if he was glad to have Yenni with him for support or worried about embarrassing himself in front of her.

Beside him, Yenni wore the Prevan uniform for formal events. She hadn't had the chance to buy any dress wear before the mugging. Weysh had offered to buy her something, but predictably, she'd refused. It was just as well—many students wore their uniforms outside of school as a sign of prestige, and as with anything she wore, Yenni wore it well. She was decked out in a long-sleeved green dress that clasped up to the neck, accented with two rows of silver buttons. She also wore black gloves, tall black boots with a small heel, and a sloping, wide-brimmed hat.

And—Weysh smiled—the ivystone necklace he'd given her.

Weysh raised the fancy brass knocker and gave the door a couple of raps. "We don't have to stay too long," he said under his breath as he waited for the door to open. "If you want to leave at any time just give me the word, en?"

Yenni squeezed his arm and smiled knowingly at him. "I will try to last as long as I can," she said, tugging at the neck of the dress. "I am eager to get out of these clothes."

Weysh bit back his own retort about getting Yenni out of her clothes.

Good. Be good.

But something must have shown on his face, because she squinted at him. Thankfully, Genie opened the door and saved him.

"Master Weysh, welcome home," she said, her eyes twinkling.

Weysh laughed. "*Master* Weysh? Really, Genie?"

Genevieve simply pursed her lips, holding in laughter.

"This has Maman written all over it. Very well." He took Yenni by the shoulders and gently guided her to stand in front of him. "May I present Mam'selle Yenni Aja-Nifemi ka Yirba."

"A pleasure to meet you," said Yenni, bowing her head.

Genevieve took Yenni's hat and gloves and led them into the dining room.

Sylvie, Montpierre, and Maman stood at the back of the room as if posing for a portrait. Weysh caught Sylvie's eye, gave her a smirk, and bowed to them. "Mam'selle Yenni Aja-Nifemi ka Yirba of the Moonrise Isles," he said again, as if announcing the empress herself.

His maman glided forward and slapped him lightly on the shoulder in reprimand. "I know you're mocking me," she said as she hugged him, then turned her attention on Yenni, and they greeted each other palm to palm. "Welcome to our home. I am Bernadette Nolan and this is my husband, Montpierre, and my daughter, Sylvie."

Sylvie curtsied—*curtsied*—while Montpierre acknowledged Yenni's nod with one of his own.

"Please call me Yenni Ajani," she said.

"Oh, Weysh, but she's lovely!" his maman exclaimed. "Come, come let's sit!"

Weysh and Yenni sat together on one side of the table, while Sylvie and Maman occupied the other and Montpierre took the head.

"Your hair is beautiful, Yenni Ajani," said his maman. "Where do you get it done?"

Her hair hung on either side of her face in her signature mini-braids, though they were getting longer now, well past her chin.

"I do it myself."

"Oh! Truly?"

"Yes, it's a common skill among women on the Moonrise Isles. My mother was forever telling my sisters and me that a proper lady must know how to braid her hair—unless she prefers to wear it shaved, of course."

"That's quite wise. What I wouldn't have given to be able to do that growing up." His maman's own loose curls were currently corralled into an updo.

"I can show you some simple styles, if you'd like," said Yenni.

Genie arrived with the precourse: slices of peppered mango and pineapple.

"So, Mam'selle Yenni Ajani," said Montpierre as he fluffed out his napkin, "what are your plans once you complete your year at Prevan?"

Thrice-damned Montpierre, could they not have just a few minutes of polite conversation first? Weysh breathed deeply through his nose and focused on Yenni.

"I'll return home," she said simply and took a dainty bite of mango. "Oh, delicious!" she exclaimed.

"Hmph." Montpierre turned to Weysh. "And do you intend to return with her?"

"Montpierre!" his maman whispered. Sylvie watched Weysh with interest.

"I have no plans to move," he said truthfully. In the days since their reconciliation, Weysh and Yenni had danced around the subject of the future. For Weysh's part, it was enough that they were finally getting along. But he knew they would eventually have to figure out how to make a life together.

And apparently so did Montpierre. He raised an eyebrow. "So you plan to live leagues apart? What will you do, visit each other on holidays?" he asked skeptically.

Yenni put down her mango and raised her chin, meeting Montpierre's eye. She gave him a charming smile. "We have not yet decided the details of our future. I know how concerning this must be to you—as a parent—but I assure you, messer, you will be among the first to know when we do."

She said it so perfectly, with just the barest hint of sarcasm, so that to anyone who didn't know her she would seem sincere. Byen above, he loved her.

Yenni let her gaze sweep over his maman and Sylvie. "Thank you so much for inviting me to your home. The food is wonderful— oh!" She lightly touched Weysh's hand. "But you cannot taste it."

His maman frowned. "What does she mean you can't taste it, Weysh?"

He winced—apparently while Harth had gone against his wishes and informed Yenni about the attack, he hadn't told Weysh's family. Weysh gave them an abbreviated story of what happened at the chapelle.

"Oh my goodness! Weysh!" Sylvie cried.

"How could you not tell this to us?" his maman cried. "Montpierre! You must book him an appointment with Healer Veronique."

"I've already been to a healer," said Weysh.

"Whomever you went to see, Healer Veronique is better," said Montpierre. He paused to cough into his handkerchief. "If it's money you're worried about, I'll pay the fee."

Weysh stiffened. "This really isn't necessary—"

"Weysh!" said Maman. "What is more important, your pride or your health?"

"How far do you think you'll make it up the ranks as a dragon with no sense of smell?" said Montpierre.

That jolted him. In his bliss over his progress with Yenni, he hadn't considered how his injury could affect his career. Panic began to spark and sputter in his chest, and he did his best to hide it as he answered. "Very well, you make a valid point, Montpierre. I'll visit your healer. Thank you."

Montpierre simply grunted.

Despite the initial unpleasantness, the rest of dinner went remarkably well. The women did most of the talking, with Maman and Sylvie asking Yenni questions about the Moonrise Isles. She answered skillfully, gracefully dodging the questions that would out her as a princess by asking questions of her own.

As Genevieve cleared away the last course Sylvie excused herself, and Yenni continued to make conversation with Maman.

"I do hope you'll visit us again," Maman told Yenni as Genevieve served dessert—a summerberry pie with the crust so perfectly browned it reaffirmed Weysh's decision to see Montpierre's Healer Veronique as soon as possible.

"It would be my pleasure," she said, and Weysh could tell her smile was genuine.

They were almost done with dessert when Weysh realized he'd seen no sign of Sylvie. Her pie was getting cold.

"Maman, Sylvie's been gone a while," he said.

She blinked. "Oh! Yes, where has that girl gotten to, I wonder?"

Weysh had a bad feeling. "I'll go find her," he said. He felt a slight pang of guilt for leaving Yenni alone with his parents, but she could more than handle herself.

"Sylvie?" he called, making his way toward the main staircase. "Sylvie?"

As he paused on the first landing he heard sniffling. The landing gave way to a small powder room, and the door was slightly ajar. Through it he saw Sylvie standing in front of the looking glass, dabbing at her eyes. Frowning, he pushed the door open.

"Sylvie?"

She spun around. "Weysh!"

"What's wrong? Who do I need to roast?"

"You weren't supposed to see me," she said, her voice wavering.

Weysh crossed his arms and raised an eyebrow as if to say *Out with it*.

But Sylvie shook her head. "Today is going so well. Even Papa is being good. I didn't want to ruin it. I'm so happy for you, Weysh, happy you've found your Given, but—" Fat tears started rolling down her cheeks again.

"But?"

"You'll definitely follow her to the Islands."

"Sylvie, as I told Montpierre, I have no plans to leave—"

"Oh, don't give me that!" she cried. "Yenni Ajani is incredible. The way she talks, and eats, even the way she moves! She's like a *princess* or something! I can't see you convincing her to stay here, and I can't see you letting her go without you."

"*If* we were to move to the Moonrise Isles," said Weysh slowly, "what's to stop you from coming with us, even for just a while?"

"And leave Maman alone?"

"She's not alone, she has Montpierre."

"Papa is dy—" Her voice hitched and she broke down into gasping sobs.

Weysh's heart just about broke as he wrapped his arms around her. "Byen, Sylvie," he whispered against the top of her head. "You've been under a lot of stress lately, en?"

"I know I'm being selfish, but I can't help it," she whispered.

"No," said Weysh. "I haven't been here for you like I should. I can only imagine what you must be going through."

"Weysh, are you sad that Papa is sick?"

Weysh was silent for a minute. "I suppose he's the closest thing I've had to a father since Grandpapa died. I'm not happy to see him suffer," he said diplomatically.

"I'm scared," she whispered. "I don't know what's going to happen when—" She closed her eyes and gulped. "And then to lose you too? It's too much, Weysh."

"You are not going to lose me, Sylvie." But even as he said it, Weysh knew Yenni would not want to live in Cresh indefinitely. Not when she was a princess of her tribe, and not after the ignorance she had experienced here. Weysh's cheeks burned with shame at the realization that he had been a big contributor to that ignorance.

But then what of his plans? His whole life's ambition had been to make something of himself in the Imperial Army, prove Montpierre wrong, and support his family without having to run Montpierre's business. How was he to do that and live with Yenni?

Kindly Watcher, show me mercy, he prayed. Sometime soon, he and Yenni would have to have a very difficult discussion.

29

Yenni had much to think about over the five-day break after mid-year exams, and she had come to a few decisions.

First, she would not to mention the Watatzi rune to her family. After endless deliberation and prayer, she'd decided it was not her place. If the Sha intended for the Yirba to have the rune, they would reveal it to the Yirba Masters. If she mentioned it, she was sure her mother would only push her for more information, especially as it had already fallen into the hands of the Creshens. She might even be able to coax the rune from Professor Devon, if she changed her tune, but she was loathe to do so. It just didn't seem right. Though she couldn't completely shake a nagging sense that she was being disloyal to her tribe, she was confident that she was following the will of the Sha.

Furthermore, she had to find a way to warn the Watatzi about Gilles Desroches. They were not necessarily an ally of the Yirba, but neither were they an enemy, and Yenni felt that if it was her tribe's runes being pilfered she would certainly want to know.

Perhaps she could write them in Creshen; *someone* must be able
to understand it if they could communicate with Desroches. And
perhaps Weysh could fly her to their Island at the end of the year,
when she was free to leave Cresh.

As for Weysh, after much deliberation and prayer she had
made no decisions regarding Weysh.

For the moment, her most pressing resolution was that she
could no longer work with Professor Devon if he insisted on
teaching the deception rune. She knew it could jeopardize her
chance to stay at Prevan, but she couldn't in good conscience
enable Devon's thievery. Her father was well, and surely the Sha
could not punish her for boycotting sacrilege. If resigning from
her position affected her status, she would simply have to find
another way to stay, because Mother Shu knew she wasn't yet
ready to leave, to say good-bye.

Professors normally returned to their offices the day before
classes resumed—with the exception of Mainard, of course, who
seemed to need no break at all. So on the last day of the hiatus,
Yenni made her way to Devon's cramped office in the basement
of the administrative tower. From the doorway she spied him
frowning over some text, mumbling to himself and scratching
notes on a piece of paper. She knocked on his open door.

"Yenni Ajani!" Devon cried, and gave her a relieved smile.
"You're a sight for sore eyes. Come in, come in!"

Yenni was about to sit when she felt the air vibrate with ach'e.

"*Ab-alfar by source's path,*" pronounced Devon.

He suddenly appeared on the other side of the desk, a few
paces away from Yenni. She pulled instinctively on her speed
runes and darted back.

"Oh, my apologies," said Devon. His face was red with exertion and his chest heaved slightly. "I take it you've yet to see a demonstration of Yasna's Teleportation, en? Advanced magic, that."

Advanced indeed! The Yirba had a rune to do something similar, but only her parents, her brother Dayo, trusted lieutenants, and of course their Masters knew how to draw it. Yenni had begged Dayo to teach her, but he had never relented. It was up to their parents or the Masters to decide if and when she ready to learn a royal rune.

"You said something I did not understand in that spell, Professor. Aba . . . abala . . ."

"Ab-alfar," said Devon. "It means *through space* in San-Uramaik."

"San . . . what?"

"The ancient language of incantation," said Devon. "Advanced spells contain words in San-Uramaik. There are even powerful spells that can be cast only in San-Uramaik. It was the language they were born in after all. So Yasna's Teleportation makes use of *ab-alfar*, through space, because it's a means of using otherspace to move instantaneously from one place to another." Devon leaned against his desk. "How went your break?"

"Very well," said Yenni.

"Excellent to hear!" said Devon. "And I'm thrilled to see you this afternoon. I must admit—"

Yenni held up a hand, cutting him off.

"Before we continue there is something I must say."

Devon blinked. "Oh?"

"Yes. If you insist on supporting the proliferation of the stolen Watatzi rune, I will have to resign as your teaching assistant and leave this class."

Devon's mouth dropped open. "But isn't that a bit extreme?"

"No, it is not," said Yenni.

"But you can't leave! Please! I beg you to reconsider!"

"You will not change my mind, Professor Devon. I will be honest: while I am grateful for your quick thinking in finding a way for me to stay at Prevan, my gratitude will not preclude me from doing what is right. I do not need this class—there is nothing you can teach me about runelore."

Devon clutched the desk, frowning in thought. After a long, uncomfortable silence he finally answered.

"Perhaps not, but there is still much I can learn from you." He turned earnest eyes on her. "I apologize. Please don't leave, Yenni Ajani. I have no say in what Gilles Desroches and the High Magus Council may or may not do, but you'll hear no more about the deception rune from me."

"Truly? Do I have your word, Professor?"

He nodded. "Yes. Whatever it takes."

"Good. Then I will stay on."

He exhaled, long and relieved. "Thank you. Now let's put all this ugliness behind us, en? We've still got the second half of the school year to get through." His brow furrowed once more. "Just four moonturns left to us. Is there nothing I can to do tempt you to stay on a year longer? I really do enjoy having you here."

She shook her head. "I'm sorry, Professor, but I'm needed at home."

"I see," he said sadly. "Well, we must do what we must do. I'll simply have to learn what I can from you in the time we have left."

"I'm happy to be of service, Professor. And thank you for your understanding. I'll see you in class tomorrow."

"I look forward to it."

Yenni left Professor Devon's office in high spirits. Perhaps her initial assessment of him was true after all. He was one of the few Creshens she'd met who even *attempted* to hold the runes of the Sha in the proper esteem.

She went straight back to her suite, intending to spend the next few hours reading ahead in her magic texts. Weysh was coming that evening to take her on one last flight before classes started. She was looking forward to a semester of learning, free of the stress of her father's illness and the confusion of politics back home.

Until the post arrived an hour later.

Yenni was out on her little balcony, curled up as best she could be on the wooden chaise longue the school had put there. She longed for the soothing sway of a softgrass hammock, but she'd thrown the bed cushions—which she never used for sleep anyway—on the outdoor lounge and done her best to make do. The fresh air and view of the green, drooping trees lining the southern walkway were worth the mild discomfort. She was deep into lesson twenty-two of *Defensive Spellcasting: A Modern Overview* when a metallic creaking from inside alerted her to the arrival of the post.

Yenni grinned with excitement: perhaps this was finally news from home! What had those devious sisters of hers been up to? And Dayo, he must be so relieved now that their father was well and could resume his normal duties. And her younger brother, Jumi—was he taking good care of Ofa? He'd better not be flying the poor creature here and there every day, tiring him out. And what of her mother? At the thought of home Yenni opened her palms, happily examining the runes her mother and father had drawn.

A moment later that happiness was leaking from her like blood from a mortal wound. Yenni blinked and brought her hands right up to her face, her eyes darting between each palm. She was mistaken. She couldn't be seeing this, not now. It *couldn't* be true.

It was.

Her father's rune was as strong as ever, but the rune on her right side, her *mother's* rune, had faded.

How long ago had this happened? She hadn't been paying much attention to the linking runes since her father's recovery, and she certainly hadn't been comparing them, but clearly she should have been.

"Why?" Yenni gasped as she scrambled up from the chaise longue. "Why, Almighty Sha? What have I done wrong?"

She dashed through the open balcony doors and came to kneel before her letter box. Yanking the door open, she found it—at long last—stuffed with brown papua rolls. Yenni plopped down on the hardwood in front of the door, frantically opening and scanning each message to find the one from her mother, until she tugged on the twine holding one of the rolls and it resisted. She tugged and tugged, but it held tight. Confused, Yenni held up the roll and inspected it, and found a strange rune painted there, one that was oddly similar to the calligraphy for *Yirba*. She pulled ache to her fingertips and sent it into the rune. It glowed, and the twine fell away.

Yenni's eyebrows rose. Well *this* was new. What was so important it needed to be shielded so? There was little chance of Creshens being able to read their discourse in Yirba, so what were her parents trying to hide? She unrolled the scroll and found a message in her mother's tight handwriting. Yenni devoured the letter with her eyes.

Oh, my brave and precious child,

It was a day of joy to rival the awakening of the sun
when you were placed in my arms. Because of your
counsel, your n'baba has regained his strength. You
were right to go abroad, my daughter. This concept
of divine ach'e leading to sickness is not something we
Yirba could have fathomed.

On your advisory, I gently suggested to the men
of the Healers' Guild that drawing on ach'e could be
contributing to the chieftain's fatigue, and through their
testing they discovered something quite alarming. It is
not ach'e that causes this illness, but a spirit that feeds
on it.

Yenni paused at that. "A *spirit*?" she whispered.

The more ach'e runs through the body, the more this
spirit feeds and grows, but it is never sated. When the
host is not pulling on runes, this evil spirit will simply
turn to the body's network for ach'e, weakening it, so
that by instinct the body turns to muscle, breaking it
down to bolster the body's waning magical system. We
have not yet discovered a way to destroy the spirit, only
to lure it to another host.

"Oh, Iyaya, no," said Yenni aloud, gazing sadly at her mother's
faded rune. She sighed and continued to read.

By the time this message reaches you, you may have

noticed that the rune of linking from me has faded. Be not afraid, my sweet child. I have simply taken on your n'baba's burden, to give him time to heal and rest. He has been pulling runes for many moonturns, fighting a threat we have been forced to hide. Even shielded as this missive is, I dare not say too much. I will simply leave you with the wisdom of our ancestors, who say to be wary of encountering malicious spirits, for where there is one there are four more.

Oh, my Yenni. My heart cries out to have you home again, but you may well be safer in Cresh. If nothing else, you have pledged a year abroad to the Sha, and you must complete your Orire N'jem. But we will see each other again soon. Your n'baba sends his love as well.

May the Sha smile in your direction.

Your iyaya,
Jadesola Iyunde-ola ka Yirba

"What?" Yenni whispered to herself. What was her mother talking about? What threat? Why would she be safer away from home? She dove back into the papua rolls. Perhaps one of the other messages, from her father or maybe Dayo, would provide some answers.

The next letter she picked up was in fact from her brother Dayo, and it did nothing to ease her distress.

Kebi, he wrote.

I have missed you. You have done well, and I'd expect nothing less. The Sha have blessed us with Father's recovery, but still I urge you to be careful. With Father's health improved, those who were counting on the chaos of his death to make their move may now turn their attention to you. Yes, we have cordial relations with the other tribes, for the most part, but if history has proven anything it's that there are always those in each tribe who lurk unfulfilled, imagining themselves revolutionaries and hungry for power. And for such opportunists a princess of the Yirba would make for valuable bargaining stock. Though I have faith in the Almighty Mothers and Fathers, and faith in you, my strong and stubborn kebi, please proceed with caution.

The rest of the letter was an update on life in the palace compound and on the main Island. He ended the letter by saying he hoped to see her very soon. It mentioned nothing about this threat her mother had mentioned. Perhaps he wasn't aware of it.

I miss you dearly, Kebi, wrote her sister Ifeh in the next letter. *We are already planning a huge feast in your honor upon your return.*

Natahi ka Gunzu has been by to pay his respects to N'baba, wrote Jayeh. *He seems quite taken with you. I think you will receive a special present from him soon.*

Yenni's breath caught in her throat at that, for what else could her sister mean but marriage beads? It was the custom among the Northern Sha Islands for a man to send a beaded necklace to his intended. An acceptance of the necklace would be a tacit acceptance of the engagement. To reject the proposal she would have to snap the necklace and send back the scattered beads.

Time was running out. Yenni cradled her head in her hand, sighing. If only she knew more about this threat her mother referenced. How could she put her family and her tribe in further danger by rejecting a prince of the Gunzu? And what would it look like, her engaged to a common Creshen? What would people think?

Who cares what people think?

She did. She shouldn't, but she did. The comparisons to her sisters, the comments that she was unladylike, that she should grow up and settle down, they infuriated her.

And shamed her.

Wearily, Yenni reached for the last unopened roll.

Agbi, wrote Jumi, addressing her as "big sister." *I want to visit but Iyaya and N'baba won't let me. By the way, I have been flying with Ofa every day since you are not here to stop me. I am sure he likes me more than you now. He will not want to fly with you once you come back. Ha! Ofa is mine!*

To Yenni's surprise, instead of irritating her, Jumi's teasing helped relieve the aching tension between her eyes, and left her with a sharp longing for home. She gathered up her letters and took them to her writing desk, where she took out a sheet of heavy paper and a pencil and began her letter back. She wrote to her mother.

Iyaya, she began. She wanted to keep the letter informal, a daughter pleading to her mother. *You are right, I was quite scared to see that your rune had faded, and your news of a threat to our Islands alarms me. Please take care, both you and N'baba. If there is anything you can tell me, anything at all, please let me know.*

Perhaps there is something I can learn here that will help. The Sha are not done with me yet.

Tell Dayo not to be too concerned for my safety. I have met

She paused. Now would be the time to mention Weysh, but how could she even begin to explain him to them, when she wasn't even sure what he was to her?

I have met a dragon and we are Given, and we will eventually marry.

No, no, they would not take kindly to that at all.

I have met the world's only Island dragon, and we must rethink my engagement to Natahi ka Gunzu. It may be more prudent to align ourselves with dragonkind.

Too mercenary, and they had been working to build relations with the Gunzu for far too long to simply switch alliances for something unknown.

I have met the world's only Island dragon, and we are bonded as Given. I believe this may be the reason I was compelled to undertake Orire N'jem.

But then what of her father's illness?

Not one of those statements felt right. Yenni grunted in frustration—clearly she wasn't yet ready to tell her family about him.

I have met strong friends here, dragons. And as always I am able to protect myself. I learn more about Creshen magic and battle every day. Tell Ifeh and Jayeh I look forward to their feast, and tell Jumi that no matter how much he flies with Ofa, my field sphinx will never forget me.

Yenni sighed and scanned her letters again. There was a folded note on cream-colored paper she hadn't noticed in her haste. She flicked it open.

Lovely,

*Meet me in the library, our usual table under the split
birch tree. I have a surprise for you.*

Weysh

Speak and the spoken appear, as the Creshens said. Strange, he
usually came to get her from Riverbank Chambers. But it was just
as well—she could certainly use a surprise. Leaving the unfinished
letter on her desk, Yenni went to change into her riding clothes.

Δ

She found Weysh just where he said he would be, absorbed in a
book. Normally he would glance up when he smelled her coming, but now he didn't even notice her until she called to him,
poor thing.

"Weh-sheh."

He looked up, smiling, then stood and bowed to her.

Kalele meyen, he said. In Yirba. *Good evening, my princess*—or
at least that's what he'd tried to say. Mother Shu, he could be adorable when he wasn't being exasperating. She put a hand to his
cheek, and he leaned down so she could kiss him.

"Where did you learn that?" she asked.

"Partially from this," he said. He held a book in one large hand.
"You've been learning so much about Cresh, I figured it's time I
start learning about your culture. Did I say it right?"

"Not really."

"Byen, Yenni, can't you let me have this?"

She laughed. "Well, you said you wanted to learn my culture."

Weysh took her hand. "Come, I want to borrow this book. It's an encyclopedia of kingdoms on the Moonrise Isles, pretty much the only book I could find with anything useful."

Once he'd checked out the book and stuffed it into his hip-satchel, they strolled aimlessly from the library, neither concerned where they were going as long as they were together.

"Now, lovely, tell me where I went wrong."

"Well, you pushed the words together, to form two words, when really it should be four or five."

"Four *or* five?"

"Yes. You said, *kalele meyen*, but it should be *kale'le mm'e'yen*."

"Kale-le meyen, like this?"

"Almost, but you need to draw out the *mmm*—this is how you say *my* in our language."

"How?"

"Like this. *Mmm*."

"I'm so sorry, sweet, I need one more demonstration."

"Mmm—" She stopped when she realized what he was doing and slapped his arm. "Weh-sheh!"

He chuckled. "I do like how you make that sound, lovely."

"Why must I be constantly subjected to your perversions?"

Weysh took her hand and kissed her palm. "Yenni," he murmured, rubbing his thumb over the area he had kissed. When he flicked his eyes up to her they twinkled with mischief. "This is nothing."

Her cheeks burned. Weysh affected her like no other man had, and every day it became harder and harder to picture a life with Prince Natahi, or any prince for that matter. But how could she make a life with Weysh, especially given today's revelations? They had so much to discuss, and it was time to stop running.

"Weh-sheh, we have much to talk about. My parents—"

"Oh!"

They made the turn onto the path that led to the lecture halls and Yenni found herself caught in Carmenna's dismayed gaze.

"Weysh, Yenni Ajani, excuse me." She gave them a small, awkward bow, her hair falling forward to obscure her face, and began to hurry away.

"Ah! Carmenna, just a moment," said Weysh hastily. "Have you seen Noriago recently?"

"Not since that day in West Castle West."

"Do you know what that Noriago did?" said Yenni. "He attacked Weh-sheh with some kind of powder and now he cannot smell. If you know something you *must* tell us!"

Carmenna glanced down at their joined hands, and guilt pooled in the pit of Yenni's stomach. She let Weysh's hand go.

"I heard," Carmenna admitted. "Everyone is talking about it. I'm so sorry, Weysh. That's just horrible."

Yenni saw Weysh sniff the air instinctively, trying and failing to read Carmenna's scent. "You truly don't know anything?"

She glanced once more between the two of them. "No, I'm sorry," she said softly.

"I see," said Weysh. "Well, please be careful, Carmenna. Noriago is clearly unhinged. Academy security have him on a watch list, and every dragon on campus has their nostrils open, so to speak, but off campus try not to be alone, en?"

She nodded. "I'll be cautious. Thank you for your concern." She paused and glanced between their two faces again before she said at last, "Congratulations."

"Erm, thank you," said Weysh. He cleared his throat. "So, I don't suppose you've learned of a way to heal pimentel damage in any of your classes, en?" He said it jokingly, but Yenni could sense the desperation underneath.

The look Carmenna gave him was full of sincere pity. "Nerve damage is some of the most difficult to heal, Weysh," she said sadly.

"Weh-sheh will be just fine," said Yenni confidently. "He's going to his stepfather's healer and—ah!" The mention of Weysh's sick stepfather reminded her of her own, and of the wither-rot. "I have some news! My tribe has discovered the cause of the wither-rot!"

"What?" cried both Weysh and Carmenna. Without going into too much detail, Yenni explained that her mother had relayed Mainard's information to the healers back home, and what they had deduced.

"So it is this spirit that is making people sick," Yenni finished. She watched Weysh and Carmenna expectantly, but they were both giving her a familiar look—the same uncomfortable shifting of the eyes some did at the sight or mention of runes.

"What is it now?" Yenni cried.

"A spirit is causing this illness? You mean, like a demon?" asked Carmenna.

"Yes! A demon."

Weysh blew out a breath, and Yenni rounded on him. "You do not believe me?"

"No, no! It's not that, lovely. It's just, well, it's hard to believe in general, en?"

"But why is that?"

"Well, no one has encountered a demon for over a thousand years, if records are to be believed," said Carmenna. "If demons have returned to the realm of folk, well, we have much bigger problems than the wither-rot."

"Nevertheless, that is the cause," said Yenni with utter finality.

"Yenni, my heart, perhaps it's best we keep this to ourselves for now, at least until your people have had more time to investigate and gather more information—"

"There's no time for that!" said Yenni, throwing up her hands. She pointed accusingly at Weysh. "Your own stepfather is ill! In fact, I think I will go to see Professor Mainard right now."

"No!" yelled Carmenna and Weysh together.

"Yenni Ajani, you and I both know what Mainard is like," said Carmenna. "He'll want hard proof before . . ."

She trailed off at Yenni's dismissive hand waving. "He can gather all the proof he needs. I'm simply letting him know what our healers have discovered. It's the right thing to do—many lives could be saved. We haven't yet discovered how to kill the parasitic spirit; we merely lure it from one body to the next, but perhaps with Cresh working toward the same goal, a solution will be found faster. Come, Weh-sheh, it shouldn't take long. Good-bye, Carmenna, thank you again for everything." Yenni put her fingertips under her chin and bowed to Carmenna before taking off for the administrative tower, consumed with her new mission.

"Be well, Carmenna!" she heard Weysh call behind her.

"Good luck?" Carmenna called back uncertainly.

30

Yenni asked Weysh to wait at the bottom of the administrative tower. It would be hard enough dealing with Mainard *without* an audience. Still, she held out hope from her last encounter with the taciturn professor. He'd given her more information about the wither-rot, after all, and perhaps he still held some goodwill toward her after she had, well, saved his life.

Despite her nerves, she was able to work the lift up to Mainard's office, and was soon standing in his open doorway, once more confronted with all of his glorious clutter. She spotted him pondering a shelf crammed with books, his back turned to her.

Yenni knocked on the open door. "Professor Mainard, I would like to speak with you."

He jumped and spun from the shelf. "Mam'selle Kayerba?" He frowned. "Oh, you would, would you? Hmph, have a seat, I suppose."

Yenni settled on the sofa across from his desk, perched between a pile of books and the armrest. One would think a man so obsessed with rules and order would be more organized, but apparently not. Mainard took up his seat behind his desk, watching her impatiently over his tented fingers. The less time Yenni spent in close quarters with Mainard the better, so she got right to the point.

"Professor Mainard, I know what is causing the wither-rot."

Oh, but his face! Mainard fixed her with the most incredulous glare she had ever seen. He didn't speak—it seemed he was so shocked he *couldn't*, so Yenni went on.

"The illness is the result of a parasitic demon. It feeds on the body's magical system, weakening it, and pulls strength from the muscles and flesh of the body."

Mainard rubbed at the bridge of his nose and let out a long-suffering sigh. "Not this claptrap again. Mam'selle Kayerba," he said patiently. "If demons had returned, surely I, a Magus Grande and member of the magical council, would know about it. This illness has a perfectly scientific explanation that, I will admit, eludes us, but we will find the answer soon enough."

"It's true," Yenni insisted. "My father has made a recovery thanks to the work of our Healers' Guild, but they haven't yet discovered how to destroy the spirit—they have only lured it to another host. But with Creshen healers *and* Island healers working toward a solution we can figure out how to defeat it, and many lives can be saved!"

Mainard's mouth puckered in disgust. "If your papa has seen a recovery, then he wasn't afflicted with the wither-rot in the first place. I've no doubt he *was* afflicted with some sort of Island parasite, but a demon? Laughable."

Yenni took a deep breath through her nose, desperate to soothe her rising temper. She needed her wits about her to do battle with Mainard. "You said, 'Not this again.' What did you mean by that? Did someone else come to the same conclusion?"

"That's none of your concern," Mainard snapped. "Furthermore, you will refrain from spreading your unfounded superstitions throughout my academy, do you hear?"

"I will do no such thing!" said Yenni, standing. "Do you not see that we can save so many—"

Mainard also stood. "Mam'selle Kayerba! I understand that things are different where you are from, but here there are rules that must be obeyed! Should you cause unrest by disseminating false information there will be consequences. *Legal* consequences. Is that clear?"

"This is lunacy," Yenni said through her teeth.

"Is. That. *Clear*, mam'selle?"

She gave him a curt nod, which was all she could manage without screaming in his face, and marched from his office.

Δ

Outside the administrative tower, Weysh took one look at her face and said, "Let's go for a flight."

He changed on the grass and Yenni fairly jumped on Weysh's back, eager to be away from stubborn Mainard, the campus, Cresh itself if she could. However, even with Weysh's warm, reassuring bulk beneath her and the wind whistling its sweet tune in her ears, Yenni's mood stayed resolutely irate. The rainbow houses of Imperium Centre passed by in a muddled blur, largely unappreciated. How Yenni wished she could reveal to that bullheaded Mainard her true status as the chieftain's daughter. Perhaps then he would show her the respect she was used to. But she knew that would be unwise. Dayo's warning was not lost on her, and even if her brother was being overly cautious in warning her not to reveal her identity, there could be Creshens who might seek to capture her for ransom. Creshens like those who had attacked her in the alley. She wouldn't go without a fight, of course, and she had her friends to help her, but it would be nonsensical to put herself in unnecessary danger. Father Ri was always ready and waiting to instruct the foolish.

They couldn't have been flying for more than a quarter of an hour when the sky began to rumble and flash so suddenly Yenni half wondered if she'd drawn the storm with her ire. Weysh screeched, letting her know they would have to cut their flight short. He glided a few minutes more, his neck bobbing and stretching as he scanned the landscape, until finally he shrugged his wings and let out that familiar cry that meant he planned to descend.

They landed among the ruins of some Creshen structure. Yenni slipped off Weysh's back and ran through the warm spring rain, which hissed and splattered on the cracked stones of a wide pathway. She darted past rows of chipped white arches that bordered the path on either side, and headed for the relative shelter of a high and crumbling dome at the path's end. As she ducked inside she heard Weysh's splashing footfalls behind her. Yenni stood in a dry corner under the arched ceiling, folding her arms as she surveyed their temporary shelter. Broken stained-glass windows revealed the overcast sky of the storm and stubborn blades of grass pushed up through the cracks between the floor.

Weysh sat against the wall beside her. "Apologies, lovely. I can usually smell a storm coming. We'll have to stop here for a while. Lightning and flight are not a terribly good mix."

"What is this place?" she asked.

"It was a chapelle—a place to pray and worship. Some rich noble must have built it but then fallen on hard times and couldn't afford the upkeep."

Weysh patted the spot beside him, but Yenni was too full of restless energy to sit. She paced back and forth in the small dry patch where the high dome of the roof didn't leak.

"How can he be so stubborn?" she fumed. "Not only did Mainard dismiss me, he says I cannot tell anyone about the demon that causes the wither-rot, or I will be reprimanded legally." She jerked to face Weysh. "Is this true?" she demanded.

"Erm, I'm no barrister, but I believe there is some law against the spread of harmful information, yes. Mainard has something of a reputation for being self-important—I had him as an instructor myself for one of those mandatory first-year magic classes, but it's not completely unfounded. He *is* a Magus Grande. He has clout, Yenni, and power."

"Unbelievable! So many deaths could be prevented—your stepfather's, for example! But this disease will continue to fester and grow within Cresh, all because of the idiocy of one man. So be it, but if our Yirba healers should find a way to destroy this evil spirit instead of merely shuffling it from host to host, I *will* make it known."

She continued to pace, muttering to herself about how these closed-minded Creshens would be the cause of their own demise.

"You're making my head spin, lovely," Weysh said. "Come, sit with me."

She settled in beside his warmth, and his rough fingers stroked the back of her neck. "Relax," he said softly. "Listen to the rain."

It sighed and pattered heavily against the chapelle's roof,

landing in musical droplets in puddles on the floor where the roof failed to shield. A black lizard, maybe the size of her hand, crawled almost shyly across the floor toward them, coming in fits and jerks. When it was about two strides away from Weysh it burst into flame.

"Ah!" cried Yenni, jerking away from it.

Weysh ran a comforting hand down her arm. "It's only a salamander, sweet. Nothing to be afraid of. Sometimes they come out and ignite when it rains."

"Oh, truly? Even though they are creatures of fire?"

"Consider it the wisdom of Byen—they ignite only in the presence of water. Imagine what would happen if salamanders were igniting all over dry fields in the heat of summer. I suppose the flames keep them warm in the rain or some such. If they get too close for comfort just use Yoben's Rainfall to put them out and they'll scamper away."

Another eruption of flame caught her attention somewhere to her left. Then another, by the entrance. The creatures slowly made their way toward them, illuminating the chapelle like candles. One got close enough for Weysh to touch, and he ran his fingers through the flames sprouting from the creature's back while Yenni gaped at him. "Does that not hurt?"

"Not if I concentrate," he replied absently. "Then it simply feels warm. The perks of being a dragon," he said, and winked.

"They like you, they know their own kind," Yenni teased.

"Erm, Yenni, you should never call someone dragonkind a salamander. It's considered very rude."

"Oh! I'm sorry. I did not realize."

Thunder crashed outside, and Weysh wrapped an arm around her shoulder, giving her a squeeze. "Don't trouble yourself, my heart. You didn't know. Oh! Speaking of culture clashes, these salamanders remind me of something. Do you have your paint with you?"

"Not *my* paint; Professor Devon's mixture. But, yes, I always carry some."

"Well, remember that conversation we had in the library some moonturns back, when you painted me with a rune? Why not try painting me in dragon? We've got some time to kill after all."

"Oh!" said Yenni. "Yes, let's try it!" She welcomed the distraction.

Weysh pushed off from the wall and made his way to the center of the circular chapelle, right among the rotting wooden benches that ringed the space. He spun slowly, judging the distance, seemed to come to some conclusion, and the next moment he was in dragon, errant raindrops plopping on his scales. There was just enough room for Yenni to scoot around him. She stroked his face and kissed his warm nose bridge, smiling at his low, delighted hum. Taking out her paint from her satchel, she bade him lie flat. She painted the rune for wind right there on his nose bridge, ach'e welling in her throat as she softly sang the hymn.

"There, now try to activate the rune."

Yenni watched, breath held with anticipation, for the familiar glow, but nothing happened. "Weh-sheh? What's wrong? Can't you do it?"

He closed his pretty jewel-tone eyes and let out a soft, hissing sigh. *Let me focus.*

She watched him, silent before the rain's serenade. He breathed deep, his large body expanding, then exhaled. The rune flickered and glowed, and a burst of warm wind fanned her face.

"You did it!" Yenni cried, and clapped her hands together. "Incredible! Come, let's try it again."

She tried painting a wind rune under his chin, and after a few moments of concentration he blasted her with that one as well. Yenni shuffled around him, painting different parts of his body—his leg, a wing, his tail—dodging and shooing curious salamanders as she went. She sent a silent prayer to Ib-e-ji that the creatures wouldn't set the rotting benches ablaze, damp as they were. In fact, she drew two quick water runes on the backs of her hands just in case. But whether the Sha had heard her, or just by their own natural instinct, or perhaps fascination with Weysh, the salamanders stayed clear of the wood.

With some effort, Weysh was able to use all the runes Yenni painted. She found that the bigger the rune, the more fierce a gust he was able to produce. It seemed his bigger body needed a bigger anchor.

"Well, this has been a great success!" Yenni said happily.

Weysh changed and grinned at her. "That it has! Casting magic in dragon, who would have ever thought it. We should show this to General Sol—she's head of the dragon division at Prevan."

"Absolutely!" said Yenni.

"And I'll have to practice so I can put on a proper demonstration for your family, en?"

"Oh, yes."

"And when might that be?"

Yenni paused, her silence filled by the crackling flames from the salamanders, until finally Weysh crossed his arms and grunted. "Have you even told them about me?"

"Not yet."

"I see."

That stung him, she could tell. As always she could see his emotions plain on his face. He was warring with himself. He likely wanted to challenge her as to why, but was reluctant to undo the progress they'd made by starting an argument.

"I need time," she said before he could speak further. "To decide—"

Decide what? If she wanted him? She could no longer deny that she did. If she was brave enough to bring him home? If her happiness was worth a war?

"—how to tell them," she finished.

She knew that answer didn't make him happy, but he nodded all the same. With each day that passed she came closer to the crossroads, to the decision she knew she must make.

But not today.

"The storm has passed," said Weysh, and in truth the rain was nothing more than a light drizzle now, the crashing thunder long gone. "Shall I take you back?"

"Oh, so soon?"

"Yes, I should get in some melee practice."

"Oh, all right."

Strange, it was usually her who suggested they head back. Nevertheless, he led her out of the chapelle ruins, changed to dragon, and took her back to her residence. She paid the toll, and he received his fare with enthusiasm, but watching him wing away to the training sands, Yenni couldn't shake a strange sense of unease.

31

In the following weeks Weysh found himself somewhat subdued. His recent success with Yenni had been cause for elation, but there was still much they needed to overcome. Their conversation at the chapelle ruins was a sobering reminder that she hadn't truly pledged herself to him. He'd been plagued by strange fits of melancholy since Noriago's attack, and it wasn't a pleasant feeling to know the one you loved didn't quite feel the same way about you. Coupled with how she'd dropped his hand like a hot coal when they'd bumped into Carmenna, he might almost believe she was embarrassed by him.

So it was with a troubled heart that Weysh flew to the offices of Montpierre's Healer, Veronique, but he did his best to remain optimistic. She was quite in demand, and it would normally have been a few moonturns before he could see her, but after hearing the nature of his injury she'd decided to bring him in as soon as possible, and even then it took a good three weeks. Weysh wasn't sure whether to be relieved or anxious about her urgency.

She kept her offices in a three-story townhouse in the upper-class district of Empress Way. The main floor was manned by a pale and pointy-nosed clerk who directed him to fly up to the rooftop and wait for the healer there.

She clearly had experience with dragons. The rooftop was paved in the same soft mixture as the roads of Sir Lamontanya, and surrounded by a simple wrought-iron fence. Weysh lounged in dragon, waiting. At last a short, plump woman of perhaps sixty years emerged from the rooftop door. Her crisp, gray Healer's robes were accented by a white stole that drooped over her shoulders, denoting her as the highest order of Healer Magus. Weysh rose and bowed to her.

Her blue eyes were sharp and assessing as she examined his nose. She had him sniff a few vials and shone a light up his nostrils, looking for Watcher only knew what. Though Weysh worried he might accidentally sneeze and roast her, she went about her examination fearlessly.

She had him change to a man and sniff the same vials, asking him if he could smell or feel anything, which he could not. The way she clucked and hummed at his answers did not fill him with confidence.

"Yes, it seems both of your bodies are affected," she said. "This is often the case with nerve damage or injuries to the brain in dragonkind. It's one of the biggest blows to the theory that the dragon body is a separate entity hidden away in otherspace.

"I won't mince words, Messer Nolan: the damage is quite extensive. I've only come across two cases similar to this in all my time as a healer. I can prescribe you a sniffing potion I came up with. It's infused with old magic, spells completely in San-Uramaik. It will stimulate the nerve endings in your nose, encouraging them to regenerate. I should have it ready for you in the next two days. Sniff it for five minutes in the morning and again at night, both in human and dragon."

"And that will repair my sense of smell?"

The healer clucked her tongue at him again in a motherly way. "I hope so, but it will never quite be what it was, I'm afraid. We're attempting to bring the dead back to life, after all."

"I see." Weysh had to close his eyes against the sinking despair that suddenly engulfed him. He would never be a whole dragon again. Never fully smell spicy-sweet Yenni, or metallic Harth, or flowery Maman.

A warm, soft hand squeezed his upper arm, and he opened his eyes to Healer Veronique's sympathetic gaze.

"Walk with Byen, Messer Nolan," she said softly.

Back outside, the bustle of the city and the sunny day seemed to mock him. The hope that his sense of smell might come back, which had buoyed him through the days after the attack, fell apart like paper in the rain, until he found himself stumbling like a drunk, his legs weak. It was all he could do to direct himself to the alley between two overpriced boutiques and sit with his head between his legs.

He felt dizzy and sick, as if he'd spent the night before drinking barrels of beer. Could emotion truly affect someone so physically? What was to become of him now? His future, his post in the Imperial Army? How was he to protect Yenni? He was a *dragon*, he was not used to this *helplessness*! The idea that someone had come along and just taken something so important from him, just *taken* it, and there was nothing he could do—the buzzing, maddening violation of it was overwhelming. It was a new, unbearable form of pain, but one that made him want to scream all the same. This was his life now—the world as he had known it through sharp and magnificent scents was lost to him forever.

He sniffed, then frowned. Why was his nose running? A reaction to the sniffing vials? He wiped at it, and felt more moisture collected right at the crook of his nostril. Tears. He was crying. When was the last time he'd cried? From *sadness*? Weysh tipped his head back to try to stop them, but that only sent them cascading down his neck, into the collar of his shirt. So he simply gave up and let the tears fall.

$$\Delta$$

When Weysh at last dragged himself from the alley and changed to dragon, even that took none of the edge off his misery. When he set out from the city center he'd intended to go home, skip his classes, and lick his wounds. But in the end it wasn't his townhouse rooftop he closed in on, but the familiar red brick of his family home.

Why am I here? he thought, even as he knocked on the door. Genie opened it and welcomed him warmly.

"Is Maman up?" Suddenly he realized he very much wanted to see her.

"Bright and early, as per usual. She's having a morning cup of coffee in the back garden—whatever is the matter, Weysh? Your face is as long as a horse's!"

Weysh shook his head. "Nothing I'm too eager to get into now, Genie. Don't worry about me, I'll be fine."

A lie.

Genie led him through the house, clucking and tsking her concern the whole way, but she didn't press him. His maman was

sitting on one of the white wicker chairs scattered among the pav-
ing stones. She turned, her face surprised and then warm at the
sight of him.

"Weysh, lovely! Come sit," she said, reaching for him. He took
the seat across from her.

With her free hand she squeezed his. "I do love it out here
in the mornings," she said, and breathed deeply, as if she could
inhale the low, musical cooing of doves, the green of the trees, the
red of the roses, the cool, dewy grass of the lawn.

Weysh kissed her hand. "Good morning, Maman."

"I'll leave you to it, then," said Genie, bowing. She left them
in private.

"To what do I owe this pleasure?" asked his mother, and Weysh
was gratified to see she looked genuinely happy to see him.

"I just came back from Healer Veronique."

"Oh!" She put her coffee cup down with a clink on her saucer.
Her brows scrunched up in concern and she seemed, at last, to
catch the gravity of his expression. "And?"

Weysh did his best to swallow the stubborn lump in his throat.
"It seems I'll never fully regain my sense of smell."

The pity on her face nearly undid him all over again. She
reached over and stroked his stubbly cheek. "My Weysh, I'm so
sorry."

"I hate this feeling," he snarled. "It's the most maddening
thing, Maman, like . . . like . . ."

"Like someone has stolen something you did not even know
could be stolen."

"Yes." Yes, that was it. Like life as he'd always known it had
been suddenly and swiftly stolen from him for good. "Everything
is different now. What about the future? My career? Now that I

can't smell, it's as if I'm worth . . . less." He stared at his hands, fingers hooked loosely together between his knees, as he struggled to articulate what he felt. "As if I'm not as important, or valuable, en? Do you know what I mean, Maman?"

"Yes I do, and I also know you're wrong. You're still *you*, my heart. What's more, you're still a flying, fire-breathing dragon. I'm positive the army will find something to do with you." She slapped his arm playfully, and Weysh knew he should reward her attempts at humor, to cheer him with a laugh or smile, but he simply couldn't muster it. The mirth left her face, replaced by something hard and serious.

"You listen to me, Weysh. No matter how others may look down on you, or try to tell you you're somehow diminished, devalued, or incomplete, they are *wrong*."

There was fervor in her the likes of which he'd rarely seen, and it struck him, clear as a pealing bell, that she was speaking to herself as well. Her eyes went suddenly dull, and she slumped back into her chair, defeated.

"Maman?"

"I'm sorry," she whispered. "I always told myself I'd never treat my own children the way I'd been treated growing up and yet I should have protected you better. From the world. From Montpierre." She said her husband's name so softly Weysh practically had to read her lips. She inhaled a shaky breath. "I have not been a good mother to you, and I know I can never undo that, but from here on I want to be more supportive of you, of my child. Can you forgive me?"

"Yes," Weysh said instantly, warmth tingling all though him. "I think I can understand, if only a little, how hard it must have been." She took his hand again, and they sat just like that for a while, mother and son, while the morning birds chittered and chirped above.

But at last Weysh broke the silence. "I think I'll get going before Montpierre awakes. I've been through enough for one day."

Guilt and sadness crossed his Maman's face like a shadow, but she said only, "Take care of yourself, my love. Shall I tell Sylvie?"

Weysh shook his head. "I'll let her know when I'm ready." He stood and kissed his mother's hand before letting it go. "Thank you, Maman. It was good to talk to you," he said, and to his amazement he meant it. He never would have thought it possible, but he was actually leaving a visit home feeling *better* about himself. The knowledge that he would never smell like he used to was still devastating, but something was back, and pulsing under the despair like a heartbeat.

Hope.

32

The season of rain has given way to the heat of summer, and Yenni breathes deeply. Home. The air smells of home—of tangy tamarind and sweet-spice and grilling crab. Of dust and soil and clay. And the people of the market sing, even as the women kneel and the men lie flat to the ground at their passing.

"Here is our princess! Welcome, welcome, Princess!" *The song is taken up, drowning out the calls of food sellers, the lowing of cattle, even the drums in the distance. They sing to Weysh too.* "Oh praises, our dragon, our dragon has returned—oh! Our dragon has returned!" *He is close, just behind and a bit to the left of her, never letting her out of his sight. The roads are wide enough for him to pass, as they are made to accommodate goat and cattle herders, donkey carts, field sphinxes, and fleet cats. The message of the drums mimics the voices in the market. Boom bam boom!* "Our princess is here!" *Boom bam bam boom!* "Our dragon is here!"

The royal market compound rivals the jungles and bao plains for places that own Yenni's heart. Perhaps it is because she spends so much time here that her family has put so many resources toward it: soldiers to keep the streets safe, servants to keep the streets clean, carpenters and artisans to keep the streets beautiful. It is full of activity, with farmers and herders, fisherwomen and sailors bustling to and fro. They carry urns full of water or baskets of fruit or fish on their heads, though they quickly lower them to prostrate to her and Weysh. She touches the fingers of one hand underneath her chin and gives them a small bow, as is proper.

As much as Yenni enjoys the farmers and fishmongers market, the best is yet to come. High up on the palatial hill, right beneath her home, the artisans converge. Instead of buckets of crabs and bundles of bananas, the stalls and shops are hung with hundreds of reams of colorful fabric, woven in prints that tell the story of their history. Figures with no faces represent the Sha, and above hang masks of imps and elephants and even dragons. The entrance to the artisans quarter is marked as the dusty road turns to deep green tiles. The clucking of chickens recedes to be replaced by the high cries of blue and green peafowls. The shouts of foodmongers fade to murmurs of civilized bargaining—though no one has ever bargained with her. Most artisans push their wares on her free of charge, much like the woman before her.

She has rich, dark skin that shines, and her gown and head wrap are of a matching pattern of green and yellow. She kneels before Yenni, holding out a sculpted figurine. It is a naked woman, carved of heavy wood and painted a deep brown-red, overlaid with a pattern of white flowers, and Yenni knows her instantly as Mother Ya—Mistress of Storms.

The figure is surprising, as few worship Mother Ya any longer. Young women of her tribe are encouraged to build relationships with Mother Shu, the facilitator of love, or Mother Ye, who protects babies in the womb. But, oh, how Yenni is drawn to this figurine. She runs her fingers along the smooth wood, lost in the pattern of delicate white flowers. So entranced is Yenni that it is a while before she notices—under the distant singing, soft bargaining, and pounding drums—that Weysh is growling.

Yenni spins around. "What is it?" Weysh is crouched low on the tiles as if ready to spring, and all of his sharp teeth are bared. No one is singing now, and the drumbeat has changed to something faster, urgent.

"War!" they cry. "Attack! Attack from above!"

The sky, once clear and blue, is now fully, impossibly, crowded with sleek, black war sphinxes.

The Shahanta Sky Fleet.

Weysh roars and, flapping his great wings, takes to the sky.

"Weh-sheh, no! They have arrows!"

The Shahanta may not have the population or the political heft of the Yirba, but everyone knows of their sky fleet. They are rigorously trained, all female, and attack with bows and fire runes. They have always filled Yenni with fascination, but now they fill her with fear. White focus runes are painted across their eyes, and they wear caps with tall white horns, in honor of their dragon kin who died three hundred years earlier. But dragon kin or not, they train their bows on Weysh, their focus runes glowing.

Weysh screeches and lets out a beautiful plume of fire, sending their mounts scattering. People scream and dash around Yenni as her eyes trail Weysh. The sky archers regroup quickly, but by the time they do, Weysh is above them. Acting on some signal Yenni cannot catch, the women fire all at once, sending a volley of arrows into the sky. Weysh pulls his wings close and dives, dodging them, then spreads his wings wide again and veers for the nearest cluster of archers, blasting them with fire. They fall, burning, from the sky.

Deep, booming war cries vibrate in Yenni's chest and make the ground tremble. Foot soldiers charge up the market road. Yenni gasps. They wear Gunzu battle attire—shields and short spears, and little in the way of armor. Their chests are bare and they wear animal fur wrapped around their arms, legs, and waists, as if to say that excessive armor is unnecessary for a proper warrior.

One soldier grabs a trembling cloth seller and stabs him through the middle.

NO!

Yenni's spear is in her hands and she twists the mechanism, extending it. She pulls on her speed and focus runes, feeling the warmth of them on her arms and legs, across her eyes, and she rushes the soldiers. They do not expect her. Yenni thrusts around the first man's shield, stabbing him in the side. She darts back, whirls, and slashes the throat of another. She pierces the back of a third, flares her strength runes, and pulls her spear free, making him scream. She sweeps the legs out from under a fourth attacker and stabs him through the middle even as he is falling to the ground. She knocks away the short spear of a fifth man and stabs him in the chest. But now she has lost the element of surprise, and the Gunzu warriors' runes are glowing. She runs.

Fire and destruction whiz by on the edges of her vision. Her beloved market is up in flames.

I did this. Mercy, Almighty Mothers and Fathers, I did this.

Where are the Yirba soldiers? Where are their fleet cats and swordsmen? Their sky force? What is her brother doing? She must get to the palace.

Yenni's speed runes give out when she is almost at the top of the hill. She stops right before the wide walkway—tiled and lined with *coconut trees—that leads to the main palace compound. Screams and war cries accost her from below, but ahead the palace seems cold and empty, ominously silent. She takes only one step before an anguished, screeching cry cuts through her, leaches all warmth from her. She snaps her head up. Weysh's wings are riddled with arrows, and he is falling from the sky. Above, the Shahanta Sky Archers are singing a low song of mourning and loss.*

Yenni does not think, only runs, pulling vainly on speed runes that have faded away. She must reach him, must protect him.

I did this.

Weh-sheh. Weh-sheh!

"WEH-SHEH!"

The sound of her own shout woke Yenni from sleep. She took a deep, ragged breath and sat up in her bed, clutching the sheets. Bed. Sheets. Cresh, this was Cresh. She summoned a lantern and tethered it in front of her face, checking her palms by its light. They were the same as they had been when she checked before sleeping.

Yenni let out a relieved breath. Three weeks had passed since she received her mother's letter. In that time her mother's rune had grown stronger while her father's faded once more. However, armed with her mother's explanation, Yenni wasn't nearly as anxious as she could have been.

But what a dream! Oh Mothers and Fathers, was it simply a cruel culmination of her worst fears over the last few weeks, or was it a warning?

Despite her sister's insinuation, she had yet to receive anything from Natahi ka Gunzu, and she wasn't sure what to make of that. Perhaps he was waiting until she returned home to make his move. Or perhaps—but there was no way he could know about Weysh.

Was there?

Across the room her spear leaned against her armoire, glinting in the lantern light.

Yenni slipped from bed, full of nervous energy. She needed to work off this restless feeling. First she drew on her runes, using the rune hymns both as a means of magic and worship. Her song for pain ward was also of praise to Father Ba, who listened to the fears of men and women. As she sang to infuse her speed runes, she sang to Father Sho, the divine hunter. And as she sang the hymn for strength, she venerated Father Gu the warrior.

An image from her dream suddenly flashed through her memory—the figurine of Mother Ya. Yenni paused—to dream of the Sha could be a very good omen, or a very bad one. What could it mean that she had dreamed of Mother Ya? The temperamental deity was known to conjure furious winds and lightning, and her anger resonated with Yenni's own simmering frustration. So on the backs of her hands Yenni drew wind runes, and though it would likely make her people cringe, she offered up her wind hymn to the Mistress of Storms.

When she was satisfied, Yenni changed into the half-shirt and pants of her battle uniform, grabbed her spear, and made for the training sands.

Δ

The night sky hid behind a veil of clouds, and the moon was a shy, shining crescent that peeped out only occasionally to glint off Yenni's spear. It was quiet but for her sandals scraping the sand and the thud of her spear as it hit the wooden dummy. Her voice echoed in the silence with every little yell and grunt. It felt good to train. Though her problems were nothing she could confront with a spear, the weight of it still felt comforting in her palms.

Yenni spun, bringing her spear around, and whacked the shaft against the dummy's side, practicing a blunt attack, but her hit landed a little lower than she'd intended. Frowning, she backed up to try again . . .

. . . and gasped as a quick, sharp pain zipped through her abdomen. The warning rune flashed bright white on her bare stomach. She glanced up. Darts of steel came flashing at her.

Yenni dragged on her speed and focus runes. Her arms were a blur as she twirled her spear, the air echoing with metallic *pings* as she deflected the darts.

Yenni crouched low and brought her spear before her, heart thudding. She squinted into the entrance to the training ground, but the lantern she'd anchored above the training dummies did more harm than good in this case. Outside its radius of light it simply created deeper shadows in which her attacker could hide.

"Show yourself!" she yelled, but no one answered; there was only the croak of a nearby toad. Very well, she still had a trick or two, but she would save her best for last. Yenni shuffled in the direction of the entrance corridor. Pain lanced her stomach again, and she dove and rolled behind a dummy. Darts sank into the wood with a *thud, thud, thud.*

"Coward!" she shouted. Fear and anger churned in her chest. Who was attacking her? Why? She had to get to the entrance.

The dummies were spaced out in rows. There was another one a few feet away, beside her, but she needed to move forward. Yenni pulled on her speed runes, ran, and dove for the dummy diagonally to her right, and the darts passed so closely she felt the wind of them on her arm.

She huddled with her back to the dummy and her spear held close, and peeked around the wood. There was one more row left, and then about ten paces of open space to the entrance, through which she would have to defend herself.

Once more she tugged on her speed rune, and winced when she felt how weak it was. A glance down showed that the paint was almost completely faded. She'd drawn it with Devon's mixture, intending to save her own for the dangers of town, and it wasn't nearly as potent. She had to move now or she'd be stuck.

She rolled and scrambled for the dummy diagonally left, darts whooshing right past her ear. She regrouped, took a deep breath, and charged.

The darts came instantly. She spun and ducked and twirled, darts pinging off her spear. But she was slowing down, and there was still a good distance to go. Shocks of pain zapped her stomach, and another volley of darts came. She ducked and dodged and whirled her spear but one got past her and sliced her thigh. She cried out and gritted her teeth, drawing on pain ward to soothe the sting, but she wasn't close enough to the entrance— she couldn't use her wind runes just yet.

She yelled and made one last desperate charge for the corridor, taking another slice to the side, and one to her bicep. She was almost there when a dart bit into her shoulder. She screamed and jerked back, but praise Father Gu she held on to her spear. Surging her strength and pain ward runes, she dashed forward. A volley of gleaming darts flew right at her, threatening to pierce her in ten places.

Yenni stopped short and slammed the butt of her spear into the ground, grabbing it with both hands. Her wind runes faced the corridor and she dragged on them, releasing a fierce blast that sent most of the darts scattering, but also sent some of them spinning haphazardly back the way they'd come. As she'd hoped, it took her attacker by surprise. She heard a shout come from the corridor, but over the screaming wind it was difficult to tell if it was male or female.

Yenni pointed her spear forward and dashed up the steps, ready to skewer whomever she found at the top. But when she burst into the corridor she found it empty.

She stood panting and sweating and bloody. The coward had run off, but Yenni doubted this would be their last encounter.

It seemed that someone wanted her dead.

33

Weysh paused with his hands in his hair, blinking through the downpour. He strained to hear over the water spattering against the porcelain of his tub. Was that knocking? Who could be calling this early?

"Source-drawn rain dry up and cease."

The rain stopped and evaporated from his tub, his body, and his hair, returning to otherspace. His shower disrupted, Weysh grabbed his silk sleep pants from the bathroom floor and pulled them on. The knocking started up again as he jogged down the stairs. It sounded urgent. If only he could smell who it was—no. No, it did no good to keep dwelling like that. He would know who was at the door when he opened it, like so many others.

It seemed to take an eternity to reach his front door, but at last he murmured the spell to unlock it, then yanked it open.

"What—Yenni!"

She threw her arms around him.

She let out some kind of oath in her language. "I would have been here sooner, but I had to redraw my speed runes."

"Not that I'm not thrilled to see you, but what in the world are you talking about?" Weysh gently removed her arms and stepped back to look at her. "KINDLY WATCHER!" he shouted. "Why are you all cut up?!"

He gripped her and turned her this way and that, examining her injuries—four that he could see. Some of her blood had even smeared onto him.

"I am sorry. I didn't have time to tend to my wounds."

"I . . . what . . ." Weysh closed his eyes, tipped his head back, and breathed deeply, fighting his racing heart and the panic that made his skin tingle with cold. Yenni was here, alive, in his arms. That was all that mattered.

"Are any of your cuts more than superficial?" he asked, forcing his voice to be calm and strong.

"I don't think so," said Yenni. "They sting, but I don't feel dizzy, or faint."

"There's still the risk of infection," Weysh said again, willing his voice not to tremble. He took her hand, pulling her inside. "Come, I'll magic you a bath."

Weysh set Yoben's Rainfall above his bathtub while Yenni stood shivering next to his commode. He took her gently by the shoulders. "All right, lovely, from the beginning."

"Someone tried to kill me, and I think they may try to kill you," she said.

"Someone—" Weysh pinched the bridge of his nose, struggling once more to suppress his alarm for Yenni's sake, but it was no use. The idea that someone had tried to hurt his Given made him want to roar, to rip and tear. He bared his teeth and growled.

"Oh!" said Yenni. "I did not know you could make that noise as a man."

"Yenni," said Weysh. "Who. Tried. To kill you." He would know, and he would incinerate them.

"I don't know." She explained the nature of the attack, and how her adversary had run off. Weysh's head spun and swam. He felt like he wanted to crawl out of his own skin as he took in Yenni, bloody and shivering. Who would dare attack her on academy grounds? How was he to keep her safe? Especially if he could no longer track her scent?

One thing at a time. "*Source-drawn rain cease and remain.*" He cut off the rainfall, grabbed a washrag, and dipped it in the bath. "You should get yourself cleaned up," he said, wiping her blood— Yenni's *blood*—off his skin. "I'll leave and give you some privacy."

"Stay close," she said quickly.

Byen, was she afraid? "As you wish, but you're not concerned I'll see you disrobed?"

"No, it's more important that I know you're nearby."

"All right, my heart."

Weysh leaned, arms crossed, against the wall outside his bathroom, listening to Yenni wash and splash as the light of sunrise filled the hallway. Who, by all that was holy, could want her *dead*?

It couldn't be Carmenna. She had too soft and sweet a heart, in spite of everything. Could Montpierre have hired someone? No, he wouldn't dare. He had to know that Weysh would slash him to ribbons, Maman or no Maman. Montpierre was far too smart for that. What of those thieves? The ones who'd attacked Yenni in the alley? Perhaps they were free and seeking revenge. Or—the hair raised all along Weysh's arms—Noriago was still out there somewhere.

But this didn't *seem* like Noriago. He'd be more likely to snatch Yenni than anything. Did he even know how to attack with magical darts? Weysh certainly had no idea what spell that was. Weysh stood ruminating until Yenni stepped from the bathroom wearing nothing but the nightshirt he'd left behind, which fit her like a gown. The silk clung to her, showing the outline of her body underneath and chasing all thoughts of anything else from his head.

"Erm, ah—"

"Do you know a spell that can heal shallow cuts such as these? I know of a rune, but I cannot use it to heal myself, of course, and I do not have my paint here besides."

"Ah, no. Sorry, lovely, but healing isn't exactly my area of expertise. However, I do have a balm against infection. Wait here, I'll retrieve it from the kitchen."

She's injured. He chided himself as he rushed downstairs. *Now is not the time.* But Byen *above* did she look tempting in his nightshirt. When he came back upstairs with the container of balm she wasn't in the hallway. "Yenni?" he called.

"I'm here," she said from his bedroom. He found her sitting on the edge of his bed, her legs dangling. "I apologize," she said wearily. "Everything caught up to me at once and I needed to sit down."

"No need to apologize, my heart," Weysh said, and went to kneel in front of her. She reached a hand out for the balm.

"It will be more effective if I apply it," he said. "It's soft poppy and mimel infused with healing magic to stop the bleeding and well, you know, Law of Self-Preservation and all that."

She squinted at him. "Truly?"

"Truly. I wouldn't lie to you about that. But if you'd feel more comfortable putting it on yourself you're free to do so."

She watched him a second more. "No," she said at last. "I trust you. Please apply the balm for me."

Weysh nodded. "Where?"

She pulled the loose shirt sleeve up her right arm, revealing a red welt on her bicep. Weysh scooped up the balm, feeling the magic of it tingle on his fingers, and spread it on the wound.

"*I'pa!*" Yenni whispered and sucked in a breath.

"Shhh, I know it burns," Weysh said soothingly. "But it will help. Now, where else?"

She let the sleeve drop and pulled the neck of the shirt down over her right shoulder. Weysh focused on applying the balm to the small stab wound there while suppressing all other thoughts, especially the strong urge to trail kisses along her collarbone.

He almost sighed in relief when she hitched the shirt back up over her shoulder, until she pulled the hem of the shirt up, revealing her right thigh.

Cursed Movay, why must you torment me!

Weysh spread the balm, doing his best not to think about the soft, curvy roundness of her.

"And one more, on my side. I'll show you."

Weysh scooped up more balm and Yenni took his hand, guiding it up under the shirt to a spot against her curving waistline.

Byen, I can't take this.

He hastily slapped it on, pulled his hand free, and shot to his feet.

"There. All done."

But Yenni held his gaze, and rose to kneel on the bed. He was helpless as she slid her arms around his neck and pressed her soft lips to his.

Weysh groaned in surrender and responded with deep,

devouring kisses. He swept Yenni's legs out from under her and placed her gently on the bed, never breaking the kiss. Her small hands slipped under his hair and played over his bare back and shoulders. He reached up and pulled down the neck of her night-shirt, and released her mouth only to finally plant that line of kisses along her delicate collarbone.

"Weh-sheh," she sighed, and he knew it was innocent: she didn't know how dangerous it was to breathe his name like that, how it was fuel to an already raging fire, but he simply couldn't stop himself.

He growled against her neck and shoved his hands under the nightshirt, running them down the smooth skin of her back, over her round behind, and back up along her waist. Yenni jerked and cried out.

In pain.

Weysh froze, his smoldering ardor doused by icy horror. He scrambled up and away from her, and her wincing expression was like a lance through his heart.

"I am so, so sorry, my love," he whispered.

"I'm all right," she said breathlessly, but he still felt like the world's tiniest rat prick.

She patted the bed. "Come lie beside me."

He had passengers to ferry in less than an hour, but he did as she asked, and she snuggled under his arm. He held her gently, terrified of hurting her further, and placed a soft kiss on the back of her neck.

"Your appointment was today, was it not? I didn't hear from you—how did it go?"

Ah Watcher, why did she have to remind him? He couldn't begrudge her concern, but for a brief few moments he'd merci-fully forgotten that he would never smell properly again.

"The healer prescribed a sniffing potion, but she said not to expect too much. My sense of smell will never be what it was, if it even returns at all."

She turned in his arms, and she looked as heartsick as he felt. "You do not deserve this," she said as she gently stroked his cheek. Weysh leaned into her soft caress. It had taken so long to get here, but she was finally his. He would do anything, *anything* to protect her. Including . . .

"Perhaps you should go back to the Moonrise Isles."

Her fingers fell away. "What?"

"If someone here is trying to hurt you, you should go."

"I cannot."

"Yenni—"

"I *cannot*, Weh-sheh. I am on Orire N'jem."

"O-reer . . . come again?"

She went silent, and when she finally spoke again Weysh sensed a weight to her words, as if she was revealing something secret, judging him worthy of it. "Orire N'jem is a sacred journey, undertaken to honor the Sha—our gods. I must complete the task they assign, and in return my tribe will receive their blessings."

"Ah, and what task is that?"

"I came to Cresh to seek knowledge of Creshen magic, in the hope that the Sha would heal my father. I have pleased them, it seems, as they have revealed the cause of my father's illness, but I pledged them a year of study in Cresh, and I cannot leave until that year is complete, or I will have broken my vow, insulting and angering them."

"Oh," said Weysh. Simply "Oh." He pushed down his first instinctive reaction—that Creshen notion that Islanders were notoriously superstitious. He knew for a fact that Yenni was neither ignorant nor uneducated, and truth be told her father *had* made a recovery. Perhaps he should be challenging her harder, but he didn't particularly *want* her to leave.

"Very well, if you won't go home then you will live here with me, and I won't hear otherwise." He steeled himself to do verbal battle, but to his surprise she agreed.

"Yes," she said. "I must be close by to make sure you are safe."

"En? Erm, all right, then. Good. I'm glad that's settled."

"Weh-sheh," she said softly. "I had a terrible dream that you were dying. I watched you fall from the sky. I worry that this attack came from the Gunzu—the tribe I am meant to marry into. I don't know how it can be possible, but they may know about you. I could never leave you behind, at the mercy of Gunzu assassins."

"Is this other tribe why you haven't yet told your family about me?"

She turned away. "Partially, yes."

Partially. Hmph.

"Yenni, we need to figure out what we're going to do once the year ends. Would this prince really wage war if you rejected him?"

"If he could convince his mother and father, and rally other tribes to his cause, it is possible. Never underestimate the pride of a prince."

Weysh fit his chin in the crook between her neck and shoulder, far too aware of how good she *didn't* smell, and kissed her cheek.

"I can't fully blame him. I wouldn't kill thousands of innocent people, but I'd at least want to land one good blow on the man who stole you from me. If I let him get in a free punch, right in the gut, do you think that would appease him?"

"Oh, Weh-sheh," Yenni sighed.

"I hate this," Weysh grumbled, dropping his humorous façade. "It's like you're being blackmailed, like my maman. How can your family allow this?"

"It's the way things have always been done," she said simply.

He squeezed her. "Yenni, I'm only one dragon—I doubt I can fight off an army, though if you asked me to, I'd try. And I'm not the heir to some long-lost kingdom, as much as I might wish it. But I promise you this: I will do my best to listen to you and take your needs and concerns to heart. I will respect you and cherish you as no other man will. Life with me will be tenfold better than life shackled to this prince."

"You think I do not know that?" she whispered, as if she was afraid to say it too loudly.

Weysh ran his fingers through her hair. She'd taken to braiding it back and tying the braids up in a horsetail, in anticipation of flying. "Then why are you hesitating? We're Given, Yenni. Everything will work out in the end. It must; it's the will of Byen."

Yenni sighed. "The reason my father was sick was because he has been pulling too heavily on runes, strengthening the parasitic demon that is making him sick. He has been fighting a threat to our Island, but my mother cannot tell me what. And then for the Gunzu to potentially strike while my parents are already distracted—" She shook her head. "Weh-sheh, if you truly know me, then you know that until I am sure my family and my people will be safe, I cannot prioritize my own selfish desires."

"I know," he said glumly. "And I wouldn't be as thrice-damned loony for you if you could. So be it. Once the year is done I'll fly you home, we'll sort out the nature of this threat, and I'll do everything in my power to help defeat it. Then we'll deal with this prince."

Excellent: now he had a plan.

But Yenni sighed again. "I know you are a big, strong, powerful dragon, but if this threat is giving my parents—the chieftain and chieftainess of the Yirba—such trouble, I doubt there is much you can do. If it was something that could be defeated with fangs and fire our armies would have dealt with it by now."

And just like that it was back, the sinking shame, that old heavy ache of not being enough. Weysh let her go and sat up on the edge of the bed. "Well at least I'm trying to find a solution. I should get ready. I have a run to make."

He heard the bedsheets whisper as she sat up after him. "What is it? What's wrong?"

He turned back to her. "Do you even *want* a future together?"

"Yes," she breathed. "Yes, I do, I truly do, but this is not a game, Weh-sheh. Someone *attacked* me."

She was right, and the sobering truth of it chased back his ego. "I'm sorry," he said, and kissed her forehead. "Stay here until I return and we'll report this to the peacekeepers." She raised her eyebrows at him. "Please," he added. His diminished pride made room for insecurity and fear. A large part of him wanted to lock her away inside his house for the rest of the year, irrational as it was, but he knew what would happen if he smothered her. She could take care of herself, and he had to learn to trust her.

"All right," she said, acknowledging his plea.

"Thank you, and in future try not to be anywhere isolated, and don't be afraid to ask Harth or Zui or anyone for an escort when I'm not around."

"I will," she said, and hugged him. "You as well, Weh-sheh. Be careful."

Weysh frowned as he stroked her back. No way in the deepest level of hell could someone try to kill his Given and get away with it. He *would* get to the bottom of this.

34

Weysh flew Yenni to a blue building with a white roof and sturdy white columns—the local peacekeepers headquarters. She gave her report to a stern-looking man with a bushy moustache, and then Weysh escorted her to the academy security building as well. At last he dropped her off at Devon's runelore class, and took her right up to the door.

"Be safe," he said, before gently collecting his flight toll. Devon cleared his throat and Yenni broke off the kiss, her cheeks heating. Weysh simply winked at Devon and made his way to the lawn before changing and taking off.

"Good morning, Yenni Ajani," Devon said stiffly. He jerked his chin at the sky, in the direction of Weysh's retreating form. "What did he mean when he said you should be safe?"

Yenni told Devon about the attack.

"Watcher above!" he cried, and his eyes scanned her up and down, concerned. "Are you all right?"

"I am a little cut up, but otherwise fine. The worst of my wounds should heal in a few days."

Devon cringed. "I truly am sorry you were hurt, Yenni Ajani, but you're a strong, resilient woman of the Isles. I'm sure you'll bounce back just fine, en?"

"Ah . . . yes." Once again, Yenni experienced that strange uneasy sensation, so common since coming to Cresh. Devon was complimenting her, so why did his statement raise her defenses, like when doing verbal battle with her cousins or rival royalty back home? What was he saying without saying?

She didn't get much chance to contemplate it, as his next statement *definitely* raised her hackles. "I thought you should know, my mentor, Gilles Desroches, heard back from the High Magus Council regarding the deception rune."

Yenni crossed her arms. "Did he," she said flatly.

"Yes. And not only did they refuse to acknowledge the superiority of the rune to its Creshen equivalent, they've declared it unsanctioned magic, so now it's illegal to use it within the Empire!"

"Wonderful!" said Yenni. She must still find a way to warn the Watatzi about that unscrupulous Gilles Desroches, but at least the rune would not be publicized.

Devon's eyebrows flew up. "But doesn't that bother you? This is blatant prejudice! The deception rune is clearly a better alternative to Ibeena's Sensory Illusion. They've only outlawed it to further perpetrate the notion that Creshen magic is superior to all magic!"

Yenni shrugged. "If your Magi's own ignorance keep them from reaping the benefits of a stolen rune, so much the better. Either way, there is nothing to be done about it now."

"Oh, Yenni Ajani," said Devon, and he shook his head in disappointment. She didn't hold back from rolling her eyes.

"We should begin preparing for today's lesson," she said.

"Oh! Oh yes, of course." He stepped aside and Yenni entered the dim, creaky schoolroom. She went to the store cupboards and took out all the herbs and sap for runepaint, setting herself up on the long, wooden table up front. She felt Devon's eyes on her, and caught him watching her intently, as if he had something more to say.

"What is it?" she asked him.

"I worry for you. But you'll be just fine." He nodded firmly to himself. "Just fine."

Δ

At sunset that day Weysh flew Yenni to mail home a letter that updated her family about the attack. She hated that she would cause them concern, but she was also concerned for them. If it truly was the Gunzu who were out for her, had they attacked her home as well? Praise all the Mothers and Fathers for her n'baba's foresight. The runes on her palms, largely unchanged, were all that allowed her to sleep at night.

And sleep that night she did, at Weysh's.

After mailing the letter, he took her back to his townhouse. As she prepared for bed Yenni's stomach fluttered with nerves. The last time they had been alone in his bedroom he was being so kind and caring that Yenni had kissed him in the heat of the moment, and then things had escalated so quickly. But truth be told, a large part of her was scared to take things further. Though there was no proof she'd been ambushed by the Gunzu, she couldn't help linking her dalliances with Weysh to the attack, as if it were a punishment for ignoring her obligation to her tribe. And so she felt that should she take the next step with him something worse would occur.

She needn't have worried, though; he simply kissed her and left her in his bedroom, telling her he would sleep on the rooftop in dragon.

Yenni lay alone in Weysh's bed for long, anxious moments. She knew her worry for him was silly: he was a giant, fire-breathing beast. But she couldn't forget the image from her dream—Weysh screeching as he fell from the sky. At last she grabbed the soft blanket off the bed and went searching for him. As he said, she found him curled up on the rooftop garden in dragon, his eyes closed and his large body moving up and down with his slow breaths.

"Weh-sheh?" she called softly.

He opened one glittering eye and let out a low, soothing rumble. *Come.*

It was foolish. Yes, they were on a rooftop, but they were still outside—it would be so much easier for assassins to reach her here. But the notion that the Gunzu might be after her didn't fill her with fear as perhaps it should; it filled her with fury, made her reckless and rebellious. Her whole life felt molded around them and this cursed alliance. With all her skills—runelore and tracking and battle—everything she'd learned and hoped to learn, was it truly her destiny to be nothing more than a link in her own shackle? She had hoped a year away might slake her thirst for freedom, but it only seemed to have made it worse. And right then she didn't want to hide from Gunzu assassins; she wanted to be with Weysh. So she snuggled into the crook between his neck and shoulder, telling herself she would go back inside when her eyes began to droop. But she slept there until morning.

Δ

Only a week after the attack, Yenni was growing weary of being chaperoned. Two weeks after, she was decidedly annoyed. Three weeks and she could no longer hide her irritation from her friends. It was even worse than her security back home, with Harth or Zui or Weysh or Diedre always waiting to shuffle her from place to place. She could take care of herself!

But though the constant surveillance was driving her mad, she was also touched by how concerned everyone was for her safety. Zui was constantly late to other obligations because she wanted to see Yenni safely off. And Yenni knew much of her frustration came from feeling like she was a burden. She'd also heard back from her family, and as she'd feared, all their letters were tinged with worry, begging her to stick close to her friends and letting her know they were praying for her safety. Her mother and Dayo wrote nothing about the Gunzu—good, bad, or otherwise—and she took that as a positive sign.

A pleasant side effect of being chaperoned was that she and Zui had been growing much closer. Yenni quite liked her and admired her demure strength. Still, her friends must have sensed her frustration. No doubt that was why Zui invited her and Diedre out to a nice tavern in the dragon district while they waited for Weysh to finish his classes and fly her home.

The entrance to the tavern was an alcove high up in the middle of a tall building, and it could be reached only by flying. The three of them were mostly done a bottle of what the Creshens called white wine, and Yenni was finding it more and more difficult to resist gawking at the crowd of colorful people around them—many green, but some with skin of an orange hue, or deep blue, or even shimmery gold.

Diedre was affected, too, if the way she kept sneaking looks at Zui was any indication. Curiously, whenever Zui was around, Diedre's personality did a complete switch. She became shy and even coquettish in a way that left Yenni scratching her head in confusion.

But drinking and chatting with them set Yenni at ease. It felt like three friends enjoying each other's company, rather than two friends guarding one from attempted assassination. At least, Yenni *hoped* they were enjoying themselves. Who knew what responsibilities they were neglecting to be with her?

"I am sorry to impose on you two like this," she said, feeling suddenly ashamed.

"Impose what?" said Diedre. "Listen, mams, I'm here because I want to be. Is two of us know you can more than protect yourself. If anything is you should be body-guardin' for me."

"Yenni," Zui began, "we've known each other only—let's see, we're just heading into third-quarter exams so—almost six moonturns now? And believe me, I say this out of kindness, but I've noticed you tend to take things on alone when you don't need to. I can't begin to imagine how it must feel to know someone out there wishes you harm. I know it would rattle me, and I'm dragon-kind." She covered Yenni's hand with hers. "I want you to know that you have my support."

"Same for me," said Diedre.

"I—thank you." Yenni swallowed against a lump in her throat. She wasn't sure what she had done for the Sha to bless her with such kind friends, but she was incredibly glad to have them. "It is not a good feeling knowing that someone wishes me dead," she told them. "What's worse is that I worry for my family and my tribe." In the weeks since the attack, Yenni had confided her status as princess of the Yirba to both Harth and Zui. "I couldn't bear it if they were in danger because of me. And—"

"And what?" asked Zui.

Yenni licked her lips. "I could not stand it if the petty judgments against me turned out to be true."

"Judgments like what, mams?"

"Well, because I am a woman who enjoys hunting, and learning about runes, and learning about combat, people act as if I am strange and unnatural."

"Hmm," Diedre and Zui said as one.

"But it was once very common for women to do these things. You know what I think? I think it is everyone else who is unnatural."

"Yes!" cried Zui. "Who creates these arbitrary rules? A so-called friend of mine told me I couldn't become an instructor at Prevan because I don't spit fire like Creshen dragons."

"What? That's ridiculous!" said Yenni.

"Did you take them out back and *give* them some instruction?" asked Diedre.

Zui laughed. "I wanted to, but instead I told them we would have to agree to disagree."

Diedre sighed. "Meh folks would say I'll draw the eye of the Mistress of Demons practicin' runelore."

Yenni shook her head. "I still do not understand why."

"Is what they were taught," said Diedre, and she swigged her wine. "Still, is nowhere near what they would say if they knew—"

She cut off, seeming to catch herself, and her light-brown cheeks flushed red.

"What is it, Deedee?" asked Yenni.

"Nothing to trouble yourself with, mams. Let's talk about you. How are things with your dragon?"

Yenni noted dimly that this wasn't the first time Diedre had steered the conversation back to her and Weysh.

"Things are quite well," she said carefully. Nevertheless, she could hide nothing from Diedre.

"I hearin' a 'but' in there."

She was right. An awkward gulf had grown between her and Weysh, and she knew it was because she was keeping him at arm's length. The only time all felt right was at night when, unable to stand cowering inside, she covered herself in runes and curled up beside him when he slept in dragon. But as a man, their conversations were filled with uncomfortable stutters and pregnant pauses, to the point where they'd begun to spend less time in each other's company. Yenni would say she needed to study, and Weysh would go on long hunts in dragon for wild boar, deer, or mountain cats—both of them desperate to escape the heaviness that seemed to hang above them like an impending storm.

Zui and Diedre watched her with concern, and Yenni wrapped both hands around her wine glass. "I feel as if I'm being pulled in opposite directions. I very much care for Weh-sheh, more than I have for any man before, but how can I ignore the reality between us? I still have not written home about him."

Zui gave a sympathetic hum. "Is it because—" She shared a look with Diedre.

Perhaps it was the wine, but abruptly Yenni's frustration bubbled over. She slammed the table with her palm. "I am so *tired* of caring about appearances! Of feeling guilty and ashamed! Of catering to the fragile egos of others. I don't want to marry Natahi! I want Weh-sheh," she finished sadly.

"Oh, Yenni," said Zui, and squeezed Yenni's hand. The mood at their table was a somber contrast to the colorful happy chatter and plucky harp music that surrounded them. Diedre sighed.

"I know just how you feel, mams," she said, staring into her wine glass. "I does wish every day there was some way I could be with Nannette."

Ah! Yenni burned with embarrassment. Here she was wallowing in her own sorrows and poor Diedre was stuck in the same dirt pit. She'd completely forgotten about Diedre's forbidden paramour, but she so rarely mentioned him.

"I'd always thought Nannette was a woman's name," Yenni mused. "There's a Nannette in my Basics of Defensive Spellcasting class, but I suppose it is a name for a man as well."

Diedre looked up slowly, just her eyes, still clutching her wine glass. "No, it isn't."

Yenni blinked, confused. "Are you saying your sweetheart is a woman?"

Diedre only nodded.

"Oh."

Oh.

"That's not common on the Isles, is it?" asked Zui, watching her closely.

Yenni scrunched up her forehead in thought. "It happens, but it is not something anyone would freely admit, for fear of being ridiculed and shamed. Men cannot marry men, and women cannot marry women. Is that different here?"

"No," said Diedre. She gulped down the last dregs of her wine.

"The only exception is dragonkind," said Zui. "If two males or two females match as Given, well, that's more important than anything. It's rare, but it does happen."

Yenni sat back, flabbergasted. "But you told me Weh-sheh was handsome!"

Diedre shrugged. "He is. I appreciate the beauty in men and women both."

"I see." Yenni was floored. It was as if she were meeting Diedre all over again. Diedre watched her cautiously—no, *fearfully*—across the table, her face pinched and tense, and Yenni found she didn't like her friend looking at her like that at all. It sent a sad ache through her heart.

"Stop it, Deedee," she said softly. "This changes nothing between us. You are my dear friend."

The relief that flooded Diedre's features flowed, warm and golden, through Yenni as well, and the tautness that stretched between them relaxed. Diedre had supported Yenni since they first met. She'd cheered her up, even saved her life. She had been a true friend to Yenni, so now Yenni would be a true friend to her. Zui clapped her hands together, grinning at them.

"But if you love both men and women, why not simply marry a man to make your family happy?" asked Yenni.

The smile dropped from Diedre's face.

"Oh, I have said something foolish, haven't I?"

"This from *you* of all people? Why not marry your prince, same way? I fell for Nannette, and Nannette is a woman, but more important, she understands me."

Yenni cringed; Diedre was right. "Sorry, Deedee."

"No foul, mams, I think you get the picture now. But at least you two are Given, there must be some kind of way to make it work. If there is even a small chance, you should take it. I would," she finished softly.

Yenni took Diedre's hand, offering and receiving comfort. Zui hailed for another bottle of wine, and the three of them settled into lighter chatter: which professors they liked and disliked, and plans for the upcoming break. And though Yenni still wasn't sure what to do about Weysh, just talking about it helped her feel better, free of something heavy and straining. For the rest of the evening she simply reveled in the warmth of the alcohol flowing through her veins, and of conversation with good friends.

$$\Delta$$

Third quarter exams came and went, and after furious weeks of revision Yenni was once more in the clear, having passed everything. One morning, shortly after the last semester of classes had started, Yenni woke to Weysh shaking her. She bolted up, instinctively pulling on her runes and scanning the green rooftop.

"What is it?"

"I think I can smell you."

He proceeded to snuffle around her neck and shoulders.

She slapped at him. "Weh-sheh!" she said, and burst into a fit of relieved giggles.

He drew back. "What?"

"Why are you sniffing me like a hound, you strange creature?"

He ducked his head, embarrassed. "Ah, sorry, lovely. But I think Healer Veronique's medicine is finally working!"

Yenni beamed. It was the most animated she'd seen him in a while. She rose up on her knees and hugged him. "I'm glad."

"Me too. Like you can't imagine." He gave her a tight

squeeze, all propriety abandoned, and it felt like before, like the night he'd taken her out to the restaurant on the docks, or the night they'd kissed under the moon. They hugged for long moments, absorbing the feel of each other, Yenni listening to the sound of Weysh's deep, searching breaths, until, inevitably, he let her go.

"All right, my heart. Where am I flying you today?"

"Why don't we walk instead?"

While she loved flying with him, Yenni missed talking with Weysh. He'd been so melancholy lately, but today it seemed his high spirits might have returned.

"If you'd like. But if that's the case we'd better leave soon, en?"

About an hour later they were trudging through the Rearwood on their way to the academy. Weysh seemed oblivious to Yenni's apprehension. Forests had always been mysterious places to her, the realm of beasts and spirits. Curiously, the Creshens seemed to find them charming and romantic. Either way, cutting through the Rearwood was the fastest way to get where they were going, and they weren't the only ones taking the shortcut. Other students occasionally overtook them on the forest path. So she did her best to focus on Weysh rather than the nervous prickling on the back of her neck.

"Let's go to Suli's tonight," he was saying. "I might be able to actually taste something this time."

Yenni spied a cluster of bright-blue, bell-shaped flowers and wandered over to pick one. It had a wonderful soft fragrance. "Can you smell this?" she said, turning back to him.

But he was gone.

Yenni spun around, her heart pounding. There was no one in sight, and no sound but chirping birds.

"Weh-sheh?" she yelled. She dropped the flower and held her spear out in front of her. "Weh-sheh!"

"YENNI!" he yelled back from somewhere down the forest path. Yenni shot off after the sound of his voice.

"Weh-sheh!"

"Yenni!" he called back, fainter this time. She stopped, trying to place him. His voice was coming from somewhere in the woods, off the path. Sure enough, up ahead she saw a spot where the trees had been disturbed, the ground stirred up by large, dragging footprints.

She ignored her tracker's instincts, pulling on her speed runes and crashing through the scrub and branches. At the moment it was far more important to get to Weysh than to be stealthy. Her heart seemed to race faster than her frantic steps. What was going on? Why did he not change to Dragon?

At last she came to a clearing—a tiny spot of grass and wildflowers surrounded by thick trunks and a shivering umbrella of greenery overhead. She spun, looking for some clue as to where he could have gone, but she saw no footprints, no broken branches, nothing to indicate where to go. She cursed herself for not painting a focus rune across her eyes, but the shocked and scared looks she received from Creshens when she did had become so tiresome, and she had been with Weysh besides.

"Weh-sheh!" she shouted again.

Her answer was a pinch of pain on her stomach.

Yenni dropped into tortoise stance to defend herself and held her spear in front of her. A familiar, wooden clacking echoed through the clearing, and Yenni gasped. Cold sweat slid down the side of her face.

Oh divine Mothers and Fathers, not this.

She wondered if she was having another dream as out of the trees of the Creshen forest, tall, dark, and horribly surreal, stepped a rune puppet.

35

It loomed, and was made completely of blackwood, with its pointed face ringed in straw. The thing's movements were jerky and inhuman, but that didn't fool Yenni. In the hands of a skilled puppeteer, rune puppets made for deadly assassins. Designed to mimic fearsome and powerful spirits, rune puppets were historically employed during wars between the Islands to mask the identity of a killer and thus sow political unrest.

However, as the puppet stared at her through yellow-painted eyes, its jangly arms clacking, Yenni knew it was not meant to mask her attacker, but confirm them. *If it's war you want, it's war you'll get,* it seemed to say.

The rune puppet slowly approached, holding aloft a wicked short sword and clacking with each twitching step. Every inch of it was covered in white runes: wards against all the elements plus speed, strength, runes for animation, and many others. Yenni backed up, keeping her spear pointed forward. The puppet couldn't use offensive runes like fire or lightning without damaging itself, since an inanimate creation wasn't protected by what the Creshens called the Law of Self-Preservation. That, at least, she had to her advantage.

But there was a reason rune puppets made lethal assassins. They burned runes at less than half the speed of a person, and eyeing the speed runes on the thing, Yenni knew she could never outrun it. And though normally she would have the advantage with her spear against a sword, she couldn't very well stab a creature made of wood. Nevertheless, if she wanted to save Weysh, she would have to find a way to destroy it.

Or destroy its puppeteer.

"Where are you?" she yelled in Gunzu, knowing he hid somewhere in the shadows of the trees.

The puppet's speed runes glowed, and it rushed her.

It struck, its joints clacking as it thrust and Yenni just barely brought her spear up to catch it. The sword pinged against her spear, and made her arms tremble, but she slipped back into tortoise stance and flared her strength runes as she parried, swinging the sword down to the ground. Then she pulled on speed and darted back before the puppet could respond in kind.

She dragged ach'e, feeling it buzz within her and tickle her fingers. "*Source as twine to bind my foe!*" she shouted. The puppet went rigid and fell to the ground. Yenni dashed to it, thrust the backs of her palms right at its face, and blasted it with fire.

She could see its runes glowing through the flames, and seconds later it was back on its feet and thrusting at her, still ablaze. Yenni flowed into gazelle stance, dancing and darting out of the way of the puppet's sword strikes, even as it smothered the flames with its fire wards. She gritted her teeth in frustration; she didn't have time for this! Anything could be happening to Weysh. He must be in serious danger to have left her side.

As she weaved and ducked, her runes warm on her skin, Yenni knew she could spend hours in this clearing and she would never defeat the puppet. Her runes would run out first, and it would kill her. She had to find the puppeteer.

"Come out, coward!" she screamed in Gunzu. "Don't send a puppet to fight for you. Face me!"

Her taunt served only to set off the rune on her stomach, though now it was not more than a dull twinge—it was almost used up. But thanks to the warning, Yenni turned and slashed, deflecting a single metal dart coming at her from the back. She saw the trees rustle before she turned back to the puppet, just as it swung its long, wooden arm. It hit her in the middle like a log and sent her flying. She slammed down on the grass and wheezed, drawing heavily on pain ward until she could breathe again. When she finally jumped to her feet, the puppet stood a few paces away, clicking and clacking and jerking its strange head.

He's playing with me!

Rage burned in the pit of her stomach. Yenni turned and attempted to dash into the woods, to try to find the cowardly puppeteer, but the puppet suddenly materialized right before her, slashing down with its sword. Yenni slipped into gazelle stance and darted back, the sword whizzing in front of her nose. Bright shock zipped through her; as far as she knew, the rune that allowed one to jump instantly from one place to another like that was known only to the Yirba—to her family and the Masters.

What?

The puppet disappeared, and she spun to find it behind her.

Yenni stood panting and confused. That couldn't be right. Why would her *own* tribe attack her?

No. She was mistaken. She *must* be. More than ever she needed to force the puppeteer to show himself. Her runes would not hold out much longer.

Think, think! Father Ri lend me your wisdom; Mother Ya lend me your fury—guide me!

The rune on her stomach gave one last feeble pulse and the puppet rushed her again. It attacked her with a series of savage blows that she did her best to block and parry in tortoise stance, but she could feel her runes slowing down. She had to pull and pull to keep up with the puppet, and eventually it knocked her with its hard shoulder, once again sending her soaring and tumbling to the ground.

Her head bounced off the grass, reminding her painfully of her fight with the bandits in the alley. The way the stars flashed in front of her eyes had her recalling the bright light of Queyor's Magic Lantern when she'd used it to blind her foes. But she couldn't blind a puppet.

Though she could blind the puppeteer . . .

Yes! He needed to see her to attack her. Magic lanterns would not work in the bright light of day, but if she could somehow block his line of sight she would force him to move and give himself away. Yenni struggled to her feet, leaning on her spear and making a great show of being injured, and it wasn't all an act. Her bones ached but she pulled on pain ward, fell into aggressive lion stance, and charged the rune puppet.

It met her charge, sword raised, but at the last moment she dove and rolled, bounding up, against all instincts, right behind the puppet, the drape of its cloak shielding her. It jerked and stopped as the puppeteer lost sight of her, and Yenni strained to listen to the sounds of the wood. Praises upon praises to lucky Ib-e-ji there was no breeze that day, so the faint rustling at the other side of the clearing must be her attacker.

She dragged on her speed runes and darted between the stuttering puppet's legs, under the cloak, and dashed for the edge of the clearing, chasing the sound. And when once more the puppet loomed in front of her, appearing from nowhere, she channeled swift gazelle and spun, flowing past it before finally bursting into the trees with a cry. A hooded figure jumped up from between two soaring trunks, startled, and took off into the woods.

"You won't get away this time!" Yenni snarled. She raised her spear, dragged on the last of her strength runes, took practiced aim, and hurled it.

A deep yell echoed through the trees.

Yenni ran after the cry and found the puppeteer limping through the trees, gripping his thigh. Her spear had cut but not pierced him, and lay on the ground nearby. She dashed to him and tackled him to the ground, ignoring his agonized scream, then yanked the hood from his head.

And reeled.

The shock of it stole her breath just as surely as if she'd been hit in the gut again. Professor Devon panted up at her, his eyes wild. Training, and only training, allowed Yenni to act through her horror. She shoved the back of her hand, with her fire rune, in his face.

"Do not move, and do not speak, or I will set you ablaze," she said coldly, switching back to Creshen. "*Source as twine to bind my foe*," said Yenni. Devon cried out as his arms and legs went rigid, aggravating his wound. She pulled ach'e to the fire rune, just enough to make it glow.

"Where is Weh-sheh?"

Devon licked his lips. "I wasn't trying to kill you!" he cried hoarsely. "Not really. I simply wanted to test the rune once more before you leave!"

And Yenni thought she had been shocked before. She gawked at him. He'd attacked her to *test the warning rune*? And test it once more, he'd said. So it had been him at the training sands as well, though he'd fussed and fretted and pretended to fear for her safety.

Was he truly capable of such selfish depravity? Was she such a bad judge of character? In all the time she'd known Devon, worked with him, she'd never seen so much as a hint that he could do something so vile.

Yes—yes, she had. It hit her with the force of yet another blow.

"You tried to kill Mainard as well," she whispered, disbelieving. It was he who had set that sharp metal instrument toppling, straight for the crown of Mainard's head.

"I had to do *something*! And it worked, did it not? Besides, I knew you would save him, just like I knew you would save yourself. You're so strong and resilient—"

"SHUT UP!" Yenni screamed, spitting all the pain of his betrayal at him. She pulled more ach'e to the fire rune, igniting it, and held it just close enough to Devon that he could feel the uncomfortable heat of it. He breathed hard, sweat dripping down the side of his face.

"Where is Weh-sheh, Devon. Where. Is. My. *Given*."

Devon's eyes glimmered faintly with runelight. Yenni pulled hard on ach'e, ready to set him on fire, until she heard a deep, pained dragon's screech right above them. Instinctively her eyes darted to the sky. She squinted through the trees but she saw nothing.

Because she was being deceived.

She whipped her eyes back down to Devon and found the rune puppet looming over the both of them. Its sword hurtled down toward her, about to cleave her in two. She had half a moment to make her decision. She placed her life in the hands of the Sha. Yenni raised her face to the sword, watching it fall, then watching it pass right through her without stirring so much as a breeze. Just like before, when the puppet in the clearing had seemed to move from one place to the next within moments, *this* puppet was merely another illusion.

"Oh hells!" cried Devon.

Enough. Yenni pulled back her arm and punched him hard in the temple, putting all her disgust into the swing. His head snapped to the side, and his eyes fluttered closed. Yenni jumped to her feet.

"Weh-sheh!" she called again.

"What in the world is that thing?"

"I heard someone shout. This way!"

Two of her fellow students came crashing through the trees toward her.

"Whoa!" one of them cried at the sight of her. The other one narrowed his blue eyes and drew his sword, pointing it at her. "Hands on your mouth."

Yenni cocked her head to the side, confused. "What?"

"Is that—I think that's a professor!" said his friend. He shot Yenni a look of alarm and drew his sword as well.

"Hands on your mouth!" the first one yelled again.

"But he is the one who attacked *me*!"

"That's for the peacekeepers to decide. We're taking you in."

"Ah!" said Yenni. "This is lunacy! I am going to academy security." While a panicked part of her wanted to run through the woods looking for Weysh, she knew she would have more luck with the help of the peacekeepers. They could more effectively interrogate Devon. She gestured to his unconscious body. "Pick him up and bring him. Mind my spear."

The two students glanced at each other in uncertainty.

"Quickly!" snapped Yenni. They sheathed their swords and scurried over to Devon. Just then she heard a faint, familiar flapping. She gasped and looked up. A moment later a high dragon cry echoed through the wood. Yenni glared at Devon, but he was out cold.

"Weh-sheh!" she yelled up at the trees. Yenni took off for the clearing as the two students shouted after her. She spotted Weysh gliding above the canopy of the trees.

Oh thank all the Mothers and Fathers! "Weh-sheh!" she called again, waving her arms frantically. He dove into the clearing, changing a few feet in the air. He hit the ground running and swooped Yenni up into his arms.

"Kindly Watcher, thank you," he breathed, squeezing her.

"*I'pa!* Weh-sheh . . . you're . . . hugging me too . . . tightly."

He let her down. "Sorry."

Yenni slapped his arm. "Where did you go?!"

"Where did *you* go?" Weysh retorted. "One moment we were walking together, the next you took off into the trees and I had to chase after you. Then you were just gone!"

"Erm," said one of the students from behind.

Weysh's face went dark. "Who are they?" he said, and took a step toward them. Yenni put a hand on his chest.

"They are helping me bring my attacker to justice."

He looked to her in alarm. "You were attacked again? By who? Where are they?"

"Weh-sheh, please calm down and I will explain. We were deceived." She laid out how Devon must have used the deception rune to separate them.

Weysh clenched his fists, breathed hard, and let out a menacing dragon's growl. "This never would have happened if I could properly smell!" he shouted. "I'd have noticed if your scent was in one direction and your image in another. Where the hell is Devon?"

"We're taking him to academy security. Actually, now that you are here we can fly him there much faster. Change, and we will put him on your back."

"Not just yet, I want a word with him."

"No, Weh-sheh, he is dangerous and we need to get him to the authorities before he wakes up."

"Before he—you knocked him out?"

"Yes."

"A professor? You incapacitated an accredited professor of magic? On your own?"

"Professor or not, he could never best me at runelore. Now hurry, he—Weh-sheh!"

Weysh had gathered her up in his arms again. "Watcher above, but I love you," he murmured against the top of her head.

"I love you, too, but now is not the time for this! Change, quickly."

He backed away, grinning strangely from ear to ear, and changed to dragon. Yenni could only shake her head. For all his virtues, her Weysh could be a real oddity.

Next, one of the students staunched the blood flow with a basic healing incantation while Yenni collected her spear. Then came the task of hauling him up onto Weysh's back. It didn't help that Weysh kept nuzzling and sniffling her as they worked, until at last Yenni had to tap him on the nose and hiss at him to stay still. Yenni climbed up behind Devon to hold him in place.

"You two bring the rune puppet there," she said to the two Creshen students. They glanced fearfully at it.

"Don't worry, it cannot move without someone controlling it. Think of it as a giant doll." How Devon had even come by it was another baffling mystery.

She turned her attention back to keeping Devon in place. "Let's go, Weh-sheh!" she called. He flapped his wings and they were off.

$$\Delta$$

The academy peacekeepers took them all into custody until a high peacekeeper could reach the academy. They split them into separate rooms, and Weysh was the one who had to keep Yenni calm when the academy officers tried to pull her away.

"They only want to question us, lovely. You're not in trouble."

Still, the room they put her in was horrible and stifling, and not simply because it had no windows and just one uncomfortable chair. The Creshens had done something to the room to dampen ach'e. The air felt heavy and soupy, and when she tried to pull ach'e it tingled painfully under her skin, like little knives. It would be difficult indeed to use runes or incantations.

She waited for endless minutes until at last the door opened and a green-skinned woman—a dragon—stepped into the room. She held a book and ink pen.

"Mam'selle Kayirba?" she said, tucking a lock of her chin-length green hair behind her ear. "I am High Peacekeeper Huisa. I'll need to ask you a few questions. The quicker and more truthfully you answer them, the sooner you will go free. Now, are you, in fact, a royal of the Yirba tribe of the Moonrise Isles?"

Yenni sighed. So much for keeping that secret.

"I am," Yenni confirmed. "I suppose Weh-sheh told you?"

"Your Given? No, in fact it was Emmanuel Devon who made that claim."

"What? But how could he—"

Because she had foolishly told him only the Masters knew how to draw the warning rune. Such a rare rune would normally only be bestowed on someone quite high ranking within a tribe, after all.

Yenni sat, seething and embarrassed, as the high peacekeeper explained that Devon had not wanted to kill her but to test the accuracy of her rune and report back to his mentor, Gilles Desroches, who had also loaned Devon the rune puppet, having pilfered it from the Watatzi.

Yenni in turn revealed everything about her trip to Cresh— from who she was to why she'd come. The clock bell tolled twice while she was stuck in that oppressive room, answering question after question, until finally the high peacekeeper called in her subordinates to escort Yenni out.

They led her to the high-ceilinged foyer of the security building, where Weysh was waiting.

"Right then, you two are free to go," said the first peacekeeper.

Yenni went over to Weysh, and he put an arm around her in

a gentle hug. She rested her head on his chest and sighed heavily against him.

"What is it, lovely?" he asked, stroking her back. "You're shaking."

"I feel so foolish," she said, and explained to Weysh the plot hatched by Professor Devon and his mentor to test her rune.

"Those bastards!" Weysh thundered. "Who in Movay's name does something like that?" He looked past her down the hallway like he wanted to rush into the interrogation room and do some interrogating of his own.

"Still, I suppose it was silly of me to trust Devon as much as I did. Perhaps I got what I deserved."

Weysh took her by the shoulders and frowned at her. "You may have been a bit naïve but that doesn't mean you deserved to be attacked! Those two are insane! And furthermore, I should have been there to protect you."

"You couldn't have known," said Yenni.

Weysh grunted. "I have to admit I'm rattled by how easily I was deceived. As a dragon I suppose I'm used to feeling somewhat invincible. Divine warrior and all that. Thank the Watcher you can handle yourself." Suddenly he grinned at her.

"Ah . . . what?" asked Yenni.

"You told me you love me."

"I did?" Yes, in the clearing. She'd said *I love you too*. So easily she'd barely noticed. "I did." She cupped his cheek. "I do."

Based on the stark terror that had struck her when he disappeared, she could no longer deny it. She loved him very much.

"I think I must write another letter home," she said.

36

Yenni did not get so much as a day of respite. The next morning in Foundations of Magical Theory students were once again staring brazenly, only this time it seemed to be in awe. For a while none were brave enough to come up to her. But as she was getting her books ready, her classmates began congregating around her seat. One of the braver ones—a familiar girl with a long brown horse-tail trailing down the back of her green uniform dress—finally addressed her sheepishly.

"Erm, hello, Yenni Ajani. Erm, my name is Celine. I'm also in your runelore class."

"Ah. Nice to meet you, Celine," said Yenni.

"I was—we were—wondering . . . is it true that you're a princess?"

A dozen pairs of light-colored eyes assessed her. Yenni swallowed her sigh. "Yes, it is true."

Her answer triggered an avalanche of questions and comments from her classmates.

"I knew it!"

"What's it like to live in a palace?"

"I never agreed with Devon, you know. I was on your side the whole time."

"Are you all right? I'm so sorry you were attacked like that."

"Please don't think all Creshens are like Devon and Desroches."

Yenni's eyes darted from person to person, unsure whom to respond to first, until at last she was saved by the arrival of Professor Mainard. His commanding voice rang out so sharply that Yenni assumed he must have amplified it with some incantation.

"What in Byen's name is all this hubbub? This is a classroom, not some sort of sporting arena! Everyone to your seats, immediately!"

The crowd dispersed, Mainard took his place at the podium up front, and class went on as usual. That day they reviewed the theory of time manipulation, the principle of spatial maneuvering, and the theory of intended focus. Then they learned a new incantation: Allard's Restoring. The purpose of the spell was simply to transport something back to its original place. But as Mainard pointed out, *original* had a broad definition. He left them with a cautionary tale about a farmer's wife who, when attempting to send some unused eggs back to the icebox, heard very curious squawking from her chicken coop a moment after her eggs had vanished.

The rest of the class was spent practicing the incantation under Mainard's watchful eye. He told them to place their writing pencils on the left side of their desk, physically move them to the right, and use the spell "*Starting spot by source restored,*" while invoking the theory of focused intent to make sure the pencil went back to the *intended* starting point. However, about a third of the time Yenni found that her pencil ended up back in her bag, rather than the intended placement on the left side of her desk.

At last class came to an end, and Yenni noticed another little crowd attempting to form around her, but Professor Mainard called out to her from the front of the lecture hall.

"Mam'selle Kayerba. A word, if you would."

She stepped down through the rows of seats to meet him. "What is it, Professor?"

He paused and frowned at something behind her. "Do you not have classes to attend next hour? If not, you should be studying. Off you go!"

Yenni turned to see a bunch of her classmates scurrying out of the room.

Mainard cleared his throat and adjusted his robes. "Now then, believe me when I say I am thoroughly appalled at the actions of Prof—*ex*-Professor Emmanuel Devon. I pride myself on finding the best and brightest to teach at Prevan and, well, I suppose I should have known, what with his eccentricities. And Gilles Desroches! A Magus, of all people, participating in this nonsense. But then he's always been something of an embarrassment to the establishment." He shook his tufted head. "I bowed to pressure to include unfounded magic in the curriculum. Prevan is meant to be at the forefront of magical theory after all, but I simply knew nothing good would come of it.

"Bah, but that is neither here nor there now. The class is in place, and someone must teach it. You no doubt received the notice that the class has been put on hold indefinitely, but disrupting a class in the final semester is far from ideal. As I said,

I want only the best and brightest on my staff. Who better to teach runelore at Prevan than a princess of the Moonrise Isles? Mam'selle Kayerba, I'm extending to you the very prestigious offer of employment as a professor at Prevan Academy."

Yenni crossed her arms, cocked her head to the side, and smiled, then smiled wider, then burst out laughing.

"What on Byen's hallowed soil can possibly be so funny?" blustered Mainard. He'd pushed his chest out, displaying his affront, and his face had gone splotchy red.

The smile quickly fled from Yenni's face. "You insult my culture in one breath, calling runelore unfounded and anyone who shows interest in it eccentric, and tell me I am among the best and brightest in the next? I wonder—would you be so bold as to march up to your own castle and extend to one of the princesses of Cresh an offer to *work under you*?"

Mainard clutched nervously at his robes. "Erm, well, I mean to say . . . but Prevan is the most celebrated school in the world! Mam'selle Kayerba—"

"Your Highness," said Yenni coolly. "Since my secret is out you may address me by my proper title."

Mainard looked like he would rather bite out and swallow his own tongue, but he bowed his head. "Your Highness," he said. "I meant no offense."

"And yet you somehow always manage to give it," said Yenni. "If I know nothing else, Professor Mainard, I know politics. And therefore I know exactly why you want me to teach your class. This is already a scandal for your school, and I doubt my royal family will take kindly to the fact that someone attempted to kill me, serious or not. You need my forgiveness, and my endorsement. You need to control the damage to Prevan's image. But what you also need is to understand that I am a princess of the Yirba, and I am not your tool.

"You are right about one thing, however. The class needs to be taught, and by someone who knows how to teach it properly. So, I am willing to become your new professor under two conditions. The first is that you give me a real office and classroom—nothing like that forsaken dungeon where you stowed Devon—plus pay me triple Devon's wages."

Mainard stared at her, stone faced, for quite some time. "Triple," he said at last, his voice flat.

"Yes, my wage, and one additional equivalent wage for each attempt on my life."

"I see. And the second condition?"

"You will seriously consider that a demon may be the cause of the wither-rot, and launch a full investigation."

He was already red, but he somehow went redder with the effort of containing his anger.

"Do we have a deal?"

"It will be done," he ground out. And he would do it, Yenni knew. For all his considerable flaws, Mainard was not a man who gave his word lightly.

Yenni smiled. "See that it is." She placed her hands under her chin and bowed to him. "Have a blessed day, Professor." She left him fuming at the front of his lecture hall.

Δ

The rest of the day went much the same, with half of Yenni's classmates whispering about her from afar while the other half engaged her. It wasn't as if she disliked it completely—some of them seemed to genuinely want to know about her and her homeland. But it had been a long while since she was the center of attention, and it soon became exhausting. It was with great relief that she climbed onto Weysh's back at the end of the day and let him whisk her away to his townhouse.

As they passed over the city, which glowed with sunset, Yenni ran her hands along Weysh's scales, tipped her head back, and prayed.

I love him, she told the Sha. *I know it could bring war and ruin to my tribe, but I love him. Wise Father Ri and loving Mother Shu, all-knowing Mother-Father Ool . . . if you mean for me to marry Weh-sheh, please, please show me that it is so.*

She stayed like that for some time, reveling in the secure safety of Weysh underneath her and the warmth of the last rays of the sun on her face, until Weysh let out an excited screech.

Yenni opened her eyes. "What—oh my!"

A group of fantastic creatures surrounded her—turtles that somehow glided on the air! At least, Yenni thought they were some sort of turtle; however, their hard shells flashed between green and gold in the waning sunlight. Yenni twisted and turned, counting them. Five in total, soaring along with their legs outstretched, no wings in sight.

"Mother Shu, Father Ri, is that you?" she whispered. Green and gold were Father Ri's colors, and Mother Shu's favorite number was five. One of the creatures floated up close enough to touch and watched her with an unblinking golden eye. Yenni reached out and stroked its shell. It let out a hoarse cry, and to Yenni's astonishment, began to fade before her eyes. Glancing around, she saw the others slowly disappearing as well, until the sky was clear once more.

Shortly after Weysh swooped in on his home, touching down before the gate as always. Yenni slid from his back and he quickly changed.

"Yenni! Yenni did you *see* that?!"

"See what, Messer Nolan?" asked Georges, the gate boy.

"Great golden sky turtles!" shouted Weysh.

Yenni laughed. "'Great golden sky turtles'? That sounds like a Creshen expression of shock."

But Georges's mouth had dropped open. "Hey, now, Messer Nolan, it's not nice to mess with the help."

"I swear it!" said Weysh. "They even flew with us for a while!"

"I touched one," said Yenni.

Both Weysh and Georges rounded on her. "You what?!" they said together.

"Do you know how rare that is?" asked Weysh.

"What did it feel like?" inquired Georges. The both of them waited expectantly.

"Oh, well, it felt smooth, like metal."

"I knew it! Their shells really are made of gold!" cried Georges.

Weysh shook his head. "Only you, Yenni."

"Are such creatures not common in Cresh?"

"Well, that depends on how you define common. If you consider a sighting once every one hundred and fifty years or so common, then yes, I suppose they're common, Yenni," said Weysh. "They largely stick to otherspace."

"Incredible," breathed Georges.

A nervous, excited fluttering began in Yenni's chest, and she couldn't keep from smiling.

That evening, Yenni sat at the little desk in Weysh's bedroom, writing a letter home while Weysh bathed. She had much to report, and was so lost in her thoughts that Weysh's knock against the doorframe startled her. He stood shirtless in his sleep pants, his dark hair free and flowing.

"I'm going up to the rooftop," he said. "Coming?"

Yenni looked him up and down. The light from the fire formed deep shadows in the dips of his muscular arms and stomach, accentuating them.

"Yenni?"

"No," she said. "Let's sleep here."

He furrowed his brow, confused "En? But I can't fit in here in dragon."

Yenni laughed as she slid from her chair. She took Weysh's hand and led him to the bed, where they lay facing each other. Yenni twined her arms around Weysh's neck and tangled her legs in his.

"Good night, my heart," said Weysh.

"Good night, my Given," she replied. Weysh smiled deeply, the corners of his eyes crinkling.

"How was your day?" he asked, trailing his nails down her back in a way that made her want to purr like a field sphinx. She told him about Mainard offering her the spot as professor of runelore, assuming she would jump at the chance, and her demand for triple Devon's wages.

Weysh laughed that laugh she loved so much. "Of course you demanded triple the wage. Never, ever change, my sweet," he said, and stroked her cheek. Yenni closed her eyes, relishing not only his fingers on her skin, but the closing of the gulf that had opened between them.

"I received a lot of attention today," she said.

"It will only get worse, I'm afraid," said Weysh. "I'm surprised none of the dailies have tried to get in contact; they must not yet be aware. But once they are, and the news gets to the general public, it will be a thrice-damned circus. We'd better enjoy the last of our peace for a while. Byen above, that reminds me—we'd better visit Maman. I'll never hear the end of it if she learns that you're royalty from the dailies instead of us."

Yenni bit the inside of her lip. "The Creshen Imperial Family may be upset I have not visited them. I do not think they will understand the rules of Orire N'jem."

"The Imperial—" His eyes went wide. "It's really beginning to sink in—you're a princess! Byen, does that mean I'll be a prince?"

"In name, I suppose, though I have to say I've never met a prince like you before," Yenni teased.

Weysh went quiet, his face serious as he studied her.

"What is it?" she asked.

"So you'll marry me?"

"There is still much to figure out, but yes, Weh-sheh, when the time is right I want to marry you."

He gave her that happy, boyish smile again. "I love you, Yenni."

"I love you, too, Weh-sheh."

His eyes dropped to her mouth, and the happy grin shifted to something far less innocent. And just the sight of it, that mere suggestive quirk of his lips, sent the blood rushing hot through her veins. He leaned forward but didn't kiss her. He put his nose to her neck, just under her jaw, and breathed deep.

"Oho," he rumbled, his lips just barely brushing her skin.

"What is it?" Yenni whispered, her heart pounding. "What do you smell?"

"I can't be sure," he drawled, making sure each word caressed the sensitive skin of her throat. His fingers started a lazy, looping trail up her leg, along her outer thigh. "Perhaps you're sleepy?"

"No, I'm not sleepy," Yenni breathed.

He sniffed again, making her giggle. "Maybe you're hungry?"

"That's . . . closer."

His fingers skimmed the underside of her bottom and she made a high little noise before jerking against him. He froze, and then his tongue flicked out to leisurely taste the spot where his nose had been.

"I see," he purred, and kissed her there, sending a spark of delight to her abdomen. Her eyes fluttered closed as he trailed stinging kisses along her jaw, each one leaving a warm echo, and her hands sought to tangle themselves in his hair. And all the while his fingers brushed languidly over her skin. Finally he claimed her mouth. His kiss, in contrast to his gentle fingers, was urgent, seeking. Yenni moaned and squirmed, and he nudged his big thigh between her legs as if he knew she needed to feel something, *anything* there. The sheets whispered and crinkled as she undulated against him.

He broke off the kiss only to graze his lips along her cheek, up to her ear. "Yenni," he whispered, his voice hoarse.

"Yes, Weh-sheh?"

"If we continue like this, I *will* make love to you."

"Yes, Weh-sheh."

He paused, then rolled them both so that he was on top of her, resting on his forearms. His hair made a curtain around them, flashing violet in the flickering light. He nuzzled her nose with his before touching his forehead to hers. "You're sure?"

She loved him, and the Sha had given their blessing. "I am sure."

The smile he gave her could only be described as wicked. "Well, great golden sky turtles," he said, making her laugh. But his thigh was still against her, and he moved it as he took her mouth, sliding his tongue in to meet hers. And she was no longer laughing.

$$\Delta$$

Yenni sighed, wonderfully content. She turned to Weysh and smiled, wondering how he could sleep, sprawled out and snoring, while every last inch of her body tingled and buzzed with sensory memory. She slipped from the bed, pulling on Weysh's nightshirt against the room's chill, and went back to the little desk by the window to finish her letter.

The words poured out of her in a long and constant stream as she explained the nature of the attacks, her new position as a professor, and her observations about Cresh and its people. But at last she ran out of things to say, and it came time to tell them about Weysh. She grabbed the pendant of the necklace he'd given her—she'd taken to wearing it at all times—and though her pencil shook in her hands, she made herself write.

But my biggest news is that I have met a dragon by the name of Weysh Nolan, and we are promised as Given. This means I am his one true mate in the world, and he is mine. Iyaya, N'baba, my brothers and sisters, I tell you: at first I thought this dragon-man a lunatic, and his interest in me to be the work of that trickster, Father Esh. But over time my heart has softened to him in a way that can only be worked by the gentle hand of Mother Shu. I am forever loyal to our tribe, and I want nothing more than to bring us glory and prosperity, and yet I cannot give my heart, my soul, or my body to another. So if you have designs for me to wed someone else, I have no choice but to object.

Weysh Nolan is part Creshen and part Southern Islander. He is technically the only Island dragon known to this world. I believe that one of the reasons I was compelled to undertake Orire N'jem was to meet him, and eventually to marry him, for in truth I don't want to marry anyone else. I cannot guess what blessings our union will bring to the Yirba people; I can only trust in the divine wisdom of the Mothers and Fathers.

I pray you will not find this news distressing, because above all, I am happy.

All my love and blessings,

Yenni

37

The circus was in full swing.

It took perhaps three days before news of Yenni's attack and Devon and his famous mentor's arrest hit the news. At first it was only poor Yenni being harassed and questioned. She was stopped outside classes, and when academy security put an end to that, they pestered her on her forays into the city. Sketches of her—some flattering, others not—showed up in every daily. They painted the sad story of an exotic princess of the Isles come to experience the majesty of Cresh only to be horribly attacked by a deviant professor. But when that well ran dry, the dailies shifted their attention to Weysh.

He was utterly baffled when one day, at the gate to his townhouse, a man and a woman with notepads ran up to him. The woman squinted and sketched while the man bombarded him with questions. *How does it feel to go from delivering packages to being a prince? Where will you two live, the Moonrise Isles or Cresh? We've learned you have Island heritage, officially making*

you the only known Island dragon—do you think it's fate that your
Given is a princess of the Moonrise Isles?

Weysh never answered a single question. He and Yenni were
having a tough enough time figuring things out *without* the dailies sticking their noses into their relationship, and it was easy
to escape the reporters when he could fly, but they still found a
way to spin the rags to riches story of his life. Whole interviews
appeared that he'd never given, some of them quite entertaining.
Harth certainly enjoyed them.

He'd come running up to Weysh, daily paper fluttering in
hand and summarize the latest nonsense. Loudly. "Weysh, how
can it be, in all the time we've known each other, you never told
me of your secret ambition to design extravagant hats made of
your shed dragon scales?" Or "Weysh! Watcher above, I had no
idea you were so self-conscious about your residual dragon tail!
You know that little stub that remains for some reason when you
turn back into a man? You should have *confided* in me! Good
thing Yenni doesn't mind it, en? It seems you fell head over *tail*
for her when she accepted you just as you are, stub and all. It's all
right here. What a love story for the ages—ow!"

Weysh boxed him on the ear for that one.

At last, in an effort to get some peace, when they both had a
free afternoon Weysh flew Yenni to a nice, hidden area on the
bank of the River Noureer where it cut through the south of the
campus. And now, at Yenni's insistence, he was practicing using
runes in dragon, *again*. They worked with a wall of green trees as
their backdrop and the rushing water their musical score. Yenni
sang the hymn for wind as she painted the scales of Weysh's nose
bridge. She sang to infuse the rune, but he knew that she also sang
to him. Weysh closed his eyes, enjoying her voice.

Yenni tied off the rune with a low, soothing note and Weysh sighed, his whole bulk shifting up then down. She laughed softly and gave him a kiss on the nose before reaching for her spear. "All right, Weh-sheh," she said as she unscrewed the sharp metal tip. "Let's begin." He would practice his runes while she would practice her Creshen spellcraft.

She attacked with her spear, augmenting herself with Creshen spells, and he was supposed to be calling on the runes she'd drawn to defend himself, but he constantly forgot, switching into the old defensive strategies that had been drilled into him over the years. He'd never been particularly adept at magic in human, and in dragon it was incredibly difficult and awkward.

"Great golden sky turtles, Weh-sheh!" Yenni would yell every time, exasperated. "*Use your runes!*" But he would only lumber over and nuzzle against her until she was no longer annoyed.

They worked at it until the sun cleared the horizon, with Yenni chanting *Use your runes* like a mantra, until at last Weysh flew them home. *Home.* He loved that the word had new meaning now. Home for him *and* home for Yenni. They didn't sleep outside anymore, preferring to curl up together in bed instead, as they did that night. Exhausted from the day's events, they fell into happy slumber.

Δ

Yenni's voice is strong and clear as she sings, as she paints, even though the wind screams and slaps her braids against her face, even as the sky cracks and flashes. The storm is not meant to harm them. Weysh stands before her in dragon, and she paints him in great swaths, singing of wind and of lightning, singing to Mother Ya.

The storm rages, but she is not afraid. It fuels her runes. It offers protection.

It drives her, and she paints with abandon. Soon Weysh is covered in white runes that glow all over his dark scales. Yenni's heart swells with pride. He is beautiful, and he is hers.

But what is this? A strange discord interrupts the grand music of the storm. She listens.

As the rumble of thunder subsides she hears it again, under the singing wind. A rage-filled dragon's roar.

Δ

Yenni gasped awake, and Weysh bolted up beside her.

"What? What is it, Yenni?"

Why was her heart pounding?

"I'm right here, lovely." He stroked her braids and kissed her forehead. "Another bad dream?"

She'd been having night terrors, and no wonder, after all she'd been through.

"What was it this time?" Weysh asked soothingly.

She shook her head. "I don't remember." All she knew was that anxiety and fear coursed through her blood. The dream had something to do with Weysh, and runes. She scrunched up her brow. "But I want to paint you."

"En?"

"In dragon. It would give me some peace of mind to know you were protected by runes."

"Now?"

Now, yes, now. "It will help calm me, I think."

He slid from the bed and they went to the rooftop, where he changed.

Yenni unscrewed the top on her runepaint and took up her brush, almost sighing at the comforting feel of it in her hand. She went to start the wind rune, but somehow it didn't feel right. Something about the air, the humid stickiness of it, reminded her of a summer storm, made her want to sing of lightning. She moved all around Weysh, singing him the lightning hymn, feeling a secret, thrilling connection to Mother Ya, the formidable Mistress of Storms. The hymn was fast, zipping up to sudden high notes at times, or rumbling and low at others. She seemed to fall into a trance as she worked, the hymn hypnotizing her so that when at last she was done and she took in Weysh, she reeled back.

He looked fearsome, his dark scales covered in jagged white lightning runes—just as in her dream. Yenni took hold of his face and he lowered it, so that she could press her forehead to his.

"I love you," she whispered.

The next morning Yenni awoke feeling rested and calm, like a weight had been lifted from her. Weysh flew her into the academy, dropping her off at the library, and as she was dismounting a dragon called to them from the steps of the library.

"Oho! Weysh!" cried the blue-skinned young man. He was differently blue-skinned than Zui—darker, with eyes like sapphires. "I heard the good news! Congratulations!"

Weysh looked apprehensive, and Yenni knew he was wondering what fresh lunacy the dailies had written about him.

"What news is that, Sween?"

"About Noriago!" he cried. "Don't tell me you don't know? I thought they'd have told you first! He's been apprehended! I heard it from Clairette."

"That's wonderful!" cried Yenni.

"Yes, everyone's talking about it."

"En? Truly? Excellent! I expect I'll hear from the peacekeepers

soon." Weysh collected his "flight toll" and left Yenni to her studies, joining his classmate and questioning him about Noriago's
arrest as they ambled down the walkway. Yenni exhaled a happy
sigh. With the last looming threat taken care of, it felt like she
and Weysh could breathe. At the very least they could sleep outside in peace if they chose. For the first time in weeks, perhaps
since she'd come to Cresh, Yenni had a carefree day. She started
by preparing for her runelore class later that week, then she met
Diedre for lunch at the dining hall, and she didn't even have to see
Mainard at all, as he taught none of her classes that day.

In the evening she went to Riverbank Chambers to check her
messages. It was far too soon to expect anything from back home,
but the academy would also leave memorandums and reminders,
not to mention sometimes Diedre left her funny little notes about
her day, which Yenni loved to read.

But when she checked her letter box, she found something
she'd never expected: a note from Carmenna.

Dear Yenni Ajani,

*I want to say I'm sorry for how things ended between
us. I abandoned you when you needed me most, and I
feel terrible about that. I hope that you will allow me to
take you to dinner this evening and apologize in person. I know a wonderful place in the Southern Quarter.
If you agree, please meet me at student services at the
eighth hour of the evening. As well, there are some
sensitive things I want to discuss with you, things that
would be difficult to say in front of Weysh, so I'd very*

much appreciate it if the two of us could meet alone.

Sincerely,
Carmenna

Yenni, too, was unhappy with how things had ended between them. She held no ill will toward Carmenna, and had never quite shaken off her guilt at breaking her promise to not fall for Weysh, though the arrogance of her promise seemed ludicrous now. She was glad the other woman wanted to talk. But she remembered the clock tower chiming seven a while ago—it had to be close to the eighth hour now.

She wrote a quick note to Weysh that she would be meeting Carmenna and would find her way home. Then she painted on her runes, including focus—no matter what these Creshens thought, she would not be caught unawares again. Then she grabbed her spring-spear and set out.

$$\Delta$$

"I know it's a bit off the beaten path, but all the best places are."

Yenni had taken the tram into the city with Carmenna, and now they were skulking through the Creshen Southern Quarter, which was an interesting place, to say the least. It was much quieter than anywhere she'd been in Cresh, not nearly as crowded. It felt shadowed somehow. There were gas lamps lining the streets as opposed to magic lanterns, and the homes and shops were largely dark, no warm light glowing from within. Yenni had to hurry to keep up with Carmenna's long-legged strides.

Carmenna took her up a set of dark steps, between cold, empty houses that seemed long abandoned. The way they squeezed in on her reminded her uncomfortably of the alley where the Creshen thugs had robbed her.

"What is this place? It seems like there is nothing here," said Yenni.

Carmenna only laughed. "That's what everyone says, but you'll see. We're almost there."

The stairs opened to a flat, grassy landing that cut off abruptly. A drop to the canal lay ahead, while empty, staring houses loomed behind. *What, by all the Mothers and Fathers was going on?* There truly was nothing there, certainly no place to eat. Yenni whirled to face Carmenna.

"What—"

"*Sleep by source, wake no time soon.*"

38

The world jerked and swayed around Yenni, pulling her from sleep. Was she dreaming, or did she hear muffled screams? Her shoulders and hips hurt and she could tell she was lying on something hard but supple, like a hammock but also not like a hammock. Fighting through the fog of sleep, she opened her eyes.

She was outside, that much she knew. Humid night air clung to her skin, but her tired, disoriented brain could make little sense of the strange landscape surrounding her. Dark, forested mountains loomed in the distance, but there were also little patches of forest on thick, plateaued pillars all around her with wooden bridges, many of them broken or rotted away, connecting them like some massive spider web.

Clunky footsteps approached, shaking whatever she was lying on. A shadow blocked out the moonlight.

"This is a princess? Not at all what I was expecting. You're nothing more than a painted savage. Is that bird shit on your face supposed to be beautiful?"

It was a man's voice, and not one she recognized, though something about how he spoke was familiar. Yenni tried to sit up, but her wrists and ankles were tied. She tried to pull on her runes, but her groggy body refused to obey. Ach'e simply stirred lazily under her skin. She groaned against her cloth gag. The man grabbed her by the braids, and something sharp scraped her scalp painfully. He turned her to look at him, and primal fear rose up in her. His pupils were slits, black horns jutted from his forehead, and bat-like wings drooped from his back.

"Still, when one marries a princess, no matter how loose the definition, I suppose he must become a prince."

His face contorted angrily, and Yenni knew why people feared dragons in half-change. With his sharp teeth barred and snake-like eyes burning with hate, he looked positively demonic.

"NO!" he bellowed at her, and Yenni flinched. She heard another muffled scream. "Not. Him." Yenni's pulse rushed in her ears. What was he talking about? What was going on? The dragon studied her dispassionately. "I wouldn't struggle too much if I were you. This bridge is fairly old. It's a miracle it's held until now. Besides, there's nowhere for you to go."

With that he spread his wings and took off, rattling the bridge just as he'd warned her not to do. She strained against the sleepiness holding her like a weighted net, and at last sat up, though her head lolled to one side. She sat suspended on a bridge between two of the giant, forested pillars that jutted from the dark gorge below. By the light of the open moon she could see that jagged slabs of rock took up the entirety of the gap below, a massive stone forest. What was this place?

Someone was making muffled sounds at her. Ahead, on the far side of the bridge, a figure with long, dark hair was tied up and gagged like she was. Was that Carmenna? The last thing she remembered was walking through the city with her to some Creshen pubs and . . .

. . . and Carmenna had used that sleep incantation on her, the same one Diedre used on the thugs.

Realization dawned like a red sun, the outrage of it burning away her lethargy. Yenni dragged on her strength runes, which lit up under the sleeves of her school uniform, and strained against her wrist bonds. When the pain of rope digging into her flesh made her eyes water she drew on pain ward as well, until the ropes burst at last.

Yenni ripped the cloth from her mouth, untied her legs, and stood, wobbling on the shaky bridge. When she reached Carmenna the other woman had tears running down her face. Yenni yanked her gag free. "I'm sorry!" she cried. "He threatened me! He said—"

"Be quiet." Yenni said it softly, but Carmenna must have heard the tirade underneath as she hung her head, silent. Yenni removed Carmenna's ties, then surveyed the surroundings as Carmenna stood, rubbing her wrists. Their bridge stretched between two of the huge plateaus, both of them, impossibly, with grand trees growing out of the rock. The trees were sparse enough that she could see through them with the help of her focus rune, and it was clear that on either plateau there was no other connecting bridge.

"We have to get out of here before Noriago returns," said Carmenna.

"Noriago?" cried Yenni. "That was Noriago? But he was apprehended!"

Carmenna sniffled. "He wasn't. It was a ruse. He told me to

mention that he had been apprehended around one of his class-mates and the rumor would spread, and Weysh would let his guard down."

"Mothers and Fathers!" Yenni shouted in Yirba.

"What?"

"Ah!" she said, angrily waving Carmenna away. How were they to get free? Dread pooled in her stomach as she surveyed their situation. The only way out was down, a *long* way down to sharp rocks that thrust up like stakes. The edges of the gorge seemed impossibly far. "Do you know of a spell that can make us fly?" Yenni asked, because that was what it would take to reach them.

"No," Carmenna whispered. "It would take a Magus's skill to get across. I was hoping you had a rune."

"Even if I did, my satchel with my paint is gone, as well as my spear." She rounded suddenly on Carmenna, her frustration reaching a crescendo. "Why would you do this?!"

"I'm sorry! I'm so sorry! He knows where my family lives. He said if I didn't do as he said he would he would fly straight to my home and set it ablaze with my brothers inside, long before I could alert the peacekeepers. And I thought even gagged, you could escape with your runes. I planned to go straight to the peacekeepers once he let me go, but he must have guessed and he kidnapped me too. I—" She cut off at Yenni's upheld hand.

"None of that matters. We must now find our way out of this gorge." And they would have to do it on their own, because the one who could have rescued her could no longer track her scent.

Δ

With Yenni gone to dinner with Carmenna, Weysh decided to

visit with Harth and his family. It had been a while since he'd seen them—as a child he was always there, another escape from his home life. And though he would never admit it to Harth's annoying green face, he was looking forward to seeing his friend as well. He'd sent a note by quick-post that he would be coming, asking what was for dinner. Harth had written back: *Roast duck with hot-berry jelly and champagne tarts for me, Zui, and everyone else; leftover scraps from the wild boar I hunted the other day for you.* Weysh was looking forward to showing up and eating both his and Harth's share of the roast duck.

Weysh had just put on his boots when he was overwhelmed by a terrible dread that washed over him like a wave of cold water. What by Byen . . . he jerked up straight. His alarm! That was how the magic of it worked, by sending a blast of horrible, unsettling anxiety through the owner if someone unauthorized entered his home. Weysh glanced around. He'd heard no one enter the door, which could only mean someone had breached his rooftop. Harth or Zui? But they'd been to his place enough times that the magic was attuned to them. Fighting back that sucking dread Weysh clomped up the stairs to the rooftop and threw open the door.

"Who's there?" he demanded. There was, in fact, a figure hidden in the shadows of the trees. "Show yourself!"

He did. Smirking, Noriago stepped into the light of one of the magic lanterns.

Weysh felt a moment of numbing shock, and then instant, painful cold, like needles of ice all over his body. Was this some sort of nightmare? Noriago should have been rotting away in a prison cell, not here on his thrice-damned rooftop!

Noriago let something slip from his fingers, dangling. Weysh's shock crystalized into brittle horror—it was the ivystone necklace he'd given Yenni. He lunged for Noriago, but the snake darted back, leapt from the roof, changed, and took off. Weysh changed and dove off the roof after him.

Where is she? Weysh roared. In response Noriago let the necklace fall, the chain of it fluttering as it fell to the city below. Heart racing, Weysh beat his wings harder. He screeched after Noriago, lit up the night sky with fire, but just like in class, Noriago continued to gain the lead. Weysh was frantic. He had no clue if Noriago was leading him toward Yenni or away. All he was sure of was that he couldn't track her scent, and only Noriago knew where she was. But if Noriago thought he could lose Weysh, he was badly mistaken. That rat shit might be faster, but Weysh was used to marathon flights. He would follow Noriago to the edge of the world if he had to.

For terrible, agonizing minutes Weysh beat the air, hot in pursuit. He followed Noriago out of the city, clear to the mountains. Where were they going? Where was Yenni?! In no class, on no flight, had Weysh ever shot through the air like he did now. A cocktail of terror and fury fueled his flight. Noriago flew over the southern mountains, to the infamous Spider Pass. They soared over an old confection of platforms and bridges built long ago, suspended above tall, craggy slabs of rock. Noriago let out an angry, unintelligible shriek, then let loose with flame, setting fire to one of the forested platforms. The trees burned, turning their stone pillar into a giant torch. What was he doing? Weysh didn't have much time to wonder, as the other dragon looped in the air and rushed him.

Weysh was more than ready. For weeks he'd been longing to sink his claws into Noriago, rip into his throat with his teeth, shred his wings. They clashed, kicking and snapping at each other.

Δ

Oh unholy shadows, the trees were ablaze!

"*Source-drawn rain here come and fall!*" yelled Carmenna. Yenni followed suit, but their contained rainfalls did little to stop the fire racing down branches, jumping from tree to tree. It had erupted too quickly, and there was simply too much fuel. Soon the heat of it became painful, and the smoke burned Yenni's eyes. Carmenna coughed beside her and they stumbled to the edge of the plateau by the bridge. Screeches and roars and bright gouts of flame pierced the air above them. Yenni gasped. Weysh was *here*, fighting Noriago. She swung between relief and terror, pausing even as the heat sent sweat rolling down her back.

"We must move to the other platform," she shouted to Carmenna at last, struggling to be heard over the crackle and roar of the flames.

"The moment Noriago sees us he'll light the bridge up! We should wait for Weysh."

"Weysh cannot smell! He likely doesn't know we are here. If we want to live we must get across this bridge as fast as possible and cut it away so the fire does not spread. Do you know speed magic?"

"It's not my area of expertise, but—"

Yenni hunched down before Carmenna. "Then get on my back."

Praise Ib-e-ji, Carmenna didn't argue, as Yenni was quite tempted to leave her among the blazing trees. She hooked her arms under Carmenna's thighs and hoisted her up, flared her strength and speed runes, and ran.

Δ

Noriago closed his wings suddenly, plummeting to escape Weysh's assault. He wheeled in the air and rushed back toward the copse of trees he'd set on fire. Weysh followed, and saw a blur streaking across the bridge. That couldn't be . . .

Yenni!

Weysh screeched her name and dove after Noriago. The rest happened in seconds. Noriago hovered in the sky, his chest swelled and glowing, ready to let loose with fire. Weysh slammed into him, sending him spinning away in a spiral of flame. Weysh dove for the bridge, then roared as searing pain traveled up his tail, wrenching his spine. Noriago had latched on to his tail and now, beating his wings, he fairly whipped Weysh around and flung him in the opposite direction. Weysh heard an eruption of flame and turned back to see that the forested plateau at the other side of the bridge—the very place Yenni had run to for safety—was also on fire.

Before Weysh could even think to go to her Noriago was on him.

I want you to see! I want you to see! he screeched over and over as he flapped and snapped at Weysh. *You don't deserve it! Not you! Not you!*

Get out of my way! Weysh roared back.

He sank his teeth in wherever he could, scraping off scales, mania taking him over. And when Noriago howled and Weysh tasted blood, he relished it. Bloodlust and vengeance crowded out his training and he completely forgot to protect his wings. Noriago saw his opening and slashed with his claws, ripping through the tough membrane. Pain sizzled through Weysh even as Noriago struck again, making another, searing slash in the same wing. Weysh tried to stay aloft, but his wing simply wouldn't obey him and catch the air. And it *hurt*. Every flap of his injured wing was agony. And so he tumbled, spinning on one wing, doing all he could to aim for the platform with Yenni. He even locked eyes with her as he crashed straight through the bridge, sending rope and planks tumbling with him.

$$\Delta$$

Yenni screamed. *Oh Mothers and Fathers,* please *Mothers and Fathers*—to see Weysh falling from the sky, exactly like her nightmare, and her helpless to stop it, was enough to drive her mad, to make her forget the flames threatening to curdle and melt her flesh from her bones.

"Watcher above!" Carmenna gasped. "Weysh!"

"Don't you call his name," Yenni snarled, even as she peered desperately over the edge of the plateau, but she must have said it in Yirba, as Carmenna seemed confused more than anything.

Please, please, please Mother Shu. I love him, I love him, I love him.

Mother Shu answered her prayer. Weysh's dragon call sounded from the darkness below.

Yenni! I'm coming!

"Where are you?!" she shouted back. Her eyes adjusted to the dark and she caught a glint of moonlight on scales. Weysh clung to the side of the huge pillar, climbing toward them. But Noriago spotted him at the same time. He roared and dove for Weysh.

"Weh-sheh! Your runes!" she screamed at him. He was even now covered in the lightning runes she'd painted the night before. But if he heard her he didn't heed her; he only climbed faster. By the cursed shadows, he couldn't remember to use his runes at the best of times, he'd *never* call on them now. It was up to her to help him.

When she and Carmenna had first burst into the copse of trees she'd seen her satchel and spear strewn on the ground, just in time to watch her satchel and paints ignite with the forest around them. Her spear, however, she had been able to snatch free. Now Yenni twisted it, extended it, drew on her focus runes, and took aim. She sent it flying true, straight for the other dragon's throat.

He dipped his neck and dove, beautiful and terrible, and her spear sailed over him, into the darkness below.

$$\Delta$$

Weysh dug in his claws, hauling himself up the rocky pillar to Yenni. He saw her spear go flying, saw Noriago dodge it, and then she was screaming at him. But she was still so far! He couldn't hear her over his own blood thudding in his ears, and over Noriago.

Die, Nolan! Noriago screeched. Weysh strained and climbed. If he could only make himself go faster, like he sometimes did as a man! If only he could use—

MAGIC!

He could use *Yenni's* magic. That's what she was always yelling at him.

Use your runes!

He did his best to concentrate through his desperation, against Noriago bearing down on him. He pulled source to the runes. It came slowly, like syrup, but at last he felt his scales warm. Noriago was right on top of him. Weysh flared source through the runes and let loose.

Lightning whizzed, making the strangest sound he'd ever heard, like a buzzing note of music, and crackled through the darkness. Noriago let out a wail the likes of which Weysh had never heard, so awful it gave Weysh no satisfaction. The lightning coursed through Noriago, illuminating him from the inside so Weysh could see muscle and even bone. Then Noriago fell twitching to the jagged rocks below.

"Weh-sheh!"

Yenni's frantic voice echoed above him and he remembered. Fire! Weysh scrambled up the column and hauled himself onto the plateau. Yenni was on him in an instant, kissing and stroking him. The trees burned and popped against the night sky. The heat must have been terrible for her and—was that Carmenna? She'd been stolen away as well?

It mattered not; he had to find a way to get them free of the blazing plateau before the fire consumed their edge. Every second it burned closer. But how? Climb down the pillar with them on his back? That had its own risks. He was built for flying, not climbing. Suppose he should slip? He'd never be able to right himself. Or suppose one of them should lose purchase hanging on to him? But what other choice did they have?

$$\Delta$$

"Weysh can shield us from the fire with his body until it burns out," said Carmenna.

Yenni coughed, her eyes burning. "But he cannot protect us from the smoke. You must heal his wing, Carmenna."

"I-I don't know if I can! Healing works best when spells are infused into balms or potions, healing straight through spellcraft is primitive and difficult." She waved her hands uselessly.

"Try! I will keep the smoke back," said Yenni. "Hurry!"

She pulled on her wind runes, blowing back the acrid smoke. It took quite a bit of force, and the smoke was only increasing. The fire continued to eat its way through the trees, as if sentient and hungry. She could hear Carmenna chanting behind her, words she couldn't understand, likely San-Uramaik, the old magic language. Yenni blew and blew at the fire, but she could feel her wind runes failing, her body tiring.

"Carmenna!"

The chanting picked up in volume. Yenni glanced back and saw that the gashes in poor Weysh's wing were much smaller. A loud crack echoed through the darkness, and a large tree fell toward them. Yenni pulled—fire wards, pain wards, and strength runes—and heaved the tree aside before it could land on Carmenna.

"The trees are collapsing!" Yenni shouted. Carmenna's voice became ragged, desperate, and Weysh rumbled and moaned as she worked.

"There!" she cried at last. Yenni turned in time to see the last of the ragged rip in Weysh's beautiful wing disappear.

Weysh crouched down and Yenni hopped nimbly onto his back, as she had so many times before. She reached out hand to help Carmenna. Carmenna held out her arm but then froze, and screamed.

Yenni followed her gaze. Impossibly, against all that was good and right, Noriago rose up out of the gorge. He roared, his wings spread wide. Weysh crouched at the edge of the platform and snarled at him, the runes on his nose bridge glowing brilliant white as he readied another attack. Noriago roared, enraged, and turned tail.

Time to go, Weysh called to them. They hunched down and Weysh dove off the platform. Rushing wind cooled the sweat on Yenni's heated skin, and she took deep, wheezing breaths of the fresh night air. Weysh arced around the pillar and took off in the opposite direction from Noriago, toward the cliffs that bordered the mountain pass. Yenni knew his main goal was to get them to safety, but she hated to know that that *rat prick*, as Weysh would put it, was escaping once again. She turned on Weysh's back, watching him go.

Please, Mother Ya, must he escape justice?

Something large and winged streaked through the air like a whistling spear, colliding with Noriago. Another dragon! The two went spinning to the rocks below. Weysh landed on the other side of the gorge and spun around, so that the women wobbled atop him.

Harth! he bellowed.

Harth? She pulled on her focus runes, strengthening her vision to match Weysh's dragon eyes. Sure enough, the other dragon was their green friend.

"Har-tha!" Yenni screamed as well. Weysh crouched, growling. Yenni could see he was anxious to go help, but he also didn't want to leave her. A small figure leapt off Harth's back and a moment later Zui twisted and writhed in the sky. Harth dipped and zoomed and harried Noriago while Zui, for her part, attacked Noriago with those deadly streams of hers, aiming for his wings. Noriago could protect himself from Harth's fire, but not Zui's jets. Harth distracted him while with practiced aim, Zui pierced each of Noriago's wings.

Noriago fell, screeching, and crashed onto a platform below. As they watched, he tried to get up, flapping weakly before falling back to the trees. Again and again.

Zui flew over while Harth perched on the platform across from Noriago, screeching at him.

Zui touched down on the cliffs and changed. "Yenni!" she cried and hugged her. "I'm glad to see you're okay!"

Yenni squeezed her back. "And I'm glad to see you! How did you find us?"

"Harth became quite suspicious when Weysh was supposed to show up for dinner and an hour later his plate remained unaccosted. We went to Weysh's place to sniff him out, and caught Noriago's scent instead. So we followed."

Weysh let out a soft dragon moan. *Thank you so much, both of you.*

"Weysh, take Yenni and Carmenna back to safety and bring the peacekeepers. We'll watch him."

Weysh screeched his thanks to his friends and dove off the platform, speeding them back to the city.

39

The next couple of weeks were a tempest of activity. Noriago was well and truly arrested, and finally locked away in an Espannian prison. Yenni and Weysh gave testimony at the trials for Gilles Desroches and Emmanuel Devon—open and shut affairs due to the mountain of evidence against them—and they too went away.

The case for Carmenna's involvement had been heard as well. She'd tearfully admitted her guilt to the peacekeepers, drawing shock and disappointment from Weysh. But due to Noriago's coercion, her sentence was not as severe. She was not imprisoned, but tasked with serving the community as a voluntary healer for the less fortunate.

"I know I can never atone for what I have done," she told them when they saw her last at her hearing. "But I want you to know that I've solidified my focus of study, and I'm going to specialize in dragon physicry. Weysh, I will make it my life's goal to bring back your sense of smell."

It was only now, two weeks later, that things were beginning to die down. Yenni had settled into her role as acting professor of runelore and between studying for her own classes and teaching others, she was constantly tired, though she had a good bit of help from her teaching assistant and best friend, Diedre.

Still, exhaustion was not the word for what weighed her steps that evening. She was so tired she didn't even trust herself to use speed runes to run home, afraid she would pass out. Luckily, her classroom was not as far away as the previous runelore classroom had been, but just a short walk from her residence at Riverbank Chambers. At last she flopped down on her bed, not caring that it was too soft, and settled in for a few hours of well-deserved sleep before her next class.

Her head had just touched her pillow when a familiar metallic creaking chased away the first tendrils of sleep. It took her half-drowsing brain a moment to realize it was her letter box.

Her letter box!

She darted up in bed, adrenaline fueling her to wakefulness. When she checked, there it was, a brown papua roll. Her family's response to Weysh.

Yenni hesitated, biting her bottom lip. She wondered: What would they say? Would they welcome a dragon into their midst, even if he was only part Islander? Would they lambaste her for shacking up with a strange Creshen man? In fact, she no longer stayed at Weysh's townhome since Noriago had been caught. She'd told him she needed to be close to the school for her professor's duties, but in truth he could be quite a distraction. A wonderful distraction, yes, but a distraction.

She worried: would her parents demand she follow through on the marriage to Prince Natahi? Perhaps she should go back to bed and wait until she could read it with Weysh.

No, she was not a coward. She would read the letter now.

She opened it to reveal her family's crest—a white field sphinx. The letter itself was quite short. She frowned as she read:

Daughter,

Praises to all the Mothers and Fathers that you are once again safe. You must bring this dragon with you when your pledged year abroad is complete and you return. We will form a strategy then. Write no more of this. Love from your iyaya, your siblings, your tribe and me, your n'baba. May the Sha guide you safely home.

What? That was it? That was all?

Yenni turned the paper over, even shook it, as if she could shake free more words. How frustratingly vague! What did her father mean by "We will form a strategy"?

Still, it seemed as if her family had accepted Weysh. They wanted her to bring him back with her. That was a good thing, was it not? So why did the letter fill her with such apprehension? Just what would she find on returning home?

$$\Delta$$

Weysh screeched his arrival as he landed on his family's lawn, but he was surprised when his maman, not Genie, answered the door, her eyes puffy and her smile brittle. She hugged him long and tightly, and he didn't need his sense of smell to tell that something was very wrong.

"How is Montpierre?" he asked, already knowing the answer.

"Come, let's sit," was all she said. As he followed her to the den, Sylvie hurried down the stairs to join them. She attached herself to Weysh's side and didn't let him go until they reached the winged armchairs and sat down.

Maman sighed. "Montpierre is not well. He was too exhausted to rise from bed this morning."

Weysh took in their haunted expressions and felt nothing but sadness. "I'm sorry," he said.

She waved at the air as if she could flick away her sorrows like swatting a buzzing fly. "But what about you, sweet? Where's your princess?"

"Professor Yenni Ajani is teaching a class at the moment," said Weysh, smiling fondly. Weysh made small talk with them, updating them on his life in a way he never used to, until eventually his maman rose. "It's time for Montpierre's next dose of medicine. Excuse me," she said, and glided from the den.

Sylvie stared after her, eyebrows raised in concern.

"How are you holding up, conductor?" he asked her.

She laughed softly. "You know, it's funny you should say that. I made some new friends, and a couple of them are tram enthusiasts like me."

"Truly? That's wonderful, Sylvie!"

"Yes, I like them a lot," she said, and her smile warmed his heart. "We're all part of the same group: Sainte Hosha Girl's Society of Magical Advancement."

"Oho! Sounds impressive! What sorts of things do you discuss?"

"All kinds of interesting things! We read journals on experimental incantations, theoretical applications of existing magical spells—it's fascinating, Weysh!" As Sylvie went into detail about her new friends, some of the color came back to her cheeks and her eyes brightened. "Weysh, I've been thinking about some- thing. If I tell you, will you promise not to mock me?"

"Of course, Sylvie. What is it?"

"I want to be able to take care of Maman too. I think when I'm done second school I want to go to Grande Magus Academy. I want to become a magical engineer and work on the trams, per- haps even develop a new type of tram or maybe even a flying machine!"

Weysh blinked. She held her chin up, watching him defiantly. Weysh had always thought of Sylvie as the little sister he had to support and protect, but she was growing up before his eyes. He'd told Yenni she would be much more than simply someone's wife, and it dawned on him the same was true of Sylvie as well.

"A flying machine? So you're trying to put me out of business, en?"

"Ah! Well, I didn't think of that—"

Weysh laughed. In truth he'd been itching to get out of the ferrying business of late, especially after today's run. He'd flown a stuffy young merchant couple to their villa on Sainte Ventas. They were the type of passengers Weysh liked the least but were unfortunately most common: not quite high enough on the social scale to have dragon relatives but flush with new money and something to prove, so they insisted on riding dragonback. They were slow to heed his signals, complained about the wind, and took forever to dismount when they finally landed hours later. Weysh didn't trust himself to change from dragon to man and bid them farewell. Thank the Kindly Watcher they'd paid in advance through credit at the bank. He had only to deposit them at their gaudy summer house, sketch them a shallow bow, and take off.

"You know what? If it makes you happy, I think that's a fantastic idea, conductor."

"Yes and it makes me feel better, the idea that I can take care of myself and Maman. I'm still scared for Papa but knowing I'll have some sort of purpose when he's gone, makes things . . . not *better*, but less terrifying. And you'll be free to live with your Given."

Weysh reached across the coffee table to take her hand. "Lovely, no matter what happens, and no matter where I live, you can always count on my support."

This was what Montpierre didn't understand. Weysh could never just abandon his family, and he couldn't on principle let the man go to his grave thinking so ill of him. Weysh stood.

"Where are you going?" asked Sylvie.

The look he gave her was resolute and sober. "To visit with Montpierre."

Δ

Weysh had to hold back a grimace upon entering his parents' bedroom. Montpierre was sitting up in bed, supported by a pillow. His face was pale, marked by blue-black shadows under his eyes, and the white duvet covering him was speckled with flecks of blood. On the left-side night table a stick of incense sent wispy trails of smoke into the air, and Weysh knew that if he could smell, his nostrils would be clogged with the herbish bite of cam-cam weed.

Montpierre's eyes went wide when he spotted Weysh, then narrowed.

"Do you not knock before entering a room?" Montpierre rasped. "I was under the impression that your Given was engendering within you some much-needed civility, but apparently I was wrong."

Weysh met Montpierre's eyes boldly, refusing to be cowed, and for the first time in his life he saw something in the man's face he'd never seen before. Perhaps it had always been there, and it was Weysh's own brush with tragedy—his fears of a future with no sense of smell—that finally allowed him to see the stark reality. Behind that rage-filled glare was raw, agonizing terror.

Weysh felt slim fingers close around his wrist. "Now is not the time, my heart," said his maman, trying to tug him away. But Weysh stood firm, his eyes never leaving Montpierre's.

"Why are you just standing there, staring like a lackwit?" Montpierre barked, and though such disrespect normally caused Weysh's blood to rise, today it provoked only pity, because Weysh knew instinctively that the terror eating Montpierre alive was not directed at him. It was far too sinister for that. It was the terror of a man about to lose everything he'd ever worked to build, and everyone he'd ever deigned to love.

"Weysh!" his mother said firmly, tugging him again. But he put a hand over hers and turned to her.

"It's all right, Maman," he said softly. "I'm not here to cause trouble." He focused once more on his stepfather. "Montpierre, I only wanted to say this: whatever may happen, Maman and Sylvie can always count on me for protection and support. I would never abandon my family. So, on that front, at least, you have nothing to fear."

That gave Montpierre pause. The tension fled him, leaving him sagging against his pillow. "You had better not," he grunted.

Weysh crossed his arms. "Maman told me everything," he said to Montpierre. "I know now why you hate me."

"Montpierre doesn't hate you, lovely—"

"Yes, I do."

Weysh had to physically flex, as if taking a blow. He'd always suspected Montpierre despised him, but to have the man say it to his face, in front of Maman? That hurt. It was the type of strike that crashed through every layer of defense to his core, to the small boy who used to pray every night for a way to make Montpierre like him.

"Montpierre, how can you say that? Weysh is *our son*!" She'd shouted the last two words, and when, shocked, Weysh looked at his maman, he saw that her cheeks were red and tears made tracks in the powder on her face.

"I'm sorry, Bernadette, but I do. And if you would be honest with yourself, you might find that you do as well."

At that, she clutched Weysh by the arm. "No!" she spat. "Never!"

Weysh hugged her and smiled against the top of her head. She was literally standing with him in opposition to Montpierre. "Thank you, Maman."

Montpierre watched the two of them for a moment, then nodded wearily. "Fair enough. Women are vastly superior to men when it comes to this sort of thing, mothers especially." He looked again at Weysh. "I may hate you, but that is due to my flaws, not yours. You have—" He fell into such a fit of hacking coughs that Maman rushed to his side. Weysh cringed in discomfort. When at last the fit passed, Montpierre lowered the bloodied handkerchief from his mouth and continued. "You are a permanent reminder of how dismally I failed the woman I love."

"Oh, Montpierre," she whispered, cupping her husband's cheek.

"And yet," continued Montpierre, "I don't believe you to be a beast. The creature that sired you is a special kind of evil, and despite what I said in anger, I've never seen that in you. I apologize."

The words *I apologize* sounded so strange coming from Montpierre's mouth it took Weysh's ears a few seconds to register them. And the amount of vindication Montpierre's apology brought Weysh was equal parts soothing and irritating. He'd hoped by now that his stepfather's opinion wouldn't matter as much, and one quick "I'm sorry" in no way made up for the years of torment he'd suffered at Montpierre's hand, so why did receiving an apology from him have to feel so thrice-damned *good*?

Of course, Weysh kept his whirling thoughts and emotions from his face. He simply nodded. "Thank you, Montpierre. I accept your apology."

Quite suddenly Weysh felt drained. More than anything he wanted to collect Yenni from her classes, fly her home, and fall asleep with her in his arms.

"I need to be going," he said. He bowed to Montpierre and kissed his maman on the cheek.

"When will you come by again?" she asked.

Weysh smiled. "Soon," he said. "I promise."

Δ

At last the sun was setting, and Yenni was home. A new type of home, curled up with Weysh on the rooftop, watching the sun paint Imperium Centre gold and pink. Who knew home could also be a feeling, rather than a place?

"I received a reply from my parents," Yenni told him.

Weysh perked up. "Oh? And?"

"They have told me to bring you home, to the Yirba islands."

"En? But that's wonderful!"

Yenni bit her bottom lip.

"That's not wonderful?"

"I'd expected more resistance. I'm happy they are being so accommodating, but I'm nervous as to why."

"The threat," Weysh said darkly.

"Yes."

He sighed. "I hope that I can be of use as I am."

Not for the first time, it saddened Yenni to hear him talk like this. Before his injury Weysh had always been so sure of himself, too sure of himself at times. But these days he often had episodes of melancholy and self-doubt. He'd never completely bounced back after he'd lost his sense of smell, but she hoped that with time he would.

"I couldn't even track you when Noriago snatched you away."

"And yet you saved us, and used your runes to do it. Whatever you may think, I'm proud to call you Given, Weh-sheh. I love you."

He rested his forehead to hers. "And I you. So what's the plan?"

"Well, tomorrow I'm meeting Deedee's sweetheart Nanette for the first time."

"Nanette—but that's a woman's name."

"Yes."

"I see. Well, I quite like Diedre. We should all go four go out together sometime. But I meant the plan for our future?"

"I think once final exams are done, *and* we've graduated the year, *and* you've graduated your schooling, *and* you've taken your post, *and* my Orire N'jem is complete, we make for the Moonrise Isles, so you can meet the *rest* of my family."

"The *rest* of your family, my heart?"

"Yes," Yenni whispered. For in her time at the academy, Weysh, as well as Diedre, Harth, and Zui, had become her family, her home away from home. They had been with her through the most trying year of her life. And whatever challenges awaited her in the future, whatever the Gunzu might throw at them, she'd have family to help. Her iyaya. Her n'baba. Jayeh and Ifeh and Dayo and Jumi.

And Weysh.

Though she stood at the chasm of something great and unknown, she knew she wasn't standing there alone.

The End

ACKNOWLEDGMENTS

Thank you to my family: my parents, immigrants from whom I derive my adventurous spirit, and who worked so hard to give me the best shot they could at success. To my sisters, Nik and Lee, and my cousin, Thayne, who indulged my earliest writing attempts with wonderful enthusiasm.

To my writer's group and beta readers: Victoria, Katie, Aya, and Justin. Your feedback and insights were invaluable, and this book would not be what it is without you.

To the Wattpad editorial team: thanks for the Wattys! You made me think I might just be good at this writing business. To my editor, Jen, who was right there with me in the trenches gunning for the deadline.

To my Wattpad readers: your votes and heartfelt comments brightened dark days and kept me going.

And finally to that intangible, god-given something inside me that must be expressed, and won't let me quit.

ABOUT THE AUTHOR

Nandi Taylor is a Canadian writer of Afro-Caribbean descent based in Toronto. Her debut novel *Given* garnered over one million reads on the online story-sharing site Wattpad and earned a starred review from ALA's Booklist. Nandi graduated from the University of Toronto with a degree in English literature and a diploma in journalism and has worked as a travel writer while living abroad in Japan. Her works are an expression of what she craved growing up—Black protagonists in speculative settings with themes of growth, courage, and finding one's place in the world.

BONUS CONTENT

Glossary and Phonetic Pronunciation Guide

CHARACTERS
Carmenna: Kar-men-nah
Diedre: Di-eh-druh
Harth: Hard *th* at the end
Mainard: May-nar
Montpierre: Mon-pee-air
Natahi: Nah-tah-hee
Noriago: No-ree-eh-go
Weysh Nolan: Waysh No-lahn
Yenni Aja-Nifemi ka Yirba: Yeh-nee, Ah-jah, Nee-feh-mee, ka Yeerba
Zui: Zwee

COMMON TERMS
Ach'e (Ah-chay, hard *ch*): The energy that runs through all things, magic
Agbi (Ag-bee): Big sister

Duvvies (Doo-vees): Creshen currency

Iyaya (Ee-yah-yah): Mom, mum

Jabdanu (Jab-dah-noo): A form of wrestling usually practiced by women

Kebi (Keh-bee): Little sister

Magus/Magi (May-jus, Mah-ja-ee): High-ranking magic practitioners in Cresh

N'baba (En-bah-bah): Papa, dad

N'kun (En-kun): Older brother

N'ne (En-neh): A gazelle-like creature with speed magic

Orire N'jem (Oh-ree-reh En-Jem): A sacred journey abroad to please the gods

The Sha: Gods on the uncolonized Islands

GODS

Byen (Bee-en): Also known as the Kindly Watcher, Cresh's God figure

Father Esh: Trickster god of the Islands

Father Gu: Warrior god of the Islands

Father Ri: Island god of wisdom

Father Sho: Island hunter god

Mother-Father Ool: Island god from whom all others came

Mother Ib, Father Ji: Twin gods of fortune on the Islands, together Ib-e-ji

Mother Shu: Island goddess of love

Mother Ya: Island goddess of storms

Mother Ye: Island goddess of women

Movay: Also known as the Mistress of Demons, Cresh's devil figure

PLACES

Cresh: An empire to the north of the Sha Islands, Weysh's home

Espanna (Eh-spah-nah): Large nation to the west of Cresh

Fuboli (Foo-boh-lee) Islands: Home of the Fuboli people

Gunzu (Goon-zoo) Islands: Home of the Gunzu people

Imperium Centre (San-truh): The capital city of Cresh

Minato: Large empire to the east of Cresh

Northern Sha Islands/Sunrise Isles: Islands not colonized by Cresh

Sainte Ventas (Sant Ven-tas): Biggest of Cresh's colonized Islands

Shahanta Islands: Home of the Shahanta people

Southern Sha Islands/Moonrise Isles: Islands colonized by Cresh

Watatzi Islands: Home of the Watatzi people

Yirba (Yeerba) Islands: Yenni's home, domain of the Yirba people

READING GUIDE QUESTIONS

1. Choose one of the following to answer as an icebreaker:

   a. What did you think about the book cover? Does it invoke any of the feelings one might feel while reading the book?

   b. If you were making a movie adaptation of this book, who would you cast?

   c. Which character did you relate to the most and why?

2. Consider the concept of "Given" and how it affects Yenni and Weysh's relationship. Does knowing they are destined for each other cause more strife than if they were unaware? What does this say about fate vs. free will?

3. Take a look at Carmenna's character—how does your opinion of her change over the course of the book? How does the concept of "Given" affect her as someone outside of a Given pairing?

4. A dragon is far more deadly by comparison, but Yenni feels better equipped to be vulnerable with Weysh's dragon form than she is with Weysh's human form. Why do you think Yenni is initially reluctant to get to know Weysh the man vs. Weysh the dragon?

5. As his Given, Weysh expects Yenni to be on board with the idea of being together without question. What does this say about the way Weysh's character has been raised to consider other women? What does it reveal about the way Weysh views his own masculinity? How does his character change and evolve by the end of the book?

6. At multiple points in the book, Yenni is referred to as a "foreigner" (p. 61) by other Creshens. Her appearance as well as her rune magic are often regarded with suspicion, surprise, or morbid fascination. Do you see any similarities between how the Creshens treat Yenni in the book and our present reality? Although the fantasy world lacks terms for xenophobia, racism, and cultural appropriation, how do these concepts still manifest throughout the book?

7. Finally, what was your favorite part of the fantasy world of Given?

(Optional) Research question: Consider the colonial history within the world of Given. Cresh sees itself as a large imperial power with advanced technology and magic, and it's people think of the Moonrise Isles's tribes as uncivilized. Yenni mentions that the dragons of the Sha Islands "were exterminated by Cresh

during the Colonial War" (p. 38) and at another point defends
herself as "not some uninformed savage who needed to be coddled when confronted with 'civilized' technology" (p. 203). How
does this situation parallel the history of our own world? Can you
find any specific examples from history?

Out of This World: Shining Light on Black Authors in Every Genre

Nandi's *Publisher's Weekly* Op-ed, February 26, 2020

This February saw numerous articles and lists touting the work of award-winning black authors and works that have quite literally shaped the narrative for black people of the diaspora. We'll hear names such as Zora Neale Hurston, Maya Angelou, Toni Morrison, Frederick Douglass, and Langston Hughes. Their contributions are and should be forever venerated in the canon of literature.

What we didn't hear as much about are the writers of genre fiction: thrillers, romance, and, in particular, science fiction and fantasy. Why is this relevant? In the last decade, sci-fi and fantasy narratives have taken the media by storm. Marvel has been dominating the box office, *Game of Thrones* had us glued to our TVs and Twitter feeds (Black Twitter's #demthrones hashtag in particular had me rolling), and people are making seven-figure salaries playing video games online. It's a good time to be a nerd. The world is finally coming to appreciate the unique appeal of science fiction and fantasy. It's wondrous, fun, escapist and whimsical, dazzling and glamorous. It takes the mundane and makes it cool. And for the longest time it's been very Eurocentric. With sci-fi and fantasy growing exponentially more popular year by year, it's necessary that, alongside black fiction's rich history of award-winning literary giants, we also shine the spotlight on black works of speculative fiction.

There is a curious phenomenon surrounding black stories, where the ones that see the most mainstream success are also the stories where black people suffer most. I've received comments on my own writing that boil down to some variant of "there wasn't enough racism." Is this simply that old journalism adage "if it bleeds, it leads" at work in the literary sphere? Or is it something more sinister?

Narratives like *Roots*, *Beloved*, and *Twelve Years a Slave* unflinchingly depict the horrors of slavery. It's a historical fact that black people were traded like sacks of grain, bred like cattle, put down like disobedient dogs, and, to this day, the legacy of chattel slavery lingers like cultural radiation, poisoning black communities in the form of economic disparity. Practices like redlining, gentrification, and the prison-industrial complex maintain the wealth gap between blacks and whites. But when the only stories about black people that are given prominence are the ones where black people are abused and oppressed, a very specific and limiting narrative is created for us and about us. And this narrative is one of the means through which the world perceives black people and, worse, through which we perceive ourselves.

It should be noted that black literary fiction does not focus exclusively on black suffering—far from it. The beauty of black literature is that black characters are centered and nuanced, and sci-fi and fantasy narratives can build on that. Through sci-fi and fantasy, we can portray ourselves as mages, bounty hunters, adventurers, and gods. And in the case of sci-fi narratives set in the future, as existing—period.

Sci-fi stories in particular are troubling for their absence of those melanated. Enter Afrofuturism, a term first used in the 1990s in an essay by a white writer named Mark Dery. In a 2019 talk on Afrofuturism at Wellesley College, sci-fi author Samuel R. Delany breaks down what the term meant at the time—essentially fiction set in the future with black characters present. Delany also explains why this is potentially problematic: "[Afrofuturism was] not contingent on the race of the writer, but on the race of the characters portrayed." As previously stated, science-fiction and fantasy have historically been overwhelmingly Eurocentric, and sci-fi and fantasy authors, largely white men, have not had the best track record for writing black characters of any depth. They had no skin in the game, after all—no vested interest in doing so.

But as the term used to describe fiction about us has been claimed by us, it has been refined and remade. Afrofuturism now invokes the glowing towers of Wakanda and the plight of Janelle Monáe's android fugitive Cindi Mayweather. In response to the erasure of black people in sci-fi and fantasy, the parameters of Afrofuturism have been solidified, and the expectation now is that Afrofuturist narratives not only contain black characters but specifically be about them. And who better to lovingly craft fantastical worlds and cultures rooted in black and African traditions than black authors?

That's why this Black History Month, in addition to Zora Neale

Hurston, Maya Angelou, Toni Morrison, Frederick Douglass, and Langston Hughes, we must also mention Octavia Butler, N.K. Jemisin, Fiyah Literary Magazine, Jordan Peele, and as many of the growing number of sci-fi and fantasy authors and creators we can manage. Because in spotlighting black speculative fiction, we're creating new narratives for black people. Narratives that are out of this world.

THE POWER BETWEEN THE PAGES

Nandi's *Bookriot* Op-ed, January 14, 2020

Good fiction can do a lot of things. It can entertain us, inspire us, comfort and delight us. But most importantly, a fiction story can simultaneously reflect and shape what we believe.

I'll let you in on a trade secret: the subconscious mind can't tell the difference between what's real and what's not, and as storytellers, we're counting on that. It's how we make you love and hurt for characters that ultimately don't exist. It's how we make you wish you could visit Hogwarts or Wakanda. Cultures the world over have used folktales to pass along social norms, warnings, and morals. There are books, comics, and movies with fandoms bigger than the population of small countries.

See, we authors know that a really good book will wrap you up inside it, make you feel warm and cocooned, lower your defenses, and, while you're in that soft and vulnerable state, it will seep like melted chocolate into the recesses of your mind.

Now, this can be a wonderful thing. In fact, one of the greatest virtues of stories is how they can reassure us, pat us soothingly on the hand and say, "You thought you were bad? Just look at this guy." Think of your favorite book or movie, the one that you can quote almost line for line. What makes you love it so much? Chances are it speaks to something deep within you, possibly something you didn't even know existed. If Hiccup can fumble and bumble his way into leading an army of dragon riders, maybe it's okay that you can't keep a white shirt stainless for longer than the time it takes to unwrap a black bean burrito.

We use stories to feel alright. At times it can seem like the only person who understands us is the one dealing with an absentee mother while living in a dystopian regime, or learning the importance of friendship while on a quest to destroy the One Ring. But what happens when someone hardly or never sees themselves on page or screen?

Ah, well, here comes that well-meaning yet simple-minded friend of ours again, the subconscious. The one who loves to jump to conclusions. When none of the characters in the stories we adore look like us, think like us, move like us, or love who we love, our subconscious minds receive the message that maybe we're not so all right after all.

But most dangerous of all are the stories that grab lazily at half-truths and stereotypes. These stories paint ugly, clumsy portraits, wrap their arms around our necks and draw us close, pointing and whispering, "You see? You are in fact the abominable freak of nature you always feared."

In her famous TED talk "The Danger of a Single Story," author Chimamanda Ngozi Adichie says: "Stories can break the dignity of a people, but they can also repair that broken dignity."

There's a reason everyone loves a good underdog story. To our subconscious minds, the triumphs of our characters become our triumphs, their redemption our redemption. And it's no coincidence that with the rise in diverse representation in the last decade we've seen leaps and bounds as a society in our tolerance for those who don't fit the dominant paradigm—people who are not straight, cisgender, white, or neurotypical.

The relationship between art and life is symbiotic: one feeds the other. As representation of marginalized segments of our society has increased, so has respect and tolerance for those segments of society, which has led more accurate and nuanced portrayals of marginalized people, and today we find ourselves with a wealth of diverse mainstream media and heartening advances in human rights.

We live in an age where anyone with a computer can reach a global audience, and this makes stories exponentially more powerful than ever before. So it is vital as authors and storytellers that we strive to tell stories that reflect truth and foster dignity, and it is imperative for readers to enjoy these stories to their heart's content.